"This book contains ideas that should be taught ... country in the world. It is not only a great novel a... ... demonstration of how we learn to create the shell of the title - around our feelings, our intuition, and our ability to connect with other people - and then how to break it down. It is, in essence, a book about communication. I found this book resonated very deeply with me, and I for one would love to see it widely read. Everyone should read this book."
Paradigm Shift Magazine

"An excellent book that weaves spiritual teachings into a modern context in classic storytelling style. The Breaking of the Shell is a powerful story filled with hope and transformation."
Yoga Magazine

"For anyone struggling with difficult circumstances in their own life, this book illustrates how everything happens to us for a reason. In Alexander's life, we see the jigsaw come together. Every significant event in his life has a part to play in shaping his future. This is a book which convincingly deals with the fabric of the universe and the great mystery of coincidence and consequence."
The Feel Good Magazine

"Hard to put down".
Kindred Spirit Magazine

"Spiritual Fiction at its best. Full of wit and charm and a style similar to JD Salinger's classic 'The Catcher in the Rye', this novel captivates from the very beginning."
Spirit & Destiny Magazine

"Reminiscent of international bestseller Paulo Coelho's works, Barry Durdant-Hollamby has managed to capture the beauty of the process whereby facing our deepest and darkest wounds, we are often able to undergo profound and inspirational change. A real page-turner."
Prediction Magazine

The Breaking of The Shell

Barry Durdant-Hollamby

Second Edition 2012

First Published 2010 in the United Kingdom by:
The Art of Change
Bramble Corner
Park Road
Forest Row
East Sussex RH18 5BX

Second Edition published 2012

www.artofchange.co.uk
email: artofchange@msn.com
ISBN 09530063-5-2
978-0-9530063-5-9

A Cataloguing-in-Publication record for this book is available from the British Library.

Special thanks to Wendy Brown

Printing and binding:
Lightning Source UK Ltd.
www.lightningsource.com

The Breaking of the Shell

Barry Durdant-Hollamby

Author of
So It's Tough Out There, Is It?
The Male Agenda
Stepping Stones
The Truth about Illness, Unhappiness & Stress?

Contact: artofchange@msn.com
Tel: (+44) (0) 1342 823809

1

"Are the ministers here yet?"
"Yes. Yes, they're all here."
"Will we all fit in alright? It's going to be a bit of a squeeze."
"We'll all fit in fine."
"Right, well, this is it. Are you ready?"
"Ready as I'll ever be."
"Let's do it then."
"Yep, let's do it."
"I love you."
"I love you too."

2

On those days when I have both the time and fortitude to peer back through the veils that try, usually unsuccessfully, to shroud my recall of my former self, I find I'm almost in awe of the ignoramus that once masqueraded as me. I see now that I was pig-headed, often to the point of stupidity. I so wanted what I had been taught and what I had learnt to be the only way. I so wanted to be right about everything. I feel like I'm just beginning to be able to let go of that.

There was no place in my life for the grey and foggy world of uncertainty and the unknown. I was an 'if-you-can't-prove-it-then-it-isn't-worth-giving-time-to' man. While I had never considered myself to have any form of relationship to a God, I had never really thought myself an atheist either, if only because that might have suggested that I cared at all about the whole God debate, which of course I didn't.

And yet, who I am now is not who I was. The richer colours and fuller depth of field I am now beginning to see, hardly bear any resemblance to the shallow and fallow world I used to observe with these exact same eyes. But then, I also now realise that seeing isn't just about eyes, is it? Oh God, listen to me – I sound like I'm addressing a bloody congregation.

Let me get one thing straight. I used to hate – and I mean hate with a capital H, any form of emotional discomfort. Physical pain I could handle. But things that made me upset – problems with partners, family, or colleagues - I can still feel the tightening of the wrench as it grips my stomach and starts to squeeze my brain.

The first time I can recall being in a state of such discomfort - abject terror would be a more accurate description - was when I was about three years old. I was in a strange room with some other children when I suddenly realised neither of my parents was around. I remember scanning the room over and over again in disbelief that I had been abandoned by the very people to whom I had entrusted my life.

Although I can't remember the exact sequence of events that day, I can almost reach out and touch shock-wave after shock-wave of despair. I screamed – that much I do know. To the teacher I was probably just another terrified child to be tolerated, soothed and ultimately broken like a horse. I was put in some sort of pen, because I remember standing up, clinging to some wooden bars while shouting for Mumma and Dada for all I was worth.

I think they did finally come for me that day – the shrieking must have eventually had the desired effect. Or maybe it was just time to go home. It seemed like an eternity had passed. I screamed myself hoarse; God knows how anything else got done with any of the other children, although I probably howled myself into a sort of soporific state after a while. And that state of despairing resignation would be the sign to the trainers that the horse had indeed been broken.

That day marked the time that I first started to lose my trust in life and, more importantly, in those people closest to me. The truth was that my parents had deserted me, and at the time I had no knowledge as to whether they would ever come back.

Looking back now, I can see that this relatively minor pre-school incident, replicated in the western world probably several hundred thousand times a day, could be considered the wobbliest of foundations for trying to build a life based on trusting the essential goodness of mankind. After all, if you can't even trust your parents, what chance does anyone else have?

I was five-and-a-half years old when I next remember being drowned in hellish emotional feelings. Typically of such a young child, I wanted it known that I was *five-and-a-half* rather than five, and on certain occasions when I needed to be really bossy, I was nearly six.

I had made a friend at school called Tom. I either never knew his last name or wasn't interested in it. I'm not sure last names have much meaning for five-and-a-half year olds. I was 'privileged' enough to go to a preparatory school for boys, and had managed to survive the trauma of first day blues almost entirely due to Tom being in a much worse state than I was. He clung to his tiny mother at the classroom steps like a limpet clinging to a rock, and as the tide of tutorial grandeur which was Miss Baines tried to separate the inseparable, Tom howled. And I found his howling reassuring; it reminded me of something in myself that I had wisely left behind. My pre-school experience had taught me that my parents weren't there for me, and I had barely even uttered a goodbye to my mother as she walked me to the portakabin that was apparently to be my educational home for the next few years.

Like the rest of the class, I think I probably giggled at Tom's misfortune. Eventually, the inevitable separation happened, aided in part by the appearance of Tom's ruddy-faced dad, who, it turned out later, offered Tom one whole pound to go into class. Tom surrendered under the full force of physical cajoling and financial bribery. Ah yes, we were taught from an early age that fear could be mastered with the right amount of cash.

Tom was to share my desk, and I was more than pleased that, for at least the first ten minutes of that first class, faces kept turning round to peer at my desk partner's distraught face. I was getting attention, and Tom had made it possible.

Over the coming weeks, as Tom was gradually broken in the same way I had been a couple of years before, we became whatever it is that nearly-six-year-old boys become when they form some sort of allegiance. We were becoming friends, and forging a bond that would be unbreakable.

That is, until the incident with the garden shed.

There is not much to rival the inquisitive nature of a young child's mind. Itches exist everywhere that just have to be scratched, even if that involves taking the top off some rather painful spots. For Tom and me, the world we inhabited then was alive with temptations and excitements.

Some days, we'd decide Miss Baines was the evil stepmother from one of the fairy tales she sometimes read us, and our mission would be to save the rest of the children from her dastardly deeds, a job we'd normally manage to get sorted during the milk-break. Other times, she might be a creature from outer space, and we'd draw rockets and make paper cages stuck together with spit to transport her back to the outer reaches of the universe.

One afternoon in school, just before the bell rang, I could see the grown-ups gathering outside the door. I remember seeing Mumma talking to Tom's mum. The bell rang, and, being boys, and knowing that the great outside world awaited us, we jumped up from our seats to shake hands with Miss Baines before running out of the class.

"Tom, Alexander! Come back here – you know the rules. We leave in order, don't we, children? Row one first, then row two, row three and row four. You boys are in row three, so you must wait for rows one and two first. One, two, three, four. You remember how to count, don't you, boys? Now then, back you go." Miss Baines delivered her commands in such a way that you had no doubt whatsoever that she must be correct. Still, it had been worth a try, and small boys forget systems very easily.

We finally got out, and that was when I took my next step towards becoming a man. Mumma told me that Tom's mother was going to take me back to their house for tea, and that I could play with Tom for the rest of the afternoon. I felt that wrench again in the pit of my stomach. Go back to Tom's house? But, but I'm fine just coming back to my house. I've seen Tom all day – why on earth would I want to go back to his house to see him for even longer?

I don't remember Tom being that keen either. Not that either of us showed it. After an initial despairing look at Mumma, I gave her my satchel, she gave me a kiss, and I then reached out my hand to Tom's mum who was going to walk us home.

She didn't even see my hand; she just took Tom's, and they walked slightly ahead of me along the narrow pavement as I tried to keep up with them. I quickly put my hand in my pocket, hoping that no-one had seen me reaching out. Tom and his mum were mumbling something or other about school, but I barely heard them – I was still seething at the heartlessness of my own Mumma.

The feeling in the pit of my stomach had subsided by the time we reached Tom's. It's interesting what you learn as a child when you first visit other people's houses. That afternoon I learnt as much about my own house as I did about Tom's. I learnt that my house was quite big. I learnt that not everyone has a back garden large enough to double as a football pitch. I learnt that other people keep real animals in their houses, not just ones made out of china. And I learnt that not everyone has a television.

At first, I don't believe either of us had the faintest idea how to behave with each other outside of school. Our familiar, everyday environment had been swapped with this world-according-to-Tom. I knew where nothing was; I had no props on which to fall back, none of the usual things around us to make jokes about. I felt naked, embarrassed and awkward. And although this was Tom's world, it seemed as if he didn't really know what to do either.

"It's lovely outside boys, why don't you put your shoes back on and go into the garden. I want to hoover, and you don't want to be stuck inside with that noise going on." Tom's mum shooed us gently out of the house. I think she was called Sheila or something and she might have had black hair, although it could have been red. Dada said she was pretty.

Tom and I dutifully obeyed, and found ourselves outside. The sun was shining that afternoon, but it was still quite cold even though the last crumblings of brown winter leaves under our feet had already surrendered to the spring surge of yellow flowers. The garden, which I still remember well to this very day for reasons that will soon become apparent, was a long, narrow strip of lawn, bordered by flower-beds, with a concrete path bisecting the middle and leading to a garden shed.

For all the impressive size of our own garden, and I told Tom there and then that I thought ours to be at least a hundred times bigger than his, we didn't have a garden shed. Dada had a workshop; a dark, smelly, brick-built room attached to the garage that I yearned to spend time in, but which was, apparently, not for young boys. In it he kept all manner of fascinating tools and devices, in perfect order and hung on hooks, brackets and nails, according to size and weight. Shelves were filled with jars of nails and screws, and Dada even had a couple of circular contraptions hung on the walls which had metal spokes going out to even more jam-jars containing even more nails, screws, nuts and bolts.

This was part of Dada's secret world; a world I longed to inhabit but which, according to some rule or other that I didn't understand, I would not qualify to be a part of for quite some time.

"I'll know when you're ready Alexander – I'll know" he used to tell me when I tried to follow him in to his workshop on one of his important missions. Or "Not today, Alexander – not today. I need to be able to concentrate – this is man's stuff you know. You'll understand when you're a bit older."

That afternoon, Tom and I went down to the shed. I marvelled at the fact that he was allowed to go into it. It was pure heaven in that shed. Tom's dad had run an electric cable down the garden so it even had a light in it. It was not only full of *stuff*, but it had that wonderful *smell* of stuff. An Aladdin's cave of treasures, awaiting discovery by intrepid explorers.

"Look, look, Tom. Look at this. This newspaper's really, really old. It's all brown and stuff at the edges. And here, look, I bet this is one of the bolts that used to hold a pirate ship together." I was in my element, finally, I was really in a man's world, and it felt good.

"Hey, Alexander, my dad's got a dart-board here. No darts though." If Tom was disappointed by the lack of darts, I didn't notice. I was far too busy trying on a huge pair of gardening gloves and hat that I'd found.

"Ha, ha – you look just like my dad now" said Tom with a big smile on his face.

"I know – I'm going to be the Fire God Vulcan that Miss Baines told us about - and you can be Superman trying to save the world. My gloves are made of metal and shoot fire from the fingers, and my hat is my crown. You've got to try to get the crown off my head before I set the world on fire. I'm going to stay in the shed and count to ten and you've got to go and hide in the garden."

While I stayed in the shed, Tom went off to hide. Inside my new heaven, there was a lawnmower; a filing cabinet on top of which were the old newspapers; a petrol can; a spade, fork and some other heavy tools that I didn't recognise; a couple of trays of mixed up screws and nails and nuts and bolts – not at all like my Dada's beautifully divided compartments. There was even some old carpet and a couple of funny-looking chairs; and nestling on the window-sill was a box of matches. The forbidden fruit of the under-nines.

I counted to ten, but not before quickly opening the box of matches to see if there were any inside. About six little, thin strips of wood, with their perfect pink heads, lay snugly in their wooden bed. I heard Superman call, and quickly put the matches in my pocket before heading off on my quest.

Having looked up and down the garden and inside the conservatory, I must have gone back to the shed. Superman, it turned out, had somehow managed to climb onto its rickety roof, and was holding a fishing net on the end of a bamboo cane with which he was trying to catch my crown as I investigated around the outside.

Once I had seen him, the real battle began. He dropped his rod and pulled a small, blue plastic water pistol from his pocket. I felt inside my own pocket expecting to find nothing; but to my delight found the box of matches. While Superman was trying to squirt me into submission, I took out a match, placed it between the index finger of my left hand and the scratchy bit of the box, and then raised the box up towards my left eye. I cocked my right index finger on my thumb right behind the match and took aim at Superman.

Flick.

In mid-flight the match got sizzled by Superman's water ray, and I quickly lined up another. With his water pistol already running low, I managed to take a perfect aim. And once again I fired my weapon at the helpless superhero. Now I'd show him who was the strongest.

But my aim was not as good as I thought. The flaming match disappeared out of sight and Superman quickly recovered his fishing rod and netted my crown in a swift and brilliant manoeuvre. I had lost all my super power; he was the ruler of the world.

Smoke started to rise up from inside the shed and in the same second that Superman wobbled to his feet on the roof of the shed to pronounce his victory, the shed roof gave way and my special friend Tom disappeared into the smoke-filled interior. I'll never forget the look on his face as he fell through the rotten timbers.

I was paralysed with fear. I had not only been stripped of all my super powers, but even of my ability to move or to utter a single word. Tom's mum must have stopped hoovering by now, because within seconds of hearing his screams, she was battling with the flames in the shed and pulling his smoking body from the fire.

I ran. I ran and ran and ran and ran and ran. I ran out through Tom's side gate, I ran down streets of unfamiliar houses and past cars and people and cats and dogs. I tried with all my might to escape from the terror of what I had just done. If Vulcan was a

God, then I despised and hated God in those moments with all my heart.

I had no idea where I was running to, or how Mumma eventually found me. I know there was a kindly-faced old man involved, who sort of reminded me of my Grandpa, my Dada's dad and only living grandparent, who was in a building far away with a lot of other old people. I ran into him as I headed round the corner of a street. I remember talking to him through my tears and feeling better because here was a man who was taking me at face value. He didn't know my dark secret – that I had just set fire to my best friend.

I do know that a part of me didn't want to be found. I wanted it all to be a mistake, a dream. I wanted to cocoon myself like a caterpillar in some warm, thick, protective covering which would stop me from ever discovering that what I had done had really happened.

Later that afternoon, back at my house, I met my first policemen. One of them was a woman and there were two men who were very, very big and very, very scary. I had shut myself away in my bedroom, unable to take in this new reality. All I knew was that it wasn't good. It wasn't good at all.

Mumma came up with the woman first. I refused to move. I curled up like a ball in the corner, not wanting to face the world. I could tell by Mumma's voice that she was very upset, and that made me even more worried. The woman sat in my bedroom with Mumma and started talking to me.

"Alexander, we need to talk to you about what happened this afternoon. Could we do that, do you think?" Her voice was soft and kind. But I was still terrified. Downstairs I could hear men's voices – the policemen must have been talking to each other because Dada was still not home from work. What would my Dada say when he found out about all this?

"Can Dada not find out? You mustn't tell him. Tell me you won't tell him, Mumma?"

Mumma came over, wrapped her arms around me and started crying.

"Dada already knows, Alexander – I had to call him at work. But don't worry - don't worry about anything, darling. Just tell the nice lady what happened."

"Your friend Tom is in hospital Alexander, but the doctors are hopeful that he'll be okay. Does it help to know that?" The policewoman was trying to be kind, which seemed odd considering what I had done.

But when it came to trying to tell her what had happened, my mind became a complete blank. In that moment, I desperately wanted to tell her everything. I wanted to shed my burden, as if telling the story would somehow rid me of my pain and suffering. I wanted to be free of the sight of Tom disappearing through the roof, free of the sound of his screams, free of the memory of the flames that seemed to appear from nowhere. But I couldn't. I was not to escape that easily from my inner torture.

I could remember playing in the garden, I could remember something about the shed and I remembered doing some running. Or was it a game of chase? The more I tried to remember and describe things, the more confused and upset I became. No amount of questions made any difference – I had pushed the whole experience into some very deep and dark hole that I had no desire to try to find for a very long time.

I didn't go back to Miss Baines's class. Dada told me soon afterwards that he had a new job and we had to move away from my familiar surroundings. I didn't ask about my best friend Tom and I didn't find out the truth of what happened to him that day until many years later.

3

"Oh – oh, help me, help me."
I had only left the room for a minute, but in that minute the pain had gripped him again. I ran back into the small bedroom to see his grey and wizened face grimacing under another attack.

"Would you like another painkiller, Dada?"

"What? Would that help? Are they good? This pain, it's - it's very bad. Yes, oh yes, that would be kind. Oh, oh. How's the weather? Is the cat in?"

"Yes, the tablet should help Dada. As for the weather, well, it's dull and grey, so there's a change – you're not missing anything. And we don't have a cat any more. She died last year – remember?"

I fetched another couple of codeine tablets from the kitchen counter and he somehow managed to choke them back with some water – a miracle considering he hadn't eaten properly in weeks, and his lips and mouth were dry. A mixture of milk, water and sheer bloody-mindedness seemed to be the only constituents keeping him alive.

"They should kick in pretty quickly."

"Did you say something?" His grey-blue eyes were watery and not able to focus; they wandered round the room, scanning the walls and door and furniture as if in search of something.

I raised my voice slightly. "I said the pain-killers should start working fairly soon – the pain will go; you'll be okay in a minute, Dada".

"Oh good, good – thank you Humphrey. Thank you so much. You've been so kind. How's the weather today?"

I didn't need to answer him again. Not because I was unkind, but simply because his eyes showed that as soon as he had asked the question his mind had gone elsewhere, to Humphrey's world.

Dada was staring into that dimension to which those nearing death seem to be granted access. I longed to see through those eyes, even for a few seconds, to catch just a glimpse of that other place that he now seemed to inhabit more and more.

His illness had somehow softened him. He had started using the words 'thank you' in a way I had never previously heard. He had developed a new smile; one that seemed to spring from a deeper place than just his facial muscles. And he had also had to learn to accept my help. At last. After years of telling everyone what to do and how to do it, after years of running from pain and trauma, my Dada had finally had to learn to stay in one place and be humble.

4

The spring and summer of Nineteen Seventy-Five were like none I had experienced before, and none I have experienced since. It turned out that Dada's new job was in a place that he described to me then as 'overseas'. At first, I didn't really take in what that meant; I hadn't done much travelling abroad by then, other than a week's holiday in Jersey the year before. I hadn't much idea of what, or where 'overseas' was.

We were now living in a new, much smaller, house which I was told to take great care of, as it didn't belong to us. I didn't understand why, or how, we were able to live in a house that wasn't ours, but did my best to comply with instructions. Being very important in his job, Dada was always frighteningly good with instructions.

He would go away for what seemed like interminably long periods, leaving Mumma and me to pass the time together. We were in a modern house, surrounded by a mixture of other little box-like houses that looked exactly the same as ours, and on the outskirts of an unfamiliar town that we had to get to know together. The town was called Guildford. Having previously lived in a village, it seemed huge to me.

Mumma had explained to me that it had been too late to get me into a new school for the summer term, so I would be staying at home and doing some 'learning' with her. I asked her when I would be going back to Miss Baines's but she would only say that I'd be going to a new school 'soon'.

I loved Mumma. She was always so kind to me, even when I had got really dirty and taken lots of mud into the house. She was kind if I got a spelling wrong, or failed to recognise a word when we were reading. She was kind when I complained I had no friends to play with and was bored with playing with her, because she didn't understand the rules of the game that I'd just invented.

In the mornings, she let me climb into bed with her, and quite often if I had had a bad dream, she'd come into my bedroom and snuggle up next to me to help me feel safe. I almost looked forward to having bad dreams, so that I could feel comforted and cared for. And, although I adored him and worshipped the ground he walked on, I almost began to resent Dada when he came home from one of his long trips, because he got to keep Mumma.

After one of his long trips that summer, Dada came home and told me that he had a special present for me. He must have been excited about giving me this present because it was the first thing that came out of the boot of the taxi that had brought him home. In fact it was the only thing that came out of the boot, because it was so big.

It was rectangular-shaped. The taxi driver had to help Dada lift it out and into the house. Amazingly for such a big box, it was all wrapped up in Cowboys and Indians wrapping paper. The Cowboys, in all their brown finery, were riding beautiful chestnut horses and shooting big guns towards Indians, regaled in rainbow headdresses and carrying axes.

I waited for Dada to pay the taxi driver and come back in with his own bags, before carefully tackling the wrapping paper which I wanted to preserve in all its magnificence. As I prised the paper away from the contents it was disguising, I soon became aware that this present was not only big in size, but big in meaning.

It was a large, dark brown trunk with the words 'Alexander Baker' inscribed in gold lettering across the top. It had its own brass combination locks. There was no doubt that it was a thing of majesty. A serious present.

With Dada's encouragement, I opened it up and peered into its empty interior. I wanted to feel excited, I wanted to feel grateful and I wanted to be able to hug my Dada and thank him so much. But I couldn't. I was experiencing that wrench in my stomach again. Something was feeling extremely wrong. And when I looked at Mumma's face I knew I had reason to feel nervous. Her soft, beautiful smile had been replaced by an awkwardness and falseness that I had seen once before. The same evening that the police had come round to ask me about the fire.

I managed to get some words out.

"Thank you Dada. It's big." I paused, wondering how to phrase my next question.

"What is it for?" I asked innocently.

Dada seemed pleased that I had said something at last.

"Read the label – you haven't read the label, Alexander."

Amongst the now carefully re-folded wrapping paper, I found a small piece of card with a smiling cowboy face on the front. Inside, in Dada's writing, was the message that, in its own subtle way, signified the beginning of the end of my early childhood. I read it slowly and with an intensifying feeling of dread:

To our darling Alexander – to help you on your journey to becoming a young man. With all our love, Mumma and Dada.'

I didn't know why, but I had to get out of that room. I excused myself and locked myself in the toilet and cried and cried. Something terrible was about to happen, that much I knew. I just didn't know what.

It was clearly quite a big thing that was happening, because both Mumma and Dada accompanied me on my first trip to Hebbingdon Preparatory School for boys. In the boot we had the infamous tuck box, which Mumma had said was crammed full of goodies, including a half-pound of my favourite American hard gums, as well as some stationery items. There was also another case containing my uniform, which I would need to put on without Mumma's help from now on, and games and outdoor clothing and shoes and boots.

Mumma hadn't seen the school before; only Dada had been to visit. On the journey they talked a lot about all the good things that happened at the school – but I didn't want to listen. I could tell from Dada's voice that he was close to tears. Although I didn't see him very often now, I still loved him and he still loved me. And I can see now that driving his seven-year old child to a strange place, where he would be left for ten days before seeing either of his parents again, must have been crucifying him.

When we pulled up to the school – to me it seemed like a vast, unwelcoming, pointy-topped building – Mumma was doing her best to be brave. The wrench in my stomach was now so tight that I almost couldn't feel anything. I could see tears forming in the corners of Mumma's eyes, and even thought I saw a slight moistening in Dada's. At that point, I remember deciding not to make any more eye contact with them. It was then that I started to switch off.

It wasn't a switching off over which I felt I had much control. It was just my way of protecting myself. There was absolutely no way that I was ready to be ripped from the comforting protection of my parents. There was absolutely no way I was ready to be waking up every morning in a 'dorm' with other strange boys, as opposed to my own room with my Mumma, and sometimes my Dada, in the next room. And there was absolutely no way I was ready to start getting myself dressed in my school uniform every morning without the gentle, loving help of my Mumma.

I had no choice but to put a lid on those terrors, and the myriad others that sought to wrest complete control of my infant mind and body and reduce me to a blubbering wreck. Suddenly, we were joined by a tall man, who was introduced to me as Mr Gardiner. I thought he must have been quite important because he had silvery hair and a large, grey moustache, which made him look as if he had stepped out of the pages of an old book.

And so, the great separation happened and the shell that would prevent me from feeling painful emotions started to close around my heart. Mr Gardiner showed all three of us around the school buildings, and later introduced me to Mrs Weston the matron, a round lady who was probably not as ancient as I thought. When we were introduced, she smiled at me in a way that made me want to cry, as if she had seen this devastating ritual played out countless times before. Hindsight tells me she probably had.

But I wasn't going to cry. I had learnt a new skill. Under the watchful eye of Mr Gardiner, Dada shook my hand, kissed me once on the cheek and told me not to eat all my goodies on the first night. I took control of my almost overpowering desire to weep, so that those telltale tears couldn't give away that, inside, my childhood world was on the edge of oblivion. This must have helped Mumma too, because she managed to give me a quick squeeze goodbye and whispered a quiet "I love you and I'll see you very soon" before quickly turning her back and walking away, arm-in-arm with Dada towards the car.

And that was it. My parents, my loving, beautiful, protective parents had abandoned me again, this time for so much more than just a day, and to a strange world full of strange new people and customs. And all I had to sweeten the pill of this gut-wrenching separation was a half-pound of American hard gums, a few other sweets and a new comic.

I'll always remember my first school assembly at Hebbingdon. I had spent two nights as a boarder before the term started, and we had to don our own school uniforms for the first day. Matron was evidently used to having very young boys struggle with this task, and as one of three seven-year olds in the boarding house, I derived some comfort from the fact that all three of us required her assistance in doing our ties and laces.

Charles Fox and James Statham-Marks were the other two 'newbies' as we had been called by some of the older boys. I remember Charles being very small with an almost incontrollable urge to laugh. It didn't matter what he said, it was invariably followed by his giggle, which reminded me of the woodpeckers I had heard many times on walks with Mumma. James was much taller, seemed extremely confident (although not confident enough to do his tie) and was either putting on a good show, or was genuinely at ease in his new surroundings.

They both had the enviable advantage of having older brothers who were also boarders at the school. And because I was Charles's and James's friend, these older boys became as much my champions as theirs.

I was told that we would be joined that day by the other 'newbies' – the day-boys. These boys actually got to be dropped off by their parents in the morning and then picked up again later in the day to be taken home, just like I used to be at Miss Baines's. Home. My heart nearly broke at the thought of it. I suddenly longed again for just five minutes with Mumma in the morning before school. The wrench tightened up several notches as I tried to steel myself again and, even before meeting a single one of them, I became intensely jealous of these daily visitors.

After breakfast that morning, I remember staring silently out of the window as car after car arrived, and a host of tidy, uniformed boys said their goodbyes to their own Mummas and Dadas. I saw how some boys hugged their parents, but the majority seemed simply to make a hand gesture and, with schoolbags and briefcases weighing them all down, walked heavily into the school building.

Until the 'day-bugs' arrived, the noises of the boarders and staff had echoed around the school building, but had never disturbed its holiday slumber. After all, there were only about twenty-five boarders in total. Now however, the building seemed to take on a different presence as it awoke to the sudden onrush and excitement caused by the arrival of over one-hundred and forty boys. I could almost sense the walls, photographs, desks and curtains coming alive as talk of holiday adventures and mischievous pranks resounded down the corridors. Even Mrs Weston seemed to look different as she appeared in the dorm to make sure that we three newbies were all ready for the assembly.

James's brother Peter, who must have been at least nine years old and seemed almost like a grown-up to me, took us down to that first school function. My stomach was getting tighter and tighter as we wound down the spiral staircase and walked along the boarders' corridor to the main hall. I kept blinking my eyes shut, to try to escape for a magical moment back to my summer world with Mumma.

We entered the cavernous hall, which was by now already filling up, and we were immediately abandoned by Peter. A man I hadn't seen before, with chalky hair and a dusty looking suit, muttered something about the front row. I was relieved to be following Charles as I wouldn't have known what instructions he had given. I blinked my eyes closed even harder than before, but the escape never came. Within seconds I was sitting down, cross-legged on the floor, within a few feet of a line of grown-ups that I presumed to be teachers. Near the middle of this line was Mr Gardiner, the man who had greeted me on my first day.

The hall was filled with chatting and banging and coughing and sneezing. At least it was until a bell sounded, and the big doors at the side opened and through them walked the tallest, thinnest man I had ever seen. But for the sound of his shoes on the wooden boards, you could have heard a pin drop. I was gripped with fear and it was no comfort to know I probably wasn't the only one.

" Good Morning boys" bellowed his voice, the words bouncing forcefully off every corner of the packed hall. The whole school, except for me and the other newbies, replied as if one.

"Good morning, Headmaster."

Mr Aitcheson, as I would later find out he was named, continued. "For those of you who are new today…"

His pale blue eyes alighted on me and the other seven-year olds sitting in the front row. I felt sick to my core as he made a gesture to us with his hands to rise.

"…please stand so that we can all see who you are."

My knees and legs felt like jelly. My heart was pounding and I felt sure I could feel drops of sweat rolling down my face. Although I wasn't generally given to vomiting, I was certain I was about to be sick.

But then Charles farted – not particularly loudly, but with deadly consequences nonetheless. Not that anyone else knew it was him, but I did because I was standing right next to him. It was one of the smelliest farts I had ever encountered. Its rank odour quickly permeated not only our row, but apparently that of those directly behind us, as I could hear people shuffling and stifling giggles.

And then, almost immediately, and before we had returned to the sanctuary of our sitting positions, he did it again. And this time it was louder. And this time I couldn't help but laugh. The whole room suddenly became silent but for my pathetic sniggering. Mr Aitcheson took three steps forwards and bent the full force of his mighty gaze upon me. He motioned to the others to sit, leaving me the only boy standing up in the hall.

"What's your name, young man?"

If I've ever in my life experienced a feeling of such panic and embarrassment as the one I experienced in that moment, when nearly two-hundred pairs of eyes bore down upon me, I can't remember it. Doubts bounced around my mind. What was my name? Who was I? What was I doing in this strange place? Why was this happening to me?

I replied with a quiet voice that belied the screaming little boy who was terrorising my inner landscape.

"Erm, it's Baker sir."

"So, we have a Master Baker amongst us do we? Mr Gardiner, make sure cook knows we have a master baker amongst us this year, will you? He could come in very handy when we need fresh bread." The auditorium burst dutifully into laughter.

"Well then, Master Baker – have you never heard someone drop wind before?" The headmaster left a pause that seemed long enough to carry on into eternity. During that silence, the screams of the little boy running around inside became more and more distant. I was becoming numb. I felt like a giant lump of lard standing amidst all these strangers that were my new family.

I was grateful when Mr Aitcheson continued. " Breaking wind happens quite often in a boy's school you know – particularly on special occasions like today. So, Master Baker, you'd better get used to it."

The room erupted in a symphony of laughter and full-blown raspberries.

Mr Aitcheson gave me a small smile and motioned me to sit again. I looked at Charles beside me, who was also laughing. And in that moment my insides, which just previously had been experiencing the seventh circle of hell, suddenly experienced a rush of joy and elation. I had just had my first experience of male bonding, where the innocent output of one boy's bottom had united a whole school in a celebration of what it is to be a man.

Mr Aitcheson continued as if nothing untoward had happened at all. "And for those of you who are not new, and who are a little more familiar with the local wildlife sounds that perennially contribute to the beginning of year assembly, a very big welcome back too." And Mr Aitcheson's thin face broke into a smile of such genuine warmth that I dared to hope that my time at Hebbingdon might be a tiny bit more bearable than I had been expecting.

I can see now how those first ten days at boarding-school were instrumental in shaping my transition from independent free-thinker into interdependent conformist.

I couldn't see that then. In my childish naïveté, all I was aware of was a new world opening up, both magical and frightening. I learnt to walk down corridors, not run; I learnt to do my homework on time; I learnt to call all adults Sir, Ma'am or Miss; and I learnt that farting and burping out loud, in certain situations and within reason, were attributes of which any man should feel proud.

I learnt to obey rules, because I discovered that failure to do so resulted in varying degrees of adult disapproval, ranging from enormous to gigantic. Failure to comply also resulted in any one of a multitude of punishments, the carrying out of which would upset my fragile world to such an extent that rule-breaking didn't seem worth the risk.

The hardest of these rules to bear in my first days at school was related to food. I remember the first time we had casserole. The meat was fatty and full of gristle, and the gravy was a dark brown, sticky mess. The dining room rule was simple. Empty plates to be left after every meal.

Pinner was a prefect; a boy of generous proportions, but not that tall for a top-bod (that's what we called the boys in the final year). It was his duty to check our plates at the end of the meal. I was horrified to see that I was the only one who had left any meat. How could they have eaten that stuff?

"I trust you're going to finish your lunch, Baker?" Pinner clearly enjoyed his power, and revelled in seeing the expression on my face as I realised I was going to have to chew my way through the impenetrable fat, or face the consequential punishment.

Slowly, I placed a bit of the gristly meat on my fork, and put it in my mouth. I chewed and chewed and chewed for all I was worth, and Pinner stood there watching me. By now, everyone at my table was also staring at me. Pinner turned to go and check on the other tables, and in that moment, James shoved a napkin full of gristle under my mouth and I spat out the piece that was causing me to gag. He quickly swept into the napkin the other bits of gristle from my plate as well. The napkin disappeared back into James's pocket.

By the time Pinner had done his rounds, my plate was empty. He seemed confused when he returned, but had no choice but to accept that I had completed my challenge. In that moment, I learnt that you could beat the system.

By the time my parents came to pick me up the following weekend, I had changed. And so had they; or at least my perception of them had altered. Mumma in that brief period, had lost her role as my sole, female protector. Matron had muscled in on the act and made me see that, for quite a few requirements at least, any woman would do. Mr Gardiner, who it transpired was my house-master, had moved in on Dada's territory. It seemed like I had spent more time with him in the last ten days than I had with my Dada in the whole of the previous summer.

So quickly had the transition happened that I remember one night when Mr Gardiner came in to the dorm to announce lights out and wish us all good night, I replied 'Good night Dada'. There was some stifled laughter from the other boys and I pulled the blanket over my head, cringeing at my foolishness.

5

The most recent trip to the hospital had been the most distressing yet. Dada was now very frail, and the pains he had been experiencing in his stomach had become, at times, excruciating. Like most men his age, he hated the idea of going to hospital and seemed to fear meeting with doctors to such an extent that he never took in any of the information that they gave him. Added to that, was the increasing erosion of his short-term memory, with the consequence that I had to attend every doctor's meeting and make a note of what was being suggested.

On this occasion, it had been Helen who'd had to call out the ambulance. I was out and she had taken a day off work to be at home with the old man. She told me later that Dada had rolled over on to his side and fallen on to the floor. Being of slight build, Helen found Dada, despite his recent weight loss, was too much for her to deal with. She had tried and failed to get him into bed, and ended up making him as comfortable as possible where he lay, although he was clearly in pain. All the while she was trying to help him, he was chattering away in between occasional yelps of anguish. Discussing the situation on the phone, we concluded that hospital was the best place for him.

My father's decline had been steep; this had been the third time in as many months that he had been whisked off in an ambulance. Yet, so far, all the doctors had been able to diagnose was an enlarged prostate. He was on some type of pills for that, and they were trying to avoid any form of surgery at this stage, as much due to his age as their own uncertainty as to what they were dealing with.

The funny thing is, when you really start understanding the language of the dying, you get to learn when death is just a stone's throw away. And, even though I had no medical training and knew little about that infamous 'old man's disease', I knew for sure that my Dada was dying. I knew it, because he knew it. Everything about him had changed in these last months and if ever anyone had relinquished the will to live, it was my father. People unacquainted with him would never have known; he still put on that same old show of grit. But I knew, and I found that both scary and strangely reassuring. It was our silent language.

By the time I got to the hospital, Dada had already been examined by yet another different doctor. As I entered the ward, I looked around for his bed. I immediately recognised the back of his head with its now scrappy shock of white hair. He was curled up in the foetal position, facing the man in the next bed. The inevitable wires and tubes had been attached, placing their spider-like grip upon his weakened body.

I should have been ready for the deterioration in his appearance; it happened each time he came to hospital, and always hit me with fresh horror. Now, at least, I was able to meet it with more compassion and a little less outrage than I did that first time I had been obliged to come and see him in a hospital bed all those years ago.

Was this the same man though, that I had said goodbye to earlier that day? Was this the same man who had, at his peak, had the capacity to petrify politicians, business leaders and entertainers alike? Here he was, shrivelled up like a walnut in his blue pyjamas – thank God he had at least something familiar with him – with his eyes closed if only to hide himself from the reality of where he was and what was happening.

"Hi Dada - what a shame, eh? What was up – did you get bored of the service you were receiving at home with me?" Like a million hospital visitors before me, I tried to lighten the cloud of depression that enveloped each new patient's world.

Silence.

"More like you fancied coming and getting some personal treatment from some of the nurses, eh? I bought you a paper by the way."

His eyes remained shut. I didn't know what had happened that day, what drugs they had put him on, but he was already holed up in some far-away chamber that my voice couldn't penetrate. Was it a conscious choice he had made to flee the terror? Or had the drugs and pain forced him into a premature escape from this loathsome environment? Either way I could hardly blame him for switching off, and I felt that speaking more would only serve to drag him back to a reality of which he had no desire to be a part. I left the paper by his bed, kissed him goodbye and went off in search of someone who could give me some information.

It was early evening; the doctors had all completed their rounds and disappeared for the day. The ward sister was kind enough and did her best to answer my questions, although being harassed by a combination of telephone calls and other inquisitive visitors. It turned out that when Dada was brought in, they had not been able to locate his notes in time, and so yet another doctor, clueless about his case, examined him. I had visions of Dada being pushed and prodded while all the time in agony and not saying a word. Not understanding that expressions of pain actually helped the doctors to diagnose, I knew that the old man would strain every sinew to breaking point to ensure that he was a Good Patient who didn't cause trouble. I bet that examination cost him dearly. He had been alone throughout, and I hated to think of that.

What a change. Me, the son he all but forgot he had as he tiptoed his way through the minefield that was his high-profile career in television, now becoming upset at the thought of his father being alone in hospital. I suppose my mother's treatment of him had always helped me to be sympathetic towards him. Even so, I had many reasons why not to care, and yet I don't believe I ever cared more. I had changed from the insensitive young man of my early twenties and I felt immense compassion for this morphing body that was my father.

The examining doctor had recommended a bone scan and also had a catheter hooked up to Dada as he was having trouble urinating. He had also given him a morphine drip for the pain. No wonder Dada had seemed so distant when I went to see him.

I wouldn't be able to find out until at least the next day when the bone scan was to take place. I thanked the ward sister, who by then was already stuck into her next enquiry, and headed for the comfort and familiar surroundings of my car. The freshness and aliveness of the air hit me the second I walked out of the hospital. The joy of being able to walk out. I could crawl, jog, run or even jump up and down if I wanted. I was free. And yet only a few hundred yards away was my Dada, a reluctant guest in an environment that was intended to be kind and loving, and yet which somehow engendered fear.

I smiled at the people I passed who were on their way into the hospital, pleased to be the one who was leaving. I wondered who they were visiting and what they were preparing themselves to face. I had come to realise that the smiles on faces of people entering a hospital are subtly different from those who have just exited. As if they are breathing in when they smile as opposed to breathing out; the body language of those haunted by the fear of the unknown.

And I wondered how differently I would be dealing with all this had I not been going through my own, almost terminal, implosion. For certain I'd be fighting the nurses and doctors for information, demanding results, pushing Dada into every conceivable treatment available. The old me would have had no idea of the meaning of the language that the deeper part of him was using to communicate; the little signs, gestures and unusual requests that I would previously have put down as the rantings of a mad old man. And in so doing, I would have thrown out more babies than bath water, for I had learnt so much about him, about us, about our relationship in these last few weeks.

Was it really just a few weeks? You get to middle-age without really knowing your father at all, and then, in the space of just a few conversations, you start to build up a picture of your self, of your family, that begins to deconstruct the myth of the life that you thought you had lived.

6

My memories of being a boarder at Hebbingdon, and my previous school, are scant, considering my above-average ability of recalling the minutiae of life from a very early age. It's as if there exists a general wash of colour that is my time there, but on the background itself, only a handful of images have been finished. This blanking out of what was presumably a fairly significant chapter in my life, only started to bother me in recent years when I began to wonder why I would forget so much about a period of over seven years of my early life. I have since come to the disappointing conclusion that maybe there wasn't that much of merit to remember.

Those recollections that have not disappeared, seem to be mainly focused upon my achievements, or my failure to achieve. This has been reinforced over the years by the occasional refreshing read of those documents brimming with astute psychological insights, peer positioning and predictive future direction: the school reports. I wonder now whether I started to form my character, my self, out of these decisive and unquestionable judgements that my parents read out to me at the end of each term?

Mumma and Dada seemed to set great store by them, even establishing an official school report reading ceremony. According to how well I had done, this ritual would be followed by one of three things. For what Dada would call a brilliant report, I'd get to go to see the latest film in a London cinema, a treat which was always followed by a meal out in an Italian restaurant called Giuseppe's. For a good report, I'd be taken out to our local Chinese restaurant for a meal, and for anything worse than good, I received nothing. Not a bean.

A brilliant report was the only desirable result, but even that had its downside as the meal at Giuseppe's always seemed to last an interminably long time, and Dada never seemed to understand my desire to eat and get back out into the vibrant streets of London. The local Chinese reward was much worse, because not only did I not get to see a film at Leicester Square, but the meal was always undertaken with a sense of my not having done well enough, and therefore the food never tasted as nice as it could have done. As for the third option, I determined from a young age, once I'd got the hang of the system, to avoid this judgement by any means possible.

The words of these reports would reverberate around my mind for days, if not weeks afterwards. Was I not trying hard enough, or was I simply bored by certain subjects? With the right levels of concentration and determination, was I really a potential captain of industry? Did I have a sound grasp of French grammar and algebra and a natural gift for chess (a game I'm sure I never played at school), or had my teachers just mistaken me for someone else? And what did it mean to be ranked eleventh out of a class of twenty-two other boys? What did being 'average' mean, when applied to a person?

All I knew was that when I scored average marks and comments on my report, I didn't get my trip to London, or even to the Chinese. And for me, that became intolerable. My parents, in particular my father, demonstrated a complete lack of interest in such limited achievements, and gradually I developed a resolution that I would not remain someone whose only impact on others was that of indifference.

So, like many other good and ignorant boys before me, I allowed myself to be shaped into a mould by these experts. I bowed to their superior knowledge and allowed them to decide what it was that I was good at, and what it was into which I should put more effort. I learnt how to buck the system, by plagiarising books, hiding gristly meat, feigning illness and last-minute swotting up. And as I rose up through the ranks to the giddy heights of school prefecture, I began to experience what it must be like to be Dada, or one of those teachers, as I dished out warnings to vulnerable newbies and became confidant of senior masters such as Mr Gardiner and the Headmaster. I had become malleable, and in so doing I became more able to resist whatever mysterious forces existed inside me that wanted to walk in a different landscape to the one busily being manufactured by those who knew best.

And there were aspects of this new landscape that I began to crave. Of those events and developments not directly related to my achievements, the transition of the innocent boy into the sexually gluttonous youth is another image firmly fixed upon the rather uninteresting canvas.

After I confiscated a copy of Arena in my prefecture year at Hebbingdon, I had discovered the joys of masturbating. The first time I came, I was deeply shocked by the eruption from my penis. I remember wondering in fact if I was normal – if a part of me hadn't just burst in some way. Sex education had not yet appeared on any curriculum of mine, and Mumma and Dada avoided talking about it at all costs. I vaguely remember existing in an atmosphere of mild terror for some days, until I finally discovered that all was well when I read some of the stories in the magazine, and talked to one or two of my most trusted friends.

I soon developed a voracious appetite for pornography and would work even harder on achieving better school results in order to receive the cash bonuses from my parents that would finance the objects of my desire. I ran the gauntlet of embarrassing discovery on more than one occasion, and soon found that this added an extra frisson to the whole experience. I'd even try to make sure that the young, blonde female assistant was serving in the newsagent when I went in to buy my latest copy. I wanted her to be a part of the transaction and imagined her getting horny at the thought of my buying the magazine. In my mind, we would make out behind the counter, while confused customers would look around the shop wondering about who to pay. Buying from a shop meant there was also the added excitement of my being well under age. Still, they never seemed to mind – it was all money and they must have been used to a stream of schoolboys following a similar path.

As I became more enveloped in this new, voluptuous and shiny world of perfect women, I would take greater and greater risks. On one occasion I very nearly fell foul of discovery in mid-come by Miss Fuller, the young assistant matron at Hebbingdon. I had returned to school early one Sunday because Dada had to drop me off on his way to the airport, and no-one else was back in our dorm. That weekend I had bought a new copy of Mayfair, and had read a story about an orgy, where a whole group of people were having sex together out in the open air. I was inspired with the idea of masturbating outside and, checking that no-one was around, I hid my magazine inside my coat and walked excitedly down to the small wood beside the cricket-pitch. It must have been the summer term, because I walked through the wood to the field beyond, and remember that it was knee-high in grass and wild flowers. I went a short way into the field and lay down on a soft bed of greenery. I flicked through some pictures and started playing with myself; one woman in particular held my attention and I remember wanting her to hold me, to speak to me, to make me come. As my excitement neared fever-pitch, I suddenly became aware of the noise of someone walking near the edge of the wood. Peering through the grasses, I could see the young woman whom many of us older boys had dreamt of screwing.

I lay as flat as I could and couldn't stop masturbating except now I rubbed my hand up and down in rhythm with what I perceived to be the movement of her own body. She unwittingly became a part of the act; my first shared sexual experience. I imagined her finding me and joining me in the grass. I kept as quiet as I could as the footsteps came nearer. I wanted to hear her breathing, but I could not. A part of me even wanted her to discover me, but she did not. She must have passed within just a few yards of me and just as she was at the closest point to me, I shot my load all over the magazine and the grass that was acting as my bed. It was everything I could do not to shout. I was never able to see Miss Fuller after that without feeling sexually aroused. She was my partner, and we had nearly done it together.

The trouble with magazines was that they regularly needed replacing – the same old images failed to hold their magic for long, and that required ever more financial resources. And so I pushed myself ever forwards into greater achievements, driving myself harder and harder to get higher and higher marks, which resulted in bigger and better rewards. Whether I really had a passion for even one of the subjects was irrelevant; it was all about whether I could tick the boxes and secure the approved of results. Like my father before me, motivated by a group of questionable driving forces, I became fully focused on my goal, and by the end of my last year I gained a place at Freestone, a public school of considerable repute.

7

It took Dada precisely two days of being back at home before he had managed to rip out the catheter. His memory being as it was, he had simply seen some wires in the way of his life and decided to tidy them up. I had winced when I discovered it, but he seemed fine and unbothered. At first, I thought this must be bad news. Not that my concern was for my own inconvenience in having to deal with bedwetting. My worry was for him; for his discomfort in not being able to urinate; for his loss of pride when accidents happened.

When Doreen, the visiting community nurse, arrived that morning, she suggested that I provide him with a bottle to pee into. He was no longer able to make it to the loo, and this could provide a temporary solution while they tried to figure out a better method. Dada, surprisingly took to it straightaway – in fact his first deposit was so large he nearly filled the bottle to overflowing which was extraordinary considering he seemed to be drinking so little.

He had been in hospital this time for five days. They said he had been as quiet as a mouse. They put his quietness down to politeness. I put it down to his terror at being in a strange place with unknown people constantly coming up and touching him, talking to him, demanding things of him. For an old man with a weak grasp on reality, but still with a strong grasp on his pride, it must have been very confusing. And, unsurprisingly perhaps, his confusion levels were worse following each visit to the hospital.

I had to wheelchair him out for the first time, and he seemed smaller and greyer and more detached than ever. I could tell that his first foray into the outside world was as if he had just landed on the planet. I clumsily manoeuvred the chair round to face the passenger seat in the car, and saw that his face was slightly tilted towards the sky and his eyes were tightly shut as he experienced the refreshing and scary sensation of the strong north wind upon his institutionally-numbed face.

The bone scan was booked for three weeks hence. It is true I could have pushed for a private scan and got it done much quicker, but somehow all this exploration seemed like unnecessary intervention for a man who only wanted to be left alone. Dada was beyond making his own rational decisions, so I was having to trust my own instinct more and more.

Hmm, trusting my own instinct. Not something in which I had received even the tiniest amount of education during my years at either Hebbingdon or Freestone. In fact I'd go further than that – I'd say I was actively taught to distrust my own instinct, learning to rely exclusively instead on that pillar of western societal thinking, the intellect.

The next couple of days involved further home visits from two different doctors on call; one who was slightly familiar with Dada's case, and one who didn't know it at all. They were both noticeably surprised by the incident with the catheter, and his subsequent ease at peeing on demand into his bottle, and fortunately, made no suggestions to re-connect the intrusive device. Of greater concern to me was that Dada was still in pain, great pain at times, although when we could get him to focus on breathing properly he did manage to alleviate his symptoms a little. I talked to both doctors about this pain and they were still both invested in trying to sort out what was wrong. Understandable of course, considering a doctor's role is to save lives.

But they didn't know Dada. I knew he was beyond fixing. I didn't know it with my head, I knew it with my heart. This wasn't a time for diagnosis, it was a time for death management. I listened to the doctors and nodded my head at their respective suggestions for future hospital tests and referrals; and then I insisted that they give him what he needed to be out of pain.

At times I could feel the massive responsibility I was taking on his behalf. Me, a man with little understanding of the complex workings of the body or serious illness, was daring to suggest that I knew better what my Dada needed than the professionals. Me, a man once so out of touch with the real value of friendship and so ignorant about emotion, that he had let the most important relationship of all gather dust in a cupboard, while the trophies of material success took pride of place on the mantelpiece. And yet this same man was now taking a leading part in the evaluation and interpretation of what many view as the scariest, or biggest, or most sacred, of all human events; a person's dying process.

And so I nodded my head in the general direction of the doctors and their desire to diagnose and fix Dada, while all the time believing that the one job I had to do now was make sure I didn't miss any of the signals that might indicate how we could ease his passage out of here.

One night, quite late, as we were watching television, I heard Dada call out. He sounded agitated. Jumping up to his calls had become a reflex over these last few weeks, but this particular appeal sounded more urgent in its nature.

"Hi Dada – what's the matter? Can't sleep?"

"Are they here?"

"Who's that Dada? Are who here?" My mind was still on the Eighteenth Century costume drama I'd been watching.

"The ministers of course. Are they here yet?"

"Oh. Right, the ministers. Let me go and check".

"Come back with a notebook, will you – this all needs to be documented."

"Right you are Dada – will do."

I left the room and went into the lounge. Helen had started to record the programme we'd been watching and looked up at me. She had been an angel throughout this illness of Dada's, and she had also been quite firm in making sure that I dealt with as many of the hospital and doctor's meetings as possible. It would have been so easy for her to slip into the role of nursing my father, but after all we'd been through she understood that this was about him and me. This was about our relationship. This was about the stripping away of everything I had believed once to be my father, and Helen knew that. It was no more or less a part of her journey than it was the visiting doctor's or nurse's. She supported me, I supported Dada. So logical, so right. And so many millions of miles away from how I would have once handled it.

"So, what does he want?"

"He wants to know if the ministers are here. And he wants me to take notes."

"Well, you better let them all in and put on your best secretarial act, Alex."

I went to the solid walnut Edwardian desk that we had brought from Dada's when he was forced to move in with me, and pulled out the large centre drawer that now contained my notepad. I took a gel pen from the little glass of pens that sat beside his large blotting-paper pad, a pad still decorated with the first blue and black scratchings of newly filled fountain pens from down the years.

I returned to the room and his eyes were shut. I turned to leave, but was restrained by a voice that sounded clearer and more certain than it had in a long time.

"So, are they here?"

"Yes Dada, they're here."

"And you've got your notebook?"

"Yes, I have my notebook."

"In that case, Mr Edwards, ask them to come in and let's begin."

8

My first inkling that all was not well between my parents came in the summer holiday that separated my lives at Hebbingdon and Freestone. When you're in a relatively confined space for a concentrated amount of time it is that much harder to hide differences and disagreements. Our holiday that summer was in Puglia, a part of Italy almost undiscovered by the increasingly ubiquitous English tourist.

Now that I think about it, even agreeing on the destination had been a problem. Dada wanted to go to the South of France, but Mumma was bored with exploring Nice and Cannes and was probably bored with Dada ogling all the beautiful young women whom I had first started to notice on last year's trip. So Mumma got her way and had selected, in her own words, 'the part of Italy that time forgot'.

We were staying in a hotel which stood high up in the white city of Ostuni. The trip had been difficult, with a long delay at Heathrow which had resulted in us all boarding the plane and then getting off again and waiting for a further two hours in the departure lounge. The flight was uneventful, but after we had arrived in Italy it was discovered that our luggage, and that of various other passengers, had gone missing.

I don't believe I had ever seen Dada so furious. I suppose a combination of the delay at Heathrow, a few on-board drinks, a holiday destination about which he had been more than suspicious, and now this horror in the heat, were all too much for him to remain calm. While all the other passengers stood dutifully in line, waiting for the Italian staff to find out what had happened, my Dada stormed back out through the customs gate we had just come through and down the steps onto the tarmac. By this time he was being followed by at least two airport staff and a rotund member of the carabinieri. They were gesticulating and shouting at him, as was Mumma, but he was ploughing on back towards our plane, which stood motionless in the hot sun.

By the time he reached the foot of the steps, the other men had caught him up. Not knowing what else to do, Mumma and I had followed, although neither of us could keep up with the men. I was terrified. The carabinieri had a gun which he had pulled out of its holster and was now brandishing in Dada's general direction. The two airport staff were trying to hold Dada's arms, but all the time he was shaking them off, and pointing to the plane's hold.

I wanted to run. I wanted someone to turn back the clock so that we were all sitting on the plane again, chatting about the white-peaked mountains we had just flown over. Dada had committed the cardinal sin as the parent of a teenage boy – he had embarrassed me. Although somewhere inside I could hear a distant voice shouting in support of him, a very large part of me wanted to disown him.

He didn't speak any Italian and the Italians seemed unable to speak any English. They tried, in increasingly loud voices, to explain to each other the whys and wherefores of their respective actions. Growing ever more impatient with them, Dada broke free of the men's grasp, and just as he did so, there was the shocking sound of a gun being fired, followed by Mumma's scream. At this moment I felt the wrench begin to tighten around my stomach, to the extent that within seconds I couldn't feel anything other than a deep loathing for my Dada for putting me and Mumma through hell. And all for a couple of suitcases.

At almost exactly the same time as the carabinieri had fired his gun into the air, two uniformed men emerged from the plane. Judging by their caps I assumed they were the captain and the co-pilot. They were both English and recognised Dada at once. In spite of the horror of what had just happened, the two men smiled and approached him, signalling to the carabinieri to remain where he was. The policeman was studying his gun as if it had been the first time he had ever had to fire it.

Within a couple of minutes, all the men were gathered around Dada and they were all in animated conversation, punctuated by laughter. Mumma and I were left a few yards away, close enough to feel we could not go anywhere, yet far enough away to feel outsiders. I watched as the men did what men do, and hated the fact that we were left as curious bystanders. I could tell that Mumma was forcing back tears. I wished I could feel like her; I yearned for the healing release of this emotion that had by now burrowed its way deep into my inner recesses. But the clamp had done its work and my emotional constipation was already established.

As ever, Dada was right. He had seen the luggage being put on the plane. It turned out that there had been so much baggage on that flight, that the handlers at Heathrow had had to use the spare hold normally reserved for special cargo. As the missing suitcases were disgorged from the interior of the Boeing, Dada and his new cronies shook hands and he walked back towards us. Mumma started to turn away even before he reached us.

We walked back into the airport, where a small crowd of passengers had gathered to watch the saga unfold. As we entered the building, one of the men from our flight started to clap Dada, and before long a whole crowd of people were clapping him. He was still behind us. Mumma seemed deaf to the applause. I turned around and could see how he was loving it. Smiling from ear to ear. Our fellow Brits followed us to the luggage collection point, and by the time we got there, the whole room was reverberating to the sound of 'For he's a jolly good fellow.'

Dada had saved the day – at least for the people who had been told that their luggage was still back at Heathrow. But he hadn't done much for his marriage.

And, although I wanted to feel pride in his achievement, and for having the courage to storm through the barriers of accepted good behaviour, I could not. I only had to look at Mumma to know that the hero was also the villain, it was merely a matter of perspective.

The holiday crawled by. That part of Italy was definitely undiscovered by the English, which might have been nice for the adults, but not so for a thirteen-year old boy. Being stuck in a posh hotel with mainly middle-aged, and presumably middle-class, Italians, and just my parents for company would not normally have bothered me. But this time it did, because of the silences, heavy with meaning, that now pervaded my parents' relationship. They weren't just not speaking, they were becoming openly hostile towards each other, particularly once the red wine had begun to weave its sinister spell.

I noticed that Mumma was getting up later and later in the morning; she complained of not having slept well to me and needing to lie in, but even if that was the truth, I knew there was a reason why she wasn't sleeping well. Dada started to spend a lot more time at the bar round the pool, and quickly made friends with anyone who would listen to his appalling Italian or try to interpret his embarrassing sign language. He often struck a lonely figure, sitting up on his bar stool, his eyes forever searching for...

For what? For who? For Mumma? For another opportunity to become the centre of attention? For the beautiful women he had become accustomed to in Cannes? Exactly what was Dada always looking for?

As for me, I lost myself in Alistair Maclean. I yearned to be one of his heroes, battling it out with the forces of evil, often with not much more than their bare hands. I'd spend hours plotting my escape from this luxurious hell that was our holiday, an escape carried out by abseiling down sheer cliffs and lying low under over-hanging rocks that reached out in to the deep blue waters. I'd imagine myself having to stay silent while all around me were the frenzied voices of the hotel staff who were festooned with guns and knives.

I started to dread our shared meals. Mumma was becoming more and more distant and Dada was drinking more and more. They didn't so much talk to each other as at each other; that is when they used words at all. Listening, or making an effort to be civil, seemed to play a negligible part in their relationship now, and they didn't much seem to care whether I knew it or not. Silence became my greatest enemy, containing within its impenetrable walls all the secrets of my parents' ailing relationship.

Any time the conversation flagged, I would try to start it up again with stupid comments about the hotel, the staff, the food and even the weather. Not that there was much to comment on as far as the weather was concerned. "Oh look, it's another glorious day." My feeble efforts afforded little relief to the volatile atmosphere that permeated the biggest family event of the year. And when I started to think about their relationship, I became increasingly aware that I hadn't seen my parents happy together for ages. When I returned from school on long weekends, Dada was often away working or playing golf. Mumma had told me it was just the way the calendars clashed.

Recently there had been a few occasions when Dada had been the one to come and get me – once we even went off to a country inn for the weekend because he said that Mumma was visiting some friends of hers. Dada was proud of himself for laying the whole thing on, but ended up spending much of the weekend in the bar talking to the woman who owned the inn. Of course she was beaming at having a celebrity in her hotel.

Dada had said that now I was becoming a young man we needed our own spaces, and, much as I appreciated the splendour of having my own room, I also felt pushed away. If I was going to be with him, I wanted to be near him. I knew I could learn if I could only watch him. I think that a part of me was desperate for some male guidance on how to move from boyhood to adolescence. Or perhaps I just wanted to spend some time with my Dada. Either way, the anticipation of these occasional weekends with him never matched the result.

I did wonder if that was what that Italian holiday was partly about. Maybe the reason Mumma had selected such a boring place for a teenage boy to holiday, was because she wanted me to see exactly what was going on in their relationship. Or, maybe she was just trying to get one over on Dada, knowing he'd hate Puglia all along.

Try as I did to lose myself in books, as the holiday wore on so the shell continued to close around my heart. I had no desire to face what may be happening between Mumma and Dada. I couldn't even look forward to getting back to the now familiar environment of Hebbingdon, as the day was fast nearing when I would be thrust into the hallowed halls that were Freestone.

We came back from that holiday with tans but not much else. I hadn't even bought myself a present; we had hardly moved away from the hotel and the couple of shops that we did visit were all full of the same postcards and books in Italian. I got so bored that I did buy a postcard and sent it to myself, just to see how long it would take to arrive back in England. Other than my name and address, I wrote three words on that postcard. 'I'm so-o-o bored.'

For the rest of that school holiday before my arrival at Freestone, the three of us shared the same space at home on probably no more than a couple of occasions. I was told by Dada that he was having to work hard now to pay for the holiday we had 'enjoyed'; when I asked Mumma why Dada wasn't around at weekends, she told me simply that he was working. It was all an act, but I didn't know it then. I hated the fact that Dada was having to work so hard to earn the money to pay for a holiday which we had all detested. I felt guilt and regret that it was therefore partly my fault that he was being driven away from home, away from us. Mumma and he needed to be together to become friends again like they used to be.

With a growing sense of dread inside, I sought escape through whatever means I could find. I tried my first cigarettes. I took my bike out on long cycle rides, pushing myself to ever further lengths, studying my mileometer regularly to see if I could break my distance and or speed records, feats that I achieved just often enough to sustain my interest. I tried some of the spirits in the cocktail cabinet while my mother was out shopping and found that I had a penchant for vodka, a drink we seemed to have in particularly large supply. Well, I say a penchant; what I really discovered one night, when Mumma had left me alone for the evening while going to the cinema with a friend, was that it seemed to get me drunk quickly. In my drunken state that night, I noticed that my worries about Mumma and Dada and Freestone all seemed to have evaporated. And, although I did throw up in my bathroom later that evening, I was pleased to wake up in the morning without any dire side effects. What's more, I'd got away with it; no-one had witnessed my shameful and self-inflicted loss of control.

But then no-one was witnessing anything that I was up to during the remainder of that holiday. One of the problems of being at boarding-school was that friends were geographically scattered far and wide, which meant complex arrangements had to be made if I was to get together with anyone. My closest friend, John, who lived on the other side of London, and with whom I would have spent at least a weekend, had been taken out to California for six weeks by his parents and was not returning until after my departure for Freestone. So I was, to all intents and purposes, alone.

There must have been some good films on that summer, because Mumma went to the cinema a few more times in the last few weeks of the holiday. Mumma had become much quieter during the day once she had got out of bed, which seemed to be getting later and later; but, on the nights when she was going to see a film, she became more like her old self. In fact she became more like a Mumma I never knew. She'd disappear into her bedroom and bathroom for at least an hour and would come out looking elegant and stylish. Her mood would be transformed and I was so happy for her, although I desperately wanted Dada to see her looking so good, and for them to be going to the film together.

I got excited during the days that she was planning her evening treats; for me it meant a night alone with the vodka bottle, television and my porn mags. I'd anticipate spending the whole evening immersed in a two to three hour feast of gradually increasing ecstasy, an evening which would make the most of every solitary minute and come to a climax maybe just a few minutes before Mumma would walk back in through the door.

The experience never matched the expectation. Within about forty-five minutes or so of being left alone I would find myself staring gormlessly at the box having guzzled some food and booze and wanked off to whichever celluloid beauty had captured my heart for that particular night. I'd go to bed feeling bad and somehow guilty, in my heart if not in my body, although not understanding why.

When I went out on my cycle rides, I'd fantasise about meeting a beautiful girl like the ones in the magazines. Sometimes I'd cycle through the housing estates just to raise the chances of spotting girls out on their streets or in their gardens. Of course, whenever I did find any, they'd invariably be in groups and I'd be so nervous that I'd cycle straight past them as if heading purposefully for a known destination.

On one such occasion, I was cycling towards a group of four girls who were walking towards me on the other side of the road. Don't ask me why, but I stopped about fifty yards short of them and pretended to be testing my brakes. As I knelt down with one hand on a brake the other on the saddle, I peered under my crossbar towards the oncoming group. To my partial delight and partial horror, they crossed the road and kept coming towards me. Once they were about thirty yards away, three of them disappeared into a house, leaving the fourth heading straight for me.

I thought I'd better make this look good, so I turned my bike upside down to balance it on its handle bars, and, half-crouching, rolled my sleeves up to reveal my bare lower arms. The girl kept walking towards me, and I could feel my heart speeding up with every step that she took. I was pressing brake handles, spinning wheels, turning pedals. And my insides felt like they were doing much the same.

"Got a problem wiv yer bike?" Oh God, she spoke to me. Now what?

"Erm, yeah – yeah I think my brake calliper needs adjusting."

She giggled. "Ooh, er, listen to you. I bet your brake calliper does need adjusting – just what I would have said was wrong."

We both laughed. I felt a wave of relief wash through me as I had my first simultaneous experience with a girl of my own age; synchronised laughter. I was just beginning to enjoy the way this new relationship was developing - potentially into something serious - when my hopes were dashed.

"Oh well, can't hang around here all day talking to you can I? Gotter bus to catch." And I watched, heartbroken, as my first love disappeared as quickly as she had arrived, heading off into the arms of the waiting number forty-seven bus which had, to my chagrin, somehow manifested twenty feet from my pretend breakdown.

A few days later, and very close to the end of my last ever school holiday of being thirteen years old, Mumma announced again that she was going to the cinema. This time I questioned her more about her plans for the evening; what was the film? Which cinema was she going to? Who was she going with? She didn't seem to enjoy the questions, but I put this down to the fact that she had not long since got out of bed. Eventually I managed to get the information I needed, and I got to work on my plan.

Dada didn't like me calling him at the office, but I didn't do it often and I felt sure this time he would understand. It was usually okay as long as I didn't call when he was about to go into the studio.

"Hello Alexander, what's the problem?" His voice sounded more formal than when he was at home. I was talking partly to my Dada, partly to a current affairs television presenter.

"Hello Dada. I won't bother you for long. How's work?" All of a sudden I was nervous again and I could feel my stomach tightening more. I didn't want to dive straight in with my idea.

"Well, I'm very busy actually, Alexander, so if you could make this quick?" I could almost touch his disapproval with my fingers. I took a deep breath and plunged into my newly-hatched scheme.

"Dada – can we go to the cinema tonight? Could you get down here and we'll go out – you and me?"

The silence was deafening. It probably only lasted a few seconds, but I couldn't bear it. It reminded me of those moments on holiday when Mumma and Dada would say nothing to each other and I felt compelled to fill the spaces. I babbled on nervously.

"It's just that I start the new school next week, and this might be our last chance to do something."

This last bit of filial blackmail must have done the trick, because Dada spoke again.

"Yes, yes, alright."

My plan was very simple. I wanted Dada to see Mumma all dressed up and looking so stylish. I wanted him to fall in love with her again and for everything to be alright, like it must have been once. I wanted to go off to my new boarding school, knowing all was well at home and that I had helped to fix things.

I arranged for Dada to come home to pick me up at six-thirty. Mumma never normally left until six forty-five. I had found out the name of the friend with whom Mumma was going to the cinema and, when she was lying in bed that morning, had managed to decipher the friend's number, which had been scrawled in Mumma's spidery writing in her address book. I called and left a message on the friend's answer-phone to say that Mumma couldn't make the film that night.

I had even booked a table at our favourite Chinese restaurant, the one they took me to when I got decent reports. I'd saved up enough money to be able to pay for it; this was to be my gift to my parents. My way of saying, '*thanks for all you've done, and in return please will you spend more time together, and be happy for ever.*' I had bought a bunch of white lilies, Mumma's favourite flowers, which I had hidden in my wardrobe to be brought out at the end of the perfect evening, and whose smell would continue to remind us all for days of the successful reunion.

43

At ten past six, as I was up in my room deciding what to wear, I heard Mumma coming up the stairs. She knocked on my door.

"Yes Mumma, come in." My heart almost burst with excitement – she looked better than ever. She was wearing her white jacket, which was partly buttoned up, and underneath it a dress I had never seen before, a dress which I couldn't help but notice revealed the beginnings of her cleavage.

"Wow, you look – you look beautiful, Mumma."

Mumma seemed almost embarrassed by my compliment; she smiled at me and gave me a hug.

"Well, thank you, Alexander. I just threw it on – I'm only going to the movies you know."

"Yes, I know – with Georgie. Remember? You told me."

Mumma bustled around as she spoke, tidying things on my chest of drawers, and putting away clean underwear that I hadn't got round to filing.

"That's right, you have a good memory for names, don't you?"

Outside the house I heard the sound of a car pulling up outside the house and the engine being switched off. My heart was thumping. The moment had arrived earlier than I had expected. Dada must have raced through the traffic to get here so early. What would they say when they found out what I had plotted?

Both Mumma and I headed for the window.

"Well, Georgie's here already – that's her car."

I couldn't believe what I was hearing or seeing.

"But it can't be – it can't be Georgie."

"Alex what on earth are you talking about? Of course it is. We agreed to meet a bit earlier than usual tonight because we're going to a different cinema. Now then, I could be back late so don't wait up for me – you need to get plenty of sleep so that you're ready for your new adventure next week." She came up to me, gave me another hug, and vanished down the stairs.

I was speechless. How could I have possibly thought that such a naïve, simplistic plan could have ever worked? What had I been thinking? So many things could have gone wrong, and one of them duly had. Georgie had not got my message; maybe I hadn't even dialled the number correctly. I'll never know.

Dada arrived at his appointed time of six-thirty, but by then it didn't matter. I was useless and my plan had failed. I had at least had the presence of mind to call the restaurant and tell them only two people would be coming, seconds before his car pulled up outside. I then told Dada that I was hungry and had reserved a table at the Chinese for us.

I don't remember what we spoke about that night; small talk about the new school, and stories about Dada's television guests probably. The staff at the restaurant loved him because he was the local celebrity, and Dada always played up to that role for them. There was even a signed photo of him, alongside other slightly better known but more ancient celebrities, on the wall beside the counter.

And as if all this failure wasn't enough, Dada didn't even let me pay for the meal when I suggested it as my gift to him for being a great father.

Since we had eaten early he offered to take me to the cinema for the late-night showing. The cinema was not busy and we spent a couple of hours watching some comedy about a couple of northern girls who move to Torquay and become chamber-maids. It was set to a background of punk music most of which I hated; I think it had a couple of fairly sexy scenes in it too, but I never got into it. My mind was still on my failed scheme.

By the time we left the cinema it was getting late, but the long summer nights meant it never got properly dark. As we pulled up outside our house, I could see on the pavement between the car and our driveway, but obscured from sight of the house by our large beech hedge, two figures entwined around each other in a loving embrace. They broke apart quickly as the car approached.

It was Mumma. I don't know what shocked me more, seeing my Mumma kissing someone else other than my Dada, or realising that the other person my Mumma had been wrapped around was a woman.

Dada got back in the car without saying a word and drove off. He left me standing there, on the pavement, my dreams of parental harmony lying shattered amongst the dogshit, fag ends and ripped plastic bags that littered the road around the drain.

I walked straight past Mumma and her friend and into the house. I shot up the stairs, shut the door to my room and crawled into bed. There was a strong, unfamiliar smell in my room. The lilies. I pulled them out of my wardrobe and flung them out of the window. I would never, ever, allow myself to become so vulnerable again. I never, ever, wanted to feel this degree of disappointment and failure. My plan had hopelessly backfired. Dada would never have known about Mumma's secret if I hadn't invited him to spend the evening with me. I might never have known.

I had looked to Dada's actions for clues as to how I should respond. He had just walked away, and so I did the same thing. I turned my back on my dream and determined to get myself focussed on school and other serious things as quickly as possible. Families were rubbish. It was time to grow up and start sorting my own life out.

Mumma tried to speak to me in the last few days of the holidays about what I'd seen, but I had switched off. I didn't want to know. My mother was a lesbo, my parents' relationship was crap and, in my feeble attempt to make things better between them, I had spectacularly ruined any chance of their doing so. I had blown it, and the only way I could avoid being eaten alive by the guilt that I created that night, was to bury it somewhere so deep that no-one would ever be able to find it. I never wanted to trust my feelings again.

9

"They're all in here Dad. All the ministers are here." I hoped he'd not question me on this, and was not disappointed.

"Good." His voice sounded stronger and surer than for many days. He tried to prop himself up in his bed, but the pain was too much, and he wouldn't let me try to make him any more comfortable. So, with his torso tilted slightly to the left and his neck angled to try to compensate, he began what I now refer to as 'Dada's Last Testament of Will'.

"We are pleased to see so many of you here today on this very splendid occasion. We are more than pleased to see that the honourable Prime Minister has been able to attend, as well as all the senior Cabinet Ministers. You will be excited too I'm sure to know why it is you have all been called at such short notice to this meeting, and so without further delay, let us begin."

The use of the royal 'we' was intriguing. I had never heard him start a sentence like that. I tried to keep up with my note-taking, but it wasn't easy. I didn't want to interrupt his flow and yet I felt that, for him at least, this was important. I took the risk of disappearing for a moment, leaving the door wide open, and I hurriedly pulled out my voice recorder from the same desk that had held my notebook.

When I got back into the room there was silence. I looked at Dada; he was staring ahead, his eyes focussed on some target that I could not perceive. I sat down and waited.

"What's that thing?" He was shakily pointing at my voice recorder. He suddenly seemed very present again.

"It's like a dictaphone, Dada – for recording voices."

"How do you work it then?" With new strength he grasped the little machine.

"You just press this and, hey presto. Look, I'll show you. Just say something."

But he went silent. At least five minutes passed with nothing uttered. His sudden silences I had become used to in recent weeks, but not the staring thing that he was doing now. I found it mildly unsettling.

I looked at the clock and realised it was time for his pills. I took a couple of the little white capsules from the bottle and put them in his hand. He turned his head and looked at me with a gentle, benevolent smile.

"You're a good boy, Alexander. You know, I love you very, very much."

I swallowed hard. A reflex from a bygone time when I used to force down every single emotion that would have the temerity to rise towards the surface of my being. The first tear fought its way through the reflex wall, and once breached, the wall crumbled thick and fast. Tears flowed out of me as I looked at Dada, and he, still smiling, gazed back at me.

These tears communicated to me that I was already grieving for the loss of my Dada. He was still alive and yet I was grieving. Things had changed between us so much now that I needed to make no effort to hide or contain these small traitors of emotion that would once have incurred Dada's wrath.

And even with the tears, these moments with him were becoming increasingly precious to me. I knew nothing about death and yet I was engaging more and more consciously in a process that the doctors were still trying to convince us was not happening. There was magic happening here and I could almost touch it. Helen knew it too. And she gave me the support so that I could immerse myself in an experience from which, a few years ago, I would have run a mile.

The most interesting thing about my crying that time was Dada's response; he seemed at peace with it. He didn't ask me why I was upset; he didn't try to jolly me along or change the subject. He just smiled.

I went out of the room to splash some water on my face. Even as I got up from the armchair that we had crammed into his small room to alleviate the discomfort of our night-time vigils, I felt a greater sense of lightness deep inside me. These tears were like oxen carrying away with them their burdens of guilt, grief, anger and resentment.

I gave it about half an hour before returning. I'd heard a little mumbling coming from his room, but he sounded perfectly calm, so I let him be. When I went back, I was preparing myself once again to take notes, and intending to use the recorder as backup in case I got behind. But the room had fallen almost silent once again, save for the gentle rasping that betrayed his ever-increasing need to sleep. I switched off the recorder which must have been running all this time, and left him to explore his approaching new reality.

10

Freestone School was set in the heart of the Sussex countryside, close enough to the small village of Thornleigh to be considered a part of its community, but far away enough to feel fairly isolated. The main building was an imposing mansion with large windows, its front wall covered in creepers and ivy, about all of which Mumma gushed admiringly as we drove through the wrought-iron gates and parked in the car park.

Dada hadn't come. I didn't blame him. The car journey had been filled with the banal pleasantries to which I had become acclimatised over the last couple of days, and my new-boy nerves had been more than cancelled out by my desire to get away from home. But, as I stepped out of the car and witnessed another much younger boy clutching both his parents in what would be the final embrace of his childish innocence, a part of me yearned to run around and hug Mumma. Hug her, and let her know that it was okay. That whatever had happened, I would learn to be alright with it, and that I still loved her, no matter what. She saw me looking at the young boy and came round towards me offering that familiar smile that had brought me so much comfort over the years. But, at that moment I heard another boy shouting goodbye to his father, and I was suddenly jerked back into the world where my mother had cheated on my Dada with another woman. As she came close to me, I looked away and muttered something about getting the cases out of the boot.

At that moment, our relationship changed. I chose to go down the route of non-communication. I chose to punish her for her sins by not allowing her to support me at a time when I desperately needed a hug and to be told that she'd never be far away, and that if the school didn't work out I could always go home. I needed reassurance, but that boy's yell of 'Goodbye Father' had flipped the switch and I denied myself all of those things that would have given me comfort. And so we found our way to the front hall, were met by a boarding school prefect who would show me to my dormitory, and Mumma and I said our polite goodbyes.

The next couple of days before the official beginning of term hurtled by in a frenzy of introductions, building identifications and system descriptions. Entering at nearly fourteen years old as I was, there were already some boarders my age familiar with it all, and they tended to have a swagger about them that displayed their current superiority. This authority would gradually be eroded as we beginners became used to our surroundings, but at this crucial time of our initiation, new arrivals were left in no doubt that we were an inferior, or at least more innocent, breed.

I had been taken to my room by Mr Pilton, our house-master. He told me that he and his wife ran this boarding-house together, and said that if I ever needed to talk to a woman about anything, even about missing my mother, then his wife would gladly listen. He reminded me of Mr Gardiner at Hebbingdon. He was younger, but he had that same kindness in his face, and I immediately liked him. He didn't talk about rules or regulations, saying that those sorts of things would be gone over in our house-meeting on the first day of term.

I shared my dorm with three other boys. It was a fairly large room with two sets of bunk beds on either side, and a couple of two-seater wooden desks at the far end of the room, immediately under the white metal-framed window. In the spaces between the beds and the walls there were two wardrobes, a chest of drawers in which we were each allocated one drawer, and a small bookcase half-filled with ancient Latin readers and dusty Ian Fleming books.

My fellow 'happy campers' as we came to be called by Mr Pilton, were an assorted bunch. Matthew Dyer was red-headed, broadly built, and had come into the school after the Eleven-plus examination. Andrew Percival, who had also been at Freestone for two years, was unbelievably tall; I don't think I'd ever seen a boy my age of his height, and yet he had a high-pitched, squeaky voice which seemed a mismatch with his stature. Finally there was Claude Denoir, whose father had recently become the French ambassador in London, and who was completely new to the English education system. He, at least, made me feel like I wasn't the only public school virgin.

By the time the term started, I had started to feel at home in my surroundings and had begun to establish a friendship with Claude. We occupied neighbouring bunks and we were also in the same class, whereas Matt and Percy (as we discovered Andrew's school-acquired nickname to be) were in different streams. Claude's English was impressive. I couldn't help feeling it was often better than my own; he used his words so carefully. His rare mistakes were all the more amusing and endearing to me because of his strenuous efforts at correctness.

After only two days of settling in, I felt almost smug when the day-bugs and newbies started arriving on the school's official first day of term. Because our house-meeting before the first assembly took place in our very own building, a staircase walk away from our dorms, we were able to stand at the window and witness the beginning-of-year arrival, an annual ritual at which Matt and Percy were apparently old hands.

"Hey, hey – look at this kid. He looks green with terror" shouted Matt with delight, as he pointed out a boy who had been walked as far as the school gate by a woman dressed in a smart, navy-blue suit. The boy was tiny, he must have been starting year one, not year three, like me. He stood at the edge of the boundary that separated the school from the outside world, hesitating to make that step that would signal his departure from his former life into this new, unknown territory.

"Fifty pence says he pukes" said Matt heartlessly, and Percy at once took him up on his bet. We all huddled more closely round the window to see what Tiny would do. His mother gave him a gentle nudge through the gate, but it was enough to make him stumble. He fell to the ground, his bag distributing its contents all around him. His mother bent to help him pick up his belongings, and Tiny hastily stuffed everything back into his bag while looking all around him, hoping no-one had noticed his gaffe.

"Fifty pence down, but excellent value for money – Tiny wins the show so far. Now who else have we got. Cor, look at her. Is that his mum?" Matt was already sizing up his next victim as we were all still laughing at Tiny's misfortune.

We all looked at where Matt was pointing. A school bus had arrived and a mass of boys was just getting off. Just in front of the bus was a sports car and a glamorous woman had got out and was saying goodbye to her son. At least we assumed she was his mother – she looked young enough to be his older sister. Almost every boy's head turned to look at this vision as they streamed out of the bus and past her car.

"I wouldn't mind giving her one," muttered Matt, his voice sounding entirely different now that he was thinking about sex.

"Ooh, that's vile – she's probably old enough to be your mother" replied Percy, who was able to stand behind all of us and still see what was going on.

"Yes, now she is really somesing." Every now and then the occasional word would give away Claude's Gallic origins. We fell silent for a moment as we all tried to get the best view of the beautiful woman.

We were shaken from our reverie by the sound of the bell announcing the first house-meeting of term. Life at Freestone was officially about to begin.

Routines quickly became established. Much to my amazement, it turned out that the same 'Tiny' whose unlucky bag spillage had so amused us, was not a year-one student, but was in my own class. In fact James, as it turned out he was called, was six months older than me, which floored me when he first told me his birth date. He sat next to me in our first lesson and we quickly became friends, sharing as we did a love of rugby and music. His size made him a perfect hooker, and he had excelled in that position at his previous school. I had the build for a front-row forward, being stocky and reasonably well-proportioned, so we often found ourselves linked up in scrum work and joining the jostling for places in the A and B third-year teams.

I noticed during these early weeks that boys rarely spoke about their families and that, when they did, they would usually refer to their 'parents' or to their 'mothers and fathers'. Staff also used the term 'mothers and fathers', rather than 'mum and dad', and I started to adopt this new terminology. I started to feel the adult pushing through the skin of the boy. If we became upset, we were instructed not to cry; crying, we were informed, would fix nothing and only serve to make us more distressed. Since we were in an institution that was founded upon the giving and obeying of orders, we strove to follow these commands.

One night when I was feeling particularly homesick, I remember Mrs Pilton hunting me out in the house drawing-room. I had just returned from a freezing session of extra rugby practice in preparation for an upcoming trials match the following week-end, to find a note on my bed saying that I had missed a call from my father. A part of me still longed for communication with either of my parents, and my father was so busy that missing his one call was like missing five of mother's. Just thinking about speaking to him and hearing his voice was still enough to stir me up, a vulnerability that I was learning to resent.

Mrs Pilton sat down and asked me what I was upset about and I remember telling her about the phone call, and that I was missing my parents and I wanted to go home. She let me talk for a while, but then, just when I began to feel confident about opening up to her about my fears for them and for the future, she interrupted my flow, saying,

"There's no need to cry. No need at all. You're a big lad now. You'll be fine. Just give it some time. When I get feelings I don't like, I imagine I've got a bottle and I take all those nasty feelings in the palm of my hand and push them tightly into the bottle, put the lid on and pretend to throw them out to sea. It works wonders. You should try it, Baker. Your parents will be here to pick you up in ten days and by then you'll have forgotten all about this."

And in those few brief words, the emotional needs of my nearly fourteen year old self were dismissed as being unnecessary. Surplus to requirements. And, like a good boy and being keen to impress in my new environment, I rammed back those stupid emotions into the bottle from which they had apparently escaped and screwed on the lid tight. Under the watchful eye of Mrs Pilton, I threw that bottle out to sea as far I could manage and, with her congratulations reverberating around my head, I went back to my dorm determined not to allow a single tear to betray my needless wobble. I took it as a sign of success and strength that none of the others noticed my weakness that night. And I daresay that Mrs Pilton returned to her husband with tales of yet another boy whose emotional unhappiness had been consigned to sail the metaphysical seas for eternity.

I knuckled down to work and sports. Even if I say so myself, I excelled at rugby, and I, along with Goliath, who had been awarded this new nickname to add to his other titles of Tiny and James, were selected for the first team in the opening match of the season against Lancing College. I loved my rugby, and managed to lose all track of time and worries when in the midst of the scrum. In addition, the academic side started to click into place. I had always been fortunate enough to have a passable intellectual capacity, and was pleased to find that, in some subjects at least, my prep school education had propelled me beyond the current levels of my public school trained peers.

My father was meant to be there for the trials match, but something had come up and he never made it. Yet again, he had called the night before the game to apologise; this time I knew exactly what to do with the resulting painful emotions. I got that bottle out all by myself, inserted the contents, and chucked it out to sea with all my might. I tried to turn a deaf ear to the encouragement shouted by the other parents the following afternoon, and focussed on the job in hand. I played a blinder, and we hammered our opponents. My immediate sense of joy and excitement at our victory was instantly squashed at the end of the game when my fellow players rushed in the directions of their parents, mainly fathers and older brothers, leaving me, and another lonely couple of bruised and mud-splashed warriors, to tackle the half-mile walk back to the changing rooms, alone. On the way I sent several more bottles out into the ocean.

The following week was little more than a build-up to the first long weekend. Hard as I tried to concentrate, I found myself thinking of my parents, my hopes of seeing them together again, and of us eating out and maybe seeing a film. All I had heard was that they were both coming to pick me up that evening, and my hopes had soared that all their relationship stuff had been sorted out and everything would be back to normal.

I said goodbye to my fellow happy campers, all of whom were going back to their families for the weekend also. And, together with various other boarders who were returning home for the first time this term, I waited with excitement outside in the car park. I listened out for the familiar sound of the Triumph Stag engine, a noise which would unmistakably announce its imminent arrival even before the car itself could be seen.

One by one, the other boarders were picked up. I tried not to watch too closely as each boy tried, often clumsily, to manage the transition from student to child. Some hugs, some hand-shakes, some rushed disappearances into backs of cars. Some boys put their own luggage in the boots, some had an adult take care of the task. I even saw one boy climb into the driver's seat of a car with an 'L' plate on it. I couldn't believe I'd ever be old enough to do that. I thought of how many different stories each of these actions told. I imagined servants and wealth beyond my wildest dreams; I imagined boys who I knew to be quiet at school suddenly becoming loud show-offs in the presence again of their younger siblings; and I imagined boys taking into their homes their newly acquired manliness, and the shock of their parents as they adapted to their new arrival. Would they feel pleased with the early results of their long-term investment?

After about an hour of waiting, Mr Pilton came out and found me in the car park. As soon as I saw him coming towards me, I feared the worst, and I tried to look away, pretending not to notice his approach.

"Baker – thought I'd find you here."

My heart sank as his words confirmed that it was me he was looking for.

"Nothing to get upset about old boy – your parents' car broke down and they're trying to get it fixed. They've asked us to give you something to eat while they arrange how to get here."

If my heart had sunk when I first saw him approaching, it hit the bottom once he'd spoken.

"You'd better bring your bag back in with you – just in case."

What followed were some of the loneliest hours of my young life. I sat in my room and tried to dip into a book on the industrial revolution, but my brain was all over the place. I sat and had dinner in the Pilton's flat, but I wasn't really there at all. When helping with the washing-up I dropped a plate, which smashed all over their tiled floor. At that point, Mrs Pilton suggested I go back and wait in the dorm, and said they'd get me when there was some news.

That room took on a whole new feeling without my fellow happy campers. It now seemed dead, lifeless, dull. I tried lying on each of my friend's bunks to see if I could feel something different, but it didn't help. I was alone, really alone, and all I had as company was a packed bag and some faint hope of what might have been that night. I wanted to cry but I couldn't. I was dry. I was empty. I felt like stone.

It was gone ten o'clock by the time Mr Pilton came back into my room. I was still dressed and had put my coat back on, more in desperation than in hope. The news was that my parents would not get there until the following morning. They would have to hire a car and could only come once the hire place had opened. I received the news without comment other than a polite thank you, unpacked my pyjamas and crawled into bed.

It was dawning on me that I was no longer the number-one priority in my parents' lives. I probably hadn't been for a while; maybe that was why they'd sent me off to boarding school. I had let them into the deepest recesses of my heart, but they had left me shut out of theirs. How little I seemed to know about who they really were or what their lives were like. How little they had involved me in the worlds that they inhabited every day. Was this because I was considered to be too young to be interested? Was it because they never felt they could trust me again after the incident with the shed? Or was it because this is how love and relationships worked – on a sort of need-to-know only basis?

Maybe I had misunderstood the whole love thing. Maybe I let them too deep into my being. One thing seemed clear; no-one really cared for me now. There was only one person who could ultimately look after me and that person was me. No-one was to be trusted, nor promises believed. I fell asleep clenching my fists and telling myself that I couldn't rely on anybody.

The next morning found me once again in the car park, my weekend bag propping me up as I sat in the weak rays of the autumn sun. I hadn't bothered turning up before ten, no point if yesterday was anything to go by. And sure enough, another delay followed. It was nearly ten-thirty before a dark blue Ford Sierra pulled up in front of me, the familiar figures of my parents in the front.

"Alexander – we're so sorry. It couldn't be helped, the car broke down and…"

"Yes mother, I know the story. Mr Pilton told me it in detail last night." I was short with her. I wasn't even bothered about hugging her or smiling - I allowed her to embrace me, but quickly slid out of her hold and into the back seat with my case.

"Morning Alexander – sorry about last night. Still, let's get going – we'll make up for it by having a pub lunch on the way home. And, I've got a little surprise for you too." My father was reaching out in the only way he knew how, and I felt okay with that.

Mother asked me to tell them about the school, but I told her I was tired and asked for some music to be put on. Regrettably the car did not have a working radio, and we had to suffer what seemed an interminable drive with none of us speaking, other than the two of them exchanging views on which was the best route. By the time we got to a pub for an early lunch, I was already wondering why I had been making such a big deal last night about getting away from school.

We sat down at a small round table, and my father gave me an envelope to open while he went off to get drinks. Inside were two VIP tickets for the English Rugby International later that afternoon at Twickenham. He looked back at me from the bar to see if I'd opened the envelope. I gave him two big thumbs up and smiled.

"Well, what is it?" My mother seemed genuinely ignorant of what the envelope contained. I wondered for a split second if maybe she wasn't meant to know.

"He wouldn't tell me, you see – wanted it to be a complete surprise and was afraid I'd give it away" she explained. I showed her the tickets.

"But - but that's this afternoon. And that means you'll be out until late this evening, and I haven't even seen you yet or had a chance to catch up. And then we'll only have tomorrow."

My father returned with the drinks. The two of them then proceeded to have a major bust-up about this treat, seeming to be oblivious that I was sitting in-between them. It was what I would call a conservative, middle-class row of hissing whispers and frosty glares. I didn't even bother to try to keep up with the conversation, choosing instead to sip on my shandy and trust that the hole I hoped would swallow me up would soon appear. It didn't.

I was hauled out of my abortive foray into dreamland by my father's raised voice, words which would echo around my head for many years to come.

"Now is as good a time as any – what's the point of hiding this from him any longer?" He was now staring directly at me, his eyes moist and slightly red. "Alexander, we have some difficult news for you. Your mother is moving in with her lady friend and we're getting a divorce."

My mother stormed out of the pub in tears. My father took a swig of his beer and put it back on the table, before repeating the same action two or three times. We finished our drinks and meal in stunned silence.

I left the pub with two tickets for England versus France, and two parents who couldn't stand the sight of one another. I supposed that the former was meant to go some way towards lessening the pain of the latter.

11

"Alex – Alex, the district nurse is here, she thinks you should go to your father. I've called your mother – and I've also told the school. I'm going to go and pick the boys up right now."

As I stirred from yet another catnap, I recognised the soothing tones of Helen's voice. She had a mug of tea ready for me and I took a sip to help me to come to.

When I got to Dada's room, the district nurse ushered me straight back out again.

"I think he might be going. There's certainly been a big change in him since Tuesday. He's asking for you over and over again. I know you only recently went off for some rest, but I thought you'd want to know."

"Yes, yes, thank you. Right, well, I'll go in. Are you staying?"

She nodded her head and told me that she'd call the doctor out. I suggested that if she was sure Dada was going, then at this stage there was probably no point, as he would certainly not want anyone trying to revive him should he indeed be choosing this murky Tuesday afternoon to pass on. From the sounds of things, we were way past the stage of needing a diagnosis, and so she went out into the living room and left me alone with him.

As I entered Dada's room, I was aware of a marked change in his breathing. His chest sounded more hollow, and there were the beginnings of the rattle, the rasping fanfare that had, since time begun, announced the transition from one world into the next. He was not uttering a word now. I dreaded the possibility that I may have missed my chance.

"Dada?" I spoke to him, but he didn't open his eyes. I put my hand on his. His bony hand felt cool to the touch.

I glanced at his bedside table. There lay my notepad and pen and the dictating machine. I never had taken down his speech. And yet it had seemed so important to him. Was he still there enough to be able to tell me what was so important.

"Dada? It's me – Alexander, your son. The ministers are all here, Dada. They're all here. They're ready for you to begin. Can you tell them now what you wanted to say?"

He said nothing and I fell silent too. I heard the back door open and close, and the sound of the boys taking off shoes and walking through the kitchen in unusually quiet fashion. Dada still made no reply, my only companion in that room being the increasingly loud sound of his chest.

"Dada, the ministers – they're all here. You've been wanting to tell them something. Remember?"

I so wanted him to wake up. I so wanted to hear a few more minutes of his voice. I thought I was ready for him to die, but now that it was happening I didn't want to let him go – at least not before he'd completed his last speech. I wanted his final words to have meaning, to be important. I wanted to remember his passing by something insightful and majestic. A part of me needed his exit to be grand.

But he wasn't there any more. His body was making the noises, his blood was still warm, his pulse faint, but not extinguished. But he was not really there. A major part of him it seemed had already taken the big step.

I resigned myself to the certainty that he never would make that last oration, and went out to ask the boys and Helen if they wanted to join me in being with him as he passed over. Now there's something I would have never thought of suggesting a few years ago.

Daniel, at ten, was the older child by two and a half years. He took one look at Joel and reached out for his hand. I walked proudly back into the room, followed by my boys and Helen, and I felt like a captain leading out his team at Twickenham, the tears streaming down my face as I entered the final scene of my Dada's life. We gathered close around Dada, as his body continued its gradual decline into terminal inactivity.

I allowed myself to cry at his bedside in full view of my two boys; my boys who had, apart from when I had split up with their mother several years earlier, rarely witnessed their father's tears. And they also wept. For fifteen minutes or so, the rasping noise continued to emanate from the shell that had been my father's body.

And then, with no warning, he failed to breathe in again. He was gone.

I now understood what the expression 'a deathly silence' really meant. We all sat in that room for at least a couple of minutes after he had died, not knowing what to do or say. There was no noise. Even our crying had stopped. My boys were now grandfather-less and I was father-less. Just like that.

By the time my mother arrived, the doctor had already been to issue a death certificate. She came as he was leaving. It was the first time she had seen my father for over a year. She didn't have much to say, and I didn't push her to talk. She spent a few minutes in the room alone with Dada, and I hoped she had finally made her peace with him.

We lit candles for him that evening and left them alight in his room, with his favourite Frank Sinatra CD playing quietly in the background. I don't know where the idea to play Frank came from, all I knew was that it felt right. And I was becoming someone who was beginning to trust that if it felt right, it probably was right.

The next day, Dada was taken away by three men in a black van with blacked-out windows. The van was backed closely up to the house, presumably so passers-by could be as undisturbed as possible by the unseemly reality of a dead body. It seemed bizarre somehow – but then I'm not sure that the South East of England and death have ever been great mates.

Deciding to air his room, I went in to open the windows and strip the bed. Lifting up his pillows, I was surprised to see some of the white capsules squashed flat on the sheet. It turned out there were twenty-four of them; four complete days' worth of painkillers. Dada had pretended to each of us that he had swallowed them, and then deliberately hidden them. I had never dreamt that he wouldn't want to take these pills, so I suppose I hadn't paid much attention. But he had chosen a different route to one of slowly anaesthetised eternal slumber. He had chosen to remain conscious and face the pain in his final days and hours. I wondered what would have made him come to such a decision. He had been considered by my mother as something of a hypochondriac when I was growing up.

After taking out the sheets and pillowcases to the washing machine, I returned to tidy up his bedside table. His glass of water still sat there, its saliva-stained rim a messy reminder of his physical presence. I looked at the blank sheet of paper atop the notepad. I was already missing the sound of his voice and cursed internally again at my failure to record his message to his ministers.

I picked up the little voice recorder and then remembered the brief test-recording we had done when he had told me that he loved me. I so wanted to hear his voice, and so wanted to hear that all-too brief affirmation of his love. I sat down in the bedside chair, stared at the stripped empty bed and pressed play.

What happened next has become another of those defining moments in my life.

12

I don't believe my five years at Freestone passed with any greater originality than those of the countless boys who had graced its classrooms since its transformation from private house to school some eighty years previously. I had returned to its almost comforting walls after that first long weekend feeling somewhat of an orphan, and yet an orphan with a terribly embarrassing secret. My parents were getting divorced because my mother had left my father for another woman.

Mr and Mrs Pilton seemed aware that something was going on, and over those first few weeks, Mrs Pilton would seek me out to check that I was alright. Unfortunately, her initial failure to allow me to talk when I had badly needed to, had left a scar which still felt sore, and I declined her various attempts to prise information from me. She gradually surrendered the fight, and I was left alone.

My parents scarcely gave me any information about their divorce proceedings. I didn't know how much they were talking, fighting, or anything. I didn't know if they were communicating at all, although I assumed they must be about me, at the very least. I heard other boys talk about divorce, and heard stories of how the children got passed around from one parent to another as if they were hot potatoes. I remember feeling how strange it was at the time that I'd never really heard about divorce much before, but now that it was happening to my family, barely a day would go past without some mention of it. None of it sounded good, although Jeremy Mather did say that for him the best bit was that his dad was always trying to make up for splitting up his family by taking him all over Europe to see England play rugby and cricket.

According to my end of term reports, I'd become a good student and continued to excel at rugby. Golly and I – Goliath was too much of a mouthful, so we decided to shorten it – became best mates and I spent at least three weekends with his family in that first year. Golly had the most beautiful older sister called Hayley who was old enough to be wholly unobtainable, but young enough to be wholly tempting. She had the most luxuriant, long, chestnut hair I had ever seen, and a shapely body that seemed to exude sex.

On the Saturday afternoon of my first visit there, I nearly bumped into her as I was coming out of the spare-room where I had been changing my muddy clothes. She was wearing only a thin dressing-gown, and she smiled at me as she vanished into the bathroom. I stood there a moment considering this opportunity, and then quietly retreated back into the spare-room, which adjoined the bathroom. I could hear the taps being turned, and imagined her luscious body slipping off her dressing-gown as she waited for the bath to fill. I could hear her moving around; movements that were so close to me and yet so frustratingly far away. I sat on the bed and shut my eyes, trying to imagine the shape of her breasts and the taste of her nipples.

"Alexander – are you coming down?"

Crap. By now I had a major hard-on and couldn't possibly risk being seen by Golly or his parents.

"Be down in a sec – just changing."

I had previously found, that in times of urgency, trying to get rid of an erection was almost impossible. I tried to walk with it to see if it was noticeable, and was forced to conclude that going downstairs was out of the question as yet. The trouble was, it would seem odd if I stayed in my bedroom for too long either. Next door Hayley started to hum quietly. When the taps went off, I could clearly hear her quiet voice singing to me, and my excitement rose. My penis shouted to get out of its cotton cage, and I soon had my hand caressing it firmly through the thin white material of my trousers.

By now I was powerless to move, and it was too late to direct the inevitable explosion anywhere other than straight into my pants and trousers. Why did they have to be white? Just as the climax reached its peak, and the damp stains started to spread, Golly came running into the room to see why I was taking so long. I'm not sure who was more mortified.

"Oh, gross. You've - you've wet yourself. God, you could have used the toilet downstairs, just because Hayley's in this one doesn't mean you can't go down there, you know."

This would not be the last time in my life that I would suffer the excruciating feeling of orgasm-interruptus. I realised I had three problems on my hands now. One, I had to clear up my mess without embarrassing either myself or Golly too much; two, I had to somehow get Golly not to say anything to his family, particularly his sister, about my little accident; and three, I had to have a manly chat with Golly about sex. He obviously didn't have a clue.

I asked Golly to grab me a spare towel. While he was out of the room, I hurriedly stripped off my trousers and pants, wiped my legs with my own towel, and bundled up my soggy trousers into my case. I put my muddy trousers back on and when Golly returned I was just zipping them up. I got him to shut the door to my room and started to transmit some of the dubious information that I had picked up about sex from the stories I had read in my magazines. He was so intrigued he seemed to forget all about my indiscretion. As Hayley continued to sing softly in the bath next door, Golly sat there raptly listening, occasionally asking questions, most of which I couldn't answer satisfactorily. I felt empowered by the hold I had over him; I felt he would have done anything for me during those moments. And I liked the feeling that being the one who knew *stuff*, gave me.

I told him about masturbation, and how it was what porn was for. I told him that all women loved sex, and particularly seemed to enjoy giving oral sex to men, often in groups. I told him that women liked to take their clothes off everywhere, and particularly liked walking around without knickers, as this turns them on, a state they like to be in most of the time to be ready for their men. I told him that women loved being with other women, particularly in front of a man, hence why so many photos in the magazines featured women together. Unfortunately, my mother crept into my mind at that moment, so I swiftly moved on.

God knows what else I told Golly that I had gleaned from the pages of those magazines. But I had started, and wanted, to believe all those things for myself. I acted like some guru enlightening his follower, and yet it was more a case of the almost totally blind leading the blind. But he trusted my knowledge, and I didn't want to let him down. After all, I had *done* it and had been doing it for quite some time. His journey was just beginning. I wonder to this day, with a fair degree of horror, whether he ever received a more complete sex education than the ignorant nonsense that I shared with him that afternoon.

Year three led into year four, four into five. I think my parents' divorce came in year four, although it could just as easily have been year five. I wasn't involved, so what did I care? They devised a rota system for having me, which meant weekends with one or other of them, and nightmares at birthday and Christmas-time when they both wanted to see me.

I learnt to cram information leading up to tests and exams, and found I had a reasonable talent for applying the years-old methods that led to good results. Revise like a madman in the days leading up the exam; don't try to be too imaginative in your thinking; stick to what you know where possible and, if all else fails, pretend you know anyway. More often than not it seemed to do the trick, and I managed to acquire enough 'O' Levels to see me comfortably into the Sixth Form. I had discovered that 'doing well' at school was all about playing the system and I had become good at it. I realised that learning was not so much about an inner search for meaning, or the following of a particular passion, as I had thought it was at some point in the distant past, but more about learning and remembering words and systems from books and teachers, much as I learnt my lines for the school plays. The books knew best, the teachers knew best – there was no need to expand much beyond their viewpoint. The only difference between the ultimate output on the stage or in the exam room being that, in the exam room I had to trot those words out in a different way to 'make them mine', whereas on the stage I had to stick to the script exactly.

And so my ability to 'fix' problems grew. This talent helped me to create the protective shell that I had cocooned around myself to make me feel invulnerable. When a problem came up I was certain to look for, and generally find, a fix. Of course this was one thing when the problem involved a quadratic equation or identification of a body part or geographical location, but it didn't always seem to produce the same high mark when I applied the concept to my relationships.

Sixth Form was in many ways like a whole new world. Suddenly I was a student, not a pupil. Doubly exciting for all of us was that we were to be the first year in which female pupils would be allowed in to Freestone's Sixth Form, and we had sixteen girls arriving on the first day of term. Following assembly, and the first couple of meaningless beginning-of-term lessons, all the Sixth Form boys piled into the common-room for the first taste of our privileged coffees and crusty rolls, filled with cheese and pickle or egg mayonnaise. But before we got in line to purchase the chosen object of our desire, a group had run ahead of the pack and were hurriedly lining up a couple of tables by the large windows which overlooked the approach to the common-room.

We then got out a book of lined A4, I think it might have been my English notepad, and six of us formed a panel of judges, sitting alongside each other with the smugness that came with not being the new-bugs. Some of the other boys hovered over our shoulders to see what we were up to. We watched as the new girls walked along the outside path to the common-room. Sometimes the girls were by themselves, other times they were in small groups together. Only two came in accompanied by boys. No matter; we scored them all. And we scored them all for different qualities; sex appeal; bust size; the one most likely to go all the way; the one you'd least like to do it with; best body. Everyone kept their own score and then we totalled them up and passed round the scores amongst ourselves. Golly wrote the final scores in pencil on the back page of my pad.

I suppose it was inevitable that someone would spill the beans. Joanna Harding-Brown, who had come top in two categories, bust size and the one most likely to go all the way, was the first to hear about it. She had already had a brother go through the school and her confidence was formidable. Fortunately, Golly was warned by a friendly prefect so that, by the time Joanna had marched over to the tables, we had all fled to various other points in the common-room, leaving her looking for invisible clues amongst the throng of testosterone and banter. With the papers quickly crumpled up amongst the loose change and sweets of various pockets, we thought we were safe.

I hovered around the table-football to watch the beginnings of what would become the termly competition for table-top supremacy. Being by now reasonably tall, I had a good view of the room, and observed with a growing sense of concern all the girls gathering together around Joanna Harding-Brown at the tables we had hastily abandoned. I caught Golly's eye in the cheese-roll queue but he had no idea why because he was still too small to see what was happening.

One of the girls then burst into tears and ran from the common-room. It was Jessica Strang, the girl with amazing brown eyes but a completely flat chest, who had come out unanimously top of the girl-you'd-least-like-to-do-it-with category. Her dramatic departure attracted a lot of attention. Richard Windass was the new head boy and revelling in this early opportunity to impress, he approached the girls, with his vice-head boy, Rory Turner in tow. By now my heart was thumping and a thousand consequences were racing through my brain. I could feel the sweat building up inside my shirt and upon my brow.

Windass stood up on one of the tables and shouted for quiet.

"Whose pad is this?"

No way I was going to admit to that. I prayed that my name wasn't on it. It was new and I didn't remember writing anything on it yet.

"Okay, let's try again. Whose pad is this?"

There's something about a contemporary trying to be all authoritative and adult-like that doesn't sit well with fellow teenagers. Just as I was wondering how to get out of this mess, an anonymous voice piped up behind me.

"It's mine Wind-a-r-s-e."

Another quickly followed.

"No, it's mine Wind-a-r-s-e, it's mine."

"Mine, Windy. My pad. My pad."

Very soon the whole common-room was echoing to the defiant sounds of over one-hundred Sixth Form students claiming ownership of my English pad and rejoicing at the head boy's perfect public school name. Windass and Turner stood there with the girls, powerless amongst the crowd. The girls, led by Harding-Brown, filed out en-masse to cheers, cat-calls and whistles, and left us boys celebrating the victory that our combined male energy had created. I never would find out who shouted the first 'It's my pad', but what I did learn that day was that, when men stick together to defend each other, it doesn't matter whether the woman's cause is just or unjust. Man stands alongside man. That's how it has always been. That's how it is. That's how it will always be. I had unwittingly found myself the member of a club, of whose existence I had previously been unaware. It wouldn't be a club of which I would ultimately aspire to be a member.

My 'A' Level choices were a mixed bag. Business studies because I wanted to make a lot of money and wasn't at all convinced that I could follow my father's footsteps into the world of TV; English because I thought it would be fairly easy, it being my mother tongue; and history because it didn't leave too much open to uncertainty. Facts were facts written in books, and all you had to do was add your own spin from time to time. In the event I found English by far the hardest because it proved to be so subjective. I had grown to like things to be crystal clear and English allowed too much to be uncertain and vague.

The Lower Sixth was a year of experimentation and diversification. It was the year I first attempted, and failed, my driving test; it was the year I first got served in a pub without my parents; it was the year I first passed out in a pub; it was the year I first had a girlfriend – I met her at a school disco and her name was Melanie Firth; it was the year I first threw up on my girlfriend, it was just after the same disco and her name was still Melanie Firth; it was the year I first got laid, at least it was according to the stories I told my friends, the layee's name also being Melanie Firth; and it was the year I first split up with a girlfriend. Her name? Melanie Firth. In fact now I come to think of it, most of that happened in a single evening.

If the Lower Sixth was a chance to relax after the two years of solid grind leading up to 'O' Levels, then Middle Sixth was the start of the real work. In the summer between these two years, I had stayed mostly at my father's bachelor pad in Notting Hill, an environment which thrilled me and my friends who came to stay. My father had stopped doing so much work in front of the cameras and was now concentrating on the production side.

When I stayed with him for any length of time, I would start to notice things about him, about his manner, of which as a younger boy I had previously been unaware. I noticed how vain he was; he would spend a surprising amount of time on his personal grooming, and seemed to take particular pleasure in brushing down his cashmere coat with the ivory handled brush that my mother had used many times when the same coat was upon his back. I also began to realise that he found it impossible to relax. That summer was a particularly warm one, and he would come back from work, shower, pour himself a whisky, then another, and then he'd start cleaning the kitchen, or talking about supper, or rummaging through his papers or flicking through channels. He couldn't switch off. And if he ran out of things to fix, or do, then he'd turn his attention to me, demanding to know every last detail of my day, what I was planning to do the next day, how I was getting on with my studies, which university I was planning to go to.

But then it takes one to know one. In retrospect, I can see that I could no longer switch off either. And that's why I liked being in Notting Hill. There was always something going on. I was close enough to the West End to be able to go there whenever I felt like it. And my public school circle of friends, particularly the rugby crowd, had widened to such an extent that there was nearly always someone coming to stay.

We didn't talk about my mother at all. She was still with her partner, a fact which contradicted my father's assertion that her relationship was a rebound thing. She used to complain to me frequently about getting ripped off by my father in the divorce agreement. And every time she complained, I would either end up telling her to shut up or I'd just leave the room. I had neither the desire nor the skills needed to sit as either judge or jury in her was-it-fair game. Interestingly my father never raised the divorce case nor talked about the settlement that they reached. He had no photos of her anywhere on display in the house. The only hard proof that she had existed in his life at all was me.

I was struck by his ability to shut her out from his existence. I found it helpful to know that you can share so much with someone for so long, and then if it all goes wrong, you can cut them out of your life without any apparent long-lasting damage. In the same way as a car, or a house, or an employee is dispensable, I learnt that partners were dispensable too.

One night, when he had returned home from work fairly early in the evening, I asked my father how he had managed to stay so focussed on his work throughout their painful separation.

"Shit happens Alexander. You might not like it, but it doesn't stop it from being the truth. People will abuse you; no matter how hard you work, things will go wrong; women will cheat on you; friends you think you can trust will show themselves to be traitors when you least expect it. I have just learnt not to take it so personally any more. I also try to get in first whenever I can – that soon takes the wind out of their sails. Don't let the bastards grind you down, look out for number one, sort out any problems quickly and move on."

I don't recall having heard my father speak with such coldness or ire in his voice. He sat there, in his black leather executive chair with his feet up on the matching footstool, and gently rocked backwards and forwards. Alongside him, I stretched out my feet on the sofa and tried to digest my mentor's sage words. *'People will abuse you, women will cheat on you, friends will become traitors.'* So this was the world that young men had to prepare themselves to enter. No wonder my father had become such a serious man over the years. How could you remain light-hearted when every day contained such potential for disappointment and anguish.

That night I was meeting Golly and a couple of his friends at the Leicester Square Odeon. I left my father sitting in his chair and poring over the latest viewing figures for the previous month. I got on the tube which had quietened down a little from the rush-hour madness and made my way into London's pulsating heart. I waited for about forty minutes, happy to people-watch amid the cacophony of a thousand strained voices and the hum of traffic noise, on which were superimposed occasional police and ambulance sirens. Another twenty minutes passed, and still Golly and the others didn't show. By this time I had missed the beginning of the film. I found a phone box and called his house, but there was no reply.

Assuming that Golly had forgotten, which was not unheard of, I thought about hanging out by myself in the West End for the evening. But somehow, without anyone to share the experience, the idea didn't hold much appeal. Besides which, humiliating as it was to admit to myself, I found the thought of being there at night by myself daunting. Why? Goddamn it, I was a growing man and quite capable of looking after myself. And this was my playground now. Long gone were the days when I should feel satisfied by a sports field, or a trip to see England play. It was a young man's destiny to find succour in the bosom of Soho amid the spicy smells of Gerrard Street. It was normal. It was right. It was my inheritance, passed on by men like my father. Men who, down the centuries, had been cheated on, abused and trampled over, and who had created for themselves a world where the dollar speaks all languages and sentiment is an asset to be distributed or withheld entirely at a man's discretion.

I walked past various strip joints, trying to see the pictures of the naked women who welcomed visitors into their shadowy cellars. Just like that time in the field back at Hebbingdon when I had been so close to being found out by the young assistant matron, I found myself becoming excited by the danger of being seen in this insalubrious environment. The more I tried to see, the less I found myself able to. Pictures were life-size and yet tantalisingly out of reach; bare arms leading to scenes hidden behind kiosks that I could only imagine.

My pace quickened as I became more desperate to find something tangible. But it didn't materialise. I was way too afraid to go into any of these dodgy places, and I tried to justify my cowardliness by congratulating myself for saving the entry money.

Disappointed, and frustrated, I got back on the tube and headed home. By the time I got back to our house, it was still only about eight forty-five. I let myself in and heard some unfamiliar, rhythmic dance music coming from the lounge. I padded quietly towards the open door and popped my head around the corner. My father was lying on the couch, his back towards me, finishing the last mouthfuls of a Chinese takeaway, his attention fixed upon his leather armchair. On it sat a girl wearing nothing but a Cleopatra wig and knee-length, patent-leather boots. Her legs were straddled across the footstool which was pulled up close to the chair and upon which knelt another girl who was partially dressed as a schoolgirl. The schoolgirl was squeezing Cleopatra's breasts with her hands and licking her sex with her tongue.

I watched, as my father went over to the schoolgirl and started playing with her breasts. I watched, as the girls got it on with each other, and as their hands occasionally strayed towards my father's trousers. I watched, as my father watched them, and I watched as he sucked Cleopatra's toes. And at that moment I found myself in the unusual situation of wanting to orgasm and vomit all at the same time. I had to get fresh air. I crept out of the house and shut the door as quietly as I could. The music thumped on. I stood in the darkness of our side path for a few minutes while my erection subsided. I then headed off in search of – what? In search of anything.

I came to a Chinese restaurant, and stood at the counter trying to understand the menu at the same time as trying to take in what I had just seen. Confusion reigned in my head; the smell of the Chinese food reminding me of the restaurant where Mumma, Dada and I used to celebrate my reasonable exam results; the smell of the Chinese food reminding me of Gerrard Street and Soho and the nearness of sex you could pay for; the smell of the Chinese food reminding me of my father and the paid-for sex of which he was right in the middle.

I left without ordering anything. And I walked. I just walked around Notting Hill, trying to work out what it all meant. Is that where relationships take you eventually? To paid sex sessions grabbed under the cover of darkness when you think you won't be disturbed?

Maybe the possible excitement of being found out was part of the attraction for my father that night. I could relate to that. But he must have felt fairly safe that I would be out until late; I'd visited Leicester Square on at least three occasions that summer and not returned until about midnight. In fact once I didn't go home at all, because I stayed with Golly at his parents' London flat near Grosvenor Square.

The more I thought about it, the more I softened towards him. He had needs; I could relate to that too. And it was alright for my mother, she was in a relationship. And she was the one who had ended it. It was ironic of course that she was in a lesbian relationship, and I had just discovered my father with two women. Still, my earlier glossy sex education had informed me that this was normal and that women loved it, so who was I to judge?

I stayed out as late as I could bear. By the time I returned home, my father was sound asleep in his armchair. I would never see that armchair in the same light again. The room had regained its normal living-room identity as opposed to a den of iniquity, and the pulsating dance music had been replaced by Frank Sinatra. I looked at my father's face and tried to find any signs that would tell me of the satisfaction, the wonder, the joy that he had experienced that night. But all I could see was nothingness. No expression, no emotion. He had clearly done what needed doing and that was presumably the end of it. *'Sort it out and move on.'* I guessed he'd followed his own advice that night.

He was up and out of the house the next morning before I had even got out of bed. It was about ten-thirty, when a dream I was having was rudely interrupted by the sound of the phone. I allowed it to ring without getting out of bed, and tried to find my way back to the blind man in my dream. I was in my private jet heading for Chicago on business, and the jet was being piloted by an elephant in full captain's gear. The blind man was stuck to the outside of the plane's window and was desperately trying to communicate with me. His face was mine, and yet it wasn't. I knew he was me, and yet he looked so different to me. Of course being blind didn't help, but something else was different about him.

When I looked more closely at the plane, I realised that underneath its smooth interior, it wasn't much more than old newspaper and duck tape. Bits had started falling off, and holes were beginning to appear that let in the sky. I looked once more for the blind man at the window, but the window had been sucked out, presumably taking him with it. The phone went again. This time I managed to get there.

I wished I hadn't.

It was my father calling to tell me that on his way to the cinema last night, Golly had been knocked down by a taxi, five minutes away from Leicester Square. He had been rushed by ambulance to St Thomas's Hospital, accompanied by his uninjured companions. Golly was in a coma.

13

"Your Royal Highness, ministers, vegetables and Catholics. It is a pleasure to be able to share with you some information that springs directly from the source of all our – ah, ouch – excuse me, I do beg your collective puddings." Dada's voice was weak, but not as weak as it had been in many of our conversations. His tone was deliberate and he barely paused for breath.

"Prime Minister, some new ministers are needed. You must create, with immediate effect, the ministries of fun, spontaneity, light and chocolate cake. These are to take the place of defence, employment, education and health care. You'll need to resign of course, and new positions of Lord and Lady High Listener will be created. The governance of the City of London and its stock exchange is to be handed over to each year's outstanding students from the top business universities around the country. This will help avoid the inevitable disaster that is currently being cooked up by the profligate attitudes of the present incumbent chefs."

I hit pause in order to wipe away tears of laughter and sorrow. It was so extraordinary hearing the voice of my dead Dada expressing such an odd mixture of nonsense and eloquence.

"Now listen up all of you, because I'm only going to say this once, and then I'll have to go. Hello Golly – you – you'll just have to wait a few moments, thank you. I'm in the middle of an important meeting with some porcelain figures.

"I can tell you where it's all going wrong, but you've only got this one chance to put it right. Otherwise the banana will grind to a self-imposed halt, and the wheels of commerce will drop out of the sky and into the great pit of snakes below, never to be seen again.

"The job of the Lord and Lady High Listener is to educate you. By their side is the Cloth Man. He'll help smooth the waters.

Between them, they will teach you how to transform the way this world communicates. What none of you understand is that the semolina has become spilt all over the table because of how you fail to communicate. There is another way. A way that has been passed down primarily from mother to daughter through the ages. Fathers and sons got bored waiting for the pot to boil. It is known and practised by very few, and yet it has the power to tidy up all the semolina. It is power beyond your dreams. And it is free."

I paused the machine again. His voice was now so assured I could hardly believe that he had only made this recording a few days previously. This message, this last testament of will, felt important, although I didn't know why. I pressed play, and Dada's voice from beyond the grave continued.

"Your feelings of guilt create only one result – self-destruction. Your desire to blame creates only one result – destruction. Take the pineapples that bring colour to the trees and learn to forgive. Learn to forgive yourselves, because most of you have acted out of ignorance, not malice. Seek to forgive others because they too have nearly always acted out of ignorance, not badness. No-one is born evil."

Again I paused the machine, as much in shock as anything else that this frail old man had been speaking with increasing clarity and strength. Where had these words come from? How and why had he suddenly become able to speak about things with which, to my knowledge, he had had no earthly connection. And what was I to do, if anything, with what he was saying? Was I making this more than it was, simply because it was the voice of my recently departed Dada? Was I seeking spiritual comfort-food? I pressed play.

"I stand today in a golden pool of light which is the birthright of each and every one of us. It is the pool of self-acceptance. When you reach this place, you will know truly what it is to have lived as God."

God. Now he's talking about God. He never talked about God.

"You cannot live as God if you cannot first learn to listen. Do you know how much listening God has to do? Have you ever thought about what an incredible listener God is? God listens first. Right action follows as a natural consequence of right listening. Very often you don't need to do anything if you follow the path of right listening."

I went and got a glass of water. I paused for a few moments reflecting on all this. I wasn't trying too hard to analyse it, instead letting myself feel these words. In a bizarre way, they felt real. They felt inspired. Chill-bumps had been raised on my arms, hairs standing up on the back of my neck. I had no explanation for it. Weird was the only word for what I was experiencing. And there was still more to come.

"It is time for you men of war and many words to look first to a woman for the new way. She will teach her Lord High Listener the way and he will reach out to the men of the world. For the men hold the keys to power, and the power is currently being used destructively. Soon, the women will have duplicates once more. Look out also for the blind man, for he holds the first key, and, without that key, the way will soon become obscured by the gathering dusts of inertia.

"You have no choice in this matter. You have to do it. Golly is calling, and it will soon be time for me to go. Juggernauts can play cricket if the moon is overhead. Look to the Trojan, for you have chosen her to help you. She has some of the knowledge. This restaurant is closing for business. Off you go then, back to your spaceships."

And with that, Dada's oration ended. Seconds later I could hear the familiar sound of his rattly snoring. I fast-forwarded the recorder to see if he had started up again, but several minutes of difficult breathing was all I got.

14

It took little Golly four days to die. His parents eventually had to make the heartbreaking decision to turn off his life-support system, when it was clear that all brain functioning had ceased. I was furious with his parents and the doctors for not giving him the chance to come back. Golly was a fighter and I felt that he might have made a complete recovery. But the science told another story, and so it was that one Friday at ten o'clock in the morning, my best friend Golly's all too brief life was brought to an end.

The funeral took place a week after the accident. It was another swelteringly hot day. There were a few of us from school, his family and a couple of teachers. The headmaster was one of many away on holiday, including my mother and lesbo, so the attendance was nothing like the size it should have been. His body was being cremated which seemed shockingly final to me.

Golly's father came to speak to me after the service. He told me what had happened. Apparently it wasn't the taxi driver's fault. Golly and his friends had been trying to skirt the outside of the crowds of pedestrians near Trafalgar Square, and Golly had lost his footing, falling into the path of an oncoming black cab. His two mates had been in shock, and were unable to speak about the accident to anyone for two days. They were both receiving crisis counselling and were on sedatives to help them sleep.

I received nothing of the sort. Fortunately, I was now well trained in the art of dealing with useless emotions, and I bottled up all my hurt and despair, securing the lid on tightly before sending the unwanted vessel off on its journey into infinity. And any time I felt the tears or the pain begin again, I seized another bottle and repeated the process. This hurt wasn't going to get the better of me. That, at least, I owed to Golly. As my father said to me the night after the funeral, it was time for me to be strong. It was time for me to show character. It was time for me to be a real man.

And now I understood exactly what that meant.

In the first rugby match of that season, both teams stood for a minute in silence to mark Golly's passing. I was dealing with it. I was moving on. I was okay.

We were defending our unbeaten record that day – ten matches in a row without a loss. Thanks to the intervention of our rugby coach, I had been spotted by some England Under-Nineteen team selectors at the end of the previous season and a couple of them were due to be present at the game. I couldn't tell who they were amongst the crowd of parents, friends and juniors that jostled on either touch line, but the knowledge that they were there unsettled me.

I remember going down for the first scrum and locking arms with the new hooker. But it should have been Golly – not Colin Steynes. Tears started to well up inside me and I had to pull out all the stops to get them bottled up and dispatched before anyone noticed a six-foot, thirteen-stone forward blubbing on the park. As I tried to ignore the voice that was screaming out in grief inside me, I lost concentration for a split second on my hold. The Charterhouse forwards piled on top of me and the last thing I remembered was searing pain as my left shoulder was wrenched from its socket by the collapsing ruck.

That was to be my last game of rugby. Ever.

The injury was so bad they had to put a metal pin in my shoulder to hold it together. No England team selection, no more riotous bus trips and rugby tours, no more sports trophies, no more *'my special thing.'* I had lost the kudos of being the school's best forward. I was told that the one saving grace was that it was my left shoulder, and I wrote with my right hand. I was told I had been lucky. I was told not to feel upset because at least I could study.

I had now lost my best friend and my greatest talent all within the space of three weeks. My father was right. Life wasn't fair. Shit happens. Deal with it. Deal with it by getting on with stuff.

So I did. I immersed myself in my studies, particularly Business Studies. I started investigating share-dealing and, with help from my father, as soon as I hit eighteen I started to dabble in commodities.

By the time I took my 'A' Levels, I had made over three-thousand pounds from a five-hundred pound start-up fund. The taste of making money was sweet, and the taste of spending it even sweeter.

My mother was oblivious to this new development. She had tried to talk to me about Golly on many occasions during my last year at Freestone, but I had dealt with it, and I had no desire to rake it up again. She and lesbo were still together, although I didn't have to put up with seeing them together often on my occasional weekends with her. She knew I despised the choices she had made, and I had become no more accepting of her, even with the passing of time. Through a sequence of small steps, taken almost unconsciously, and out of a need to blame someone for my pain, I realised I had moved away from my mother's world and into that of my father. She provided me with food, shelter and some clothes. But we no longer went away and hardly ever went out to meals together. I found myself less comfortable in her presence in public, save for the cinema where we could sit alongside each other, without eye contact and in the dark. I had made a choice. My father was the wronged one. He was the one who needed support. He was the man. And we men needed to stick together.

The dreaded exams came and went. I had decided to have a year off in between leaving school and university. I had applied for five places, and received one unconditional offer from University College London and four conditional places from universities ranging from Dundee to Exeter. Taking a year out in those days was not as commonplace as now, and even less usual about my choice was that I wasn't going to travel, at least not to start with. I wanted to explore further my capacity to gain some financial independence, and I managed to get a job through a contact of my father's at FiveStar PLC - an international hotel group.

At first I was given the job of helping in their treasury department. I became transfixed by the numbers involved in this business and watched carefully as Steve Drayton, a Seattle-born financial wizard, juggled their assets. This was a revelation to me; I had done my own small-scale investments and had loved it, but here was a man who, via several telephone lines, was always in touch with his various contacts in the city who would then invest, reinvest or sell shares that the group had bought and needed to offload.

The company's business, obviously, was the hotel trade. And yet, much of their surplus income was generated by trading in stocks as diverse as tin, oil, even foreign currencies. I had read in my studies about companies investing in non-related businesses to bolster their profits, but now I was seeing it in real life. It made sense. Here was life in action; business in action. School had never, could never have, brought it to life in the way that being there did. It was so simple. The hotel group made money out of the hard physical grind of hiring out rooms in beautiful hotels and selling expensive meals and functions, and then critically, the money made money out of mining, lira, sugar, and government bonds – commodities and investments which involved virtually no physical work and very little manpower. Brilliant. The web of worldwide commerce.

Steve was responsible for making sure that the group's money worked hard, and work it did. And so did he. In those first few weeks, I sat by his side and learnt about hotel building and development, how and when to invest and how and when not to. His rule on this was simple. Surround yourself with the best possible brokers you can and let them do the hard work for you. Wine them, dine them, never screw them over, never renege on a deal, accept that sometimes investments go wrong and move on. He worked hard and played hard, often entertaining or being entertained late into the night prior to a six a.m. start.

During these first whirlwind weeks of learning and excitement, I received my exam results. I'd sailed through Business Studies and History gaining As in each. English was only a B, but it didn't matter; I had the choice of every university to which I had applied.

I chose none of them. I was becoming hooked on making money, on late nights in the office and on learning about this fascinating new world. I deferred UCL for another year, explaining that I needed more time to gain some life experience; reasoning they seemed happy to accept.

I'd been at FiveStar for about three months when Steve called me into his office one afternoon. He told me that he had recommended to his board that I become his permanent assistant, and they had agreed. If I wanted it, here was an offer of a full-time job, complete with salary and company car. Even though I had not seriously thought about getting into the hotel trade, I jumped at it.

Without realising it, I had arrived at a crossroads and I didn't so much as glance in the other directions. I chose to follow the path which offered instant returns, instant gratification. I didn't even think about consulting my parents; this was my time to make my own decision.

That night, Steve took me out into the West End and got me absolutely laced. I drank champagne for England in a wine bar lined from wall to wall with Hooray Henrys, devoured oysters and a fillet steak in Smiths of Piccadilly, and then got dragged off by taxicab to spend the rest of the night being manhandled by various American and Japanese women at Stringfellows as I danced my socks off.

At one point I went into the toilets and found Steve bent over one of the sinks, a couple of other men beside him. The dancing had sobered me up a bit and I could see that he was snorting cocaine. I went up to them all, and before I knew what I was doing I was bent over that sink getting my first taste of serious drugs. When it finally came, the rush was electrifying; I could feel every hair on my body, and I could step inside every single blood cell and travel up and down my limbs as if I were on the greatest rollercoaster in the world. At that moment I knew I could conquer the world, and now I could see how Steve got his incredible stamina and zest for life.

Steve invited me back to his flat after the club, and we arrived there in a black cab with two of the Japanese women that I had danced with earlier in the club. I was still feeling on top of the world and, delightfully, did not appear to be any worse off for the alcohol I had drunk. We went up to Steve's apartment, a modest two-bedroomed flat on the middle floor of a large house in Hampstead. Steve left me with the girls, disappeared into his bedroom and never came out again that night, at least not that I knew of. And I finally lost my virginity.

To both of them.

15

Over the course of the next forty-eight hours we organised Dada's funeral. I was amazed at how quickly the messenger of death spread his broad wings. I had to screen calls, I was receiving so many from people I hadn't even heard of.

BBC Television had also been in touch to say they were going to do a feature on Dada on the six o'clock news that day. He had started his long television career in their regional news department, before moving on to national TV, and his now famous travel and current affairs shows. They asked me to email over a recent photo, and I alerted my mother and made sure that Helen and the boys were both back with me in time for the show.

At five to six, the four of us sat down in the lounge to watch the show. After the main news, there were articles on a local school's programme to help the elderly, a supermarket recycling scheme and a blind man who had that afternoon returned from a charity walk across Europe and Asia and which had taken him a year to complete.

Dada was not even mentioned.

At that moment I felt cheated on his behalf; all that work, all that dedication, the promise of a tribute announcing to hundreds of thousands, probably even millions, his passing. And he got nothing. His life's work had been coldly consigned to the BBC department labelled 'no longer at this address.'

A phone call I made the next day brought an end to speculation that they had merely forgotten.

"Mandy, it's Alexander Baker. Peter Baker's son. We all tuned in last night for my father's tribute feature but never saw it. What happened?"

There was an awkward silence and the rustling of some papers.

"Oh, right, yah, hi, Alex."

I wanted to say my name was Alexander, but I couldn't be arsed. Helen was the only one who had ever been allowed to call me Alex.

"Well, yah, rahlly difficult situation, but we had this blind chap, Thomas, er, Thomas Jennings, yes that's right, and we had just found out that yesterday afternoon he was completing…"

"Yes, yes, I saw it. I know what he did. So tell me Mandy, is the article going to be screened today?"

"Well, arh, yah, don't know actually. We've got a pretty full prog on today and of course Peter's death has already been announced in the papers, so it's becoming old news, I'm afraid."

I put the phone down, knowing that if I said any more I'd probably regret it. Old news. That's all he was now. Old news. His death didn't seem like old news to me.

At Dada's request, the cremation took place in private in the Streatham Crematorium on a dull, wet Thursday morning in September. My mother was there, unaccompanied; a lonely figure in her dark grey suit and black hat. She sat a couple of rows back from the front, apparently wishing to remain as inconspicuous as possible. I stood at the front alongside the boys and Helen, with Dada's one surviving brother and his wife and sons behind me. Other than us, and one or two other close friends and work associates of Dada's, the only other attendants were the Priest and the undertakers. If we had opened it up to everyone who would have liked to come, the crematorium itself would have been struggling for breath.

From there we drove to the Church of St Anne's-in-the-Field near Notting Hill, just round the corner from Dada's favourite pub, The Dog and Whistle. We had decided to have everything on the same day as I couldn't face dragging it all out any longer than was necessary. The church service, which was to be a celebration of Dada's life, was open to all and had been widely publicised. But even so, when we turned up five minutes late, thanks to awful traffic, nothing could have prepared me for the numbers crammed inside that church.

As I walked down the aisle towards the front row with my boys and Helen in tow, I was reminded of the day I had walked back up the aisle with Helen at the end of our wedding service. Everyone turned to look at us, but with a very different energy now to that of the day of my nuptials. I imagined a chorus of 'oh poor things' escaping from the lips of the onlookers as my boys walked, with heads bowed, towards the front of the church. I wondered what those same lips were uttering as my mother made her way down the aisle, just behind us.

It struck me that my boys weren't so badly off; their Granddad had nearly reached eighty, and they'd spent more time with him than I ever had with any of my grandparents.

I wanted to go round the church and ask each and every one of the people that I didn't recognise, how they had come to know my Dada. Had they seen him a few times on the television years ago and become members of some secret fan club? Had he really been such a character that even meeting him once meant you had become his friend for life? Or was this audience made up of just a few real friends; their numbers swelled by superficial acquaintances and general hangers-on?

There were various readings, including the obligatory Psalm 23, which was read by Daniel. As he read it, and stumbled slightly on 'righteousness', I couldn't help but hear echoes of my own young voice in his. And yet his was becoming the voice of authenticity. Daniel and his brother were being allowed to grow in their own time, under the shelter of physically split, but now at least emotionally united, parents. There was no longer any need for them to find bottle after bottle into which to ram their emotions. If I had determined anything about the future, it was that, wherever possible, the sins of this particular father would not be visited upon his sons.

The rest of the service went off as Dada would have liked, ending with Frank's 'My Way'. I don't suppose there was a dry eye in the house by the time Sinatra had delivered those words *'For what is a man, what has he got? If not himself, then he has naught.'* Mine certainly were not.

What did Dada have? What had he got? I heard those words anew that day and I wondered what Dada thought about himself. And I thought about those words he had made on that last recording all alone from his death bed, words which seemed to come from the very place that Sinatra was singing about. And that gave me hope. Hope that Dada had found some kind of acceptance, that he had found a doorway through to a realm of wonder and inspiration in those last few hours of his life.

The last notes of the song echoed around the church, their finite journey ending in a silence that contained a magical presence; a phenomenon that is only possible when a large group of people suddenly fall into an impossible hush.

My mother started to cry out loud. And I followed. And soon the whole front two rows of the church were crying, leaving the rest of the congregation to hold our tears in its loving, and quiet, embrace. Five years ago, I would have waited until every trace of tear had been erased from my face before allowing myself to be seen by anyone. Now, I stood up in full flow and led the congregation out of the church. This was how to do a funeral. This was real. And the dying Dada, the one who had left the bizarre legacy of his oration, would have been pleased.

As I stepped outside, the sun broke through the rain clouds, and as if on cue to my Dada's command, a rainbow appeared directly opposite the church. I stood with the boys and Helen alongside the vicar as people filed out, nodding, smiling carefully, and doing the things that English people do after funerals.

"Who are all these people, Dada?" Joel wanted to know.

"Granddad knew everyone, Joel – he was jolly famous once you know." replied Daniel before I had a chance to say anything.

I thought about that. Knew everyone. And yet, did he truly know anyone? And did anyone really, truly know him? Did some people here today know the Peter Baker of that final, extraordinary speech?

As I was having that thought, my mother came out, preceded by an elderly couple and a middle-aged man with a white stick. They gave us their wishes and departed, leaving mother to stand on the fringe of our family group. Part of me didn't want her there, but then part of me also knew that she had every right to stand alongside us.

As the last people filed away from the church, I bit the bullet and invited my mother to join us at The Dog and Whistle for a drink. We weren't having an official wake, but had let it be known that people would be welcome at the pub after the service. When we got inside, it seemed like at least half the congregation had packed itself into the various bars.

Drinks were pressed into our hands by mourner after mourner. Eventually, we found a small table, and the five of us sat down. I suddenly realised how tired my legs were. The boys started playing on their Nintendo and Helen, who couldn't cope with pubs at the best of times, quickly excused herself to get some fresh air.

"Alexander." My mother's voice sounded frail and uncertain, in amongst the babble. I looked at her. She suddenly looked quite old, older than I had realised. But then I hadn't really been looking at her in recent years – not closely. I hadn't wanted to. For all the work I had done on myself, I still hadn't been able to forgive her for destroying Dada.

"There's something you need to know." She looked down into her glass of white wine, apparently unsettled by something.

"What? What is it?"

"Do you remember that man just now, with the elderly couple, the man with the white stick?"

I thought about everyone I had seen leaving the church, and then recalled the blind man accompanied by a couple I had assumed to be his parents.

"Yes, yes I do. Why?"

My Mother took a drink and swallowed hard.

"Well, that man's name is Thomas Jennings."

I knew that name. I tried hard to remember where I knew it from, but amidst the cacophony of the increasingly noisy public house, I couldn't concentrate.

"Should I know him? Is he famous?"

Mother continued,

"Well, yes, he is quite famous. And in answer to your first question, yes you do know him." My mother had, for the first time in years, my undivided attention.

"When you were very young, there was a terrible accident. You were playing with a friend in his garden, when a shed caught fire, trapping your friend inside it. That friend was Thomas Jennings. Do you remember Tom, Alexander? That fire blinded him. It wasn't your fault – everyone knows that – but you need to know. We've kept it from you for too long - your father made me promise that I would never tell you while he had breath in his body. Well, he's not breathing now and you have a right to know. You have a right to know a lot of things."

My inner world, whose gradual refurbishment had already been interrupted by Dada's illness, was now rocked to the core by my mother's revelation about Thomas Jennings. Tom. Miss Baines. Matches. A fire. The Police. A house move. Time off school. A new school. A new house. A new life.

A charade.

16

The loss of my virginity now well behind me - thank God no-one at Freestone knew I'd left school a virgin - I settled into my work at FiveStar, with Steve guiding me through the ins and outs of investments and the hotel acquisition business. I did a lot of number crunching and a ton of menial office jobs ranging from coffee-making to sandwich-fetching. But I didn't care. I was making money and living a fast-paced, frenetic life.

Within six months, I was making my own decisions as to when to call the brokers and get advice on moving money from share to share. When Steve was out of the country, apart from setting certain limits on what I could and could not trade, he gave me free rein, and I revelled in the independence. The brokers helped to make sure I did nothing stupid, and all I had to do was press the button.

Having been generally in excellent health up until my working life began, I was shocked when I started noticing my energy levels were not what they used to be. Some mornings I'd wake up with blocked sinuses, a fuzzy head and aching joints. I was starting to get colds, and even had the first bout of flu I could remember having in years. And when I got a bad cold, my pinned shoulder would hurt like hell.

With it becoming more necessary every day for me to keep going, at the first sign of a cold I'd go straight to my doctor demanding antibiotics, and if it was really bad, I'd want strong painkillers for my shoulder. Steve had encouraged me down this line. He knew exactly what it took to stay in the game. I felt lucky to have him to mentor to me; always advising me on how I could maintain my ability to work.

"This", he used to say on a regular basis when he could see that I was struggling physically and needed another trip to the doctor, "this is how we do it in the good old US of A. We nuke the bejesus out of any virus that has the nerve to come anywhere near our defences."

His other way of nuking any unwanted visitors to the body or of restoring energy to required levels, was by 'using.' Under his careful tutelage, coke, which he liked to call 'Bolivian Marching Powder' or BMP for short, had become a more than occasional fillip which provided me with the energy to get through those days when I had been partying until four or five in the morning.

I didn't see it then, but I see now that my once pure state of health was beginning to suffer from the complex effects of a wide range of pharmaceuticals, that were unerringly weakening my immune system.

The longer I stayed at FiveStar, the more enthusiastically I got into bed with everything that went with the Thatcher years. It was like the days of the Romans; one big orgy of materialism. I thought it was brilliant. I thought *I* was brilliant. Like so many other young men and women of the day, I felt like I could do almost anything. And when I had snorted a bit of BMP I *knew* I could do anything. I was becoming a supreme being and everything was within my grasp.

Thoughts of university had long since disappeared from my orbit, much to my mother's disappointment. Within my first year of working, Dada and my first Christmas bonus had provided me with enough cash for a five percent deposit on a small flat in Chelsea. With no real responsibilities at that time, I was left with enough over from my salary every month, after I had paid the mortgage, to cover my increasingly excessive lifestyle.

I spent my twentieth birthday in New York. Steve had invited me over to take part in a merger negotiation with a Hong Kong chain who were looking for a 'marriage of convenience' with a leading western operator. The deal would give us a share of some prime hotels in Hong Kong, and Steve had been poring over the paperwork for months. This was big – even by Steve's standards. In return, the Hong Kong company, Tang Leisure, wanted to secure a stake in FiveStar. It was Steve's job to make sure that the deal being offered was in FiveStar's favour and to assess what level of cash or share allocation adjustments might be necessary. He was also to make sure that FiveStar didn't part with any more equity than was absolutely necessary to secure the deal – a deal that the board were keen to push through due to the prominence of the hotels in the far east's greatest performing market. A foothold here was seen as a potential doorway into the massive market of China which was being predicted as the business centre of the future by a few independent thinkers of the time.

That first trip to New York was unforgettable. I had thought that London was a buzzy place, but my mind was blown away by the craziness and energy of the Big Apple. It was like being high but without the need to take drugs. Not that I would be turning down any drugs that came my way, obviously. I arrived after Steve, met up with him at a hotel close to Grand Central, and spent that evening, my birthday evening, ligging it with him at clubs and bars all over the city. I very nearly had sex in a toilet with a girl from Rhode Island; I narrowly escaped being scarred for life by a drunken Irishman brandishing a broken glass as The Pogues performed to an exclusive audience at a lock-in in an Irish Bar; I ate Sushi from a conveyor belt; I squeezed into a Chevrolet with Steve and at least six New York brokers, and watched in part-horror, part-awe as Steve and one of the others did a deal with a man near the Bronx. I didn't need to ask what they were scoring.

We all went back to a building on the Upper East Side, home to one of the brokers, Yakov Miller. Yakov was tall, dark haired and brimming with confidence. It had been he who had done the deal with Steve and the pusher. We took the plush elevator up to his place, a fourteenth floor apartment overlooking Central Park.

The spacious rooms were kitted out with designer furniture, centrally controlled lights and sound system. This was it. This was what I aspired to. This was what I had to earn. If I didn't have the acquisition bug fully yet, that visit to Yakov's apartment made sure I had it now. I thought of my little flat back in Chelsea and felt embarrassed.

The living room was surrounded almost entirely by glass. The views of Manhattan were exhilarating. I turned from the windows to see the guys assembling a couple of funny-looking pipes and spreading some off-white crystalline rocks onto a cloth on the smoked-glass dining table.

"Crack?" I asked hesitantly.

"Yep" replied Steve looking up at me as he inhaled his first breath of smoke. "Happy Birthday, Alex."

The others gathered around the pipes, and each in turn took their fill. The rush was almost instant, but first time around I exhaled too quickly and the euphoria was replaced by a strong desire for more. I soon got the hang of retaining the fumes for as long as I could, and once again experienced the sensation of being all-powerful.

At four in the morning, I found myself wandering alone through the streets of New York. I was twenty, I was out of my head; I didn't have a clue where I was going or what I was doing. I didn't know where Steve was, and I didn't know where it was I had just come from, and even though I had been up since some Godforsaken hour the day before, and had travelled across the Atlantic, I still felt indefatigable. I still felt all-conquering. In fact, I felt more powerful than ever.

But as the colours started to lose their vibrant luminosity and the sounds began to return to a duller mixture of cats, car engines and police sirens, I started to become paranoid that I was being followed. I suddenly felt like someone from a spy movie – every time I turned onto a new block I'd glance over my shoulder to see if I could spot my would-be assailant. I started ducking into shop doorways and waiting for minutes to see who would pass. No-one ever did. At least no-one who was interested in me. Not until the cops caught up with me anyway.

"Everything alright?"

I turned around, expecting to be knifed at the very least, only to see a police car driving alongside me. A policeman was hanging his head out of the window as the car crawled along by the sidewalk.

A thousand thoughts went through my head. God, did I have any crack on me? Had they given me some at Yakov's apartment? Where was my passport? I didn't have a Green Card – I'm sure I remembered someone saying once that you needed a Green Card to visit New York. My hair – oh shit, my hair, I hadn't had it cut for weeks. Was it too long? What did they want with me? What had I done, and how did they know?

I spoke at a speed which surprised even me. I could hear the words escaping from my mouth, but I had no control over them.

"Me? Oh, you mean me? Yes, yes thank you, everything's fine, although I am rather worried that I haven't got a Green Card and my passport is back in the hotel, and did you know that I'm twenty years old today?"

"Whoa, whoa, hold on sir. Are you English?" The car had kept rolling along all the time this exchange was taking place.

"English, English, yes, yes I am. Of course I am."

This time the officer who was driving leant across his partner, keeping the car remarkably straight.

"First time in New York, right?"

"Er, yes, yes it is. My first night as it happens. But I don't see what that's got to do with anything."

"Oh, well, we do sir. You have a good night now – and be careful." The two of them laughed as they drove off, looking for their next drunken or drug-afflicted victim.

No sooner had they driven off than I hailed the next yellow cab that came my way. I didn't like the look of the car or the driver but I figured I had no choice. His eyes were much too shifty and he barely spoke. I'm sure he was hiding something in his right hand which he kept still on his right leg, just below his crotch. He had a tooth-pick between his teeth which made anything he did say almost impossible to decipher. I told him to take me to the FiveStar International on Forty-Fourth and Second, and emerged from his car, relieved to have my wallet and body still intact. I wouldn't take his cab again though.

I darted into the hotel and up to my room. I went to bed that morning feeling like I had done my birthday New York style. I was becoming a real man, a lone warrior fighting for everything that was rightfully mine.

But, even with these mighty ideals, a real man couldn't sleep while being tortured by a stomach that was shouting out 'feed me, feed me' at full volume. I opened up the mini bar and stuffed my face with peanuts. I called room service, demanded a sandwich, and asked for the description of the person that would be delivering it so I could make sure I wasn't being attacked by some mugger or something.

The sandwich duly came and was dispatched to the bottomless pit that was my stomach. I tried to sleep again, but the only thing worse than trying to sleep on an empty stomach is trying to sleep on one that's full; particularly when your brain is still telling you it's empty. I ended up taking a bath to try to calm my increasing panic. I had an important meeting in a few hours with Steve and the Hong Kong team, and I needed to be alert for it.

I crawled back into bed and shut my eyes.

I was woken at about eight-thirty by a knock on the door. It was Steve, looking immaculate, brief-case in hand.

"So you got back then. One minute you were there, the next minute you were gone. That was pretty good stuff, huh?"

I was feeling weird. I had been overly cocky about my body's ability to cope with jet-lag, copious champagne, dancing and crack. I felt like I was made up of a thousand pieces, each one feeling ever so slightly dislocated from the next. But I confidently replied:

"Right, yeah, I just had to get out of there, you know get some fresh air. Once I got out I just decided to head back here and get some sleep for this morning." I almost convinced myself that I was telling it as it was.

"Always thinking of the job eh, Alex? Well, I've got to take my hat off to you. Now then, you better get yourself ready - we're meeting at nine o'clock down in the VIP meeting room. We'll get some breakfast at the meet." Steve spread out some of the contents of his case on the table and started studying some papers.

I went to the wardrobe to get out my shirt, suit and tie. Bollocks. In the excitement of yesterday I'd never unpacked. I opened up my case and pulled out my suit and shirt, both of which bore the creases of their transatlantic incarceration.

I jumped into the bathroom with them before Steve had a chance to notice and swiftly washed, shaved, and got dressed. I looked like I had just slept in my suit. I could feel a knot forming in my stomach and my nerves fraying. I had to have a shit. My conditioning at boarding school had meant that this was something at least that I didn't worry too much about with other men around. I screwed up all my nerves about that meeting and my fears about my appearance, and I crapped for England. I don't know what came out of me that morning, but it was loud and fulsome. I hoped that the ventilation system worked well in our hotels.

I came out of the bathroom, and Steve didn't turn a hair. He must have heard me. Next door must have heard me. In fact the next floor must have heard me. I told Steve I was ready, and he said we could go as soon as he had used the bathroom. Part of me was embarrassed at the thought of him entering that foul-smelling room, another part of me wanted to be proud of what I'd done.

"Holy shit, who died in here?" I could hear Steve pissing as he laughed. Maybe that's where the expression pissing with laughter originally came from. "Well, you sure know how to dump. You could get on television with that trick. Let's go."

And with that, Steve collected up his things and we went in search of the VIP meeting room. Thank God. The bathroom incident had taken his attention away from my suit and shirt. I had got away with it.

From my point of view, the meeting itself was to be fairly straightforward. I was there to watch, listen and learn and top up drinks when necessary. Steve didn't tell me not to speak, but he didn't encourage me either, unless I was offering refreshments.

My heart felt like it was pumping still well above its normal rate. I didn't want to sit, I couldn't sit, I was too nervous. The Tang Leisure representatives were there at eight fifty-nine. Two men and a woman. All three of them were impeccably presented; the two men dressed in matching dark grey, single-breasted suits with matching burgundy coloured ties, sporting an emblem I presumed to be that of their business. The woman wore a midnight-blue trouser suit with a crisp white blouse and a burgundy neck scarf. This was Team Tang and no mistake.

We greeted them, their hand shakes were inconsequential and their eyes lowered, and Steve invited them to sit down. They all smiled and then one of the men spoke to me.

"Ah, the lived-in look – nice." Smiling again, he nodded his head up and down and towards the other two.

This comment threw me. What a start. I was at a loss to know what to say. Fortunately Steve jumped in.

"Yes, Alex likes to be right on top of fashion trends, don't you, Alex?"

I fumbled for something interesting to say.

"Er, yes, yes, it's all the thing in London." What an idiot. 'All the thing in London' – who was I, some sort of third-rate fashion commentator on local radio? Fortunately they all smiled again, nodded at each other and sat down.

I offered them drinks and they all accepted an offer of mineral water. No coffee. No tea. I noticed my hand shaking as I tried to unscrew the top from the bottle; I had to hold it together, but my body was determined to show who was boss. In one terrifying moment, just as I had managed to prise the lid from its neck I thought the bottle was going to slip out of my hand and smash all over Steve's documents on the table. But, thank God again, I managed to slide my hand back down the neck and avert disaster.

To avoid risking any further problems with this simple task, I collected their glasses and poured out their drinks at the end of the table while Steve was engaging with them in what seemed like a very tedious bout of mindless small talk. I later found out that this was a traditional way of opening a meeting with people from Hong Kong before turning to the business agenda. When I gave them each their glasses with my still shaking hand, I was intrigued to see that in front of the three of them was a clear crystal pyramid, about two inches in height. No-one talked about it. It just sat there, bridging the gap between their chief negotiator and Steve.

The meeting proceeded at impressive speed. That is to say, Steve conducted himself at an impressive speed. I was amazed at how effective he could be after a night like the one we'd just had. I marvelled at his resilience and his clarity of purpose. I found myself getting drawn more and more into the story of this potential merger, and watched closely for the tricks that Steve employed as he negotiated his way through a minefield of potential contract-breakers.

As the meeting wore on, I perceived that it was Steve who most wanted to push through an agreement. The Hong Kong team, led by Yao Kuo-Rui, was almost pedestrian in its approach. Each time Steve suggested a new bargaining point, Yao would lean back in his chair and put his two hands together, with the finger tips of each hand pressed up against each other so that his hand formed a pyramid like the crystal one on the table in front of him. Throughout this he would be nodding his head, and he would continue to nod while turning his head to each of his associates.

Occasionally Yao would then ask a question, and the woman, Zhu Ling-Shun, would make notes. The other man, Ma Bo-Tian, only ever spoke after this initial question process had taken place each time, and then only in what I assumed was Cantonese.

I must have topped up Steve's and my coffees three or four times. I took Steve's lead in everything, right down to how often he took sips. I didn't top up our counterparts' drinks once. Steve became more activated as the meeting continued, and I noticed the first hint of desperation creep into his normally rock-solid, phlegmatic approach. These people were getting to him. I didn't know how, but they were. He was beginning to cave in on certain terms before they had even tried to knock him down.

After three hours of almost entirely one-way negotiations, the Hong Kong contingent, led by Yao, suddenly stood up. He picked up the pyramid and put it into his pocket.

"Thank you Steve, Alexander, this has been most useful. We call you later."

And with that simple acknowledgement, they departed, leaving Steve and me wondering what, if anything we had done to cause their sudden exit.

Steve was first to break the silence.

"Well there you go, Alex, your first negotiation with the Far East. What did you make of that?"

For a few seconds, I was confused as to whether Steve would want my honest opinion or a dressed up version. He soon let me know.

"Did you notice how I handled their silences? Clever trick that one, huh? You have to watch these guys, they're playing mind games all the time."

And that was when it dawned on me that silence could be used as a mind game. I'd never thought about that before. Neither had I been aware of Steve's use of it and, somewhere in my head, a quiet voice was wondering whether Steve really had handled Yao's silence cleverly at all.

17

I sat in stunned silence. I had developed from small boy to middle-aged man without any knowledge of what I had done to Tom, while he had been obliged to grow from being a boy who could see everything into a man who could see nothing. Not only that, but he must have had reconstruction work done on his face and possibly body too. To hurt someone so badly, albeit unintentionally, and to know is one thing; time must help you to come to terms with it. But to hurt someone, and to be oblivious of the fact; it was a choice my Dada had made, but in that moment it felt like the wrong one. I didn't want to feel angry with him on the day of his funeral, but I couldn't help it. I, Alexander Baker, had caused a man to lose his sight. I had felt low in my life, but there was a whole new level to which I now plunged.

The name Thomas Jennings bounced around my mind along with a thousand other aimless thoughts. And then I remembered the news feature about the blind man who had done the charity walk – wasn't his name Thomas Jennings?

"Alexander – Alexander?" My mother was trying to get through to me but I remained impassive, trying to understand what impact this new information would have on my life.

"Is he here?" I suddenly wanted to meet him. I wanted to talk to him again and tell him I was sorry. I wanted to see what I could do to help. I wanted to make it right.

"No, I haven't seen him in the pub. He probably left with his parents."

"Alexander – good to see you. Hello boys, very nice reading Daniel, well done. Heard every word." It was Dada's brother, Uncle Gerald. He refused to acknowledge my mother. The scars ran too deep.

My mother made it easier.

"Right, well, if you'll excuse me Alexander, I think I'll get on my way."

Ah, the joy of family politics. Mother got up to leave. We hadn't hugged, I mean properly hugged, in years. But maybe something in that brief exchange about Tom had altered something. Maybe I was just feeling vulnerable and needed her close to me again. Whatever the reasons, and right in front of Uncle Gerald, I gave my mother a bear hug. I shut my eyes as I held her close to me, and felt the tears rolling once again down my face.

"Thank you Mumma", I whispered gently in her ear. I hadn't called her Mumma in years. "I needed to know."

She withdrew a little. "I know" she said, looking into my eyes. "You always needed to know. Bye boys." She got a grunt from Daniel and nothing from Joel who was too wrapped up in the Nintendo. "I'll call you – soon." I watched as she made her way carefully out of the sea of gently swaying mourners-turned-drinkers.

A few minutes later, Helen, who had been out walking to escape the smoky bars, returned. We said our goodbyes to those we knew and some we didn't, and made our way back to the house. I felt like someone who had just been told they had a terminal illness, and who hadn't worked out how on earth he was going to tell his family. I was now carrying a heavy burden, and ached to share it with Helen. The trouble was, I had laid so much at her door already, I wasn't sure she'd be too pleased with any more revelations.

Helen and the boys had been staying with me on and off for about three weeks. She had suggested that they help me get through the funeral and then return home once it was out of the way. Things were going better now between us, but I knew I still had work to do to convince my beautiful ex-wife that the man who was her loathsome former husband had changed for good. The scar I had caused had been deep, and had resulted in her going on her own journey of self-discovery; a journey from which, out of the ashes of Helen One, an almost entirely new Helen Two had emerged.

In many ways, Helen Two was scary; she was confident, calm, firm and seemed to care for herself in a way that Helen One never did. Helen One, on the other hand, had been a bit of a walk-over; a doormat who allowed herself to suffer mistreatment from her husband and young sons without caring what damage it may have been doing to her. I was aware that I was beginning to love Helen Two in a profoundly moving way; I had started to enjoy her unusual perspective on things, and was, frustratingly, finding her sexier than ever.

And yet she was keeping clear boundaries, and these boundaries were also helping me to feel safe. These invisible walls held me and protected me from my own inner self-sabotage monster. There was no way now that Helen Two was going to turn a blind eye to my drinking or drug use; there was no way she was going to have a quick shag with me, surrendering to my male needs just to appease me like she used to, even if she was feeling horny. She had learnt how to say no, but in such a way that I no longer felt rejected. Helen had learnt self-respect.

The journey back through the traffic was slow, and I remained quiet throughout. Helen had taken us all in her little Ford, our ever-growing boys beginning to dwarf the back seats. All I could think about was that conversation with my mother. Pictures torn from the pages of an old mental scrap book flashed through my mind; a police woman's face, my new bedroom, Miss Baines - was that her name? My history, my real history, had been ripped out of me as a surgeon would cut off an infected arm or leg. But, just as so many amputees experience phantom limb sensation where they believe they can still feel their missing body part, I could still feel the pain of something from long-ago that had never been resolved. A pain that had been quietly, but relentlessly, gnawing away at me for years. Dada might have been able to take the boy out of the situation, but he couldn't take the situation out of the boy. And the boy was now a man. And the situation was now a collection of fragmented memories that had suddenly sprung to life like Frankenstein's monster at the spark of my mother's words.

We got back to the house and I fell into my favourite chair as if I had been steamrollered. I must have fallen asleep, because the next thing I remember is waking up with a blanket over me and all the curtains closed. Helen was lying on the couch with her feet up reading a book under the light of the nearby standard lamp. She had her glasses on, one of the few clues that showed the passing of the years. Something that had become clear to everyone who knew her, was that the new Helen was looking younger than ever. She was continually asked by friends what it was she was on that made her look so vibrant. I wasn't alone in wanting a part of that.

"Hello, Alex. How are you feeling?" She put down her book and was looking directly at me, smiling easily.

"Like I've been trampled on by a herd of buffalo. Other than that I'm fine. Do you fancy a cuppa?"

She nodded her head. "That would be lovely – do you want me to do it?"

"No, no I'd like to stretch my legs a bit." I went into the kitchen and put the kettle on. I could hear the boys upstairs in their room, watching the telly. While the kettle was boiling I checked my messages; the machine showed two new calls. The first was from my mother saying she thought she was going to be late for the funeral – didn't she realise I would already have gone? Oh well.

The second started to play. "Hello, Alexander. Look, this is difficult – not easy to leave a message about but, well, I thought I'd give you the chance to get in touch or not. You see I'm just leaving on the train with my parents following the service for your father. Awfully sorry by the way – deepest commiserations, I should have said that at first. Anyway, just to say, well if you want to get in touch, I'd be pleased to speak with you. By the way, bother I should have told you this first - this is Tom. From Miss Baines's class. Remember? I'm the…"

And at that point my machine cut him off.

18

I thought it odd that Steve had insisted back in London that I was the only one to go with him to New York. He had explained to the board that he felt it would be a good training opportunity for me and that, despite the size of the potential merger, he was confident in being able to negotiate the final outline deal to present to the other directors. As vice-president in charge of the treasury at FiveStar, Steve had a lot of clout.

The company probably knew nothing about his extra-curricular activities, or his penchant for drugs. All they knew was that their asset sheets were healthy and their investments of the last few years had been highly successful. Steve had been there for four of the most profitable years, so had earned the respect of his board. Of course this was also a boom time in the global economy, so it's possible that a little too much praise was being piled at his door.

Either way, Steve had the power to do much as he pleased. That morning, after the meeting had finished, he went through the paperwork again, meticulously going over all the numbers to see if he had missed a trick, or if he could offer something more appealing to the Tang group. He kept on popping pills and drinking cups of coffee interspersed with glasses of water. Lunch was delivered to us in the meeting-room; a couple of seafood salads. I made sure my notes from the meeting were in order, although there had hardly been any notes to take since Steve had done most of the talking, and had beforehand written down his entire presentation.

As the lunch hour began to eat into the afternoon, and we'd still had no call from Yao and his team, I noticed Steve becoming more agitated. He called the UK office a couple of times and asked for updates on some trading figures for a small group of our smaller hotels in Scandinavia. While he was on the phone, another call was put through on the second phone. It was Peter Carver, another senior director of FiveStar and someone with whom Steve linked very closely; he said it was urgent and so I passed Steve a note. He quickly ended his call.

"Look, Alex, I need to take this call alone if you don't mind. Just need to concentrate. Go and grab a drink or something and come back in half an hour – I've got some figures I need you to check for me."

I gave Steve his space, picked up my coat and walked out on to the Manhattan streets. How different they seemed from the streets of four in the morning. Was that really only twelve hours ago when I had spoken with the cops? I jockeyed for position on the sidewalk alongside an international mix of walkers, joggers and skaters. Someone had once said just because you've been to New York, it doesn't mean you've seen America, and I could understand what they meant. Of all these faces and rushing bodies, who was a true native?

My stomach was beginning to feel odd and I hoped to God that I hadn't eaten some dodgy shellfish. I'd only taken a couple of bites before leaving the office, so I couldn't believe it was that. I also began to notice my whole body beginning to ache and suddenly my head felt like someone had stuck a red hot iron through one ear and out the other. I found the nearest lamppost and held on to it for a while, allowing the searing pain to pass.

After a couple of minutes I felt well enough to go back to the hotel. I decided to sit in the lobby until my allotted half-hour was up. I continued to feel strange, but my stomach discomfort had subsided enough to ease my suspicions about the food poisoning possibility.

"Hello Mr Alexander" - I looked up and saw Zhu Ling-Shun staring down at me. She was not an unattractive woman, her age impossible for me to determine. She had a couple of crisp white carrier bags with the familiar stamps of Bloomingdales on their sides. I stood up to greet her, copying Steve's example at the earlier meeting.

"Hi – how's it going? Please, call me Alexander." I didn't quite know what else to say.

"Well, Alexander, it depends on what you mean by it. If you mean New York, then it's going well. I like shopping here." She paused to laugh for a moment and I laughed politely with her.

"If you mean our deal, then I'd say it is in an interesting position." Her English was perfect, and I found her confidence slightly unnerving. "May I sit down?"

I nodded my head rather pathetically.

"Mr Steve, where is he? Is he still trying hard to juggle the figures?"

"He's in conversation with London." I made sure I didn't give too much away, aware that she may not have arrived here by chance at all.

"How do you like your hotels Alexander? Do you enjoy staying in a FiveStar Hotel?"

I wasn't sure where she was going with this. Was this just polite conversation or was there another agenda at work? I suddenly found corporate blood flowing through my veins. At the exact same moment, her two associates magically appeared and, after more greetings, sat down beside her.

"Like our hotels? I love them. You know, when I was growing up I was lucky enough to have parents who could take me to some of the top hotels in the world. I knew what to look for in a good hotel and that's partly why I took this job. So far, the hotels I've been to that belong to this group are amongst the very best I've stayed in." I was getting into a flow and my physical aches began to dissolve. "And from what I've heard from Steve, your group has similarly high standards in the Far East. That's why this is such a perfect marriage."

The three of them then spoke together in Cantonese, which made me feel slightly uncomfortable. I suddenly wondered if I'd given any secrets away that could weaken our negotiating position.

Zhu continued to do the talking.

"Please tell me, what is it in particular that stands FiveStar apart from its competitors?"

I suddenly felt incredibly important. They were engaging with me, a mere scrap of a twenty year old who had been with the company for only a few months; they really seemed to want to know what I thought made FiveStar special.

I wanted to give them the perfect answer. I wanted to impress. In fact I was so desperate to answer well, that I hesitated as a dozen different potential responses flashed across my brain. Without meaning to, I found myself arching my hands in the same pyramid shape that Yao had created earlier. Yao followed suit, and soon all four of us were playing hand geometry.

After what seemed like an eternity to me, I opened my mouth.

"You see this shape?" I leant over and pointed directly at Zhu's pyramid hands, inadvertently touching her fingers.

"What about this shape, Alexander?" she replied leaving her hands positioned just as they had been.

I slowly traced the outline of her hand with my fingers as I made my pronouncement.

"FiveStar seems to recognise the significance of this shape. If the peak of this shape is the experience of actually staying in maybe one of our presidential or honeymoon suites, then the bottom of the pyramid is that of a casual visitor who stays in a cheaper room or just comes in for a one-off meal." I took my hands away, concerned that I may be breaking with acceptable Eastern convention.

"Some hotel chains seem only interested in the peak customers, the ones who are going to spend the most in the shortest possible time. But FiveStar recognises that their pyramid falls down if they don't look after, what we call in England, the bread-and-butter clients. The ones who keep the cashflow ticking along. That, I believe, is what makes FiveStar different. They value, and are in touch with, the people."

Ma, who had still only spoken in Cantonese, stood up. The other two immediately followed suit.

"Thank you, Mr Alexander." I wanted to tell him just to call me Alexander, but felt I couldn't interrupt him. "Please to tell me, can we speak with Mr Steve now?"

My heart started racing again. Oh shit, what had I said? Had I given something away?

"Er, let me go and check, I'll see if he's finished. Please, just wait here in your seats."

But the three of them remained standing. I knocked on the meeting-room door. Steve's tired voice answered.

"Come in." Steve was picking at his plate of food, papers spread out on the table in front of him.

"Ah, good, Alex. Look, I need you to go through these figures for the Scandinavian group. I've spoken to London, they're prepared to offer a small involvement here as well to sweeten the pill. I told them they were playing hard-ball. These guys are good – you've got to hand it to them."

"Steve, they're outside in the lobby, I, er - I just ran into them. They want to see you now."

Steve's already somewhat fragile demeanour disintegrated a little more at this news.

"Shit, I'm not ready to make a new offer yet. Did they say what they wanted – no of course they didn't. Why would they tell you? Okay, let's tidy these up quickly and we'll just have to wing it. Watch and learn, Alex, watch and learn."

Steve took another pill from his pocket and swallowed it down with some water. He got me to order fresh supplies of mineral water and coffee, and within a minute had transformed the table-top to pristine condition again.

"Okay, Alex, ask them to come in."

I went back out into the lobby. They were still standing where I had left them.

"Steve is ready for you now, sorry for the delay, he was just finishing a phone call."

They filed back into the meeting room. Zhu hovered by the doors, which I was about to shut when Yao spoke.

"Please may I ask that Alexander remain outside while we say what we have to say? We have asked Miss Zhu to stay outside too."

My heart nearly dropped through the floor. I had screwed up. It must have been when my wandering fingers touched Zhu's – oh shit, I knew it was dodgy at the time but I was so into my little speech. Why couldn't I have just kept my mouth shut, why did I have to speak at all? Who the hell did I think I was?

Steve looked quizzically at me but quickly jumped into his business mode.

"No problem. No problem at all. Alex, could you leave us for a minute?"

I tried to smile as I pulled the doors behind me, but failed. My first major business deal and I had blown it, big time. Hmm, maybe I would be going to university after all, albeit as a mature student.

Twenty minutes passed at a deathly pace. I waited, as requested, outside in the lobby with Zhu, who politely engaged me in all manner of small talk about my family, my education, restaurants in Hong Kong, hotels in Hong Kong, her favourite shops, films, food and books. While superficially keeping up this conversation, all the time my mind was running through the potential repercussions of whatever it was that I had said.

Like the condemned man whose time has finally come, there was a strange sense of relief when Steve finally emerged with Ma and Yao.

"We'll get the legal boys on it upon my return to London, and fax you the outline contract by the beginning of next week." Steve wasn't speaking like a businessman whose biggest ever deal had just been reduced to ashes by a young, fire-starting big-mouth.

"That's good Mr Steve, very good." Yao smiled broadly and he and Ma offered their hands one after the other as they said goodbye. Zhu then went up to Steve and also bid him goodbye. Ma approached me first and spoke awkwardly in his broken English..

"You Mr Alexander – you clever. I like you. I like you a lot. We work well together." And he shook my hand as he laughed out loud. Yao and Zhu also offered their goodbyes and I noticed that they both thanked me.

Before I had time to think, Steve ushered me back into the meeting-room.

"Shut the door, Alex."

I did as instructed, anything to delay the abuse I was convinced I was about to get.

"What the hell did you say to them exactly while you were in the lobby?"

I fumbled for my words. "Oh, it was just small talk Steve, you know about holidays and different hotels and stuff."

"Well it might have been small talk to you, Alex, but to them it was the difference between renegotiating the whole deal or going for it as is. Whatever the hell you said out there convinced them that the stake they're getting in FiveStar is worth every square foot of space that we're getting in the Far East operation. They're going for it. I didn't even have to dangle Scandinavia in front of them. Genius, Alex, genius."

At that moment I wanted to bottle my speech in the lobby that afternoon. I wanted to record the order of the words and the tone and inflection of my voice. I wanted to revisit in the most minute of details, my facial expressions and body language. I wanted to lock that magic up in my genie's bottle and have it to use whenever I needed it in the future.

"There's one other thing, Alex. Sit down – you might need a drink for this." Steve suddenly looked as serious as he had when he had been poring over all the figures earlier that same afternoon. That same afternoon, in fact just a couple of hours ago. How the world had changed since then.

"Ma is one of the top dogs in the business. He liked you Alex. Via Yao, he's asked me to make sure that you are fully involved in the relationship between FiveStar and Tang Leisure. He wants you to fly over to Hong Kong with me when the legal boys have thrashed through the contracts."

I was trying to take in what Steve was telling me. I had after all only minutes previously been castigating myself for screwing the whole deal up; I'd even been contemplating university places.

"Alex, listen up. Ma wants to offer FiveStar a deal to get your services for a few days every month to help them with their European expansion. You might not realise it, but you're a wanted man."

I felt my chest puffing up like one of those birds on a wildlife programme.

"But I can't do that Steve, I mean I'm employed by FiveStar now. And what about you? I mean, I've done nothing except have a little chat in the lobby."

"Alex, Alex, Alex. First rule of business – when you're told you've done something brilliantly, just accept the compliment. It doesn't matter whether it's true or not. Take it while you can, there will be plenty of time for knocks in the future. Secondly, having a position with Tang and FiveStar could work wonderfully for FiveStar as it gives us a foot in both camps. It's unusual, but since we're getting into bed with them anyway, it is certainly not out of the question.

"Thirdly, Ma wants me to control all negotiations between Tang and FiveStar in the future. So don't worry about me, as long as this deal is happening, I'm doing just fine. We need to iron out the details, I'll negotiate for you of course, but I reckon you'll be looking at doubling your present salary with some sort of options. Plus you'll be travelling all over the place. Sound good?"

More money, travelling to top hotels and presumably quite often to Hong Kong. What wasn't to get excited about? I went back up to my room in a state of euphoria. I had to tell someone. I so needed to share this joy, this success, this amazing feeling of power that was rushing through my body.

I called my father first. Nothing. Just his answer-phone. I started to leave a message stating my good news, but then began to feel let down by the inevitable realisation that I wouldn't be getting a verbal response which, in that instant, I so urgently needed. I muttered something about a successful trip and birthday and hung up. I started to dial my mother's number. But then the closer I got to finishing it, the more angry I felt with her again and the less I wanted to share with her my good news before I had got hold of Dada. I resented her for being the only other person I could call. I hung up the phone and lay down on the bed.

I was beginning to realise that success is fabulous as long as you can share it with someone. New York suddenly seemed like a very lonely place.

19

When Helen took the boys back to school and then returned to their small house the next day, I felt a sense of isolation unlike any I'd experienced in a very long time. New York sprang to my mind – all those years ago when I had first been informed of the job share with Tang by Steve Drayton, and I had tried to ring my father to let him know. I had become used to Helen's presence, and the expectation of the boys coming home after school. I had even become okay with having my aged father for company, and longed to hear him call out from his room for a cup of tea or a pill. But there were to be no more calls now.

The quiet gave me time to think. A commodity of which I had been short for most of my adult life. I had experienced a few strange things in recent years, but what was all this new information about? Was I meant to do anything at all about Dada's message from beyond the grave? And how was I meant to process this news about Tom? I was five years old at the time for God's sake, what did anyone expect me to do now about something that happened when I was so young?

I reminded myself that Tom's voice had sounded quite calm, and far from angry. He's obviously okay with it all. Has anyone told him the whole story however? Was it 'destiny' that I should be the one to tell him? Should I call him? And then what? What would I say? *"Oh, hi Tom, yeah, really sorry I disfigured your face and body and caused you to go blind. I didn't mean to."*

Here I was, a man who had made large sums of money out of knowing how and when to act; yet now I couldn't work out whether I was meant to do anything about what was happening to me. I decided to go out for a run on the Heath and to listen to Dada's words again on my headphones.

It was a beautiful, clear spring morning. I took my normal route near to the station, entering the Heath down by the playground. There were quite a few mums there, mainly with toddlers, their older brothers and sisters presumably sitting behind their desks at school. I got past the worst of the noise, paused for a second and pressed play on the little machine which I held firmly in my hand.

"Your Royal Highness, ministers, vegetables and Catholics ..."

I found myself more able to smile at the humour this time around. In fact I believe I was listening to the whole thing in a slightly different way than the first time. I now heard things in the speech that I had previously missed. I heard Dada mention Golly, telling him to hang on, saying that he was coming soon. This really struck me. The only Golly we ever knew was my Golly, my best friend, whose life had been so tragically cut short. Was Dada communicating with him? And if so, was this talk delusional?

I turned off the busier path, up towards the tumulus and my favourite London view, across Parliament Hill to the City. As I jogged more and more slowly up the hill, I could feel my chest beginning to move into the familiar territory of aches that would either precede a few minutes' enforced rest or a successful acceleration beyond the pain barrier and into effortless striding. As I struggled with my own breathing techniques and pain control, Dada, who at the time of the recording must have been having similar, if much more exaggerated, struggles, was rambling on about bananas and semolina and snake-pits.

I stopped for a minute and hit pause, while I made my final assault on the peak. Half-jogging, half-walking, and with the sun now beginning to bring warmth to the Heath, I made it to the top of the hill and stood there. London stretched out all around me. I hit play on the machine again and listened closely to his voice. As the speech went on, so his voice sounded different. He was not only expressing himself more clearly, he sounded clearer. As he talked about communication as a way to transform the world, I realised I was going to have to transcribe this speech, so that I could separate out the plain barmy from the inspired.

"Your feelings of guilt create only one result – self-destruction." Well if anyone knew about guilt, I did. I had been haunted by it all my life, my mother's nightmarish revelation about Tom maybe partly explaining why. But I had also done plenty of things that I hadn't

been proud of. Things that I had ended up hating myself for. Things that I still hated myself for. And although I had not destroyed myself - I was alive after all - I had come too close to self-destruction.

Pausing on this one sentence, these few words delivered so calmly by my dying parent, I felt the weight of guilt upon my shoulders the like of which I had never previously been aware. Images and words surged through my mind. I sat down on the grass, my attention turned outwards, trying to escape the sight of a jumbled mass of mental pictures that were vying for my attention. Obviously I felt guilty about Tom, but there was also Golly and Melanie Firth and Mumma and Tom's parents and business associates and Helen and Daniel and Joel and Miss Fuller and naked women ...

I stood up. I shook my head from side to side to try to loosen and relax the muscles in my neck. I bent over a couple of times and tried to touch my toes; I never could, but it felt like the right thing to do. But the attempt at relaxation didn't help. I wanted to escape. I wanted to run away from the madness of Alexander, the madness that lived inside and that had been bottled up for so long. I wanted my running to take me far from the mixed-up land of guilt that Dada's voice had brought into view. My breathing became very quick and I started to feel light-headed. There I was, on the Heath in the midst of openness and tranquillity, and yet I was in a state of panic that there would not be enough air to sustain me. I started running slowly again, but managed only a few, clumsy, strides. I fell to my knees and I wanted to cry.

And I did. Yet again I felt myself crying, without control, in a public place. But this time I wasn't mourning a parent, at least not specifically. This felt different. This felt like a small rush of air that had managed to find its way out of an old rusty pipe that had finally developed a leak. I didn't know what pipe this was, or where it led.

"Hi, are you okay?"

I looked beside me. A couple of young men in shorts and t-shirts stood there, warming down as they talked to me.

"Me? Well, thanks – actually I have been better. Just dealing with some shit, you know how it is."

The taller of the two took a couple of paces forwards and bent down.

"No offence, but you don't look great. Do you want us to help get you somewhere?"

I felt a little strength come back at this offer of help.

"No, no, I'll be fine. I just need a few minutes I think."

This time it was the smaller one's turn to talk. "You want us to stay? Don't need to talk – we can sit here while you recover."

I suddenly felt very embarrassed. And guilty. Why should my pathetic state put these guys out? Oh God, guilt - again. The feelings started to rush back. I felt myself starting to shake. Not badly, but just enough to force me to sit again. The crying started again. This was so embarrassing. Me. Crying in front of a couple of total strangers. What would they think?

"Go for it" said the taller one. "We're here. Go for it."

And I did. Again. I cried and cried and cried. And all the time I wept, these two young men sat there on either side of me, holding a safe space for me without touching me. They protected me from the worried looks of passers-by; they stopped me from rushing away from my hurt; they created an arena in which I could, in those moments of confusion and uncertainty, just be me without editing.

I thought the tears would never end, but then they simply stopped. No words were exchanged between us throughout. Just three men, two younger, one older. The young ones helping the elder through a difficult moment. No fixes, no solutions; just their unworried presence.

After a few tearless minutes, the smaller man spoke.

"Panic over?"

"Yes. Yes, it is. But how did you know?"

"Does it matter?"

I wasn't ready to know how he knew. I just smiled and shrugged my shoulders. They both stood up.

"You be okay now?" The taller man reached out his hand to shake mine. His friend followed suit. I felt better. I felt stronger. I felt loved.

"Yes, yes I think I will, thanks. Thank you both. So much." I didn't entirely know what I was thanking them for, but their part in whatever had just happened seemed profound. Just as they were about to run off, the smaller one turned round to me.

"What do you know about meditation?"

I replied a simple one word answer.

"Loads."

"Then why don't you practise it regularly?"

And with that, the two men set back off on their journey, the smaller one raising his two hands skywards as he went.

It was true, I did feel like I knew a lot about meditation. Helen Two had all but ordered me to read up on it for my health. I had read a few things but soon got bored, and hadn't seen how it was worth spending the time doing it when there were so many other more important jobs to get done. But how did this guy know that I didn't practise it? Was it that obvious? And if he knew, then did Helen realise that I wasn't meditating as well?

I took it easy on my way back down the hill, stopping for a bottle of water at one of the kiosks. I sat on a nearby bench and thought about what had just happened. Those guys had done nothing to me – many would have called an ambulance or at least got a park warden to help. But they had simply sat with me. I wondered whether their action was irresponsible or courageous and wise beyond their years.

When I got back to the house later that morning, I was still in a weakened state, although I did feel lighter, presumably for the tears. More importantly though, I had felt loved; loved by a couple of men I had never met before and would quite possibly never meet again; loved with nothing required or demanded in return.

Why was this such an alien concept, even now? Why was I so shocked to find a couple of blokes offer their support, unconditionally, to another man in crisis? What was it about me that still clung on to a view of reality that dictated that people need to get something back for the love they give?

After showering, I sat down with a cup of tea and thought about how I might have handled that situation had the roles been reversed. I wanted to believe that I could have remained calm and present like the two young men, but could I? And if I had jumped in and convinced the sick man that he needed professional help and that he should get to a doctor or hospital, what chain of events might that have started off?

I wondered what Dada would have been thinking now if he had realised the effect his words were having. Maybe this was, at some level that I certainly didn't understand, the whole bloody point.

Maybe these words were meant for me entirely. To shake me up. To force me to see myself and my life and my relationships in a different way.

The timing of his illness and death had, after all, been critical in my own journey. I was probably just about strong enough again, just about recovered enough from my own breakdown, to start thinking about, and caring for, others. I had been through months of falling to pieces and was, with Helen's help, gently rebuilding. By the time Dada needed me, I was ready to be needed again. I was still vulnerable, some of the wounds were still open, but at least I was more aware of who I wasn't. Now all I needed to do was to start finding out who I was.

The move into consultancy work had helped to some degree. It had in part helped to get me off the mad hamster-wheel that had been my career up to that point. The problem with that had been learning when to say no to new offers and possibilities. When temptations came along, it was very difficult to make the right decisions with no-one else to bounce off. Helen told me that I should have brought in a partner, but then that would have meant giving more of the pie away and I wasn't sure I could get the business to sustain another high flier. I had set the consultancy up prior to my breakdown and, by informing clients I was taking a sabbatical for a few months, had managed to avoid losing face during my crisis period.

I sat in the armchair that Dada had made his own in the early days of his stay, and thought again about those words that had affected me so much that morning. I felt my heart begin to quicken as they echoed around my head. *"Your feelings of guilt create only one result – self-destruction."* I thought about what I had recently learnt about Tom and how my actions had contributed to his leading a disabled person's life since he was five. My heart continued to race. And then I thought about the two young Samaritans this morning and how they had done nothing physical to help, they had trusted that, given the right support, I would recover. They allowed me to deal with my problem with no intervention.

So I allowed the panic to begin to build as I shut my eyes, and this time I didn't try to hide from it. Again, I experienced jumbled up images and names, voices and actions that seemed bonded together by the glue of guilt. I couldn't pinpoint individual events, I just had a general sense of disgust that past actions, even thoughts, of mine had caused pain or suffering to others.

I took some deep breaths and clenched my fists, a simple relaxation exercise that Helen had showed me but which I had not often practised. As I stopped trying to shut out the madness and allowed the new breaths in, I felt my body relaxing. Within a couple of minutes I had come out of this second panic attack through self-management. I felt pleased with myself, as if I had achieved something important. There had been something that those young men had done that had touched me, that had left an impression. And I felt grateful to them. This wasn't gratitude of the head, but gratitude of the heart.

And something else had become clear too – I wouldn't be rushing to listen through to any more of Dada's speech - yet. I didn't think I was quite ready for it.

I was brought suddenly into the moment by the phone.

"Good Morning Mr Baker, Linda here. I've got some messages for you." Linda was my very own virtual secretary. Well, that is to say, one of three virtual secretaries that I had. They had each been under instructions not to contact me for five days while I sorted through Dada's estate and got the funeral out of the way. She reeled off a list of business calls that I needed to return.

However hard Linda tried to sound posh, somehow she just never quite made it. But she had a nice voice, and was certainly friendly enough on the phone which was important for me from a business point of view. Having a virtual office had many benefits besides the endlessly happy sounding Linda, or Joy or Cheryl. The building was in Covent Garden, a good address that doubled up as my mailing address; it had a couple of small meeting rooms and a conference room that I could hire out when necessary; someone was always there to take my messages, often late into the evening, and when the desk was unoccupied, they had a decent answering system for each company; and most importantly for me, it was close to the heart of London action. I could visit my virtual office once a day or once a year and, as long as I paid my fee, it didn't matter.

"Oh and there was one more call Mr Baker. He said you might not remember him, that he hadn't spoken to you for a long time. His name sounded French, yes that's right – Claude Denoir. I made him spell it for me. C-l-a-u-..."

Suddenly my heart started racing again. It's funny how little things, sometimes just two simple words, can produce a sudden change in heartbeat, pulse and blood pressure.

"Yes Linda I know how to spell his name thank you. What did he say?"

"He asked if you could call him. Said it was very important. He's staying in London, at the Strand Hotel. Room 441. That's all Mr Baker, have a nice day."

I still found it hard to believe that 'have a nice day' had crept into the once conservative language employed by the frontline voices of industry. A thousand, a hundred thousand, maybe a million people every day were being told to have a nice day, when previously they would have had a simple goodbye. Some part of me wondered whether such an instruction was always going to be too much to ask of the British. We don't really do 'nice days'. We do 'not bad' days.

Claude Denoir. My mind raced back to that last year of Freestone; Golly's death; 'A' levels; getting drunk; trying marijuana. Somewhere in amongst all that, and somewhere in my tangled and confused past, Claude had a place. We had met up a couple of times during my early twenties, but we probably hadn't seen each other now for at least fifteen years.

I looked up the number of The Strand Hotel.

"Hello, room 441 please. Monsieur Denoir."

20

When Steve had told me to accept Ma's compliment and to enjoy the feeling of being wanted by two companies, I couldn't connect with what he was saying. When doing studies at school and taking exams you got judged on your results. That was tangible. That was easy to measure. When my father was making his TV programmes, whether he was in front of, or behind, the camera, he got judged by his ratings. Again it was tangible. But I was haunted with suspicion about both of my jobs. Suspicion that somehow I hadn't really done anything special to deserve getting them and that, as a result, I would one day get found out for being a fraud.

At school I had developed systems to avoid being found out for things. It was part of growing up and of becoming a man. I had built layers around me that had enabled me to form a whole new persona. Now, I needed to find similar techniques that would further protect me from the danger of discovery. I already had the Bolivian Marching Powder in my armoury when I needed extra energy or major escapism, and a stiff drink had also become invaluable in helping me to calm my nerves in the middle of demanding projects. Sex and pornography also became extremely useful when I needed to offset my office worries, so that I would even occasionally pay for sex in my numerous trips overseas and revert to adult channels and magazines if no physical companion could be found.

The first six months of the new working arrangement appeared to pass successfully. I was learning my trade and getting paid for it. Quite how it had become my trade I wasn't really sure, but I had faith that people like Steve and Ma knew best. The FiveStar deal had gone through with Tang, and I had been invited to Hong Kong to visit Ma and his board of directors to sign my own contract and talk through what they wanted of me. It turned out that their expectations were simple. They wanted me to visit hotels throughout Europe, and to look for any small groups or privately owned hotels that seemed to offer exceptional, and forward-thinking, service. Ma wanted to know what made these hotels tick and so I became a hotel spy. The job seemed made in heaven. I would get paid handsomely for travelling to beautiful places, staying in top hotels, writing the odd report or two, while pretending all the time I was James Bond.

On the days when I wasn't fulfilling Tang's brief, I was still working under Steve's stewardship at FiveStar. Steve continued to teach me about investments and recreational drugs, hotels and the best locations across Europe to pick up classy women.

What I didn't know then, was that I had not only opened Pandora's box, but I'd stuffed both my hands in so deep that it would take a major crisis to free them again. Each month the money flowed in to my bank account, and each month the money flowed out into luxury goods, sex, drugs and alcohol; for about eight days in every twenty I would be waltzing in and out of aeroplanes and luxury hotels as if I'd been born to it.

Days flowed into nights and nights flowed into days. Jetlag became a commonplace inconvenience; sleep became haphazard along with my health. And I just kept bumbling along, always seeking to find new tools that would enable me to become more able to survive this lifestyle and keep the wolves from finding out that I was a fraud.

I found I could do quite well on as little as four hours sleep a day, as long as that came all at once. This became one of what I called Alexander's Survival System, or A.S.S. for short. I would avoid catnapping as I was in fear of sleep taking me over. I'd use coffee and other stimulants to keep me going until the allotted sleep time came.

My twenty-first birthday was different to that of the previous year. I'd always seen twenty-one as somehow more important than eighteen. I'd imagined it as the threshold of manhood, a step once made, never returned from. My eighteenth had been a subdued affair mainly because of the loss of Golly a few months before. My twenty-first should, in my mind, have been a cause for great celebrations, a day that truly signified the ending of youth.

As it turned out, I spent most of the day at Heathrow waiting for the fog to lift. I was in the work culture now, and work didn't stop for little things like twenty-firsts. By early afternoon the weather had improved enough for us to take off and a couple of hours later we touched down at Helsinki, where I was going to stay at a hotel owned by a small Finnish group in which Tang was interested.

I finally made it to the hotel at about six-thirty. The weather was cold and grey. I checked in at reception and was taken to my room by a polite young man who was probably my age, and who spoke perfect English. The room was remarkably light and uncluttered, and the jacuzzi bath looked inviting.

Here I was, in another perfect hotel room, on my twenty-first birthday and with no friends or family in sight. I assumed the mantle of adulthood, but it sat awkwardly on my shoulders. Somewhere, deep inside, something was hurting. I ran through the various options open to me to distract my mind and first off I called in to my answer-phone to check for messages at home.

"Hello Alexander. I daresay you're off gadding about the continent somewhere or out with friends – anyway I was just ringing to wish you a wonderful twenty-first birthday. I hope you have a lovely day, whatever you're doing. I've got a prezzie for you but I'll give it to you when we meet next week. Lots of love."

For a few moments while I listened to her voice, I felt myself weaken a little. I didn't like the feeling; I didn't like it that my mother could still exercise any form of control over my emotions.

"Alexander, it's me, Dada. I'm going to be working near you in London next week, I thought we could go for a drink, have a meal, or something? And I'd appreciate it if you could get me a deal on staying in the FiveStar Hotel in Innsbruck in January, I've got a …".

The answer-phone couldn't cope with all his message. I wasn't sure I could either. Not a mention of my birthday. Bastard. She remembered. She remembered for God's sake. I didn't want her remembering, I wanted him to remember.

I got changed into some more casual clothes and went down into the bar prior to ordering supper. I sat down on one of the stools by the bar and was greeted in perfect English by yet another

Finnish anglophile. There was a couple seated a few feet away from me and a young woman by herself at the far end of the bar, talking to another bar attendant.

"Yes, sir. Good evening. Is everything okay in your room?"

I wondered how he knew that I was a new guest. Impressive. They must have some briefing system going on here.

"Yes, yes thank you the room seems fine. What champagne do you recommend?"

Before he had a chance to answer, I was interrupted by a tap on the shoulder.

"Alexander? Alexander Baker? Good grief, what are the chances?"

I knew the face, and yet I didn't. She looked familiar. Early twenties, dark brown hair, beautiful brown eyes, voluptuous figure. Not the sort of woman I'd easily forget, or so I thought. My mind flashed back over the women I'd dated in the last couple of years, but no name came to me.

"Jessica? Remember? Jessica Strang. I joined Freestone in year six."

Oh my God. The flat-chested girl who had ended up leaving the sixth form in her first year to go to another sixth form college, was now standing beside me a confident, beautiful woman.

"Jessica. You've, you've…"

"Grown tits? Yes I know."

I suddenly felt uneasy. Jessica's lack of cleavage had resulted in her winning that first day vote for the girl-you'd-least-like-to-do-it-with. Rumour had it that she never really recovered from that opening day and that she left Freestone because of stress. Still, she was talking to me and seemed perfectly sociable.

"No, no – I mean, yes you have and very fine they are too. Oh God. Look, you look amazing. What on earth are you doing in Helsinki?"

"I'm filming. I do porn movies."

I suddenly felt my birthday might be turning into something rather exciting after all. I hurriedly ordered the bottle of champagne and two glasses.

"Join me in some champagne? It's my birthday. Be nice to celebrate it with someone." We went over to a table in the window and sat down. She was wearing a body-hugging, black satin dress with a pink silk shawl draped over her shoulders. Her eyes seemed larger than ever.

The waiter brought over a bottle of Moët and an ice-bucket. He popped the cork, poured out the first two glasses and left us.

"Cheers. Happy birthday." She took a sip of champagne and ran her tongue around the outside of her lips. I was beginning to feel more than a little turned on.

"So what do you do Alexander? What brings you to Finland?"

"I work in finance now. And hotels. I do a bit of investing, a bit of advising, that sort of thing." I tried to make my life and job sound interesting, but felt I had failed.

"So how come you're not celebrating your birthday with some gorgeous woman? You're not gay are you?" There was something so different about this Jessica, from the one I had sat next to occasionally in business studies.

Before I could stop the words from coming out of my mouth, I said it.

"But Jessica, I am celebrating my birthday with a gorgeous woman. Haven't you noticed?"

She flicked her hair from side to side and smiled.

"Ah, yes, Alexander, always the charmer. Just like you were back in the Sixth Form." She had a hard edge to her voice, a coldness that was a little disconcerting. I didn't enjoy the pause and responded quickly to her question.

"Well, to be honest Jessica, I'm in between relationships at the moment. I'm working here for a couple of days – that's why I'm here on my own."

"How do you know you're in between relationships? Maybe you won't have another one." All of a sudden I felt like I was sitting opposite the Ice-Queen. Her brown eyes and sexy voice had developed a steely edge to them. The silence that hung in the air following her last words pressed heavily upon me, demanding some form of reaction. The only thing I could think of was to top up our glasses and change the subject.

"So, tell me about your work, Jessica. How on earth…?"

But she put her finger up to her lips and whispered quietly.

"Not now." She smiled again. "I'll tell you. Later. When we go up to your room."

As someone who had learnt to be quite brash with women, it came as a surprise to find myself threatened by her directness. The champagne continued to slip down, and we soon found ourselves sitting opposite each other in the restaurant finishing off what had probably been an excellent meal. To this day, I can't recall one thing that we talked about or ate. I think I must have been imagining her in too many different sexual positions to be able to concentrate on the food or conversation.

At the end of the meal she excused herself and said she'd meet me in a few minutes in my room. I left shortly after and returned to my suite.

There was no dimmer switch in the room, but there was at least some low lighting in the form of a couple of free-standing designer lights, one of which was a low, wall-lighter, and the other a taller, single tube frame whose bulb lit the top corner of one wall and ceiling. I undid the top two buttons of my shirt, splashed on a little cologne, and ordered another bottle of champagne from room service.

I thought fleetingly about that moment all those years ago when I had chosen her to be the girl I'd have least liked to do it with. I allowed myself a chuckle, thinking now of the goddess into which she had transformed. And she made porn movies. I had a sudden urge to call up my old public school mates and give them the low-down.

A couple of minutes later there was a knock on the door. My heart skipped a few beats as I anticipated my soon to be euphoric state. What would she do? What *wouldn't* she do? What new tricks would I learn tonight to take on my stop-start sexual development journey?

"Room service Sir."

Damn. Oh well, best get the champagne in first anyway. The young man came in, and yet again beamed that smile and uttered those same corporate words that I had become familiar with in the last few hours.

"Your champagne, Sir. And how is the room? Is everything to your satisfaction?"

I hurried him out of the door with a tip, while answering,

"Yes, yes it is all fine thank you. More than fine. It's excellent. Thank you very much."

"Very good sir. Have a good night." He tipped a nod in the general direction of the two glasses and the bottle of champagne. Cheeky bugger, I thought. But then he was a bloke, and blokes know this sort of thing. They understand. It's a sort of unspoken agreement that we have with each other. Don't come out with the actual words *'well done mate, looks like you're getting nooky tonight'*, just let the other man see that you've acknowledged his soon-to-be-conquest. Let him know that the brotherhood salutes him. Hence the nod towards the two glasses.

I looked outside in the corridor as he left, but no sign of Jessica the pornography queen yet.

I left the door slightly ajar so that she could let herself in. I went back inside, thought about opening the bottle and then decided against it. At that moment the phone went.

"Hi, Alexander, look, I'm so sorry, I completely bloody forgot earlier. Happy Birthday."

It was my father.

"Oh hi – listen, don't worry, doesn't matter." Why did I say that? It did bloody matter. I was furious that he had forgotten, although I did think that maybe he was just pretending earlier and that when we met next week he'd prove to me it was all part of one of his famous pranks. This was worse somehow, because he was admitting that my twenty-first had slipped his mind.

"So listen Alexander I thought we should do something special to celebrate your twentieth…"

"I'm twenty-one actually dad."

"Oh, yes, of course that's what I meant. That's why I think we should do something special. Go away somewhere maybe?"

There was a knock at my half open door. I thought about Jessica standing there, probably half naked and waiting for me to greet her with some bubbly. I pulled out the bottle and popped the cork while saying goodbye.

"As you like Dad. Going to have to go now – got an early start tomorrow. Thanks for calling. Bye." And I heartlessly hung up the phone, not waiting for his response. I was feeling weird. My sexual experiences up to now, limited as they were, had all been with girls and women about whom I knew virtually nothing. But now I was standing on the threshold of doing it with someone who I sort of knew. Well, I'd sat next to her in a few lessons. And I'd had a conversation with her tonight over dinner about something or other. It felt different. I felt different.

Pulling myself together I went over to the door. Standing outside was the same young man who had brought me the champagne. He was carrying a small silver tray with an envelope on it. I thanked him and took the envelope. I noticed this time he didn't bother asking me if the room was to my liking. I shut my door, went back into my room and opened the   envelope.

'Room 475 in twenty minutes. Jx'

Bollocks. Another twenty minutes to wait. What could I do for twenty minutes? I sat in the chair again and put on the television, flicking through various channels that I didn't understand. I couldn't concentrate on them anyway so I switched off again.

I couldn't get Jessica's face out of my head. She had become beautiful; maybe she always had been, I just hadn't seen it when all I had been conditioned to admire in women was big jugs and a tight arse. And she seemed, well, nice. And how astonishing was it, that this vision of beauty would appear in a hotel by herself on my twenty-first birthday? Of course, my mother, who was getting into all sorts of weird shit, wouldn't have said it was surprising at all. She would have probably said it was fate or destiny or that the planets had aligned to make it happen. Well, whatever it was, I was just a few minutes away from having the ride of my life with a gorgeous porn star on my twenty-first.

Porn star? How come we call anyone in pornographic movies, stars? And how the hell do you go from public school to porn movies – what sort of bizarre story must be wrapped up in that chain of events?

I tried with all my might to get the cork back in the champagne bottle, but like many men before me, failed miserably. There was something about the fizziness of a freshly opened bubbly that seemed always to be missing after the first few minutes. Oh well, I trusted that there would still be enough fizz left by the time I was in her room.

I went back into my bathroom again and checked myself out. I might have changed my shirt again had I had more clothes with me, but had no choice but to remain as I was. I fiddled around with my hair, and brushed down my trousers to remove any odd traces of fluff. God, the time went slowly.

With five minutes to go I decided I could probably risk it. I had to find her room anyway. Big decision. Should I take the bucket, bottle and glasses or leave the bucket in my room. Either way I wouldn't have any hands free. I decided to take the whole show. I went out of my room and took the lift down two floors. I found her room surprisingly quickly.

Attached to the door was another note with the word 'Alex' on it. My heart sank. Why couldn't she just be standing there waiting for me. Why all this note writing? I wasn't feeling in control any more of this situation and I didn't like it.

I read it. 'The door's open. Jx.' Happy days. I opened the door and went in.

21

"'Ello?" Claude's disembodied voice sounded more French than I remembered it at Freestone.

"Claude, it's me. Alexander Baker. I can't believe this. How are you?"

"Ah, Alexander. How nice to 'ear from you again. I'm okay thank you. And you? How are you?"

How was I? What should I say to an old school friend with whom I haven't spoken in so many years. *'Oh well, I'm not too bad, I've just cremated my father, found out that I blinded and disfigured a bloke when I was five, and am in recovery from a breakdown.'*

I opted for the traditional, English route.

"Not bad thanks Claude, not bad. So what brings you to London? Or are you based here now?"

"No, no I work in France – in Paris still. I've been there for years now. Alexander is there any chance we could meet? I 'ave something I need to share with you that I can only do face to face. Besides which, it would be nice to catch up again after all these years."

He caught me off guard with the request to meet. I had seen so little of my ex-school friends since leaving Freestone – they had all gone off to universities and I had gone into business and somehow timings of terms and work holidays rarely seemed to coincide. As a consequence we failed to establish foundations for our continuing friendships in those significant post-school years when we were becoming young adults. The odd drinking session merely served to stitch us back together for an evening. The rest of the time we were busy forming new lives, new relationships. At least I guessed they were all busy forming new relationships. I had been fully occupied in climbing my ladder.

"Sure, of course. Where would you like to meet?"

We agreed to convene in Covent Garden the next morning.

Later that evening Helen called. The sound of her voice comforted me. I had become used to her being in the house; I liked her being in the house; I still couldn't believe that I let her leave with the boys all those years ago. What the hell had I been thinking? How could I have missed the greatest gift of all, a gift which had been right under my nose, a gift that a blind man would have seen; blind man; Claude; Thomas Jennings; those two men on the Heath; God, what was happening? What did it all mean?

"Are you okay Alex? How's your day been?"

I so wanted to answer her from the heart, but still found it difficult to allow myself to be honest.

"Not bad. Had a bit of a turn in the park this morning, but I came through it okay. I'm fine now."

Even Helen's silences transmitted compassion. She had become so balanced, so able to bear my mood swings, and I loved her for it. I had always loved her I know now, but I was only just beginning to understand how to do love. She was light years ahead of me and I had a lot of catching up to do. Still, I was beginning to learn humility and that was a start.

"The boys missed you when they came back tonight. The first thing Joel did when he got into the car was ask where you were. I told them that you were fine and back in the house, sorting out Grandpa's things."

I felt tears start to build again as she spoke. I was still fragile. Very, very fragile. She could read me, even down a telephone.

"The pain will pass, Alex. Don't fight it huh? For once in your life, don't try to fix the bloody thing. There is no quick answer here. This is where you really grow up."

I knew she was right, but a whole lifetime of conditioning wanted to fight that reality. I didn't want to stay in this part-broken, permanently-on-the-edge, state. I wanted to be strong; I wanted to be clear-thinking again; I wanted to be unbreakable.

But those days had long since gone. And I now knew that, at some level, wanting to be unbreakable, wanting to be impenetrable, had been my very undoing.

I said goodbye and the next wave of tears promptly broke upon my cheeks. I sat there, Killer the cat curled up on my lap purring away, while little drops poured down my face. I'd got Killer about six or seven years ago now, and her name was a legacy of the world I used to inhabit. What sort of a world was it?

The next morning I made my way after the rush-hour to Covent Garden. By the time I got to the top of the tube station steps, Claude was already there. I recognised him immediately. He was dressed in a long, dark blue overcoat and jeans, and wore a traditional French beret upon his head.

"Alexander – how good to see you." He reached out to hug me, I quickly offered my hand in exchange. "Ah, yes of course, English public school. No hugging! I wore the beret to help you recognise me, do you like it?" He smiled and pushed me on the shoulder in jest.

"Claude, you look just the same as you always did. What are you doing these days?"

Claude shook his finger at me.

"No, none of that just yet. Let us find a nice café and we can talk about things."

We went off in search of somewhere quiet, and ended up in a small sandwich bar that had six stools looking out onto Langley Court. Claude said he liked the feel of this one, though I didn't get why or how.

We went in and ordered; Claude, of course, went for the Espresso, and I had a Cappuccino. We took the two end stools and Claude spoke first.

"Do you remember when we last met, Alexander?"

I had thought about that very question after I had heard about his message yesterday.

"Yes, it must have been when we were about twenty-six – it was in Paris. We met up with Matt and Andrew for the England game."

Claude smiled. "That's right."

"We stuffed you if I remember rightly."

"You certainly did. Thirty one thirteen. Please do not remind me." The waitress brought our coffees.

"Alexander, do you remember what I was doing then?"

I was suddenly on the spot. God, what was he doing then? Something about law?

"Well now, we had a few drinks that night I think Claude."

"Yes, you did. I had already given up drinking by then."

A vague memory of a far, far off conversation about Claude wimping out on the drinks began to dance around my head. Matt, Andrew and I would have got lashed, that's for sure. But maybe Claude didn't. I think we probably put it down to him sulking at the rugby result.

"When we met that day Alexander, I had not only given up drinking, but I'd also given up my embryonic career in law to join the Church. I told you all this, but don't believe any of you were particularly interested at the time."

I shuffled awkwardly on my stool. While I couldn't remember Claude saying any such thing, I could imagine me not knowing what to say if he had informed me he'd gone into the Church. And I could easily imagine Andrew and Matthew being useless as well.

Claude made no effort to break up what was an obviously painful pause. He had been looking at me when he had been talking, now his eyes followed the activity on the street outside.

"Look, if that's what this is all about Claude, well, I'm, I'm sorry that I didn't ask you more about it. I have absolutely no problem with you being in the Church."

He looked at me again, and took another sip of his coffee.

"That is not what this is about Alexander. Not directly anyway. Let me tell you why I got into the Church. I entered a legal firm in Paris after university, but it quickly became clear to me that I wasn't a lawyer. The people there were perfectly nice. The money was good. Some of them even seemed content with their work. But something inside me did not fit. It was like I was the square peg in the round hole.

"I started worrying about why I felt so bad. I started having conversations with a local minister, Père Varne, a rather frail old man with an occasional cough which irritated me. Père Varne listened to me in a way that I don't believe anyone had ever listened to me before. He suggested that I give the practice a little more time, I was after all only a year into my new career. He told me to go into work imagining each day to be my last day there. He said this would help me to work out whether to stay or not. We met every week."

"And what happened?"

"It was very interesting. To start with I was really excited about it possibly being my last day at work. I'd leave in an inner state of bliss, imagining never needing to go in there again. I know that I worked better during those days. But, as the weeks passed, I found that this state of bliss started to turn to frustration that it wasn't my last day."

"And then what?"

"One day I was coming home and I got really angry that I would have to go to work again tomorrow. I called Père Varne and told him about my rage. I am not, you may remember, a generally angry person even when France gets beaten by England, and this came as quite a shock to me."

As I thought back to our school days, I could now recall that Claude was rarely angry. In fact he often helped to sort out disputes to such an extent that he acquired the occasional nickname 'Joan of Arc'.

"What did this Père Varne chap say?" I was mildly intrigued by the story although I had no idea where it was going.

"He told me that I was now ready to quit. That I had now found out at least one aspect of who I wasn't."

Those last three words magnetised themselves to some recent conversation I had had with myself, and that was still somewhere in my head. Hadn't I recently just said something very similar about finding out who I wasn't? Claude could tell I was contemplating his words.

"This sounds familiar huh? I was told it would. Let me continue." I nodded my head and took another sip of my Cappuccino.

"So the next day I handed in my notice. As soon as I did, I felt as if the world had been lifted from my shoulders. I felt free; I felt capable of achieving anything. That night I ran most of the way home from work, which was funny because it was pouring with rain. But I didn't care. I felt like I had escaped from certain oblivion."

"So what did you do?" I was now getting into Claude's story. He spoke with so much honesty. He chose his words carefully and was in no hurry to rush through his tale, frequently taking pauses to finish up his Espresso while it was still hot.

"Well, that weekend I visited my parents in their house just outside Lyon. I told them about my conversations with Père Varne and my decision about my job. My father in particular struggled with my wanting to throw away my legal training, but as we talked it over that weekend, they realised how unhappy I had become doing law. They suggested that I speak further with Père Varne, since he had helped so much already."

"Another coffee?"

Claude nodded his head and the waitress came over to take our empty cups away.

"So you went back to Paris?"

"Yes. And I arranged to see Père Varne the following day. I went to meet him in his house. His door was opened by a young lady, Fleur, his granddaughter. She told me that Père Varne had collapsed at the weekend and was now very weak and in his bed. But he had specifically asked to see me if I called.

"She showed me to his room and he was sitting up in bed. His eyes were half shut and his breathing very heavy. I couldn't believe how much he had changed since the week before. Fleur had shown me into the room and whispered in her grandfather's ear. He immediately opened his eyes and smiled. Fleur then left us alone."

The waitress reappeared with new coffees. Two young men with loud voices came and sat on the two far stools. I resented their presence, not wanting anything to get in the way of Claude's story in which I was now wrapped up.

"Père Varne told me I was to go to him every day that week at the same time for just a few minutes. He said I would find out what I needed to know by Friday, in order that I could make the next step. He said I was to go back home each night and sit in silence for half an hour after every meeting. When thoughts came into my head I was simply to observe them. I was most specifically not to try to do anything with the thoughts. I was not to drink any alcohol. And then he sent me away."

"So he didn't give you any words on that first night?"

"Those were the words, although I didn't realise their significance until I went home and sat in the quiet for thirty minutes. At first my brain went mad; thoughts jumped in everywhere, about my career, about my ex-girlfriend, about my car. But I did as he said; for the first time in my life I didn't react to these thoughts, I tried to let them exist in the quietness. And as I let them exist so I began to feel a state of unease. This state of unease grew and grew. I was aware that I was struggling to catch my breath, worrying that I would no longer be able to breathe at all."

This began to sound alarmingly familiar. My mind jumped to the Heath and my two young friends.

"Go on Claude." My voice was quieter, my words less hurried. Even I noticed it.

"Okay, well, I was determined to follow the old man's instructions. So I stayed in this place of uneasiness and as I did so, it finally began to relax its grip upon my sanity. And as I felt the grip relax, so I became aware of a great sense of compassion for Père Varne. It suddenly hit me that he was dying, that he had been dying when I first started speaking to him, but I had been so involved in my own world that I hadn't allowed myself to see.

"The next day I went again at the allotted time. Once again Fleur showed me in, and Père Varne opened his eyes and smiled. His breath was a little shorter, but he still seemed entirely present when he spoke. He asked me what I had noticed the night before and I told him about my feelings of compassion for him and how I felt I had failed to notice his own difficulties because I had been so absorbed by my own."

Mysterious as the story was, I reminded myself that this was my old mate Claude telling it, and he had always been a regular guy. I encouraged him to continue.

"On the second visit he said just five words. *Stop looking for the answers.* And then with a smile and flick of his hand he waved me away. I went back home again and sat in the silence once more, reflecting on these five words. That night I found my inner stillness to be more profound than the night before. When thoughts came, I was more able to detach from them and not go inquiring after them. By the end of thirty minutes I felt more peaceful than I had in a long time. In fact I felt peaceful at a level I had never experienced. It was as if he had given me permission not to go trying to solve the world's ills and to stop trying to get my life right; and for a few minutes I had been able to sustain that state of mind.

"So on the Wednesday I went to his house again. He was a little lower in his bed, but yet again I got a smile. He pointed to his glass, indicating that he wanted me to put some water onto his dry lips. This I did, and with some difficulty he asked what I had gone through the night before. I told him that I experienced a profound sense of peace when I had contemplated the idea of no longer looking for answers. He muttered something about telling someone to wait, that he was coming, and then he said slowly, but quite clearly, '*Two ears and one mouth. Use them in the proportions God intended you to.*' And again he waved me away.

"That night my silence was filled with images of when I had failed to listen to people. I saw how Janine, my ex girl-friend had tried to get me to listen to her, but how my fear of finding out things about myself that I didn't want to hear had got me using my mouth too much. I found myself crying throughout the silence as I saw how I had misused God's tool in the past and screwed things up for myself and most importantly for others."

I was beginning to remember Dada's speech. There were familiar themes here. It all started to feel a bit freaky. I took a large gulp of coffee as Claude continued.

"On the fourth night he was very frail. He could no longer speak, resorting instead to whispering. I knew to tell him what had happened the night before. He smiled. I leant over so that my right ear was near his mouth. He simply said '*Guilt destroys. Blame destroys. No-one has ever done anything wrong, we were all just ignorant.*' This time he even managed a very quiet laugh. I took his hand, which he squeezed remarkably tightly, and I left him.

"I went home that night and again sat in the silence with which I had become increasingly familiar. I thought of all the guilt I had, the guilt I had experienced the night before; I thought about the blame culture that is the world in which we live, and I felt an explosion of joy as I thought of a life free of guilt and a world free of blame. I sensed a rainbow in my heart and saw Père Varne at the end of it, waving his hand to me, that precious smile lighting up the glorious colours of his path."

A few moments passed where nothing was said. We both looked out into the street ahead. Claude was in a different state to the one in which he had started the conversation. I sensed a slight disturbance in him. Sadness? Or an anxiety that hadn't previously been present?

"What happened on the Friday – the fifth night. What was his final teaching?"

Claude was looking outside at a street artist who was clowning around outside the window. He smiled again.

"I was forgetting to smile again. I tend to take these things too seriously. That's why he sent the clown."

I wondered for a minute if Claude was maybe not all there any more. Maybe he'd lost the plot somewhere along the way.

"Père Varne, he sent that clown to remind me to be light. He was always telling me to lighten up. He does that sort of thing from time to time. Anyway, yes the Friday. Well, I turned up and Fleur opened the door. She smiled at me and told me that Père Varne had died a little while after my last visit."

"So you never got to hear the final words?"

"Ah, well that's what I thought at first. But Père Varne had told me quite specifically to go back and sit in silence every evening of the week. So I did. And that Friday night as I was sitting in the silence, I became clear that I had to help people to find this place of peace in themselves that Père Varne had helped me to find that week. I had to teach people to become self-accepting because in doing that we would become more accepting of each other. What better place to start than the Catholic Church – an institution whose history is littered with the tragic repercussions of guilt and blame. His final lesson was in my silence, so that I could find what I needed to do at that time. His final lesson was simple; I no longer needed his words, I just needed to find my own."

Outside the clown had moved on; I hadn't seen him leave but he was no longer there. Claude was smiling again and finished his Espresso. I asked the obvious question, the one I had heard asked in a hundred or more films.

"So what's all this got to do with me?"

Claude laughed. He must have seen the same movies.

"I have been in the Church now for nearly fourteen years. I have learnt the ways of the Catholic Church from the inside so that I might bring in some of Père Varne's wisdom into its teachings. It is where I belong and I am quite content with that. But, like anyone, I sometimes doubt the choices I have made, or whether any of this really happened even. Every now and again, and this might sound even more strange, I have a sense that Père Varne is with me, talking to me, guiding me, reminding me who I am and what I am here to do. And, as with the clown just now, reminding me to be light with all this.

"Last week Père Varne appeared in one of my silences. He looked just as he did when I first met him."

I hardly knew what to make of this statement. How could I believe in the literal truth of what Claude was saying? My old impatience was getting the better of me.

"And I repeat Claude, what has all this got to do with me?"

Claude looked straight at me.

"He was with another man. Tell me Alexander, what news of your father?"

I swallowed hard. I could feel the blood draining from my face, as fast as air disappearing from a punctured balloon. I had specifically opted not to tell Claude on the phone about my father's passing. I quickly reasoned that he could have found out from Linda. This was weird and I was not liking it very much.

"He passed away last week. Linda told you I presume?"

Claude looked quizzical.

"Who's Linda?" And then the penny dropped. "Ah, your secretary. No. No I'm afraid not Alexander. No, I asked that question in all earnestness."

I took a deep breath and clenched my fists a couple of times. I put my stress right into the middle of those clenched hands as I had been taught and breathed out gently.

"My father died last Tuesday."

Claude reflected for a minute.

"Last Tuesday. Exactly fourteen years to the day that Père Varne died. And then they appear together in my silence. I knew it was your father straightaway – he was looking just as he did when I used to see him on television."

Claude could see that I was becoming uncomfortable with this conversation. We had long since finished our coffees and he suggested we take a walk and get some air. As we walked down Floral Street towards Leicester Square, I looked into the faces of strangers; I wondered what they needed to forgive themselves for; I wondered who they were blaming for their poor hand in life; and I wondered which of them, if any, had already found it in themselves to get to a place of peace about their lives. Was there one person walking the streets of London at that precise moment, who had found peace? Did anyone even know what peace meant?

"Claude this is, I dunno, this is…"

"Strange?"

Strange was about the most appropriate word. It was strange – and yet, with what I had experienced with Dada and in particular with his recording, it was anything but strange.

"So, what did Père Varne say to you when he was standing next to my father? What made you come here?"

"I'm afraid that's another peculiar thing. Neither of them said anything. Your father just stood there, light shining all around him with Père Varne at his shoulder. And that was it."

I felt frustrated. "That was it? And you came all the way over here to tell me that?" I felt my frustration giving way to mild anger. What had Claude hoped to achieve?

"Alexander, I believe we can help each other. I believe this is why they appeared together. Is it not a remarkable coincidence that they died on the same day fourteen years apart? Is it not strange that your father should appear to me on the very day that he died, standing alongside a man who shared with me profound wisdom in the last days of his life?"

At these words, just as we were turning out of Garrick Street and into St Martin's Lane, I stopped dead in my tracks. Profound wisdom; last few days of his life; Dada's Last Testament of Will. This is what Claude had come for. He had come to hear the recording.

"Claude, do you have plans right now?" My anger had given way to a rush of excitement. "Come back to my place, I have something I have to play you."

"Alexander, I was hoping you would say something like that." And, just like it used to be when we were rushing to our morning lessons at Freestone, the two of us raced down the steps and into the tube station.

22

I stepped in and closed the door behind me. Jessica's room was dimly lit by one floor-lighter illuminating the corner wall. The door to her ensuite was open and her voice called out.

"I'm in the bath. Come in and join me."

Oh wow, this was really going to happen. And with her. With Jessica Strang, the once laughing stock of the school. Freestone's best kept secret now, if you ask me.

I went into the bathroom and she was lying in a bath, her naked body only partly, but tantalisingly, covered by bubbles. I felt my trouser pocket respond to the stiffening that was happening beside it, and suddenly felt rather embarrassed.

"Oh Alex, you bought more champagne. How lovely. Yes please."

I parked my glass on the floor and knelt down to the bath to use the ledge to support her glass as I poured into it. My eyes got distracted by her right nipple which had just peeped out from under some bubbles, and I overfilled her glass. She leant over and licked the spilt champagne from my fingers and the side of the bath. This girl was hot.

She took her champagne glass and ran her finger around the rim. I was so excited, I could barely contain myself. I wanted her and I wanted her right now. I daren't stand up again, my erection was now so intense. I reached for my glass and poured myself some champagne, this time being careful not to make an arse of myself by spilling it.

"So, here we are Alex. Are you going to get in here with me?"

I thought about the state of my penis. But God, this was what it was all about. And she wanted me to, so I supposed she was going to see sometime. I got undressed rather awkwardly from my sitting position and, with my glass of champagne held carefully over my manhood, I climbed into the other end of the bath.

I stretched my legs down either side of her body, and as I did so she retracted her legs so that her knees were protruding some inches above the bath water. Her right foot now rested quite firmly upon my throbbing dick, her left foot resting softly up against my balls..

"Ooh. Someone's excited about something, aren't they?" She gently rubbed her right foot from side to side, expertly retaining its hold upon my penis. I was in a confused state of massive anxiety and unbelievable joy.

Much to my relief she then took her feet away and got out of the bath. The head of my member stood embarrassingly above the water, all the bubbles choosing that moment to disappear to the furthest reaches of the tub. It was as though she got out and the bubbles followed her. I suddenly felt very exposed, and turned awkwardly on my side to face her.

Jessica's naked body was as perfect as it could have been. She just stood there, sipping her champagne, and running her other hand lightly over her lightly coloured pubic hair.

"You'd like this Alex wouldn't you? You'd like this right now. What a birthday treat huh?"

Like some gormless gorilla being offered bananas by its keeper, I could only manage to nod my head and shoulders and utter pathetic little grunts. Jessica fingered herself a little more, and again I could feel myself becoming extremely anxious that my orgasm might not make it out of the bath.

And then it all went horribly, horribly wrong. The next thing I knew the remaining contents of her champagne glass were dripping down my face.

"Well if you think you're going to have sex with me you must be fucking joking. Anyway, you shouldn't be disappointed. I was, after all, the-girl-you'd-least-like-to-do-it-with. Have you any idea what that piece of paper did to me? No failed exam results or bad reports could ever have shattered my self-esteem like those few words written by a bigoted seventeen year old. You and your so-called friends were the reason I had a breakdown. You were the reason I had to leave Freestone and you were the reason why I went into therapy at the age of seventeen. It's taken me nearly four years to transform my life, but transform it I have, and no thanks to you lot.

"And another thing you should know, Alex. Your body's not that great, in fact some women might be quite disappointed with you, if you know what I mean. Looks like you've let yourself go a bit since your rugby days." All the time Jessica was venting, she had been drying herself, and now she put on a towelling dressing gown. She threw a towel at me that landed in the bath water. "Now get out of my bloody room."

I lay there for a few seconds in that bath, my previous state of arousal now replaced by one of total, numbed shock. I pulled the plug, squeezed out the towel that was now heavy with the water we had just been so intimately sharing, and dried myself quickly with another dry towel that barely stretched around my waist. Just as I tried to tie it around my waist, she came back into the room and the towel dropped to the floor, leaving me facing her fully naked.

Jessica addressed herself to my lower half.

"No, not that impressive at all Alex."

I pulled the towel up quickly and this time managed to secure it. All the time I was pulling on my clothes, she stood there watching, enjoying the spoils of her victory.

"So, all that, tonight, that was all just an act?"

Jessica's eyes hardened. In that moment I felt a piercing pain shoot through my head.

"Yes. It was all an act Alex. As soon as I saw you in the bar I knew this was my chance."

"And the porn movies?"

Jessica allowed herself a small smile.

"Oh my God, you arsehole! Men! You'll believe just what you want to believe won't you, however unlikely it is. Of course I'm not in porn Alex – shit, how shallow can you be?" Jessica left the bathroom, shaking her head. " You know the way out – feel free to use it. Thanks for the champagne and the meal. It's the least you owed me."

I'm sure I did, sort of, deserve this treatment, and yet knowing that didn't make it any easier to endure the sadness of that moment. In a few brief hours, I had not just lusted after Jessica, I had allowed my heart to open to her. She was gorgeous, and I enjoyed her company. I liked that brief time of getting to know her, albeit so superficially. And in my history with girls, that was the equivalent of a long term-relationship. Sure it would have been great to have sex; and yes, my imagination had got carried away with the idea of her making porn movies. But none of the physical pleasure would have come close to the joy of waking up next morning and finding I had someone to talk to. And if she had only given me a chance, I could have shown her that I was more than a shallow idiot in pursuit of an easy lay.

I picked up the nearly empty champagne bottle and my glass, and went back to my room, tail firmly between legs. I got back to my room, lay on the bed with my back up against the wall and poured out the remainder of the now somewhat flat champagne. I flicked through the TV channels and ended up staring at a Finnish sex romp. The stereotypical big-busted women were providing a man with all his possible sexual wants. There was no heart exchange going on here; no complications; just a bit of a chase and then the inevitable outcome. The problem to be solved wasn't 'whether' it was simply 'how'.

I finished off my glass and drank a few last drops straight from the bottle, throwing the glass on to the floor up against my door in a rather pathetic act of defiance. This was my Keith Moon moment, I guess. Everyone gets fifteen minutes of fame, and everyone gets a Keith Moon moment. This was mine. It wasn't going to make the front pages of the tabloids, but at least I'd done it.

For some reason, my father came into my head. Was tonight an example of the indirect advice that he had given me about relationships, about women? He hadn't specifically ever told me not to trust them, not in so many words, yet that's what I felt he had wanted to say. After his experience with his wife, I suppose he had good reason not to trust them. I shut my eyes and tried to imagine him saying *'Don't trust them, son.'* Was that what he would tell me, if he had one bit of advice to give me? *'Don't trust women an inch Alexander, they'll take a mile. Use them carefully. Don't let them come too close.'*

'Use them carefully? Don't let them come too close?' Where the hell had those thoughts come from? Was that Dada's relationship counsel, distilled from years of being a fully grown man? I flashed back to the time that I had found him with the schoolgirl and Cleopatra in his house and suddenly, in that Moët influenced state, relationships

according to my Dada did make sense. Use them and don't let them come too close.

Some twenty-first birthday this had turned out to be. I determined not to let another woman have power over me in the way I had allowed Jessica to have that night; and an already well-developed shell closed a little more tightly around my heart.

The pressure of providing Tang with their reports and carrying out FiveStar's brief as well, soon started to weigh me down. Trips to my doctor had become so commonplace that I soon became on first name terms with each of the receptionists. My various complaints; flu, heavy colds, lack of sleep, bad coughs, occasional shortness of breath, were put down to a mixture of 'bad luck', 'a lot of it being about' and 'overwork'. I was prescribed antibiotics (often one course after another), sleeping pills, stronger sleeping pills, rest (which, because it didn't come in a bottle, I found impossible to swallow) and was even referred for a couple of chest x-rays which showed absolutely nothing.

Conversations with colleagues reaffirmed that this seemed to be part and parcel of getting work done and so I just stumbled blindly on, assured by my doctor that I was doing everything necessary to ensure my continued health. Everything apart from the resting of course.

The trouble was that one day's absence from work instantly put me in an awkward position with my two employers. Who then got my next day? When would the last one be made up? When there were flights booked already by Tang, there was little choice, and it wasn't long before this disparity started to show itself to Steve. He started to become colder in his exchanges and more demanding. I tried harder and harder to get my work done, to be the good and responsible employee, but found my body continually unable to cope with the demands of both companies.

As I had moved away from being under Steve's total control and authority, I had gained a degree of independence, and I had felt for a while that this independence threatened him. I had even found myself my own dealer, so I was no longer dependent upon Steve for my occasional forays into the world of narcotic escapism.

Things started to come to a head when a large project I had been working on for Tang, which had involved checking out a chain of hotels in the embryonic holiday resorts of Croatia, was nearing a critical point of the negotiations. I had been over to visit all the hotels and had been asked by Yao to talk to the Croatian owner about a possible Tang Investment. He told me that Ma had suggested I might get a sizeable bonus if Tang ended up securing a deal, as the Croatian market was being seen as a future goldmine.

Imre Jaksic, the hotel group owner, was on a visit to London to talk to possible investors and so I arranged to meet him in his suite at The Berkeley in Knightsbridge to sound him out about a possible merger with Tang. Steve had already booked me for that day, but I told him I had a doctor's appointment in the morning and that I wouldn't be in until after lunch. He'd left a message on my desk about a meeting he wanted me to join him for at three-thirty, but I'd been so busy preparing for the Croatian meeting I hadn't had a chance to go through it. I knew I could attend to that, and all the other messages that would be waiting for me, once I got into the office.

Imre was a small, tanned, rough-skinned man probably in his late forties. His face and voice bore the signs of years of smoking, and he was dressed in black chinos, a black shirt which was open almost half way down his chest, revealing a hefty gold cross on a gold chain which hung around his neck. He looked like he belonged amongst the extras on the set of a seventies American TV cop show.

"Alex Baker, I presume – how good to meet you – sit down." He sat down and began to play with an ornate gold ring on one of his fingers. "So, Alex, what can I do for you? If you don't mind me saying, you seem a little young to be conducting big business?"

If there was one thing that I hated, it was being called young. I was nearly twenty-three. For success in business, how old did you need to be? Didn't Richard Branson start when he was sixteen? I struggled to regain my composure.

"First of all Mr Jackson..."

"Jaksic Alex. My name is J-a-k-s-i-c. But it's okay, you can call me Imre."

"I'm so sorry, Mr Jaksic. Imre. I have visited your four hotels in Croatia, and I represent a company called FiveStar..."

Shit. I wasn't there representing FiveStar, I was there representing Tang. What a start. Got his name wrong, got my own company name wrong. Imre looked confused.

"But Alex, surely you are not FiveStar?"

I was desperate to correct my mistake.

"Er, well, no and yes. Anyway, no I'm here today representing Tang Leisure from Hong Kong."

"So why did you mention FiveStar?"

"I have no idea. Must be the antibiotics I'm on at the moment. I've stayed in a few FiveStar hotels and, of course as I'm sure you know, Tang has an interest in FiveStar."

Imre seemed pacified by my answer.

"But they also act totally independently upon acquisitions sometimes, yes?"

"Oh, yes. FiveStar and Tang have a mutually beneficial relationship which allows them both to continue to pursue their own goals independently. Five Star makes it possible for Tang to have a foot in the Western leisure market, and Tang makes it possible for FiveStar to have a foot in the Eastern market.

"Imre, Tang would like to know if you would consider a cash offer with options for a share in your hotel group. They would like to send over their financial team to Porec to go over your figures with your team and to suggest ways in which, with Tang's backing, you may be able to develop your hotel group throughout Croatia."

I didn't know what it was about Jaksic, but there was something that made me feel uneasy. It was no more than that; just a feeling.

"Alexander, I would be very happy to receive your colleagues from Hong Kong. Let them get in touch with me directly and I'll sort out the dates. I return to Croatia after the weekend - they can contact me from Monday." He got up and shook my hand. My father had been hot on handshakes, saying that a slippery handshake was the sign of a slippery person. Jaksic's grip would have jumped straight to the top of the wet handshake scale.

I reasoned my suspicions away, and by the time I had reached FiveStar's offices, I had fully convinced myself that this would be a good investment for Tang. I naturally didn't admit to myself that my reasoning was influenced by the thought of a fat bonus.

When I arrived, I went straight to my desk and went through my messages. The one from Steve about the meeting was buried under a pile of expense requests from accounts. I pulled it out and read through the hastily scrawled note.

'Tomorrow – 3.30 in the conference room. Interesting meeting – Mr Jaksic from Sunsure Hotel group, Croatia. He's looking for a heavyweight partner. The board want this one. Can you bring any info on Croatia including competition? Thanks, Steve.'

I sat back in my chair in stunned silence. What the hell was I to do now? Tell Steve that I have been checking out this group for Tang? Tell Tang that FiveStar were after the same fish as they were? And then what? Would Tang think I've tipped FiveStar off? Would Steve think I'd tipped Yao the nod? I had to do something and I had to do it quickly. I had less than two hours until the meeting.

At that moment my phone rang. It was Steve.

"Ah, great, I'd heard you had finally come in. Alex can you come up – I need you to go through some financials for this Croatian meeting this afternoon." And the phone went down, before I had had a chance to say anything.

I studied the figures that Imre's accountants had put together for his trip to London, the same figures presumably that he would present to Yao and his team. I felt like a spy getting first peek at a top secret document. In my mind, these numbers became a jumble of meaningless symbols. I was panicking about how I would explain my way out of this. I couldn't feign sickness again, could I? I'd only just been to the doctor's that morning, as far as Steve knew.

As I was wondering what the hell to do, the door opened and in walked Steve followed by Imre Jaksic.

"Ah, you see Imre – just as I said, Alex is already running through your figures. Alex this is Imre Jaksic from Sunsure. We're looking at getting involved with his wonderful chain. Help them grow. Fancy a trip to Croatia Alex? Play your cards right and you never know!"

I stood up to greet Imre for the second time that day. I wondered how he would play this.

"Hello Alex. Nice to meet you. Yes, we'll have to get you over to Croatia – I've got a feeling you'd like it. I can see that you are working hard."

"Er, yes, yes Mr Jaks…"

"Jaksic Alex. But you can call me Imre."

"Er, right, Imre. Nice to meet you."

There were only two things I can remember about the meeting after that. By the time it ended, Steve had absolutely no idea that Tang was pitching for the same group, and he was clueless that I had already stayed in each of the Croatian Hotels. A very muffled voice somewhere deep inside was shouting to me to tell him these things. I think.

But maybe that was just my imagination.

23

By the time Claude and I had got back to my house, we were both in need of something to eat. I sorted out a couple of sandwiches and offered Claude a beer.

"No thank you, no alcohol now. I don't drink it any more."

"I'm sorry – of course, you already told me." I apologised. I was so unused to a man turning down the offer of a drink.

"It is not because of my position. To begin with I was guided away from alcohol by Père Varne. Through personal experience, I have discovered for myself his reasons; it muddies my mind, makes me less able to think clearly or feel my emotions."

I gave Claude his sandwich and we sat in the living room, which looked out onto the small terraced back garden which I'd had hard-landscaped about three years ago.

"Do you mind if I say Grace?"

For the second time in just a few seconds I felt unnerved. No alcohol, and now he wants to say Grace. Why did I feel threatened by such a choice and such a request? Why did I feel like I needed Claude to drink? Why did I feel awkward at the thought of Claude expressing a few words of thanks before eating his food? Was it because I felt he was trying to push his beliefs onto me?

The silence while I was thinking was obviously telling.

"I've said my Grace in silence. No problem."

I suddenly felt small. I felt uncharitable and judgemental. I felt I had failed Claude. All he wanted was to express his gratitude. Was that so much to ask?

We ate our meal in relative silence. I wondered if Claude was feeling the same anxiety from our pre-lunch exchange as I was.

"Look Claude, about Grace, I'm sorry, I just didn't know how to react."

"It's okay Alexander. This is possibly part of why we are meeting. The recording, can we hear it now?"

I piled the lunch plates on the table alongside the empty beer tin and crisp packets from the night before, and I found the recorder. I wired it up to the stereo and reset it to the beginning.

"You're a good boy, Alexander. You know, I love you very, very much".

I had no idea that this was how the recording had started. Dada must have said this when I was showing him how the machine worked. These words killed me all over again. Claude stood up, his tall frame towering over me on the couch.

"Stand up Alexander, let me show you how real men hug."

I stood up and he took me in his arms. He held me in a way that made me realise how starved I had been of man love all my life. For all his warmth, Dada wasn't a hugger. Not a fearless hugger. Not like Claude. Claude held me in a way that I imagined a God would hold a fallen angel. No judgement, no fear, no fixing. Just love. Just pure, strong, physical, grounding love.

My tears continued their relentless quest to join up with some mythical ocean; and then, as quickly as they'd come, I felt no more need to cry. We must have been standing there for at least two or three minutes; whole minutes of being held by another man for the first time in my life. And in those moments I became grateful that Claude had become a man who desired to say Grace; and I became even more grateful that he had had the wisdom to follow the instructions of a dying old man.

The recording had been playing all this time; suddenly a few indecipherable mutterings gave way to a much clearer sounding, determined voice:

"Your Royal Highness, ministers, vegetables and Catholics…"

Claude listened in silence. He shut his eyes most of the time, his head rocking gently to and fro. By the end his eyes were moist and a broad smile stretched across his face.

"And this is why I had to come to England. So you could play me this. Now it is beginning to make sense. Tell me Alex, do you know what this all means?"

"Do you think it does all mean something? I've thought over the last few days that maybe it is just the mad jabberings of a dying man."

"This is so similar to what Père Varne said as he was dying. So similar. You remember what Père Varne said about guilt for instance. It destroys us. And don't you think it is interesting that our old friend Golly is mentioned by your father as waiting for him? Your father actually says *'hold on Golly, I'm coming'*. Père Varne said someone was waiting for him and he said *'I'm coming'* also."

I remembered how Dada always liked Golly; he used to say he reminded him of his best friend at school ages ago.

"Are you telling me my best mate Golly was waiting to take Dada through the pearly gates and into heaven? Are you asking me to believe in some sort of life after death?"

"I'm not asking you to believe anything. I'm just saying that it is interesting that when Père Varne was dying he muttered something to someone about waiting a moment for him, and that your father said almost exactly the same thing to a dead friend of ours as he was nearing death. It should be reassuring for you to think that a friendly face might be waiting to meet you on the other side Alexander. But anyway, that is not even the exciting bit."

Claude had a way of responding that put me at ease. He really didn't seem to have an agenda, at least not one that I could discern at the moment. I wasn't challenged so much by what Claude was saying. I was challenged by my thoughts. To be precise, I was challenged by my reaction to the possibility that the dying may be approached by dead acquaintances to help them through the final stages of leaving the body. Because that meant something left the body and the existence of that something then brought into question everything that I had, or hadn't, believed in. The trouble was, Dada had definitely asked Golly to wait while he finished what he had to do. And, according to Claude, Père Varne had also asked some disembodied figure to wait as he issued his final instructions that week. Was there a connection here?

"Have you transcribed your father's speech, Alexander?"

I shook my head. Claude asked me to get him some paper and a pen. He asked me to go back to the beginning, and he started writing.

Fifteen minutes later Claude had written the whole thing down. I put the kettle on and made some tea. When I went back into the lounge Claude was standing up looking out of the window.

"How are things with your wife, Alexander?"

Where did I start with that one? What did I tell him – how things are now, or how things got to be how they are now?

"Now – now, how are things now with your wife?"

"How do you do that Claude?"

Claude looked puzzled.

"How do you know what I'm thinking?"

"Forgive me – I haven't learnt yet always to give people time to answer. It's one of my weaknesses I think. I sense what they might say and then jump in and say it."

"Hmm, some people would call that psychic, Claude."

"Semantics, Alexander. So, how are things - now?"

"Well, now they are improving. But she's not my wife. We divorced. A few years ago. It was hell. But, well, there's a lot you don't know about me Claude. I have had a bit of an emotional crisis since the divorce. We've got our boys though, thank God, and Helen's been an angel. She's been quite tough with me, but honestly it's probably what I needed years ago."

"Has she got a new partner?"

These words travelled through the air and landed like a barbed arrow in my heart. Although she didn't have one, the thought of her having another partner was not a happy one. And I wondered how different the last couple of years might have been had I not been able to cling on to the rock of hope that was the two of us one day getting back together.

"No. No she hasn't. Why do you ask, Claude?"

"No matter. Not yet. And you Alexander. This crisis you have had – would you say your life has changed in any particular way since you became weakened?"

A full description of how my life had already changed since my breakdown could fill the pages of a small book. I tried to select my words carefully.

"Claude, my breakdown, to give it its proper name, is probably the best thing that has ever happened to me. I was fucked. My life was fucked. I had screwed the important things up to such an extent that there was practically nothing left for me to screw up. The thing was, it was only when I crumbled that I started to realise what the important things were."

"And they were?" Claude's voice was calm but insistent.

"Are. They are relationships. Nothing more or less complicated than that. People."

Claude and I sat in silence for a couple of minutes taking sips from our tea. I felt both relieved to be reaffirming my own new found values, and churned up to be standing on the precipice of the pit of memories that contained the final remaining proof of what a jerk I had been for much of my life.

"How has your work changed in this time, Alexander? I mean how has your approach changed?"

I delved back into my recent biography.

"Five years ago I was still buying, selling, hiring and firing. People were expendable commodities. One day I realised I had to change my focus from being materially-orientated to being people-orientated. This realisation happened when I first started to realise what I had lost; something which took a couple of years to filter through following the divorce. Instead of getting the most amount of money for a sale or buying something at the cheapest price or trading another dollop of shares, I started wanting to teach executives how to get the best out of themselves and out of their employees. I knew there was a huge market for it and I knew I'd be good at it. I wanted to give something back, and this seemed the obvious route."

Claude was sitting down, listening intently.

"How have you found it? I mean, how do you help get the best out of people?"

"I've learnt to become a better listener I guess, and a better observer. I've learnt quite a bit from how Helen has been with me. I suppose I've carried some of this with me into my consultancy."

Claude was now sitting on the edge of the chair, his eyes fixed upon me.

"Alexander, what does Helen do? Does she have a job?"

"Sure – she has her own practice. She was a nurse before we were married. Then she gave it up to be with the boys while they were young. She's a natural carer and now she's a counsellor, specialising in communication. She's practically taught herself as far as I know, although she has often spoken of her books and her spiritual teacher. I think she probably did quite a lot of work on herself in the last few years of our marriage and when she needed to earn more following our split, it was a logical progression for her.

Although I don't know too much about what she does, I'm told she's good."

Claude stood up with his pad and went over to the window. He turned around to look at me.

"Alexander, listen closely to me. I think your father was giving out instructions to you, just as Père Varne did to me fourteen years ago. He says here *'new positions of Lord and Lady High Listener will be created.'* I think you and Helen may be the Lord and Lady High Listener. Oh I'm not saying that the two of you are meant to take over running the country, but it could well be a message to say that you have important work to do. Together."

Instructions for life from the grave. Hidden messages in the midst of garbled nonsense. Wisdom? I still had my doubts. Claude though, seemed as earnest as ever.

"And as if that is not enough, I think your father meant for me to help you both. When he says *'The job of the Lord and Lady High Listener is to educate you. By their side is the Cloth Man'.* I think the cloth man is me Alexander. The man of the cloth."

None of my training, none of my education had prepared me for this type of information. This didn't fit into any box that I knew of, didn't make any 'sense', but then what was sense anyhow? I had lived my life according to what was meant to be sensible and I hadn't exactly created a Utopian existence.

One interpretation of the facts pointed to a dying man ranting away in a confused state, his delusions brought on by a mixture of drugs and lack of oxygen to the brain. This interpretation was easy to accept at an intellectual level and would no doubt have been validated by any conventional doctor or psychiatrist. This interpretation matched with my old way of life and made a part of me feel relieved. It also left me feeling sad.

The other interpretation was the scary one. The other interpretation meant turning everything I believed in, on its head. Against this view stood the full force of logic and science. And yet there was some evidence that suggested this alternative view could not now be so easily dismissed. At least it had to be considered; it would surely be bad science to throw it out without investigation?

It was undoubted that Claude had not known about Dada's death, and yet, because of his 'visit' from Père Varne, he had been able to tell me the very day he died. It was fact that Dada had spoken the name 'Golly' twice, asking him to wait for him. Was that in truth my old friend Golly, waiting to take Dada off into the spirit world?

Claude sat down on his chair and stared intently at his writing.

"Alexander, I am meant to be returning tomorrow morning to Paris. Is there any chance we could arrange to meet with Helen before then?"

Claude was serious about this. In fact he was taking Dada's speech a lot more seriously than I had been. I wasn't at all sure about calling Helen and I certainly didn't fancy trying to explain any of this over the phone.

"I'm not sure, Claude. She's really busy with everything right now, she's taken a lot of time off to support me through my dad's illness and with the funeral."

"Yes, yes of course, I understand Alexander. Just that impatient part of me again. Tell me, can you imagine talking to her about this at all?" There he was, second guessing me again.

"Do you know what Claude, I just don't know. I just don't know what she'd think."

"How about if there was a trip to Paris involved in it?"

I smiled. How could I not? Helen loved Paris. I'd got engaged to her in Paris; one of presumably many of hundreds of men who have dropped on to one knee on the top of the Eiffel Tower, demonstrating a temporary air of submissiveness that probably rarely entered many of the marriages themselves.

"Yes Claude, a trip to Paris might swing it. Look, I won't promise anything, but I will talk to her. Do you think I should play her the recording in the meantime?"

Claude shook his head.

"I think it might be better if she has someone present to help explain this fully, don't you?"

I imagined myself trying to communicate successfully to Helen the meaning of the tape according to Claude, as well as his part in all of this and his relationship with Père Varne. *'Hi Helen, listen to this tape. It's my dying father telling you and me to work together to help change the world and working alongside us is going to be an old school friend from Paris who joined the Church after he received some spiritual guidance from a dying priest, who also just recently appeared to him in a vision with my father standing beside him!'*

"I think you're right Claude. I think we should sit through this together with Helen."

That afternoon we went for a walk together across the same part of the Heath that had nearly been my undoing yesterday morning. Yesterday? How meaningless time seemed sometimes. It seemed like days had passed.

Claude and I reached the top of Parliament Hill and sat close to the spot where I had collapsed. We sat in silence. No words; only that very special silence in which nothing needs to be said. Like my two good Samaritans of the day before. They had said nothing. They had just let me be.

As I sat there with my good friend Claude beside me, I gave myself permission to allow the madness of everything that he was suggesting to permeate my still fragile self. I didn't fight it; I didn't try to call it nonsense or absurdity. I let it be. I let it be, right alongside the other part of me that was saying there was a perfectly rational explanation to all this. But my shell had been breaking for some time now and as I looked out towards the city of London, I knew I didn't always need rational explanations any more. I'd lived a life based on logic already; it had cost me most of my friends, my health and my marriage.

But the ultimate cost had been the effect on my spirit. I had become dull, predictable and lacking in spontaneity. The shell had shut out my joy. It had protected me from feeling pain, but in doing so it had protected me from experiencing the highs as well as the lows that constitute a real life. The concept of the unlikely interpretation, as espoused by my now ecclesiastical school friend, lifted my spirit. And that was something, I was beginning to realise, that I had great interest in pursuing.

24

That night when I got back home, I reached straight for my secret supply of BMP. My heart had been pounding ever since I had read Steve's note informing me of the meeting with Jaksic. Jaksic had, weirdly, not said anything at the meeting at FiveStar, and I had, foolishly or otherwise, opted not to say anything to Steve after we had concluded.

What would I say? *'Sorry Steve, I've taken my eye off the ball, I hadn't realised you'd been pursuing Sunsure. I've already been out there for Tang and stayed in all their hotels. Tang are going to make a bid.'*

Not only would I look a right dick, but Steve would be gutted that Tang, the very group he pushed so hard to get into bed with, was making a rival bid; a bid partly based on my recommendations.

And I had recommended the hotels to Yao; partly against my better judgement. I couldn't help feeling when I stayed in Croatia that there was an atmosphere amongst the staff that was slightly oppressive. I couldn't put my finger on it, but meeting Jaksic had only served to cement the sense that Sunsure was run with a fairly aggressive attitude, and that this insensitivity was showing in the behaviour of their employees. Something felt uncomfortable, and it definitely wasn't the beds.

But my recommendation was linked to the possibility of a sizeable bonus if the deal went through. And for that I felt I could overlook any uncertainty I may have had about the working atmosphere. Why risk such a potential prize on a mere feeling that was not based on any concrete proof?

My much-needed escape route took me far away from concerns about work. It took me to a place of almost instant relief. A place that I was finding I could only regularly get to these days with the use of drugs, drink or sex. Outside stimulus. And I was beginning to understand why I earned money. To afford the things that provided the relief that made the pressure of earning money bearable.

That night on television one of the channels was showing a Kevin Costner film, 'Field of Dreams'. It's about a farmer who hears voices in a corn-field telling him that 'if you build it, he will come'. He goes on a crazy journey that leads him to build a baseball stadium in his cornfield, for a bunch of dead ex-pro baseball players to play one final game. Ultimately it is about one man following a dream; a dream that was brought into realisation by a disembodied voice. What a crap plot.

I don't know why I watched it through to the end – the candy confused me probably. Funny thing was, when the film reached its ultimate 'pass-me-the-tissues' climax, I found myself crying like a baby. I don't know when I had last cried like that. I seemed to cry myself right into a dream state. I was being chased across some open land that separated a housing estate from some nearby woods. There was a group of shapes chasing me, but these figures weren't ordinary people, they were dark, demonic beings. Behind them a house was on fire and there were people screaming from the top floor windows. It looked like those people were my parents; they sounded like my parents, but I couldn't make out their faces.

I wanted to get back to help them but to do so would mean having to risk being captured by my pursuers. I was becoming more and more agitated, but I could not escape the simple choice that awaited me; go back in order to help rescue them and risk my own well-being; go on and save myself but almost certainly consign them to a horrifying death.

Whether I forced myself to wake up or not I don't know; it was only four-fifteen in the morning. I had only been asleep for a couple of hours. My mind was racing. I felt agitated to the point of needing to get outdoors. I threw on some clothes and went out.

The roads were deserted. There is something peaceful about walking around silent streets, streets with which you are more familiar as buzzing with activity. I broke into a jog and my jog sped up into a run. I hadn't run for ages, not properly, not since my last game of rugby. God, I missed my rugby. The shoulder. Why? Why the shoulder, God? Why take away something so important to me?

That last match – Golly should have been there. Golly should have been in the scrum beside me. Not Colin Steynes. I ran faster.

I started to develop a stitch but I wanted, I needed, to run through it. I needed to feel pain again to see that I could run through it like I used to. Pain was something I could once deal with; I was its master. I had been able to transcend my physical pain on many occasions as a young man. But now pain had become my master. The first sign of pain, be it emotional or physical, found me running for a fix. Anything to help push the distress away and leave me free to get on with life. I had developed a pretty impervious shell, a shell that Steve had taught me how to strengthen.

"Excuse me sir - can you stop for a minute?"

I had failed to notice that alongside me, driving carefully down the middle of the street to avoid the parked cars, was a police car. A young policeman was leaning out of the passenger window. I suddenly panicked – did I have any drugs on me? Had I done something wrong? Was that fire real? This all seemed very familiar.

"Yes, yes of course." I came to a halt and the police car pulled up in front of me in a driveway opening.

"Can we ask what you are doing out at this time of night sir, and why you seem to be running so fast?"

"I couldn't sleep officer. I came out for some fresh air and ended up running."

"Could we have your name and address sir? Just like to run a quick check."

"Yes, officer. Alexander Baker, 17a Radnor Walk, Chelsea."

The policeman leant into his car and spoke into his walkie talkie. I stood beside him thinking of New York and their American cousins who had stopped me on the night of my twentieth birthday. On both occasions I had taken some coke, and I was standing there, guilty as hell, while all they did was check my name and address.

"Thank you sir, that all checks out fine. Sorry to have bothered you. Word of advice though – if you're going to come out at this time of night again, get yourself one of these luminous jackets or arm bands – for safety."

I nodded at the officer and he got back into his car. Forgetting why I had originally chosen to run, I started to walk slowly in the direction of the river. I felt like a criminal who knows he has committed a crime, but who has just been given parole.

The Chelsea embankment was markedly busier than the back roads I had been running in. I stood beside the river, wanting to get closer to it, wanting to be down right alongside it, but having to content myself with the view from the pavement. The tide was coming in as the water flowed past powerfully – my father had told me once that in the Thames Tideway the water level had been known to rise by up to seven metres.

I wondered how my father was. I even wondered how my mother was. Three separate lives now; each of us pursuing our own paths, paths that had once been one. But then this was what life was about, wasn't it? Growing up, becoming independent, moving out, moving up; that was the model that the beloved Mrs Thatcher had all but stamped upon the brains of every yuppie wannabe. The model that my parents had made no attempt to condemn.

I didn't really know what either of them were doing any more. I knew my mother had got into *'weird stuff,'* according to my father. His telling me this was a tactic that succeeded in putting me off investigating further, and she had made no effort to explain it to me. My father? Well all I knew was that retirement was looming; his role as an executive producer trundled along, but as for what lit his fire now, I hadn't a clue. He used to talk to me about his travel programmes, the great places in the world that he'd visited and some of the interesting people he'd met. But somewhere that dialogue had fizzled out. I had long since lost track of the shows in which he was involved. One thing I knew for certain though, was that he'd stayed single throughout all this time since my mother's betrayal. And, possibly because of that lonely warrior spirit, he was still my hero.

I walked along the embankment towards London Bridge, and eventually came to a little riverside kiosk selling hot drinks and bacon or sausage rolls. I felt in my pockets for some change - bugger. I'd come out without a penny. The bloke serving behind the counter had already asked me what I'd wanted and I now had to suffer the embarrassment of not being able to pay for the tea I'd ordered.

"Don't worry, I'll get it, Joe."

I turned around to see a young woman in a dark blue overcoat with a hood, her light blue nurse's outfit peeking out from under the hem of the coat.

She smiled at me and handed me twenty five pence for the tea. She then ordered her own hot drink and a sausage roll. I took my tea back to the railings overlooking the river, within close proximity of the kiosk. Much to my delight, she joined me.

"Thank you. That was really kind. I feel like a tramp taking your money."

"No worries. You don't look like a beggar. And anyway, I always try to think of how I'd feel, you know, when I really wanted something but I didn't have the money with me. And I like to think that someday someone might help me out like I've helped you. I saw your face when you reached into your pockets, and I knew you was really gutted that you had no cash on you. I wanted to help. See it as a great start to your day."

She spoke quite quickly and with confidence. Her accent was clearly cockney influenced, and yet she said her tees and aitches, which led me to think she must have come from parents who shared different backgrounds. It was a bizarre blend of Eliza Doolittle and BBC newsreader. I didn't want to make too much eye contact with her for fear of scaring her off. It was so nice just to have some company for a few minutes.

"So are you on your way to work?" I asked hesitantly, hoping I'd chosen a question that wouldn't send her scurrying for the hills.

"Just knocked off. Night shift, started at six last night. Knackered, me, absolutely knackered. But I do like to walk down this bit of the Thames before I go home. And I always try to stop off at Joe's and get a sausage roll and a cup of rosy. It sets me up for a great kip."

I wanted to ask her where she lived but felt that would definitely scare her off.

"So, which hospital do you work at?"

"Guys. I get the night bus back along the embankment. I share with some friends just off West Road. What's your name anyway?"

I don't know why I was taken aback by this question but I was. I guess because I wanted to know her name and was wondering when would be the right time to ask.

"Me, oh my name's Alexander. Alexander Baker."

"Ooh, well there's posh. Very nice to meet you Alexander."

She held out her hand to shake mine and her hood slipped back, revealing a beautiful halo of blonde hair. She was now facing me directly, her blue eyes staring straight at me. Her face, even in the early morning light, seemed to radiate joy.

"I'm Helen. Helen Tanner."

I shook her hand with grave politeness, and felt alive. Her energy was infectious and I found myself smiling and wanting to exude the same positive energy that she did.

"So what are you doing out at this time of day? You don't look like you're on your way to work."

I thought about the state I probably looked in my shirt and big coat, baggy jogging pants and sneakers.

"I'm er, I'm a compulsive sleepwalker. It's amazing sometimes where I end up. I found myself outside Harrods one night trying to get served in a t-shirt and boxers."

"You're having me on, aren't you? Harrods. No – never."

I laughed. She laughed too. I liked that. I liked her laugh a lot.

"Oh well, better go. Got to get me sleep in time for the next shift."

My heart sank. No sooner was she there than she was gone. I shouted after her as she strode off across the road.

"Thanks – for the tea."

But she couldn't hear me over the noise of a couple of passing lorries. I watched her disappear into the early morning bustle, and stood there once more on Chelsea Embankment, a man alone with his thoughts.

Helen. Nice name. Nice girl. So alive. Work. Oh crap. Steve. Jaksic. Tang. Oh bugger, can't you even let me have just a few minutes of joy?

The next day was another FiveStar day. I went into the office with a sense of trepidation about the mess that I was in with Jaksic. Thinking it over on the tube on the way in that morning as I stood amidst the huddled grey shapes of the early morning commute, I had come to the conclusion that I should tell Steve everything that had happened. It wasn't my fault after all that Tang and FiveStar were going after the same fish, and it wasn't my fault that I had stayed in SunSure's four hotels already.

The only trouble with telling Steve everything, was what he would then think about me. I had, after all, sat through a whole meeting with him and Jaksic, having already met Jaksic on behalf of Tang that morning. This would make Steve look more than just a little foolish as far as Jaksic would be concerned. Steve's junior working for two competing camps. And Steve cared a lot about his reputation, that much I knew.

It was possible that there were more interested parties than just Tang and FiveStar. Jaksic was going out into the open market, and so the likelihood of it coming down to a straight fight between the two of them was quite small. It was therefore entirely possible that neither would even find out that the other was interested.

By the time I got into my office, I had changed my mind completely, now convinced that I must keep quiet about Tang's interest. Steve called me into his office at about ten-fifteen to talk about the previous day's meeting.

"So, how do you think yesterday went, Alex?" Steve was pouring himself a cup from his personal coffee-maker that was the envy of us down on the second floor.

"Good. I think. I'm not sure it's a great deal though for FiveStar." I started to hatch a new idea for getting me out of the shit.

"Really? Why do you say that?" Steve suddenly became very interested. He perched on the edge of the table with his coffee in his right hand, while repetitively squeezing his executive stress ball in his left.

"Something about Jaksic. Not sure I trust him. I don't know what it is about him. His eyes are pretty close together, that's for sure." I thought my little joke might help to relax Steve, but he started squeezing his stress ball even harder.

"I knew something was bothering me Alex, but until you said it I couldn't really put my finger on it. There's something about him I don't trust. The figures all look good. The potential for expansion is massive. It is in every way exactly the sort of deal and new territory that FiveStar should be getting involved with, and yet something isn't right. And until you said that about him, I couldn't put my finger on it. It's him Alex. It's Jaksic."

"Well now, I'm not sure. It's only a feeling."

"Yeah well, whatever it is, or wherever it comes from, I share it. I need to look at this all over again. Thanks Alex. That's all for now." And with that, Steve opened the door to usher me out of the room. That was not what I expected. It sounded like Steve might even consider pulling FiveStar out of the whole deal. I returned to my desk feeling mightily pleased that I hadn't jumped in and told him everything. It was a tightrope I was walking, but that was what business was about; you had to learn when to open your mouth and when to keep quiet. I hadn't lied, I just hadn't told the whole truth.

Later that afternoon Steve sent me a memo.

"Thanks for feedback this morning. Thought you might like to know that we're pulling out of the deal with Sunsure. Fancy some action tonight? Steve."

Twenty-four hours of stress were brought to a close by this brief note. A failed acquisition was not generally a cause for celebration, but on this occasion, it felt like it was definitely something to which to raise a glass. I accepted Steve's invitation and we arranged to meet later that evening at a club he loved called Heaven. I'd heard about it as being the centre of the London gay scene, but Steve told me it was a cool place to hang out. Anyway, I was young and open-minded. I certainly wasn't homophobic, so why not?

I got there at about eleven. The entrance was in between the arches beneath Charing Cross station, its warehouse-style entrance with big, blue metal doors giving no clue as to the intimate goings-on inside.

I found Steve by the bar; much to my relief he was chatting to two women, although the wider circle around him and at the bar was almost entirely male. Wall-to-wall men, clad in everything from leather shorts to flower-printed flares. As soon as he saw me, Steve smiled, stood up and asked me to follow him to the washroom. He was wearing a black leather jacket and leather trousers.

"Save these places for us, girls." He winked at his two companions. We walked to the loos and went over to one of the sinks where he pretended to wash his hands and spoke to me by looking at me via the mirror.

"Don't ask me any questions, Alex, try one of these." He pulled out a small blue pill from his pocket.

"What is it?" I demanded, ignoring his request.

"It wouldn't matter. Oh what the hell. Look, if you must know, it's something called MDMA. The better name is Ecstasy though."

I had heard of Ecstasy. There had been various reports on it, and rumour had it that this was to be the new designer drug of the nineties.

"What's it do?"

"You'll love everyone. You'll feel like everybody is your friend, that you could go up to anyone and talk with them without feeling like an awkward jerk. You'll feel relaxed, and - I guarantee that you'll score tonight."

"And the downside?"

"There aren't any. Trust me Alex, I've been taking these for a few weeks. They're the business."

Without further ado, I popped the little blue pill in my mouth. I was off.

I went back to the bar where we had left Steve's lady friends, and I started to sense what Steve had been describing. Everyone had a warm glow around them – not that I could see it, but I could definitely sense it. When I bumped into a bare-chested bloke near the bar, I didn't get a scowl, but a big smile and some effusive comment about my shirt. And amazingly, I didn't feel scared that he might have been wanting to pick me up, I just felt liked. And I liked him back. And that was it.

The girls were sitting on the one stool that Steve had been on when I came into the club, one on the other's lap. And that's when I realised that they weren't girls at all. Steve's two lady friends were most definitely blokes. Steve took off his jacket to reveal a white vest underneath. And that is when I realised that Steve's penchant was for other males. How had I missed it? That first night when he had brought back the Japanese girls to his flat and left me to it with them, while he went off to the bedroom. Had I ever seen him with a woman? No.

But it didn't matter. I loved Steve that night, He was beautiful, he was fun and his 'ladies', 'Eva' and 'Siobhan', loved him too. We laughed and danced and drank and laughed, and I marvelled at all the beautiful, lovely men that brought Heaven to life that night.

As the evening went on though, I found myself less and less able to remember things. Eva and Siobhan's names transposed on several occasions; I'd get drinks orders from the dance floor and forget them by the time I'd reached the bar; I even went to the bathroom once having completely forgotten that I'd only been a couple of minutes before.

It was about three in the morning when we finally made our way out under the arches of Charing Cross. We must have been quite a sight as the four of us emerged unsteadily up the steps and onto Charing Cross Road. We managed to hail a cab and Steve, Eva and Siobhan and I blundered our way into the back, the driver obviously used to picking up fares from this particular area.

"I'm going to get home Steve – can you drop me in Chelsea?"

"Tell you what – we'll head for Chelsea, and see if by the time you get there you don't want to come back to my place. Chelsea Bridge please driver."

It was at this point that I started to feel concerned about what I had got myself into. Up to now, it had all seemed like a good laugh. As Steve had described, it had seemed that everybody was my friend, and I hadn't felt required to make gender judgements of any sort. But that confidence was beginning to wilt and I started to sense a growing anxiety that I was in the back of a taxi with a gay man and two transvestites. Me, a former rugby forward. Bloody hell, these men were all gay, or bi, or whatever. Damn you Steve. It didn't help that I was crammed between Siobhan and Eva, while Steve sat opposite us on one of the little pull-out seats.

There may well have been groping of sorts in the club, but again I had not noticed anything that bothered me. The taxi ride was different however. In one movement, I suddenly became aware of one of Siobhan's hands and one of Eva's both landing upon my right and left thighs. I breathed in, and wondered what on earth to do. I'd had a laugh, but I didn't want to take this any further. No matter how strong that pill was, it wasn't strong enough to turn me gay or even bisexual with just one pop.

As we drove along the embankment my unease grew. Their hands stayed there, Siobhan's gently tightening upon my leg and, I could have sworn, moving stealthily towards my crown jewels. While they both talked to Steve about funny things that had happened in the club, I prayed for salvation.

It came in a shape I wasn't expecting. We were pulled up at a set of lights near to Chelsea Bridge and there, walking along the pavement was Helen, my night-nurse.

"Stop the cab!" I surprised myself with my forcefulness.

"Sorry all of you, I've just seen a friend. Thanks for a great evening – must be going. Bye." And without further explanation, I managed to prise my thighs away from Siobhan's and Eva's grasps and head out into the fresh night air, not far away from where Helen was walking. Much to my delight, she recognised me immediately.

"Well, well, well. If it isn't the sleepwalker. Is this a regular appointment now or something?"

My jaw suddenly felt very strange. It felt heavy and awkward. The rush of cold air had started to wake up my body, and my body was beginning to pay the price for whatever was in that little blue tablet. I spoke, but with difficulty. Or at least it seemed that way to me.

"I'd like it to be. How are you? How was the night shift?"

I was feeling weird. I started grinding my teeth. I didn't know why. Maybe it was to try to free up my jaw which was definitely locking by the minute.

"What's up with your eyes? Why are they doing that?"

I didn't even know about my eyes. I tried to focus upon them, tried to see them from the outside, but I couldn't.

"You've popped some e tonight haven't you? You stupid bastard. That's what it is. God, I had a kid in casualty two nights ago. His eyes were darting all round the place and he was convinced that me and the doctor were going to stick him in a straightjacket and lock him up in a prison cell. He said we needed to secure him so we could hand him over to the aliens. He was grinding his teeth something rotten too. He'd been given a little pink pill by a friend – turned out it was Ecstasy."

At that moment my teeth ground for England.

"Oh shit, I don't feel so good." The weight of the world suddenly descended upon my shoulders. Helen put her arms round me and helped me to the side of the pavement where I promptly threw up. In the meantime she hailed a cab.

Helen was not a large woman, but somehow she managed to manoeuvre my six-foot frame and not inconsiderable bulk into the back of a cab. I attempted to tell her where I lived, and must have succeeded, because I woke up the next morning at about ten o'clock on my couch. Thank God it was Saturday. Two days off before it all started again.

I went into the bedroom hoping to find a warm nurse tucked up inside my bed. Nothing doing. Helen was gone.

I spent the rest of the day curled up on the couch, trying to remember what had happened the night before, in Heaven and in the cab. I wondered what this meant about my future working relationship with Steve. I flicked through the sport on TV but couldn't get interested. My mouth tasted like sawdust and my stomach felt like it had been kicked.

At about five o'clock the phone went. This was a common time for my father to call; he liked to discuss the football results of the day and how his beloved Manchester United had fared. Strange, considering he knew I was a rugby man. Still it provided a rare opportunity for a father/son debate and I used to join in as wholeheartedly as I could.

"Hello?" At least my mouth seemed like it had returned to normal.

"Alex? Have you recovered?" The woman's voice at the end of the phone was vaguely familiar. I suddenly dreaded that it was Siobhan or Eva.

"Me, yes, I'm fine."

"Oh, good, because I was worried. I hope you didn't mind that I put you to bed on the couch?"

"The night-nurse! Oh, oh, I'm so sorry, I, look, erm, shit. Helen. What a prat I've been. It's so great to hear your voice. How did you get my number?"

"Easy, I just took it off your phone when I left. What are you doing later – I'd like to chat?"

I couldn't believe that this woman still wanted to see me. I grabbed at her invitation like a drowning man grabbing for the life-belt.

"That would be fantastic. Where and when?"

"I'll come to you. About an hour okay?"

"Perfect."

This was it. My own Florence Nightingale had seen me in my worst possible state and still wanted to see me. Score.

25

Claude returned to Paris the following day as planned. I had spent a couple of days afterwards, reflecting on what he'd said, and decided it was time to call Helen. Daniel answered the phone, his voice lifting once he'd realised it was me.

"Oh Dada, it's you. Hiya – I just finished reading The Prisoner of Azkaban. It's wicked. I can't wait for the film."

What I loved about the boys was that their world seemed to bear so little resemblance to the world of futures and pasts that Helen and I seemed to inhabit. For Daniel and Joel, what was happening now was all that mattered. It was something I had learnt to appreciate about them since they had ceased to be a part of my 'now' on a daily basis. Losing them had been the second most painful thing I had experienced in my life.

"Can I talk to Mum?"

Daniel said goodbye and I heard him shouting out for his mother.

"Helen, it's me. How are you?"

"I'm fine Alex. I should think it's been a bit lonely hasn't it? Must be strange not having the old boy to care for any more."

"Yes."

What I wanted to say was how dreadful it was not having her and the boys here, but I had decided a while ago that this was still too sensitive a subject to discuss, particularly over the phone.

"How's work?"

This was the safest area for Helen to ask me about. It had been the area that had dominated our married life and as far as she knew was the thing that still dominated my every thought.

"I haven't started up again yet. I've got some calls to make, but I decided not to rush back in yet. I want to get it right. I've had an old school friend over as it happens. You might remember him – you spoke a few times on the phone. Claude."

"Claude, Claude – ah French Claude. The charmer. Yes, yes I remember him. You went to watch a rugby game with him in Paris after we were married didn't you? I was furious, you knew how much I loved Paris. Going there for rugby, what a waste."

I remembered too. She was livid. My justification at the time was that we had a toddling Daniel, and there was no way he could come. I was working very hard and it was a rare opportunity to meet up with some of the gang – I hadn't seen them for so long and had started losing touch with any friendships I had once had.

"Yes, well Claude came over. He was asking about you as it happens. He didn't know about the divorce."

There was a silence in which echoed the word '*divorce,*' bouncing off the walls of a void which I didn't know how to fill. Why did I have to even mention that bloody word?

"Hmmm, well, shit happens – I'm sure he knows that. What's he up to now, anyway?"

"He's a priest – in Paris. He's invited me over there actually. And, well, I owe you a trip to Paris it seems. If you could sort out babysitting for the boys, would you, er, fancy coming? Just for a couple of days. We'd have separate rooms. "

Bollocks. I hadn't wanted to talk about Claude over the phone; and I hadn't wanted to talk about taking her to Paris without meeting her face to face. Shit.

"What did you say Alex?"

"Nothing Helen, I'm sorry. Look, I wasn't thinking. Could we meet sometime?"

"Whoa, hold up. Did you just invite me to Paris or not?"

"Well, yes, sort of."

"Separate rooms?"

"Separate rooms."

"You're on. I'm coming. And so are the boys. It will be educational for them. And they could do with seeing us getting on together. They've been through enough parental crap for one life."

I couldn't believe what I was hearing. She was accepting. And, as I thought about the boys coming too, it felt even more right. They would take the attention away from just the two of us.

"How soon can you three do it? I was thinking of going fairly soon if we could arrange it."

"Don't tell anyone, but I'll pull them out of school for a couple of days. I could so do with a break. And they could too. It's been hard for them losing their granddad."

I finished the phone call and sat back in the chair, my heart pumping hard again, but not in a stressful way. Somewhere in me a memory stirred. I shut my eyes; I was a young boy on my bike. A pretty young girl was coming towards me; she had just said goodbye to her friends. My heart was pumping. We talked, she said goodbye. My heart raced.

It must have been about half an hour later when I came to. I got to work on sorting out flights and accommodation. No free stays at FiveStar Hotels any more. It was a surprisingly easy task, thank God. I managed to get four flights, plus accommodation for the following Tuesday, returning on the Friday. We'd avoid the madness of the weekend and it would give us the best chance to meet with Claude.

It all seemed strangely effortless. When I firmed it up with Helen, she raised no problems, even though the Friday flights came back at ten in the evening. And when I later called Claude, he seemed genuinely delighted that I'd managed to get it all organised so quickly.

And so it was that a few days later, the four of us found ourselves unpacking our bags in a small family hotel just off the Avenue Emile Zola, within five minutes of the famous tower which had staged my proposal to Helen twelve years earlier. It was still September and although we'd had some grey weather in England, in Paris it was sunny and remarkably warm.

Helen had a list of sightseeing she wanted to do with the boys and she was happy to take them off to the Louvre on that first afternoon while I went off to meet Claude.

I surprised myself at how excited I was to see him again. It was like meeting my protector or something. Somehow I felt safe around him, safe and not judged. We met at a small café in the Rue Martyrs – Claude had told me it was the best coffee shop and bakery in the whole of Paris.

He was already there when I arrived – sitting just inside the window at a small round table with two wooden slatted chairs. In front of him was an empty coffee cup. He stood up as soon as he saw me and embraced me. His hug felt good.

"Alexander, it is so good to see you again, and so quickly. I didn't think you'd be able to organise things so fast."

The waitress came over and we ordered a round of coffees and he also ordered a couple of pastries that he insisted I try.

"You know Claude, I can't quite take in how easily it all happened. Mainly, I couldn't believe Helen said yes. Not after everything that we've been through. But she did and here we are. She and the boys are at the Louvre."

"So, it's as if everything has fitted into place quite easily. This is good Alexander. This means we are on the right course. Père Varne used to talk about some things happening effortlessly when they were meant to be. I think this is an example. Have you played Helen the tape?"

"Nope. She knows nothing about it. That bit I did manage to keep quiet."

"Good. Very good. Now we are going to need some time when the boys can be kept occupied and we can play her your father's oration. You are here until Friday. Thursday night is your last night so I'm sure you'd like to have your last evening in Paris together – tonight Helen may be a bit tired from the travelling and The Louvre. So that leaves tomorrow evening – you'll be busy during the day I'm sure. How about if I come to your hotel and we meet in your room?"

Claude didn't miss a trick. Even though he didn't have children, he seemed more attuned to my family's needs than I. As he worked out what would be best for everyone, I was aware of some feelings of jealousy. Where had he learnt to do that?

"That sounds great. Tomorrow night at our hotel. If we say eight o'clock, that will give us a chance for an early supper and for Helen to get the boys settled."

"Merveilleux. And now, let us enjoy our pastries." And with that, Claude took a bite of the sweet that sat untouched on his plate. It was as though he had saved his reward until he had attended to business. He had style, and I was beginning to warm to him once again as I had when we were boys. Here was the brother I had never had.

The next twenty four hours panned out as Claude had described. Helen and the boys had returned shattered from their afternoon's sightseeing and we ended up eating in a bistro near the hotel. Wednesday during the day we stayed together, combining some shopping with a trip down the Seine which took in the Eiffel Tower and Notre Dame. We had a four-course lunch beside the Seine in a Michelin star restaurant and returned late in the afternoon to the hotel where the boys watched satellite television while Helen and I both had a lie down. She came to my room, which was next-door to theirs, to rest which felt wonderful. I loved having her close and I was beginning to appreciate these moments of silence more and more. I wondered whether this was the same type of silence during which Claude had experienced his revelations; the silence about which Père Varne had instructed him.

At supper that evening I was not entirely present. I had decided to play the meeting with Claude right down as far as Helen was concerned and had not even mentioned it yet. As we finished a round of glorious, home-made crème caramel, both the boys went off to the men's room. I seized the moment to tell Helen about Claude's visit.

"Helen, Claude is coming to my room tonight – he's got some things he'd like to discuss. We were both wondering if you'd like to join us."

"Sure. The boys will be very happy to be left with the television. What does he want to talk about?"

"It might sound a bit weird if I try to describe it. Do you mind if we wait?"

Helen smiled, the smile that I had so missed in my life over the last few years.

"Sounds mysterious. Even more reason to come. I'll be there."

Daniel and Joel returned to the table. I asked for the bill, paid and we returned to our hotel in the shadow of the Eiffel Tower.

At precisely ten past eight there was a knock on my door. In between shutting my eyes for some silence, I had been staring intently at my travel clock, wishing the hands forward. It was like waiting for a plane to take off when you've already boarded, but someone else is late.

I opened the door to find Claude's tall frame standing in the doorway.

"Bonsoir Alexander. And how are you?"

I was nervous. That was the true answer. That word popped straight into my head the second he asked the question.

"Well, I feel a little on edge Claude."

I surprised myself with my own honesty.

"That is wonderful. Not wonderful that you feel on edge, but wonderful that you can admit to it. It is so refreshing to hear someone speak the truth rather than pretending that everything is fine. Your boys are very lucky to have you for a father Alexander."

'Lucky to have me for a father?' If only you knew Claude. If only you knew of all the times I had failed to be aware of their existence; of all the times when my own much more important life had come streets ahead of their own; of all the times I had failed to tell them the truth, or in fact anything like it.

But, he was right on one thing. And it felt refreshing to me too to answer a question like that honestly. For about the first time in my life, I had really heard the words 'how are you?' And instead of rushing into the knee-jerk response, 'not bad', 'I'm fine', 'mustn't grumble' – I had replied authentically. And had thereby demonstrated my vulnerability to another bloke. I felt another part of the shell, that so nobly protected my heart, fragment.

Claude came into my room and sat in one of the two armchairs. I had already figured out that I would lie on the bed, propped up with pillows and then Helen could have the other armchair.

"I have made copies of your father's words, and those of Père Varne – sometimes it's easier to read than listen. The more I study them, the more I am intrigued by the familiarities between them."

Every now and again Claude would let slip the odd word that gave away his foreign roots. I felt no need to correct him any more. He got out his copies and placed them on the table that stood between the two armchairs.

"You have your player?"

I had my little mp3 player, complete with mini speaker, all ready to go. I picked it up from the bed and placed it on the table beside the papers.

"Before Helen comes in, I just wanted you to see these words again. *'Guilt destroys. Blame destroys. No-one has ever done anything wrong, we were all just ignorant.'* Do you remember who said that Alexander?"

I recognised my father's words immediately.

"Yes, my father said that Claude. Why?"

"No Alexander, your father said *'Your feelings of guilt create only one result – self-destruction. Your desire to blame creates only one result – destruction. Seek to forgive others because they too have nearly always acted out of ignorance, not badness'.* I knew the words were similar, but I too didn't realise how similar until I wrote them down and compared them."

"It is remarkable Claude. Like two different interpretations of the same script."

Claude's detective work was impressive. I didn't yet know Dada's speech that well that I could remember it, but this refresher made me want to hear it all over again. And this time I knew I'd be able to cope with the guilt section.

We had left the door ajar, and just after this discussion Helen walked in. Although she hadn't changed her clothes, she was looking radiant.

"Helen, how lovely to meet you. Thank you so much for joining us." Claude was charming. He shook her hand and Helen responded with a smile immediately. Somewhere inside me I felt a stab of jealousy of Claude's ability to produce that smile with his first sentence. Sometimes it had taken me hours to get there.

"It's a pleasure to meet you at last, Claude. Thank you for asking me. I'm intrigued – Alex was quite mysterious about all this." She came over to me and kissed me on the cheek. I offered her the armchair and she duly sat down.

"Drinks anyone?" I had bought a couple of big bottles of mineral water at the petit magasin on the corner of the street on our way back from dinner.

"Water is always good – thank you Alexander."

"And me Alex, ta very much."

Ta was a word that Helen used all the time in the 'old days'. She either used it when she was feeling playful or when her mind was elsewhere and she said it on autopilot, as if it formed a part of some deeper conditioning that had made her who she was.

"So, what have you got for me? Why have you called us to this meeting Alex?"

Playful. Thank heavens. Because I wanted Helen's mind to be present tonight. I poured their water while I tried to work out what to say. I had been putting off telling Helen why we'd invited her until this moment; now that it had arrived I felt clueless. Claude was saying nothing.

I went over to my bed and plumped the pillows to buy some more time. The old Alexander would probably have jumped in with a huge rambling speech about how what we were going to share with her was probably all nonsense and could be a bit of a time-waster and...actually the old Alexander would never have even got this far. The old me would have dismissed the whole thing from day one and would have wiped the recording. But I hadn't. Christ. I hadn't dismissed it. I had changed. And this meeting, whatever the outcome, was as much proof as any that I was changing.

I lay down on the bed and shut my eyes for a few seconds; still Claude said nothing. I opened my eyes again and looked directly at Helen. I saw that she was wearing the pearl necklace that I had brought her back from New York several years ago. She had probably been wearing it all day, but I hadn't noticed until now.

"Helen, I'm not entirely sure why we need to meet. We've got something to play you and some words to show you. Claude, can you press play?"

Claude smiled at me. I sensed that he was impressed with how I had handled Helen's question; and I was pleased that he hadn't jumped in and saved me.

And so Dada's speech began. Helen's eyes seemed to grow in size as she realised who was speaking. Surprise soon gave way to intense concentration, interrupted by the occasional giggle when words like 'incumbent chefs' and 'bananas' squeezed their way out of the tiny speaker.

Then during one paragraph, I noticed a tear making its way down Helen's left cheek. It heralded the arrival of several more and she made no effort to hide them.

You cannot live as God if you cannot first learn to listen. Do you know how much listening God has to do? Have you ever thought about what an incredible listener God is? God listens first. Right action follows as a natural consequence of right listening. Very often you don't need to do anything if you follow the path of right listening.'

I was learning that we each seemed to get something different from Dada's words. I had been shaken to my roots that morning on the Heath, by his comments on guilt; and now, in a pool that existed in some deep place inside Helen, a pebble had dropped causing ripples to spread to its furthest banks. Perhaps it should have been no surprise that the section that moved her was focussed on the importance of *'listening'* – a talent that Helen had mastered to impressive levels. As I thought about it more, I vaguely remembered having an emotional response to the same section.

As tears gently dropped down both her cheeks, I watched as she took a tissue from the table and wiped her face. She asked Claude to pause the recording while she blew her nose, making her characteristic tiny trumpeting noise that I'd always found endearing. We each took drinks from our glasses and, with no words spoken, Claude pressed play once more.

'It is time for you men of war and many words to look first to a woman for the new way. She will teach her Lord High Listener the way and he will reach out to the men of the world. For the men currently hold the keys to power and the power is currently being used destructively. Soon the women will have duplicates once more.'

Even though I was shacked up in a hotel room in Paris with my ex-wife and old school friend-turned-priest, listening to a jumble of words spoken by my dying father, none of this seemed wrong. In fact quite the reverse, it felt absolutely right. It shouldn't have, but it did. In that relatively gloomy atmosphere that was my room, surrounded by unfamiliar things, I felt like I was coming home in some way. And I was beginning to wonder whether Dada's words were not the signpost I needed to direct me home.

The tape ended. Helen let out a sigh and Claude remained quiet. The three of us sat there for at least a couple of minutes in what felt like a mutual silence of respect. As I found out later from Helen, it was also a gap during which she was able to feel a part of herself that she had not connected with for a long time.

Claude then gave each of us a transcript of Père Varne's words, as well as the copies of Dada's. Helen studied the dying priest's wisdom carefully. She then turned to Claude.

"You're being very quiet about all this Claude. You must have some thoughts?"

"Oh yes Helen, I do. But it seems to raise more questions than anything else."

Helen leant forward towards him.

"Questions are good. Questions are great. This whole thing about listening – this is what I base all my work on now. By going through my own crisis with someone who shall remain nameless but who is lying on that bed, I had to develop my own way of responding to shit. Oops, excuse the blaspheming. Not used to speaking in front of a priest."

I hated that she referred to what I had put her through as shit. Not because it wasn't, but because I now so badly wanted to make it right. Claude waved his hand and shook his head.

"No matter. Carry on, please."

And so it was that Helen started to describe to Claude the listening system she had created. It was based on various conversations with her spiritual teacher, all sorts of books that she had read, and on her own experiences as a mother, betrayed wife, counsellor and nurse. This was the new landscape that Helen Two had created out of the ashes of Helen One's destroyed world. It was a landscape with which I was still mostly unfamiliar, having drunk from its healing waters only when it was forced upon me. I hadn't delved into this brave new world any more than I had needed, confining myself to picking up little snippets of wisdom that I occasionally applied in my own life as and when it seemed appropriate. I had learnt just enough from her to be able to deal effectively with Dada's last few weeks of life, and that was in itself a miracle considering the feeling-less place from which I had come.

I listened for as long as I could, but I was not close enough to their immediate orbit for my attention to be held by their voices. I had placed them near each other not only because it avoided either of them having to lie on the bed but also because I hoped it would enable them to communicate with each other more effectively. This positioning had worked too well and ultimately resulted in my drifting off to sleep.

The next thing I knew it was early morning, there was a duvet over me, but I was still in my clothes. I tried to move but had a stiff neck from lying in the same position for too long. The armchairs were empty. I was alone.

I looked at the clock and realised that four thirty-five was way too early to call either of them to find out what they had talked about. I wanted to drop straight back off to sleep, but my mind started to do the thing with which I had become so familiar. Thoughts started piling up near the starting line, waiting for the starter's pistol to be sounded so that they could all set off on their own crazed journeys through my inner world. This would generally result in countless attempts to reason with each and every one of them as they grabbed their few seconds of attention by blazing across the screen of my mind.

What did they talk about? What did Helen really think of all this? What did she make of Dada's tape? Was she livid about giving up an evening in Paris to discuss this sort of stuff? What did Claude think of her? Did he like her? Did she like him? Had they gone off together to her room? Did Catholic priests abstain from sex with non-Catholics? Where can I get something to eat?

I stood up and went over to the table where they had been sitting. I wanted a clue, a single line penned by Helen to say everything was fine and no she didn't like Claude *in that way*.

There was nothing on the table, but there was a small piece of paper on the floor near to where Helen had been sitting. It must have dropped out of her bag. It contained four words. Four words that sent a chill down my spine and stopped all the other rampaging thoughts in their tracks. *'Tom – the blind man.'*

26

I did my best to get the flat ready for the night-nurse in the small amount of time I had until she was due. I took a badly-needed shower and put on a fresh shirt and jeans. My hair was still soaking wet when she arrived. Two minutes later she was already drying it for me.

"You've got lovely hair, Alex."

I was still feeling uncertain of my ground, trying to work out how I should be reacting to her. This was not, after all, an opportunity for a quick bit of nooky. This was not a prey that I had stalked relentlessly and was now bringing to the ground prior to devouring. It was Helen who had taken the initiative and here she was now drying my hair. It felt strangely surreal.

"Thank you for the compliment. I'm stuck with it I guess, so it had better be good." Even as I said the words I thought how pathetic they sounded. I so wanted to say something interesting to her; I so wanted to impress. "How was your sleep?"

My God, was that the best I could come up with?

"You're funny. How was my sleep? Well, I don't really know, because I was asleep."

We both laughed, she finished with the hair dryer and then put both her hands on my shoulders as she looked at me in the mirror.

"Now listen here Alexander Baker. I can put up with a lot in a man, but there are four things I can't cope with, and if that's no good for you then let's get it over with before we start getting all silly about each other."

I sat there, looking at myself in the mirror, as this petite fireball turned the tables on the whole *male-makes-the-first-move* story that had, as far as I was aware, repeated itself down through the millennia.

"Right, of course. So what are they then?"

"No drugs. No smoking. No lying or cheating. Above and beyond that you can do pretty much as you please and the same goes for me."

I have learnt that there are some rare moments in life when you are so certain of the answer to something that you don't need to take any time to come to a decision. This was one of those collector-item moments. I stood up and turned round to face her. I reached out and took her right hand in mine.

"You've got a deal."

And at that moment she reached up to place the very first kiss upon my lips. A kiss sent by a messenger of the Goddess of Love. We kissed and kissed and kissed. I held her and she held onto me. She felt small in my arms and I immediately felt protective of her. I could sense her feeling my strength and gaining comfort in that. Love flowed through me such as I had never felt; this sensation was nothing like I had experienced from my pornography or my haphazard sexual fumblings. This was humbling. It was power. It was weakness. It was magic.

We ordered a takeaway and soon found ourselves doing all those corny things that men and women do when they find themselves in the grip of irresistible attraction; we laughed at each other's jokes; we talked and then found ourselves leaving awkward pauses which we both tried to fill; we interrupted each other and then immediately apologised; we offered food and drink to each other before ourselves and both glanced nervously at the clock as the night went on, knowing that at some point the dreaded *'I should be going'* sentence needed to be uttered.

But it wasn't. I'm not sure she ever even thought it. The fact that one thing led to another and we ended up in my bed that night was, strangely, not planned by me. I can't be sure that Helen planned it either. It just seemed to happen.

And, with my life temporarily free of worries about Tang and FiveStar, and the nightclub experience behind me, the sex was unbelievable. It seemed strangely ironic that, as I lay there in the middle of the night with Helen's beautiful, warm body pressed up against my back, I felt like I had died and woken up in heaven.

And so Helen and I began our voyage across the oceans of relationship. She had three days off and the second of those, Sunday, only served to confirm our mutual attraction. I'd once read that if a woman looks beautiful when she first gets up in the morning then you're onto a real winner, don't let her go. She got up and threw on one of my shirts which sat loosely over her otherwise naked body, her long blonde hair finding its way both inside and outside the collar. I was sold.

"Alex. I meant what I said yesterday. About the four things. No drugs. No smoking. No lying or cheating. Do any of those and I walk."

It seemed a harsh way to greet a new lover, but it made me realise she was serious.

"Yep, I got you night-nurse. No worries." I went up and squeezed her bum to try to make light of what she'd said. She was having none of it and stepped away. It was an awkward moment for such early days.

"Alex, I'm serious. I have my reasons for this stuff. I don't want to get hurt again and I don't want to waste my time if you've got no interest in taking me seriously."

I felt the wrench tighten a little in my stomach. I could do it. Sure I could. God, for that type of sex I could do anything.

I took her hand again, just as I had the night before.

"No more drugs; no more smoking; no lying or cheating. I promise."

And that was that. The subject was not raised again that day. Our relationship was off and running.

On the Monday she returned to her flat and I had to go off to Oslo for Tang. While I was there, Jaksic, who had asked for my contact details the week before, called me.

"Hello Alex. Good to talk with you."

His voice sounded as slippery over the phone as his presence appeared in real life. I hated it when people called me Alex. Except Helen for some reason. It sounded, well, nice, coming from her. It was her special name for me now. That right belonged to her. Not Jaksic.

"Mr Jaksic – good to hear from you. How can I help?"

"Imre please, Alex. No need for formalities. I'm wondering whether we couldn't help each other out here a little."

My heart sank. I knew immediately that this was going to involve some sort of payback for his finding me at the FiveStar meeting. He continued.

"I was surprised to find you last Thursday at the FiveStar meeting Alex. This puts me in a, well let's say, puts us in an awkward position."

"How so, Imre?" I wasn't sure how it did, and thought I'd buy myself some time.

"Well Alex as you know, we have been in a sensitive negotiation for a while with FiveStar. And now we have Tang interested too. Now, I've got a feeling that Steve Drayton has no idea that you are working for Tang on this deal. Am I right?"

"Yes, but what of it?" I couldn't tell where he was going with this. After all, FiveStar had pulled out. What was the problem?

"Well I'd hate Steve to find out that the same day I came to meet with you at FiveStar, you had met with me in the morning to discuss a similar proposition with Tang. I think he might find it a little odd that the same employee who has convinced him to call off the FiveStar offer, has been helping Tang to put together an offer. Don't you think he might be just a little bit angry in the future when he finds Tang's money has helped Sunsure to become a hugely successful chain throughout Eastern Europe?"

Fuck. I hadn't thought this through. Of course word would get out about Tang's investment if they went for it. I knew that, but I hadn't thought about the possibility of Steve finding out that I had anything to do with the groundwork. And what would stop him from jumping to the conclusion, the right conclusion, that I had put him off the deal in order to secure the hotels for Tang.

"And, of course, maybe the bonus system deal is better for you at Tang?"

Fuck again.

"Of course Alex, I could make it very worth your while. Let's say a generous cash payment of twenty-thousand dollars and free hotel stays in Croatia for life."

All of a sudden this cloud had a silver lining. If any alarm bells had been going off, it was remarkable how quickly they were silenced.

"Okay Imre, I understand the awkward situation we find ourselves in. What do you need me for?"

"From what I understand Alex, Ma trusts your judgement implicitly. I don't know what you have done to deserve such regard, but that is how it is. I need you to do two things. First you must praise Sunsure Hotels to the rooftops if, or when, they ask for any more feedback."

"And the second thing?"

"Ah, this is very simple. I just need to know what figure FiveStar were putting together to offer us. That should be easy to find out, being so close to Steve as you are."

Jaksic had me by the balls. I had no choice it seemed. The Tang promise was no big deal, I'd already recommended the chain, even though I had considerable reservations about them. Those doubts were being confirmed by this phone call. As for finding out the FiveStar price – that was easy. Steve had already told me what it was worth on the open market. And it was a lot more than this unscrupulous Croatian had previously realised.

"They'd have gone up to six million dollars for a forty percent stake."

The phone went quiet.

"Imre? Imre, did you hear me? Imre?"

Eventually his voice returned.

"Alex, you've just earned your twenty-thousand. Now just keep your fingers crossed that the Tang deal goes through. Have a nice day."

And that was that. End of conversation. I sat there trying to work out whether I had, or had not, just committed a crime. FiveStar were out of the game anyway, so that was okay. The truth was, I had only told Steve what I thought – which was that something felt wrong about Sunsure. And if Imre wanted to pay me a few quid because I'd helped him to realise the true value of his business, it wasn't going to hurt anyone, was it? And God knows, Tang could afford the acquisition anyway, even at the full market price.

I convinced myself that all was well, and returned to my Norwegian fact-finding mission. My double life had begun.

The deal all went through within a matter of weeks – Jaksic managing to secure just under six-million dollars for a thirty-eight percent stake in the business. Ma himself, not just Yao or Zhu, had been in touch with me to hear personally that I was happy with the chain. I think I must have been crossing most of my fingers as I gave him my approval for the deal. I remember his words clearly.

"Okay Mr Alexander. You know good hotels. Thank you. You look forward to bonus, yeah?"

Damn right. In fact I was looking forward to two bonuses. I didn't know exactly what Ma was going to pay me, but with Jaksic's twenty-thousand bucks in my account any day now, I planned to have some fun.

During these few weeks, the night-nurse and the sleepwalker met whenever they could. Helen had a busy schedule of work and I had to be away a fair amount too. I had managed to keep my promise to her without too much effort, the occasional yearning for any quick fixes of my old addictions giving way to the fear of losing this precious new development in my life.

One morning Steve, who had been noticeably less chummy with me since the Heaven night, called me into his office 'for a little chat'.

"Alex – I've just heard that Ma and his team have bought into a share of Sunsure."

Silence. He just sat there, in his leather armchair, his hands clasped together and his eyes fixed firmly upon me. All my resolve, all my logical reasoning suddenly seemed very flimsy now. I sat in my chair, guilty as charged. Or had I been charged? What was I guilty of? A shed. Flames. My parents. Jaksic. Helen. Ma. Names, images, nonsensical thoughts trying to ram their demolition balls into my new construct of success and smash it to pieces.

"Alex?"

"Sorry Steve. Wow – Tang huh? Well, I'm not sure that that is a very smart move, are you? I mean that guy Jaksic, I just don't think he can be trusted. And that runs through the hotels."

"Does it Alex? How do you know that?"

Shit.

As far as Steve knew I had never been to one of Jaksic's hotels. At least not on FiveStar time – it had never been my job to suss out their potential acquisitions. That was a job that FiveStar's Seattle based owner, Manny Williams, liked to do himself whenever possible. He didn't trust anyone else. I don't know how many airmiles he clocked up every year, but his total must have made mine look minute.

"Well, I don't know for certain, of course Steve, but isn't it obvious? I mean, if the example from the top is dubious, then everything else is going to be of a dubious nature too. I don't need to go there."

"But have you, Alex? Have you been there for Tang?"

The hole I was digging myself was getting bigger.

I thought back to my days at school; hiding gristly meat in napkins, and exam instructions that I had been given time and time again by my tutors; *Tell them what they want to hear. Nothing more, nothing less.'*

I suddenly became very scared of the consequences of Steve finding out that I had lied to him about Jaksic. So, insanely, inspired by years of questionable conditioning, I lied again.

"Good grief no Steve. I would have told you of course if I had, because I presume that would have put me in a very compromising situation with you negotiating as well at the time."

Steve remained quiet for a few seconds. It seemed like minutes.

"Okay Alex. Thanks very much. You can go now."

I left his office, taking with me considerably more baggage than I had when I had entered. I felt all those things that I had felt so many times before. My chest tightening, sweats, adrenalin pumping like billy-oh. I had to get outside. I needed a smoke, a pill, a drink, something.

A cigarette was the first thing that I could lay my hands on. I had kept a packet in my desk ever since my introduction to the candy pipes in New York. I went outside and walked around, the mild rush of nicotine helping to drown out the guilty voices that were hopelessly clamouring for attention.

I bought some mints at a local newsagent and returned to the office. I kept my head down for the rest of the day and dreaded it every time my phone rang. I was desperate to get out of there. To get away from the office; to get away from London. To escape.

At twenty minutes past five the phone went. I hesitated before answering it. I needn't have done – it was Helen.

"Hi Alex – and how is your day going?"

Another rush of guilt swept through me. The cigarette. Our promise. Bollocks.

"Yeah, I'm okay," I lied. I wasn't. Oh I could put on the mask, but inside guilt was gnawing away at me like a small, undetectable mouse patiently but unerringly, eating through the contents of an attic. I'd also just broken my promise to Helen never to lie. This was turning out to be a bad day. I had to break the cycle and take some positive action. I had to do something to deflect the conversation.

"When are your next days off, Helen?"

"Next week - Monday through Thursday. Why? Look, are you sure you're okay? You sound, I dunno, different."

"I'm fine – it's just my end-of-a-working-day voice. So listen, don't book anything and have your passport ready. I'm owed some holiday. I'm taking you away for a little trip."

Steve and Yao individually okayed my time off, Steve with slightly more reluctance. The following Monday found Helen and me in the centre of Paris. She had been there once on a school trip and had loved the place. While all her friends had only been interested in the shops and the young French men, Helen had found her appetite fired when she visited the Louvre. She had a passion for sculpture, a passion that lived inside her, that hadn't been taught at school or by her parents. She told me that she marvelled at how someone could capture an individual's very essence in such a painstaking medium as stone.

We were staying at FiveStar's Hotel just off the Avenue de Champs Elysees. It was a beautiful hotel and my staff discount meant I could make Helen feel special. We were met at the hotel doors by a porter and our small bags taken up to our room. Helen's reaction to our accommodation was worth every penny of my wages that this was costing.

"Oh. My. God." Helen stood gaping at our suite.

The porter shut the door and left us alone. She came up to me and gave me a hug whose warmth seemed to permeate the furthest corners of my being. And as her loving embrace enveloped me, I became scared that she might uncover the little lies that had lain hidden in dark corners, alongside the little gnawing mouse.

"I have to take you to the Eiffel Tower. Have you ever been there after dark?"

She hadn't. She had no idea what I was planning, and, up to that moment, neither really had I. All I knew was that I was feeling stuff about this night-nurse that I had never felt before for anyone. I wanted her. I wanted her to be mine. I had to capture her now while I had the chance. And in doing so, I knew I could silence the other voices that were beginning to question my ability to keep my promise to her. I sneaked out to the shops in the late afternoon while she was bathing and within a short space of time managed to pick up a simple, solitaire diamond ring. It would do for starters.

That night we made what became our historical climb to the second floor of the Tower, and then took the elevator up to the top. My system was on overload. Was I really going to do this? I was about to say something that might change our lives for ever. The power of a few small words: *'Will you marry me?'*

Paris and the Tower were dazzling that night. Thousands of shimmering lights, an electric atmosphere that seemed resonant with my own state. I had taken her up there in the evening because there was more chance of finding a small space to ourselves on one of the observation decks. And there, just as we approached a small look-out point that gave us a view across Paris, was indeed an area free of tourists.

My heart felt like it would explode as we approached the viewing platform. I felt in my pocket for the ring. She had no idea what I was about to say. I felt guilty even about that; my secret. And I'd been keeping it from her for hours, deceiving her every time I opened my mouth and failed to say *'I'm going to propose to you tonight.'*

She reached the view first; I walked up behind her and, without her knowing, got down on one knee, and took the ring box from my pocket, opened it and proffered the whole box with my right hand. That was what you were supposed to do wasn't it? I suddenly wondered.

Just as I was wondering she turned round.

"Alex?"

"Bonsoir Monsieur, Bonsoir Madame. Ah, merveilleux. Vous allez vous épousier, n'est-ce pas?"

From out of nowhere, a middle-aged French couple had appeared right behind me. Crap. Now what? With the wind almost fully taken out of my sails, I decided to blunder on. The French couple, with relentless insensitivity, remained at my back. In those moments, they were as parasites, sucking on the very stuff of love that should only have been shared between Helen and me. I tried to ignore the awkwardness and irritation of it all and somehow managed to utter the words that would change my life forever.

"Helen, will you marry me?"

"Ah, l'amour. Enchantant."

"What? But Alex, we've only just met. Are you sure? Have you got any idea what marriage means? I mean, why?"

I listened to her, and I didn't. There was only one thing I wanted to hear her say and until she said it, I would just keep asking her the question.

"Helen, will you marry me?"

"Il vous aime. Dites oui!"

"Alex, this is so quick. How can you be so certain?"

"Helen, will you marry me?"

"Qu'est ce qui se passe?"

Voices were building up behind me. I couldn't look.

"Un Anglais. Il veut s'épouser la fille. Elle est très jolie. Nous pensons qu'elle va refuser. "

More mutterings. I still didn't turn round. Helen was looking over my head at the small crowd of people that was evidently gathering behind me.

"What about the promises Alex? Can I really count on you?"

I quickly banished all thoughts of any wrongdoings into the loft with the mouse.

"All agreed. No drugs, no smoking, no lying or cheating."

She looked again at the people behind me. She then turned to look out over Paris. There was a deathly hush behind me. Finally she turned round once more.

"Yes, Alexander Baker, I will marry you. I will. I really will."

I took the ring out of the box and suddenly realised I had no idea which finger it was meant to go on. Why in the name of God didn't they teach you these sorts of things in school? You might only need it once, but at that moment it was about the most important piece of information you could ever have had. Helen, sensing my ineptitude, gently placed my hand over her ring finger.

I slipped the ring on, and then we were kissing on top of the Eiffel Tower, the lights of Paris stretching way into the distance, and a small crowd of appreciative strangers as our witnesses.

27

'*Tom - the blind man*'. Four small words, yet as powerful at that moment in my life as those four simple words 'will you marry me' had been atop the Eiffel Tower all those years ago.

It was now eight-thirty in the morning. I had sat awake in the chair for two or three hours, the crumpled piece of paper somehow having survived in one piece through dawn and into morning. There was a knock at the door.

"Come in." I felt as though I was stuck in my seat and failed to answer the door. It was not Helen as I was expecting, but Claude. Underneath his coat, he was wearing a cassock and collar; the first time I had seen him dressed for work.

"Bonjour mon ami. You are up – I thought you might be. You fell asleep last night, huh?"

Nothing in me could be angry with Claude. And interestingly, nothing in me could suspect him of any wrongdoing with Helen either, not that I was in any moral position to stop them from fooling around if they wanted to. God, where did all this crap come from? Had I become thoroughly neurotic over the years, or what?

"Hi Claude. Yes, I fell asleep. How did it go with Helen?"

"She is incroyable Alex. She is the Lady High Listener that your father describes. Her model for listening needs to be taught from nursery school to the Houses of Parliament, from football fields to theatre dressing-rooms. She is naturally gifted with this I think, and her pain, her struggle, has helped her to refine a talent that already existed."

I didn't really know what Claude was talking about, having not paid that much attention to Helen's career progress after we separated.

"What did she make of the recording? Does she think there is something in it?"

"You saw her cry, Alex. What more do you need to know? She wants to talk to you about something relating to it. Well, probably more than one thing, but there is one sentence in particular that we identified last night as being fundamental to how we take this forward."

'Tom the blind man.' I knew where Claude was headed. I had found the note. At that moment, Helen entered the room. It was then that I realised they must have prearranged to meet at the same time.

"I heard voices – I assumed you must be here Claude. Good morning. Good morning Alex. The boys are watching TV, so we should be good for a few minutes at least. They know where we are if they need us."

I got up to greet her. Much to my surprise she gave me a big hug. I held her and I once again felt her tiny body close to mine as I had all those years ago in my flat. I became aware once more of my physical superiority, of my power, in relation to her fragility. And yet for all that, I didn't feel like the strong one any more. She was holding me and I was receiving her. I could feel tears wanting to flow, but something prevented them from coming. Maybe I wasn't ready to be vulnerable in front of both Claude and Helen at the same time. There was no real reason to cry here, and yet I was once again reduced to that weakened emotional state with which I had become so familiar over the last two years. We separated and this time Helen sat on the edge of the bed, while I returned to my armchair.

"Claude tells me you have a brilliant communication system Helen." I almost said 'why didn't you tell me?' but fortunately managed to stop myself. She knew damn well that it wouldn't have made any difference if she had told me; I wouldn't have taken her, or it, seriously. I didn't feel proud of the fact that the only reason I was even able to acknowledge it now was because Claude had been impressed by her. The truth is, I wouldn't have known what to think anyway, even if she had described this system to me. And still somewhere inside lurked the demon that said 'the man does the important work. The man creates solutions. The man fixes.' Not even the success of The Iron Lady had managed to alter that scratched record.

"Thank you Claude, thank you Alex. Yes, we had an interesting time last night. Alex, ah Alex. Where do I start?" Helen looked straight at me, her face soft and demonstrating little sign of a late night. She cared for herself well now and it showed.

"I suppose, and this is going to surprise me, I suppose I start with another thank you. Thank you for bringing me to Paris, for taking Claude seriously and, most importantly, thank you for challenging so much of what you have been taught to be the way of things."

I couldn't remember the last time Helen had really thanked me. I had been the one doing the thanking for at least two years now. I'd thanked her for helping me when I was in the midst of crisis, for being such a great mother - and father - to the boys when I was out of it, for being a rock all the time that Dada was sick and dying. So it made a welcome change to be on the receiving end of her thanks. I wanted to frame these words, this feeling. I wanted to put them somewhere where I would always be able to access them. Funny thing was, I'd striven throughout my marriage to do things that I thought would earn her gratitude – working tirelessly to provide loads of money, fancy holidays, nice clothes – and yet I couldn't remember any of those acquisitions ever resulting in real gratitude. Not direct-eye-contact-arms-round-me-tears-in-eyes gratitude.

Helen went on.

"I don't want to sound like I'm on some ego trip here Alex, so this bit is hard to put without the risk of sounding naff. Claude and I discussed this well into the small hours last night and we're both intrigued by it all. What would you think if we said we believe that your father's speech, and Claude's experiences, might suggest that we three, for whatever reason, are being given a chance to do something very special with our lives and for our children?"

What would I say? What would you expect me to say? Before I had a chance to reply, which was just as well because I didn't have a reply, Claude spoke.

"Alexander, so much of what has happened is now beginning to make sense. Père Varne was teaching me the way of finding peace in myself. I now help people to find peace in their lives and, where possible, to find meaning in difficult events. Through helping individuals to see things differently, I hope, step by step, to help the Catholic Church to see things differently. To become less judgemental and more open. Père Varne taught me not to panic when I didn't know the answer; he taught me that looking for the answer was not necessarily what we needed to do; that what we need to do is to make sure we are asking the right questions. And that is certainly true of the Church too. To become aligned with the Twenty-First Century it needs to be asking questions of itself, instead of merely projecting doctrines, some of which may now be out of date."

Helen took up the thread.

"Alex, in my work of the last few years, I have been working on a very similar basis to Claude. Through lots of instruction and a certain amount of trial and error, I've developed a model which enables the most challenging of relationship problems and confrontations to be transformed; it's all to do with listening. Remember what your father said? *Right action follows as a natural consequence of right listening. Very often you don't need to do anything if you follow the path of right listening.* It takes a hell of a lot of self-discipline to use this model; people can't always stick to it which is a real bummer, but when it's applied consistently, mountains can move. I've felt for ages that something is missing, some step; a step that will help people not only to stay on course, but also make it easier to understand why they need to instigate a new approach in their communications.

"Your father describes, to some extent, what Claude and I are both already doing with people. Guilt and blame do destroy; he even describes how *'fathers and sons get bored waiting for the pot to boil.'* We think he's saying that these techniques have been in use for millennia but that as men advanced technologically, they couldn't be arsed with methods that didn't produce instant results. Makes sense based on my experience I have to say."

My mind wandered into the dangerous territory of self-recrimination; how many times had Helen begged me to be patient with the boys when they had done things wrong? I could now see how warped I had been to expect a five-year old or a three-year old to follow instructions, but I was determined to be the one who was 'right,' and believed they 'needed teaching.' I wanted them to be respectable, good, polite young men. I wanted them to know how to respond to instructions. Then they would get somewhere in life. They'd cope. They'd be acceptable.

"And how does any of this involve me? I mean, I haven't learnt your skills, and am not the brilliant listener that you two obviously are. Even if this stuff does all mean something, what am I supposed to do with it?" I was speaking as much from despair as anger. I was both confused at not knowing what all this meant, and angry that Claude and Helen had found some magical common ground to which I didn't think I could relate.

Claude spoke, calmly as ever.

"Alexander, don't do yourself down. You are a good listener. You have listened to your father's message and allowed it to speak to you. You listened to my crazy story about Père Varne; you've listened enough to yourself to book this Paris trip, and to risk your ex-wife's anger by bringing her over and allowing us all to meet. Maybe your listening skills have developed a little more than you realise…"

"And maybe" continued Helen, "maybe you are meant to develop them even more and show these contacts of yours in business and politics, who let's face it have the real power in this world, how to communicate with each other in a way that could demonstrate that there is hope for the human race. I'm not exaggerating here Alex, you know it's not one of my traits. I believe we may be standing on the threshold of rebirthing a system of communication that could end up filtering peace out through every layer of society. Claude and I have already started doing that, in our own way, at the grass roots level; with your leads, you could start much higher up.

"Alex, I know you well enough to realise that, if you grasp these concepts, and if we find whatever link or links may be missing to make this model complete, you have the standing and the ability to make a real impact. People do like you Alex; incredibly, I think most people who know you even still trust you. You've got something Alex, that can't be taught. You're an implausibly attractive human being. People want to see the best in you and, with our support, you can make a difference. And I think that's what your dad was trying to tell you when he made this recording."

To me these were all words, nice words some of them, particularly the *'implausibly attractive'* bit. But words nonetheless. It's true I had always felt I was here to do something 'special'. But that dream had been suffocated by the hands of time. I had occasionally connected with something inside when I'd watched a superhero movie or read of some daring deed in the papers, but that was as close as I ever came to thinking about doing anything to make a difference, at least until the breakdown. Then, through crisis, I did reconnect with that feeling, and that's why I started wanting to give something back.

The room remained silent while I contemplated what they had both said. It all threw up so many issues. What surprised me as I reflected on it was that, out of all the bizarre stuff that I had heard, the thing with which I had the biggest problem at that moment, was not whether Dada really had appeared in a vision with Père Varne; neither was it the question of whether his speech had truly come from some source of Divine wisdom. My biggest problem was with Helen's 'system,' the communication tool about which Claude and Helen were so excited.

"I don't understand the method you're talking about Helen. And if I'm going to be able to do anything with this, I'm going to need to be able to know what this magic bullet of yours is."

"Yes, I understand that Alex. And I'm going to teach you. I'll start teaching you every minute of every day that we spend any time together. I'll teach you on the phone, in the shops, in the restaurant tonight, at the airport tomorrow. I'll teach you what I have so far, so that you know it as well as I do. Claude has already helped me to understand a couple of things about it which make it even stronger, in particular in relation to silence. But, as I said earlier, I have had problems with some people either not wanting to put this system into place initially, or falling back into old patterns once they've begun, and then giving up on it because they think it doesn't work, which I know it does if you are patient. Quite often these problems have been with men – which is where you come in, Alex.

"Claude and I both think your father was encouraging us to share this with you so that you can help make it complete, and so that we can each take it out to the world. But we're missing something and we think you can help get the answer."

"Me? How?"

"This is going to be hard Alex, I know that. We'd like you to consider calling Thomas Jennings. Your dad said in the recording that the blind man holds the key to the first step. When I told Claude about what had happened to Tom, and how we'd seen him at the funeral, he instantly felt that this was the blind man your dad was talking about."

"Alexander, I have come to trust my intuition. As soon as Helen mentioned his name I felt the hairs go up on my arms. Somehow this man is important."

Thomas Jennings. My friend, blind Tom. How weird that it should be Tom's miraculous fundraising achievement that had sidelined Dada's television tribute. How weird that he should be at Dada's funeral. How weird that his name should be coming up now.

Or was it weird? Was it weird at all? Hadn't I known for the last few days that he was going to be re-entering my life in some way. Unfinished business. Was Claude's 'intuition' right? Was Thomas another part of the jigsaw puzzle that I had been - ironically - too blind to see?

"Yes, I saw your bit of paper Helen. And contacting him will be hard. But I knew when he called after the funeral that I had to talk to him. So, yes. The answer is yes. I'm prepared to learn everything you know and I'm prepared to talk to Tom. And I'm shit-scared too."

"Yes, Alex, meeting Tom will be hard."

"Oh, that's only part of it. What I'm really scared about is having you as a teacher, Helen."

The two of them smiled. Helen stood up, quickly followed by Claude who gave her a hug. They then turned to me. I stood up and joined them. A group hug; suddenly I was back in the scrum at Freestone on a freezing cold day in winter, Golly's right arm locked around me as his small but stocky frame stood its ground resolutely by my side. And now the tears that had been blocked earlier started to flow. Now my scrum was formed by Helen and Claude. It was a strangely uplifting experience. As we stood there, arms around each other, I could feel another part of my shell shattering.

We said our au revoirs to Claude and my training with Helen started within minutes, at breakfast with the boys. Helen ordered me to watch her closely, and in particular, to listen to how she was responding to them. I was not, under any circumstances, allowed to dive in with solutions if problems arose.

Eating out with Daniel and Joel had traditionally been something of a nightmare, particularly Joel, as his attention wandered off with frightening regularity. His school was beginning to raise this as a concern, but so far Helen had resisted all their attempts to make it into a serious problem, convincing them that she was as well placed as anyone to help improve things.

The small family hotel provided a simple continental breakfast every morning. Juice, croissants, coffee, some cereals. We were late down that morning. The boys were both shirty with each other as we sat down, Helen insisting that I sat opposite her at the small round table, leaving the two boys on either side of us. The boys' shortness of fuse was something that Helen had found happened whenever they started the day with television. One of her madcap theories had been that, according to 'research' she'd found somewhere, there was evidence to show that television causes alterations to the chemistry in the brain, and that some people, and children in particular, are more sensitive than others. Much as some people are more sensitive to alcohol or drugs than others. She'd been recently restricting Joel's input of telly, particularly once he went over the one hour mark, and reckoned she was already seeing the benefits. I can't say I had taken any of this too seriously.

"I don't want croissles again", said Joel. Croissles had become his favourite word in the French language in the last couple of days.

I jumped in without thinking about the deal we had just struck.

"No matter Joel, I'll see what..." I stopped as I had received a tap on my shin under the table. I looked at Helen, who remained calm and focussed on the breakfast things in front of her. She spoke with no trace of anger or frustration.

"Yes Joel, I understand, you don't want croissants again do you? You've had them two days running, are you fed up with them now?" Helen was talking to Joel while pouring herself some orange juice, there was no direct eye contact going on.

"Well, it's not that I hate them, I just don't want them that's all." Joel was fiddling with one of the boxes of cereal.

"Well, that's quite okay not to want them again. Can you see something else you'd like?" Helen was placidly getting on with her own breakfast. They were still not making eye contact.

"Not really."

"That's alright, Joel. Bear in mind that we've got a big day today and we might be doing a fair bit of sightseeing and some shopping, so you might want to make sure you've got something inside you. Can you pass the coffee Alex?"

Had I been in charge, I would probably have had the waiter over by now and would have ordered eggs on toast for Joel. I would certainly not have risked him going off for the morning without anything in his stomach. I had always thought that was bad parenting. Daniel picked up one of the croissants and was busy breaking it up and spreading it with butter and jam. Joel sat resolutely in his chair playing with the cereal box.

I was surprised at how much willpower it took on my behalf not to sort this out. It would have been so easy to get him something that he wanted. But I had made a promise to Helen and I remained silent. Even though this was such a petty thing, it took all my patience to stay out of the exchange.

No more than a minute later, Joel put his cereal box down and picked up one of the croissants. He broke it up, spread it with butter and jam and ate it in about four bites. He then took a second one and did the same thing. I wanted to say something like *'Oh, so you like them now hey?'*, or some other cute remark but held back. Helen said nothing. Even more impressively, Daniel said nothing either. I was painfully aware that, left to our own devices, Daniel and I would most probably have ended up making some jokey comment to Joel along the lines of *'told you so'* that would have backfired and resulted in a mini-scrap, or tears. And I wondered how many times someone had *'told me so'* in my life, and how much that might have contributed to the defences I had built up around the real me.

What hit me as well was that Helen did not so much as smirk in my direction. There was no desire to get one over on me or point out my failings. This was her system in action and although it was a relatively innocuous event, it was still one which could have led to a very different outcome and much more difficult start to our day. As it was, we all went up from breakfast with full tummies and no bad feelings.

I went back to my room and made a couple of notes. I wanted to start figuring this out for myself. What exactly had her role been in making that go so smoothly? There was no doubt that she managed the whole event. And very successfully. One thing that struck me was the eye contact thing. One of my rules as a parent had always been make direct eye contact with your child, particularly when you want to be certain as to whether they were telling the truth or not. But, now that I thought about it, I felt Helen had positioned us specifically so that if either of the boys looked straight ahead they would only see each other, rather than a parent.

She had also not tried to make everything alright for Joel. She hadn't rushed to the hotel staff demanding something that he would eat, which is certainly what I would have erred towards. I knew I had certainly been guilty in my life for trying to make things right for the boys, particularly since the divorce. It had been easy to appease them with the breakfast they *did* want, or the new football boots or computer game. However, I had also become acutely aware that not only did the effects of that appeasing seem to be more and more short-lived, but it also was the source of greater disagreements between Helen and me.

The divorce proceedings had hurt me financially, but I had still managed to retain an economic advantage over Helen and I had been guilty of using that from time to time to try to secure the boys continuing affection. It was only recently that I had started to see that, ultimately, this worked against me even more than it did Helen, creating as it did a raised level of expectation in Daniel and Joel that was becoming harder and harder to satisfy. This in turn had led to feelings of great disappointment for them both in the last couple of years as I had felt less able and willing to take them on expensive treats in order to maintain their loyalty. This spoiling had probably only started with an extra two pounds pocket money or a new football, but it had grown over the years into adventure park trips, short holidays and expensive, and generally unappreciated, meals out. And each time they returned from a weekend with me with tales of financial exuberance, Helen had had to deal all alone with her anger, resentment and fear that the boys would end up liking me more because I spent more money on treats for them. In the early days of the separation she used to rage at me on the phone when the boys were asleep. But, as time had gone on, I noticed that she called me less and less to vent her frustrations at me, even if I had just taken them both to another rugby game or football match.

There was a light tapping at the door. It was Joel. To me, he seemed much smaller than usual, being out of his normal context and in a strange hotel.

"We're nearly ready Dada, are you?"

"Yes, yes I am thanks Joel. I'll just brush my teeth and I'll come and join you in your room. Did you enjoy your breakfast?"

"Yep. Can I hang around until you're ready?"

"Of course. Here, why don't you count the Euros in my wallet?" I threw him my wallet which he caught easily. He had amazing reactions for a boy considered to have attention problems. I was pleased he wanted to stay with me. I brushed my teeth, got my jacket and made ready to leave.

"Four hundred and sixty seven Euros seventy."

I was impressed. He had a natural affinity with numbers and had totted up my total in no time and got it absolutely spot on.

"Another thirty five and you'd have five hundred." Ah well, not that good, yet.

"No Joel, another thirty two Euros and thirty cents and I'd have five hundred"

Joel quickly put some coins in his pocket.

"Not if you've given me two Euros and seventy for counting your money." A smiled beamed across his face and I had to laugh. He was a cheeky boy with a great sense of humour and I'd walked straight into his trap.

"You little…"

Helen and Daniel walked into the room. Helen looked straight at me.

"Are you ready?"

"Once Joel gives me my wallet back I am."

Joel gave me the wallet, keeping the coins in his pocket. I winked at him and he gave me an endearingly inept wink back.

"Let's go."

The sun had decided to grace us once more in Paris that morning. Helen had wanted to do things according to the weather, and so we started by taking the metro to Montmartre, where we took the funicular up to the Nineteenth Century church which maintains its careful watch over Paris. I wondered whether the church had been positioned in particular to cast its lengthy shadow over the familiar red light district of Pigalle below; or had someone decided to stick two fingers up at God by developing the Paris sex centre under His very nose?

Outside the church, tourists and sightseers were already crowding. Most people stopped and leant on the railings to take in the staggering views of the city. We must have been there at least thirty seconds before Joel started moaning.

"I'm bored."

This time it was Daniel's turn to beat Helen to it.

"But Joel, we've only just got here."

Helen remained serenely looking out over Paris, Joel behind her, tugging on her black jeans.

"It can seem boring Joel can't it, when you're doing things that you don't necessarily want to do?"

Joel remained quiet. Helen continued to look at the view.

"Yeah. Look Mumma, they've got a telescope. Can I have some money?" Joel had recovered from his boredom surprisingly quickly. I was watching all this and had my own idea.

"Hey Joel, your pocket, remember?" And I winked at him as I had in the bedroom earlier when he'd pocketed the extra change. He smiled back and came and grabbed my hand.

"Come on Dada, show me how it works."

I went with him to the telescope and helped him put in his change. He only got a minute or so on it, but he had forgotten his boredom.

"Hey Daniel this is so cool, you've got to try it."

And before long we were all queuing up for a go on the telescope that Joel had found and, initially at least, paid for. I could tell he was proud of himself.

"Where're we going next Mumma?"

I was beginning to grasp the first step of Helen's model. Twice Joel had started to kick up, and history had shown me that on both occasions this could have easily become a downward spiral. Potentially lousy foundations on which to build our last day in Paris. On both occasions, Helen had simply acknowledged what he had said, and this had been enough for Joel to respond positively. She hadn't changed her actions to suit him; she had merely heard what he had said. Ah, yes, she had listened to him. Really listened to him. And he had felt that. So bloody simple when you think about it. Yet why, oh why, did it seem so difficult to do?

The rest of the morning was spent wandering around the Latin quarter. After visiting the Pantheon, we had lunch in one of the hundreds of little bistros that line the pavements of Paris. Both the boys had been complaining of being tired of walking and I was beginning to be able to anticipate Helen's responses.

'Yes Daniel, it's tiring wandering around a new city isn't it? Shall we sit down at the next bench we find?' and *'I know you want to go home now Joel; do you think the airline will let us on the plane if our tickets say tomorrow instead of today?'*

What was impressive about the way she delivered her responses was that she never sounded patronising. And the boys got to sit down, or talk through whether airlines would accept wrongly dated tickets, and as a consequence felt heard and valued, even if the result didn't go the way they thought that they wanted. It was eye-opening.

For the rest of the day I acted partly on auto-pilot as I watched how Helen dealt with the intermittent protests, complaints and squabbles that inevitably go with the territory of children. Not once did I hear her dismiss either of the boys' concerns. She listened to them, often repeating back to them their words as she had heard them. *'You really don't want to go any further without a rest do you Daniel?' 'It hurts when you walk into a glass door doesn't it Joel?' 'It's hard when your dad says you can have a new pair of trainers but you can't find any that you like that fit.'*

Normally I learnt theory-based things in seminars and from books. Of course, I had learnt loads on the job so to speak early on, but these days I was more often in the role of teacher than pupil. If I wanted to expand my knowledge-base, I had assumed it was up to me to attend the right events or buy the right publication. But here was Helen, demonstrating to me in practical terms, and amidst the mayhem and excitement of one of the world's greatest cities, this very simple step towards transforming potentially confrontational situations. Helen, my former wife who, for some reason, I had let slip through my fingers. Helen, the woman who I had never known how to love, because, the truth is that I never knew how to love at all.

I could feel a part of me wanting her to be wrong, and I almost wanted one of the boys to throw a tantrum in reaction to her calm, measured approach. But it didn't happen. She just continued hearing them and asking them questions and eventually the boys ran out of reasons to keep whingeing. Sometimes one of them really needed to be angry, such as when Joel found trainers but Daniel still hadn't. Trust the cause of the greatest problem of the afternoon to be related to me; a promise I had made to both of them, unbeknownst to Helen until that afternoon, about getting new trainers *from Paris*.

"It's not fair, they're just the ones I want but they haven't got them in my size."

I dropped my guard, having been the one who had made the offer in the first place.

"We'll find another store that's got them, Daniel, don't you worry."

Daniel was quick to take me on.

"But what if we don't? How do you know we'll find another store?"

"I promise we'll find another store. Don't you worry about that."

"But you never keep your promises. Does he Mumma?"

Checkmate. Daniel stormed off out of the shop and I was about to run after him when I felt an arm on my shoulder.

"It's a bummer when one of the children is upset isn't it?"

Oh crap, she was doing it on me now. And damn it, it felt good.

"It's okay Alex, let him go. How far is he going to go? He's in Paris for heaven's sake. He just needs to let off steam, so let him. Stop trying to make it alright. It's not alright, Daniel knows it; and he also knows there might not be another pair of shoes in his size in the shops we get to this afternoon, despite the fact that his father is promising that there will be. You used to promise all sorts of things Alex but you didn't deliver. Your promises don't mean so much to them any more. And all these promises do is put pressure on you anyway. So let go of them, okay? Let Daniel be upset."

Let Daniel be upset? Why was that such an alien concept? I looked at Joel who had been quiet throughout the Daniel episode. His face had turned from one of triumph to one of seriousness.

"I wish Daniel could have these. I'm not that bothered about new trainers anyway." For such a young boy, Joel's level of compassion and sensitivity was striking. He had always been like that. In spite of his occasional attention problems, his caring for others was immense. His being unbothered about new trainers, and Daniel's problem with not getting what he wanted, made me realise that maybe my gifts weren't gifts at all, but burdens. I thought back to the holidays I had as a child and the presents that Dada brought me back from his trips. Did any of them mean that much to me? Hadn't I just wanted time and attention? Had I ever asked for stuff? I hadn't, but Dada rated it as important, and I made his story mine. I became 'Stuff Man Two'. And my boys were beginning to demonstrate the side-effects of that same education.

I had finished paying when Daniel reappeared beside us in the small boutique. His eyes were red from crying.

"I'm sorry, Dada."

His apology floored me. I was the one who needed to apologise. For years of screwed up promises. For years of conditioning him and Joel, albeit quite subtly, that if they didn't have stuff, they couldn't be happy. For years of teaching them both that one of the most important jobs a father can do is keep the new things rolling in. For teaching them both that the pain of lack is not acceptable and can, and should, always be removed by the instant and relentless pursuit of the goal. For not allowing them to experience disappointment, and therefore how to go beyond disappointment to find relief. For not allowing them to experience real life.

Helen had not said anything to Daniel. She hadn't panicked, hadn't run out after him. She had just allowed him to do the one thing that I had been too scared to allow either of them to do; to feel the frustration that comes when things don't work out as anticipated.

"Joel, they're really cool trainers. I'm glad you found them." There was warmth in Daniel's voice as he spoke. Joel smiled and the four us walked back towards the hotel. Daniel never got his trainers that afternoon and neither did he utter another word of complaint. He sat far more willingly in his pain than I ever had; and, for once, I let him.

When we got back to our rooms, Helen and the boys went into theirs, and I returned to my single room and lay down on the bed. The last time I had been here, I had been meeting with Helen and Claude. When I had committed to learn everything I could from Helen about her system, I hadn't realised that for my first lesson, all we needed to do was to go out en famille. It was the best way of learning and observing, because it was real. I had learnt today that when a problem arises, I was to use validations and questions as a starting point. Helen hadn't given me any direct instruction, I had just been meant to learn from her example. And I now had the first step, or at least the first step of her system. Dada had suggested that the blind man had the key to the first step. Was it the first step to this communication model? Was there something missing? I shut my eyes.

I must have fallen asleep because I started to dream. I was in a plane. It had a familiar feel to it, as though I'd been there before. Out of the cockpit area came the pilot, who was an elephant. He came up to me and spoke. The plane started to dip dramatically. His voice was quiet and calm.

"Your memory is like a vast cupboard, Alexander. We never forget things, we just hide things. Give up trying to pretend life didn't happen. It's okay. Listen to the prophet, he knows. Ask the blind man. Pain is the breaking of the shell that encloses our understanding."

And with that, he disappeared, the plane once again correcting itself. I looked out of the window and there pressed up against my window again was the blind man. It was Thomas.

And then as quickly as it had begun, the dream was over. There was a knock at the door. It was Helen. My perception of her was changing rapidly, and today had raised my levels of respect to new heights.

"Hi Alex, sorry, did I wake you?"

"It's okay, I was dreaming."

"Anything interesting?"

"No, no just bonkers stuff with elephants and planes. So how are you after that day out with the boys?"

Helen was wearing a purple sleeveless vest and white, wide-leg linen turn ups. She sat down on the edge of the bed. She looked so alive.

"Great. So. What did you make of today? Did you learn anything?"

Did I learn anything? They were words which once would have sent me running for cover behind my shell. A woman asking me if I had learnt anything. But things were changing. I had changed. I no longer felt patronised by her. Was that because she had changed the way she spoke or had I changed the way I listened? Maybe it was both. Maybe we had both grown up a bit.

"Yes. Yes I did learn something. I learnt a lot today. My mind is sort of reeling at it, probably because so far, it seems so simple. And yet the results; well, at least with our boys, were quite significant. Time and again you gave them permission to have their feelings and each time they came out of their pits of despair of their own accord. One question though." I was still harbouring something about the trainers and I needed to share it.

"Why didn't you shut me up when I made the promise about the shoes?"

"You were too quick Alex. You jumped in. The only way I could have done anything at that point would have meant embarrassing you in front of the boys, basically by taking over. I didn't want to do that. I knew Daniel would get over it, and maybe it was good for you to observe the difference between trying to make things right for them and just accepting that sometimes things don't work out exactly as we want."

Ouch. But damn it, she was right. I had probably learnt as much from screwing up that particular opportunity as I had from observing Helen for the rest of the day. I hadn't liked the result, or the feelings I experienced, and I would certainly think twice before diving in again with my promises.

"At least it has given you a good chance to grasp the first step of the system. If you learn to become the world's greatest listener, which you can do by continually validating others and using subtle questions- not inquisition style stuff - you'll find yourself able to transform a sizeable percentage of problems without taking any further action. It can sound far-fetched to say you can solve a problem just by listening, but it's true. Very often, through allowing someone else to express their anger or pain or frustration, you lance the boil. Questions can sometimes help to release any residual angst, and that may be all that is necessary.

"The greatest challenge people have to meet in order to apply the system sustainably, is in learning how to avoid the temptation of falling back into fix mode. For instance, you patiently watched me listening and validating the boys all day today, but then you jumped back into your habitual problem-solving father role with Daniel and the trainers. Okay, so you're very new to this. But this is where my clients struggle too. Remembering not to sort everything out just because things seem a little calmer, or they have acquired a bit more information and can suddenly see a solution."

"So you think the model can be improved?"

"Oh God yes, Alex. Why wouldn't I think that? Things can always be improved, and if that makes this tool easier to use, then bring it on." Her humility was humbling. How different we were. Was this a Helen/Alex thing or a man/woman thing? If I had developed a system over a matter of years, would I be open to other people's ideas to help improve it? Would I be interested if getting an improved result meant getting other people involved, or would I preserve the status quo, and hang onto one hundred percent ownership? *'That's mine, leave it alone.'*

"Can you make any money out of this Helen?"

Helen said nothing. She just looked at me with raised eyebrows waiting for me to continue with my train of thought. I felt like I'd dragged an angel into a grubby bargain basement.

"Well, I mean, this is good. It might have some applications in business if we could get our heads around it. I was just wondering whether you have it set out in some sort of template form?"

"Alex, I hear you. I know you well enough to know that your brain is immediately going to be looking for the business possibilities here, and there's nothing wrong with that. First of all though, it's important that you thoroughly get to know the steps we have, and then help us to complete the framework. There's something missing here; Claude and I both feel that, and we're certain your father was trying to help us to find the link."

"Alex, have you thought any more about Tom?"

Oh God, Tom again. Could I never escape this haunting figure from the past? Was I destined to be terrorised by his face in dreams, his name on people's lips, for the rest of my life?

"Sort of. Actually I was dreaming about him when you came in. I was in a plane and he was on the outside pressed up against the window."

Helen had inched a bit nearer to me on the bed.

"Well, did you manage to get him in? What happened?"

"You knocked on the bloody door is what happened."

Helen laughed. It was like having a fairy flying around the room sprinkling magic dust everywhere. Things changed. I started to laugh too. And at the same time as I was laughing, my heart started to grieve for all the opportunities I had missed down the years to have this magic as a regular part of my life. Why had I shut her out and therefore ultimately punished myself so much?

Before long, we were both laughing so much that tears were rolling down our cheeks. Another part of the shell was smashing and I liked it. I looked up from drying my eyes to see the boys standing by the door. I don't know when they had last seen their parents laugh like this, but before long they had joined us on the bed and they started laughing too. And we sat there and lay there, each of us in our different positions, laughing away. Half the room not knowing why. And as we laughed, so we began to make up for the years of lost joy out of which we had all been cheated.

28

Our marriage happened as quickly as the engagement. Once we'd got the engagement part out of the way, there seemed no point in delaying the wedding either. Helen was adamant that she didn't want a big fuss; she was estranged from her father and her mother had died when she was seventeen. And my parents and I were set on such independent courses these days that I didn't think they'd care. After all, it was only a marriage. And so it was, that by eating into our holiday allowances a little more, we took seven days out and flew to St Kitts where we were married on the beach by a rather large black woman with the whimsical name of Lorna Love, and with bikini-clad twin sisters as witnesses.

And that was it. Possibly the single most important event of my life all done and dusted in a manner of minutes amongst an audience of total strangers. Just like the engagement.

The rest of the honeymoon passed too quickly. Looking back, I can't help feeling that I arranged the whole thing just to escape from the uncomfortable feeling I had about the whole Sunsure, Tang and FiveStar deal. Steve hadn't said anything directly to me but word had got out about Tang's investment in the Croatian group and there were whispers that the FiveStar board were far from happy at missing out on this project. Especially with a recession biting and everyone looking for a reasonably safe place for their spare cash. Apparently Eastern Europe, and Croatia in particular, was thought to be a good opportunity.

What I noticed in particular during that all too brief window of heaven, or rather what I noticed once Helen had pointed it out, was that for the first time for years I was beginning to relax. And I don't mean the relaxing vibe I used to feel after a joint, a fag or a stiff drink; I mean a relaxation that came out of not pushing myself like a madman, and out of not having to be someone other than who I was. And who I was during that week, was a bloke beginning to realise that he was with the woman of his dreams.

After four days I felt like I was moving at about half-speed, and yet it felt right. The biggest decisions that faced me were issues such as *'shall we stay in bed for another hour, or get up and go and lie on the beach?'* Helen told me she noticed a change in my breathing, and once she had drawn my attention to this, I began to notice it myself. It wasn't something of which I had ever been conscious. Breathing? I'd always thought it simply happened, and when it didn't you were no longer. I remember lying on the beach alongside Helen the day before we came home, calypso music playing at a bar nearby, the Caribbean lapping just a few yards away from our sun beds, and my breathing reaching a state of such sublime effortlessness that I felt connected to everything. This was a hallucinogenic experience without the drugs.

In some ways it was a scary feeling, and not something I had ever experienced before without the use of some sort of intoxicant. But then I hadn't realised, at that point in my life, that the states of being blissfully happy and at peace are the scariest that a driven, fearful, guilt-ridden, non-feeling person can ever experience. It was as if the little Alexander who lived inside me, who up to that point had been madly driving everything in his attempt to stamp his mark upon history, suddenly found himself plunged headlong into a world of sunshine, deep blue sea and multi-coloured fish where judgements of any sort didn't exist. There was no ladder of success heading off up into the clouds; there was no right or wrong; there was only *being* in it and accepting the majesty of it all. And little Alexander had no point of reference as to how to deal with that.

Everything merged into some sort of soft-focus, boundary-less utopia. I closed my eyes, the music played on, I opened my eyes, Helen went in and out of the azure sea, I closed my eyes, the music played on and the bliss continued. If I had a chance in my life to hit the freeze button so that I could have remained in one particular window in my life, then this would have been that time.

But little me wasn't so sure; as the time passed, which I assumed it had, a mild sense of unease grew. How could I lie there and relax when there were possible problems with FiveStar? How could I lie there, married now to the night-nurse of my dreams, knowing I had already broken my vows not to lie and not to smoke? What made me think I was allowed to experience such joy when I was not deserving of it at all?

"Alex – aren't you coming in for a dip? You've been lying there for ages. The water's beautiful." Helen was leaning over me, her petite and already bronzed outline blocking out the sun. I couldn't answer. I wanted to speak but I had no words. Big me wanted to rush into the water with my new wife. Little me was shouting out that I didn't deserve it.

"Alex? Are you okay? Have you had too much sun?"

I still couldn't speak. I just lay there, like a vegetable, looking up at Helen and wanting to say yes and also knowing that I had to say no. My heart, having been so at peace previously, had started racing. I started to feel dizzy. I decided to take action and started to stand up. I didn't make it.

Next thing I knew I was in our bedroom, lying on my back on the four-poster bed that graced our sumptuous honeymoon suite. Standing over me with a stethoscope was a black man in a blue and white flowery shirt and black trousers. Sitting on the end of the bed was Helen.

"Welcome back Mr Baker. How are you feeling?"

How was I feeling? I really didn't know.

"Fine, thanks. Well, you know, a bit woozy. What happened?"

"You fainted Alex. Completely blacked out. Sunstroke. I told you you'd been in that sun for too long."

"Yes Mr Baker, you're not used to our Mother Sun. She's a powerful beauty. Take a couple of these tablets, drink plenty of water, and don't overdo it for the next couple of days."

"Doctor, we're travelling back tomorrow – will he be okay for that?"

"Oh I'm sure he will. Maybe he's done enough sunning for the moment huh? You look after yourself Mr Baker – or rather, let your beautiful wife look after you." The nameless hotel doctor left our room. Helen came and curled up beside me.

"You scared me Alex. Have you ever had anything like that before?"

I tried to think. Had I? What was *that*? Was it just sunstroke as the doctor had suggested? Or was there some other cause, linked to the struggle I'd had allowing myself to experience the bliss of that afternoon?

"Sunstroke you mean? No, Helen, I don't think I've ever gone through anything like that."

I lay there, Helen cuddled up beside me, in the honeymoon suite on the beautiful island of St Kitts, wondering whether I was already on borrowed time. This wasn't only sunstroke. I didn't know what it was, but I felt sure the sun had served only to aggravate the symptoms. This was a deeper disquiet that had been developing over time. As things panned out, its true nature would not be fully recognised for years more to come.

It seems odd to say that coming back from the honeymoon was something of a relief. But in a way it was. I was back into the world I could understand; the world of doing, dealing, fixing, sorting, rushing. There was no time to dwell on thoughts or feelings, and bliss became more of a brief encounter that happened from time to time in bed with Helen, than the expanded state of consciousness that I had experienced on the beach in St Kitts.

My father had met Helen once at this stage; my mother hadn't met her at all. I hadn't thought too much about what either of them would have to say about our marriage, which I suppose was naïve, but I didn't feel under any obligation to tell them. In part, I guess I was exercising my rights as they had exercised theirs to keep me in the dark regarding their divorce proceedings, leaving me the child of a split family.

Helen and I decided to tell them both in person the weekend after our return. We chose my mother first who was then living an hour and a half out of London. On the Saturday afternoon we got into my pride and joy, a silver 325 BMW, and drove down to her house in Winchester. I hadn't seen my mother for at least three months. Our relationship continued to be frosty at best; I had withdrawn from her many years ago now and still struggled with the idea of her being a lesbian. I had warned Helen, who had responded as if it was no big deal, which I thought a little churlish. However she did have the compassion to say that it must have been very hard for me to find that out as a teenager, and in the way that I did.

Mother had long since split up with the first 'other' woman I had seen her kissing that evening all those years ago. She had by now been living with her partner Jenny for several years. Jenny was an acupuncturist with a practice in Harley Street, which I could not help finding impressive. My mother was also into some form of alternative health, although I knew even less about what she did than I knew about Jenny.

We had been invited to stay for dinner and for the night. I felt uncomfortable with this – I wasn't at all sure I could deal with sleeping in the same house as my mother and her female partner. Helen however, had been adamant that if we were invited then we ought to accept, and I should just start learning to deal with it. And so, with our overnight bags packed in the boot, and U2, Springsteen and Bob Seger for company, we sang our way down through some light Saturday afternoon traffic to Winchester.

When we arrived I was feeling a buzz from having had a chance to enjoy the car, an opportunity that London life didn't always afford. Helen looked well and tanned from the honeymoon and seemed relaxed after our journey, if somewhat hoarse. I decided to ride the surf that I was still on from the driving, and rather than taking the bags out of the car first, I went straight to the front door, Helen beside me.

The door opened and the familiar figure of my mother appeared at the door.

"Alexander – at last!" She gave me a hug which I received with some awkwardness.

"And you must be Helen. What a pleasure to meet you. Come in, come in."

"I'll just go and get our bags."

Helen disappeared with my mother into the house and I returned to the BMW to get the cases. When I got back into the house, they were both in the kitchen, already chatting away.

"So, congratulations my dears. When did you do the deed?"

I looked at Helen who silently shook her head.

"How did you know?" I wasn't sure whether I was cross with her for stealing my thunder, or surprised that she knew.

"Oh come on, Alexander. When do you ever bring any girlfriends to meet me, let alone stay? Besides, I might be getting older but my eyes still work." She pointed to the ring on Helen's finger. "May I have a proper look?"

Helen moved closer and reached out her finger. My mother took Helen's hand in hers and looked at the ring.

"Beautiful. Simple and elegant."

Just like Helen. Beautiful, simple - meaning not complicated - and elegant. My mother reached into the fridge and pulled out a bottle of champagne that she had chilling. She'd even put some glasses in the freezer which had frosted perfectly. I put down the bags and we took the glasses and champagne out onto her patio and sat out in the afternoon sunshine.

"Where's Jenny?" I asked hesitantly, I suppose partly hoping that my mother might say '*Oh, I'm not one of those any more, I split up with her.*'

"I had a feeling we might need some time together first. I asked her to join us for supper."

I popped open the bubbly. Mother raised a toast to our future happiness.

I finished my champagne and took the bags upstairs to the still relatively unfamiliar spare room in which I had stayed no more than a dozen times. I had left Helen telling mother all about the proposal on the Eiffel Tower; they seemed comfortable with each other already. I couldn't work out if I resented the fact Helen that seemed to be more at ease with her than I.

I lay down on the bed and shut my eyes for a minute. Outside through the open window I could hear the murmur of their voices below on the patio. I noticed that if I concentrated hard I could make out what they were saying.

"Please Helen, I may be your mother-in-law but do call me Elizabeth from now on, okay?"

"Okay – Elizabeth. You know, Alex and I hardly know each other, and yet here we are married. I still can't quite believe it."

"You certainly didn't hang around, so I can understand why you find it hard to believe. As for knowing each other - when can you say that you really know anyone?"

'*When can you say that you really know anyone?*' That sounded rich coming from my mother. Certainly the woman who my father thought she was throughout their marriage turned out to be someone else entirely.

As they talked on, their voices either became quieter, or my need for sleep overtook me, because those were the last words I heard until I was woken by a gentle thigh squeeze. I turned on to my side to find Helen lying beside me. She was smiling.

"What is it with you and your mother? She's fantastic. And my God does she love you. How come we don't see her more often – is it really just because she's got a female partner?"

I wanted to say it was a long story; I wanted to talk about the years and years of torment that had followed the revelation about my mother's sexuality; I wanted to justify why it was that I had shut her out of my life so completely. But I could summon neither the will nor the words and Helen didn't press me. She just lay there, one arm round my waist, and her eyes peering into me on their way to finding the furthest secret reaches of my universe.

Supper that evening was a one-sided affair. I was outnumbered by women, and found myself horribly out of my depth amidst conversations ranging from simple issues such as how to create the perfect union of the mind, body and spirit to more vexing topics such as which film star had undergone the most plastic surgery. They tried to involve me, but I found it more comfortable to act as occasional waiter and dish-washer. Jenny was, much to my chagrin, perfectly charming and did nothing at all which could excite my continued disapproval.

After dinner, and at Helen's request, mother got the dreaded photo albums out. It's one of those moments that I think every child both loves and dreads. The delight of a new partner going '*ah, wasn't he sweet, so cute*' , and the torment of becoming a boy again, wondering whether she'll ever see you in the same light, and whether her own picture of your past marries up with the one she is now seeing in real form.

The albums were not in any particular order and the tour started with a few pictures of my time at Freestone. I suddenly wondered about their divorce and how they divided up things like photo albums. What would they have agreed? In the state their relationship was in, it was hard to imagine Dada saying '*You have them this year, and I'll have them next.*'

"So who are these three, Alex? The one on the right is cute." Helen was smiling as she asked.

I looked at the photo. It had been taken in our dorm, probably in about year four.

"Okay, these were my dorm mates. That's Matthew Dyer on the left, then Andrew Percival and the guy on the right is Claude Denoir. He's French. I'd never thought of him as cute though."

"Ooh, better not introduce him to me – French and cute. What a perfect combination."

I hadn't thought about Claude for a long time. In fact I had lost touch altogether with my Freestone days. Apart from that chance meeting in Helsinki with Jessica. Ah Jessica, if only you knew who I'd married. That would shut you up.

"And who's this with you here?"

I looked down and saw Golly's cheerful face staring up at me. We had just finished a rugby match and we were covered in mud. We had our arms around each other's shoulders. I felt a lump in my throat and an aching in my gut. Golly. My best mate. My only real mate that I could remember. What had happened to him? Oh yes, that's right. He died.

"I called him Golly. We were pretty close actually."

"And where's Golly now?"

I wasn't prepared for how much this simple question hurt. It was like I had a clamp around the answer but the answer was so desperate to escape that it was going to burst through my defences anyway, whatever the cost to my sanity.

My mother intervened.

"James, or Golly as we all knew him, died in a road accident one night in London when he was on his way to meet Alexander at Leicester Square."

Helen suddenly became very quiet. The atmosphere in the room changed almost instantly from one of mellow, post-dinner and champagne fuzziness to one of awkwardness and discomfort. At least, that was my perception of it.

"That must have been really hard for you Alex. How old were you both?"

"Seventeen." And then I felt the clamp ease back into place and I continued with the speech I had once known so well. "Yes, well, these things happen. You have to get on with life though. I don't think I've let it change me."

"Is that good?" Helen was looking directly at me. It was a look I had experienced before when she had asked me to make my promise about no drugs or lying.

"Is what good?"

Helen was not going to give this up without an answer.

"Is it good that the death of one of your closest friends hasn't changed you?"

My mother was sitting on the other side of me, remaining quiet. Jenny was out clearing up in the kitchen and making coffee.

"Well Alex, is it good?"

I didn't have the capacity to answer the question. My mind went back to the beach on the honeymoon and how I couldn't speak. I started to panic that the same thing was going to happen here, in front of my mother and Jenny. I quickly made an excuse that I needed the loo.

I sat on the loo for at least five minutes trying to regain composure. What was it with these questions? Why did they cause me to get into such a state? Was it good that I hadn't let Golly's death change me? I didn't know. I didn't have the first idea what the correct answer to that question should have been.

When I got back into the room, they had started on another album. Jenny was back in the room and I found some relief in sitting opposite her in one of the armchairs and hearing about acupuncture, while Helen and my mother flipped through more pictures. After about another thirty minutes, I felt relaxed enough again to go and sit with them on the couch and answer Helen's continuing questions about the identity of various characters in my former lives.

"So, what happens before Hebbingdon? Which album is that? I'd love to see him in his first school uniform." Helen's genuine interest was flattering.

"Oh we haven't got any pictures of him at his previous school. We just never got round to it somehow."

It had never struck me as strange until that moment. The funny thing was, there were pictures of me when I was a baby, when I was a toddler and when I went to Hebbingdon. But in-between, there was a whole chapter of my life missing. Why weren't there pictures of me at my first school? And what was it called? And why did I leave it? Dada took pictures all the time, why wouldn't he have taken pictures of me then?

Helen made nothing of it and shortly afterwards we all decided it was bedtime. But I was not comfortable with the realisation that part of my life had been wiped clean. As I climbed into bed that night I felt her warm body climb in behind me, nestling up against my back in the way we both loved.

"Alex - don't you think it's odd that there're no pictures of you at your first school?"

I shut my eyes. Images flashed across my mind. Vulcan. Superman. A shed. Screaming. Fire. The police. A new house. A new school. A new life.

On the Sunday morning we had breakfast before packing our bags and saying goodbye to my mother and Jenny. I had, reluctantly, warmed to Jenny a little on this visit, which may have had something to do with Helen's accepting presence. I still struggled when it came to hugging my mother at the car, but noticed her give Helen a very warm embrace.

"Helen, it has been a real pleasure to meet you. Alexander, make sure you treat your wife as you'd like to be treated."

I reversed the car out onto the quiet private road and glanced over to the house to see my mother standing alongside Jenny in the drive, waving us off. Why couldn't I just accept it? Helen seemed to. What made me so bloody rigid?

"So, you never told me Elizabeth was so fascinating. And you look so like her; you've even got her long eyelashes, you lucky boy."

Lucky boy.' That sounded familiar. How many times had I been told that I was a lucky boy by my parents as I had grown up? If I was so lucky, how did all this luck show itself? I hadn't seen any clear signs of luck. Having a private education wasn't luck, it was part of the great plan to shape me into a man. Losing my best friend wasn't luck, not good luck anyway. Being the son of divorced parents wasn't luck. Owning this BMW wasn't luck, it was down to bloody hard work. Marrying and honeymooning in St Kitts wasn't down to luck, it was down to doing a bit of a cheeky deal. A calculated, or not very calculated, risk.

We arrived at my father's house a couple of hours later. The Sunday morning traffic was heavy around the M25 and, as we came into Notting Hill, there had been an accident quite near to his house, which slowed us down again. As we sat in the queue near to his house, we just had time to hear Springsteen's *Hungry Heart*:

"Like a river that don't know where its flowing,
I took a wrong turn and I just kept going"

Those words jumped out at me as if I had never heard them before. Up ahead the cars crawled along, while Bruce and the boys kept on playing. The ambulance pulled away leaving a small crowd of onlookers and little else – there was no sign of any smashed-up cars. But my mind was stuck on two lines of lyrics, words that replayed themselves over and over.

The song came to an end precisely as we pulled up outside the house. Those sorts of coincidences made me smile, often making me wonder if there wasn't some cosmic genius at work after all, pulling the strings of a billion different situations to make sure that, wherever possible, there was a tidy conclusion.

"Helen, probably best if you don't mention that you liked my mother so much. I'm not sure he's quite ready to hear that."

Helen nodded.

"What makes you think I would be so insensitive, anyway? I know this has been hard for your dad."

We went up to the front door and I rang the bell. There was no reply. Strange, he knew we were coming. I went around the back and through the side gate into the garden. I looked through the French doors and could hear the radio playing inside. So he was there then, somewhere. Probably in the loo.

I banged with my fist on the French doors – the glass rattled in its old metal frames which were in need of a coat of paint. Nothing. I started to get a little nervous, a feeling that something wasn't right. This time I ran round the front again to see if Helen had found any sign of him.

As I turned the corner towards the front garden, a middle aged woman was hurrying up the drive.

"You must be Alexander." She was breathing heavily, clearly being someone unused to running.

"I'm Joyce, darling, I live across the road in seventy-four. I've known your dad for a while. Listen lovey, he's just collapsed down the road. The ambulance has taken him straight off to hospital. I was out walking with my hubby, we saw everything. He fell and dropped his papers and magazines - he must have been popping back from the newsagents. We put the bag back in the ambulance with him.

"He was conscious when he was put on the stretcher and he asked me to look out for you and tell you. They're taking him to St Mary's."

I had no tools for dealing with this. I suddenly felt like I had been abandoned at school again and that any moment Mr Gardiner would appear to start his job of fathering me all over again. But he didn't. And he didn't need to. I'd married a nurse, and Helen stepped quickly into the role.

"Thanks Joyce. I'm Helen by the way. Alex, get in the passenger seat. I'll drive." She was in the driver's seat quicker than I could even think. Joyce stood there, looking as shocked as I felt. I staggered round to the passenger's seat and sat down. Helen already had the car running.

"Hang on a minute Helen." I had just remembered the radio in the house. I found my spare key which I once used so regularly, and let myself into the house. It was alive with his energy, his smells. It was Sunday morning and whatever radio station he was playing had Frank Sinatra crooning away to the music of 'New York, New York.' He'd be sorry to be missing it. Why I thought I needed to turn the radio off I have no idea – one of those compulsive thoughts, bits of tidying up, action to take, that your mind latches onto in moments of shock.

Funny thing was, once I'd heard what they were playing, I thought it wrong to switch off Frankie in his prime. Was that what was going to happen to my father? Was he to be switched off? I didn't want to tempt providence, so I left the house to be entertained by my father's favourite.

It took us about twenty minutes to get to the hospital. Helen was in her element, this was her territory. She'd even worked at St Mary's a couple of times on short stints so she knew the layout. She had a way of talking to the staff that only a fellow nurse could have. Direct and friendly; not like a consultant, all unapproachable and demanding. But clear and not panicked.

"Your dad is going to have some tests, Alex." It felt weird hearing her call him dad and my mother mum. I used to call them similar names but something had changed somewhere along the way and now I always referred to them as mother and father. It hadn't really struck me until I started hearing Helen being much more familiar with them.

"He just blacked out. He had this bag of stuff with him. It must have been what he was bringing home. Sunday papers I think. You can go in and see him in a few minutes, when they're done. I'm just off to the loo."

I sat down on the cold plastic seat in the A&E department. I pulled out the papers from the bag and the supplements fell out of the middle. As I reached to put them back in the bag I noticed a woman's naked behind pointing out of the corner of one of the magazines. There weren't many people around but I still felt incredibly conspicuous. I carefully brought the whole pile closer to my face and slid out the magazine in question. It was, as I dreaded, a pornographic magazine. Oh God. In his early sixties and my father was still buying porn mags.

I quickly slipped it back inside the magazines, just in time as Helen reappeared.

"That was quick, darling."

Helen looked confused. I had no idea whether she had been quick or not, but needed to say something.

"Was it? Oh well, there you go. Cup of tea?"

"Yes, yes that would be great. Thank you so much."

She came over to me and knelt down in front of me, her face hovering over the plastic bag that contained my father's disgusting secret.

"He's in good hands Alex. He'll be okay." She was so caring and so certain. Why shouldn't I believe her? She reached down and pulled out the newspaper from the bag.

"Have a read while your waiting, I'm sure your dad won't mind."

Maybe there was a God, because somehow the magazine didn't slide out onto the ground as I was dreading it would. Helen went off in search of tea dispensers, and I carefully reassembled the Sunday paper and its dubious contents. I wanted to dump it there and then, but didn't want to risk leaving pornography in a public place that children frequented.

By the time Helen had returned with the teas, a nurse had told us that I could go and see my father. He had been taken to a ward bed, protesting vehemently that he had private healthcare and that he wanted his own room. According to the nurse, this would be made available soon.

Walking into that ward was a shock. It was the male medical ward and it regaled to the sounds of hacking coughs, echo-ey shoes, voices and the occasional bleeping. My father was lying prostrate in a bed, a couple of wires attaching him to various gizmos. He looked like the very life had been sucked out of him.

"Dada?" It wasn't often I had to call him anything these days, but on this occasion, maybe spurred on by Helen's approach, the word just came out.

Dada opened his eyes, clearly with great effort.

"My bag, did you - did you find my bag Alexander?"

To me, this was staggering. Here he was, laid out on a hospital bed having just collapsed from a heart attack or God knows what else, and all he bloody cares about is whether I've got his porn mag safe and sound. What the fuck goes on inside our minds?

"Yes, yes I've got your papers Dada. I'll keep them somewhere safe for you for when you're ready to look at them."

He smiled and exhaled a sigh; presumably of relief.

"Thanks Alexander. You're a good boy, you know." And with that his eyes shut. We hung around for another five or ten minutes but he was out for the count. News of our wedding would have to wait.

They kept him in for observation for a couple of nights. He got his private room, and before long was soon fussing and being made a fuss of by the staff. Most of them knew him from the telly. He had made quite a name for himself over the years with his travel work and occasional current affairs programmes in which he often became the defender of the people as he aggressively interviewed politicians and personalities.

I'd had a big internal fight about his magazine. I had chosen not to tell Helen about it, whether out of shame or not I wasn't sure, and had carefully hidden it in one of Dada's drawers when I had returned to the house the next day to turn off the radio and collect the post. I'd thought about chucking it away. But then I reasoned that I had no knowledge what it was like to be a man in his early sixties with no partner. What did you do about things like sex? Where did you get your kicks? While it might have been sad, was it wrong still to be using pornography to get in touch with that energy that presumably reminded him of his youth?

I'd moved effortlessly into crisis mode, leaving messages with Tang and FiveStar that my father had been taken ill. I had also told my mother what had happened. She at once offered to visit, but I suggested she back off since he didn't appear to be in imminent danger of dying.

Test results came back and showed no major abnormalities. A minor heart murmur and blood pressure up slightly above normal, and even those readings weren't definitive. The doctor suggested he take it easy for the next week, get plenty of fresh air, and take some sleeping pills if he had trouble dropping off at night.

And so it was that I picked him up from the hospital and took him back to his house. The house suddenly felt a very lonely place. I'd spoken to Helen, and we agreed that I should stay with him for a couple of days while he recovered his strength. This was hard for both of us, so recently returned from our honeymoon as we were, but we both had no doubt that it was also the right thing to do.

I helped him into the house, although he didn't want to be seen being assisted, and into his armchair in the lounge.

"Beer?"

"Absobloodylutely Alexander. Absobloodylutely."

I needed it just as much as he did.

"Do you remember what happened Dada?"

He took a drink of his beer - I saw how much his hand was shaking. I wondered if it was beginning to hit him that he would not live forever. Was this one of those moments when the truth of one's own mortality hits home?

"I had gone to Dilip's for the papers."

Yeah, and I know what else too.

"I was coming back, when I tripped on a paving slab and dropped my bag. We've been trying to get the council to repair these slabs for ages. Next thing I remember I'm on a stretcher with Joyce beside me. That's when I asked her to tell you."

Oh crap. Joyce said she saw everything. She must have meant *everything*. I could see it all now. Dada falls over, spilling the contents of his bag all over the pavement, porn mags and all. Before he knows it, two of his residents' committee members are on the scene and staring directly at full frontals of naked girls and headlines screaming how they like to do it. Guilt, embarrassment and shame swoop in and Dada flies into freefall, ending up in hospital. Stupid bastard.

We finished our beers, accompanied now by the one o'clock news. I made him a sandwich and soon after eating it, he dropped off to sleep. I didn't know whether I felt sorry for him, embarrassed by him, or angry at him. Whichever it was, I scrawled a note and left it by his chair.

"By the way, Helen and I got married. Thought you should know before someone else tells you."

Helen was back on nights and we soon became like ships that passed in the night. She had been livid with me for announcing our marriage to my father in that way, but then she didn't know the full story. For a few days our relationship was sticky, I put it as much down to her starting her nights again as anything else.

Since my father's fall, my mother started calling more, often talking to Helen, asking how he was and whether she could help. I knew he would never receive her help again and so took on the role of fending off her offers. Besides which, he was soon back on his feet and wanting as little fuss made as possible. And only I knew why. I wondered what he had thought when he had eventually found the magazine that caused the whole problem in his drawer.

My first couple of weeks back at work after the honeymoon had been relatively uneventful. I had caught up on various reports and been given documents relating to forthcoming projects for both FiveStar and Tang. With the recession now biting into the leisure industry there was a more nervous atmosphere, and everyone was beginning to look over their shoulder.

One Thursday morning in the spring of 1992, Steve called me into his office.

"Alex, I need to ask you a question and I need you to tell me God's honest truth."

My heart suddenly wanted to spring out of my chest cavity. Shit. The shell immediately clamped into place and I became Superman again.

"Try me."

"I have a proposal for you. But before I tell you the details, I need you to answer me one question."

The shell was straining to maintain its position against a surging tide of emotions.

"What's the question?"

"Did you lie to me about Tang and Sunsure?"

It's a question Alexander, just a question. Remember your schooling, tell them what they want to hear, nothing more, nothing less.

But what did Steve want to hear? How could you be certain as to what it was that someone did want to hear? They never told me that did they? What if they want to hear the truth? I opted for the quick, confident response.

"No, absolutely not Steve. Why do you ask?"

"Why? Because I've just been informed that I've been *'let go of'* Alex. And, while they haven't gone into reasons yet, I'm pretty sure it's got something to do with failing to secure the Croatian deal. And if it is, I wanted to hear from your own mouth whether you could admit to playing a part in that. But since you haven't, well, I thought I'd ask again anyway."

"Steve, I – I don't know what to say."

"Nothing to say, dude. You'd better get back to work."

I returned to my office feeling a level of pain that was disturbing. I couldn't remember now how much I had done wrong. I still didn't think Jaksic was to be trusted, but whether he was or not, Steve had lost his job, potentially partly because of me.

It wasn't long before I got a letter hand-delivered to my desk from one of the other directors:

'Dear Mr Baker,

In the light of recent global economic changes and company restructuring, it is with regret that we have to inform you that we will not be renewing your contract at the end of March and would be happy for you to take your outstanding holiday time in lieu of notice.

We would like to thank you for the contribution you have made to FiveStar in your time here and wish you well for the future. Human resources will be in touch regarding any other formalities.'

And that was it. My first sacking. I felt hollow and numb. I went to Steve's office, as much on autopilot as anything else.

"For what it's worth Steve, they're getting rid of me too."

Steve looked up from his desk without saying anything. The silence was uncomfortable.

"By the way, you never told me your proposal – it might be of interest now." I tried to make light of what happened, but it didn't come over very well.

"That's right Alex, I never told you my proposal." Even as he was speaking he was taking things out of his drawers and off his table and putting them into a cardboard box. "But then, to be fair, you never told me the truth. Game over."

I stood there in an embarrassed silence for a few seconds not knowing what to do. Eventually I left his office, and the building, and I never returned.

I wandered the streets for a while uncertain as to what exactly I was meant to feel. No-one had ever told me what to do in the event of being fired. Public schools weren't big on that sort of advice. Helen would have left for her shift and I wasn't going to tell either of my parents. God, they'd only just found out that I'd got married.

I ended up at the Dog and Fox and bought a pint. It was only late afternoon, and there was a motley crew of fellow suits, presumably left over from some extended lunch, and a small group of incredibly loud women at one of the corner tables, a pile of photographs spread out in front of them. I sat on a corner stool at the bar and reflected on my latest news. The beer slipped down easily and I felt I'd earned a second.

"She's just the business. I think her latest collection is the best yet. What do you think Charlotta?"

I don't know whether my ears were becoming more sensitive because of the beer or the women were becoming louder. It had suddenly become very difficult not to hear their every word.

"Oui, it ees quite stunning. Probably the best yet. I agree."

"You know Gucci are now talking seven figures for an exclusive. So the question is, how do we take the Jessica Strang brand forward?"

Jessica Strang? Jessica bloody Strang? Surely not. They couldn't be talking about the same Jessica Strang who'd done me up like a kipper in Helsinki, could they? I had to know, and a couple of pints were beginning to oil the system.

I went over to the table and interrupted their meeting.

"Excuse me, but I couldn't help overhearing. You were talking about Jessica Strang?"

A brunette woman in a dark blue suit and white blouse answered.

"What's that to you?"

"Well, it's just that I went to school years ago with a Jessica Strang. I wondered if she's the same person you're talking about."

"Well, why don't you wait a few minutes and you'll find out. She's due here any time."

My courage suddenly melted away.

"Thanks, if I can I will. I've got to be going very soon."

One of the other women tugged on my jacket as I started to leave.

"Well, can't we give her your details in case you miss each other?"

I wasn't thinking straight. I gave the girl, a fairly attractive young blonde, my card.

"And if she doesn't call you, then maybe I will anyway." She winked at me and the rest of the girls all laughed. I tried to laugh as well but I think it came out as more of a grimace. I went back to my drink and gulped the remainder. After a quick visit to the men's room, I headed off in the direction of the tube. As I got to the top of the stairs to the underground, I nearly ran straight into Jessica.

"Well, well, well. If it isn't Alexander Baker. What a surprise. You know men really shouldn't wear light trousers, so easy to spill when you're pissing don't you think?"

I looked down at my crotch. There were just a few tell-tale spots from my recent visit to the gents. Bollocks.

She walked off towards the pub, leaving me standing at the top of the stairs wondering how many other women had already noticed my trouser marks. It was like another kick in the nuts. I took the tube into the West End. I needed to score something and I needed it quick.

Two hours later I was home and in an entirely different space. I had managed to get some E and the magic pill had cast its spell. Jessica, my job and the white chinos had all merged into a fuzzy nothingness. I was getting buzzed up and needed to do something with my energy.

I still hadn't told Helen about my job. Thought I'd best leave that until she was home and had her sleep tomorrow. I wasn't due to fly out anywhere for another couple of days and then I'd be off for four days in a row, so tomorrow was the only slot.

Just as I was thinking about her the phone went.

"Hi, is this Alexander Baker?"

"Yeah, whose is that lovely sounding voice?"

"Melanie. We met at the pub earlier. I work for Jessica Strang's agency." Bloody hell. What did she want?

"So Alexander Baker, where are you?"

"Chelsea, why?"

" I'm drunk and I'm horny and you're cute. I thought it might be fun to meet up. I'm only two stops away."

The E had dissolved whatever defences I had. Within thirty minutes we were engaged in our bed in some uninhibitedly depraved sex, fired by my E, one of which she also had. In *our* bed. In my newly married bed. In the bed that belonged to Alex and Helen not Alex and some blonde called Melanie. And it was great. And it was terrible. And it was fixing my problem. And it was fucking up my life. And I needed it. And I had earned it. And from that moment on, I hated myself even more.

Miraculously, I had the wherewithal to get her out of the house and into a cab by midnight, two hours before Helen was due back. I'm not sure we even said goodbye. The sex had served both our needs, and I was already trying my hardest to believe that would be the end of it.

I tried to put the bedroom and bed to rights, opened the windows to air the place, showered, and ran around the flat checking every corner for any clues that might give away my indiscretion. Why, oh why? How brain-dead was I? Hadn't Helen made it clear enough that she would not tolerate lying or cheating? Oh God and drugs. I'd managed to break most of the unbreakables. And once again, why? Who the hell had taught me to fix the shit in life by creating even more shit? Which lesson was that exactly?

At two twenty-three I heard the door go. I breathed in as huge a breath as I could and exhaled, trying to vanquish any signs that I might be awake. Every bone in my body was shaking. I heard the light go on and off in the living room, the loo flush, and within a couple of minutes her naked body was pressed up against mine. Innocence and the Devil. Beauty and the Beast. What interesting bed partners.

29

For the next week following our return from Paris, I immersed myself in practising the new validation and questioning techniques. I found similar methods on the web that in some ways disappointed me because it made me realise that Helen's technique was nothing new. But in other ways, this only served to confirm what I was finding; that this method of dealing with people did seem to transform difficult situations. It worked. I used it on the bus, in the fish and chip shop, at the supermarket. I couldn't always remember not to blow my top when a problem arose, but when I did, things flowed more easily.

On the following Tuesday I received an urgent phone call from one of my clients. Alan Stevens, founder of AS PR, had started the business several years ago, not long before I had started my own consultancy, after coming to the conclusion that he was never going to go far as a musician. Being a pushy bastard by nature, he decided to give public relations a go. He got his first client the day of his launch; an independent label by the name of Rocco Records, run by an East-Londoner called Tony Rocco. Rocco Records had almost immediately shot to the forefront of the UK indie scene by signing a young boy-band. They were called Slipstream and their first single was used as the theme tune on a pilot teenage TV show that went on to become a cult, syndicated all over the world.

Alan had got me involved initially because he felt he was missing a few tricks with his business and wanted to grow it more quickly. He felt that while he was in a fairly high profile position thanks in particular to Rocco and Slipstream, he needed to get the word out to other potential high-flying prospects who might want a fresh PR approach. At the time he was handling a reasonably wide range of clients, but they were mainly from the arts world. He now fancied getting in with businessmen, and politicians too, as he felt this would give him a diverse catalogue with lots of possibilities for cross-fertilisation. He had visions of representing footballers who might team up with his musicians on projects; and of representing politicians who he could put together with TV and film celebrities to raise their popularity. He knew I had good business contacts, and a few in politics too, and he felt my consultancy might help him to realise his company's true potential.

Over the last few years I had built up a good network in both fields. My reputation for advising and guiding new companies had grown, and my inbox was frequently filled with communications from high-profile players in business. Interestingly though, Alan had experienced similar problems to mine over the last year in particular. His body, as opposed to his emotional state, had become his greatest source of concern. He was overweight, on blood pressure tablets and had received a major scare the year before when he had collapsed in agony at a music awards ceremony in the West End. That time it turned out he had an ulcer, a condition which had apparently now been dealt with. And I think it was probably because we had these sorts of difficulties in common, that he had felt able to stick with me when I was struggling.

I arranged to go straight round to see him. The AS PR office was on the third floor of an old regency building, about a five minute walk from Knightsbridge tube. Alan had moved to this exclusive neck of the woods in his second year, as he felt the address would go down well with prospective clients. The risk was one well taken. Clients felt safe visiting Knightsbridge, and he had secured an impressive strike rate for new business.

As I walked in to reception, I was greeted by Julie-Anne, his wife who also acted as office manager. I had always admired them both for their ability to work together, particularly in a business as pressurised as public relations.

"Alan's just finishing a phone call; he'll be with you very soon, Alexander." Julie-Anne was older than Alan, probably mid-forties, and she had kept in good shape. He had often told me that it was entirely due to her that he kept going at all. In all the time I had known her, I had never seen her angry, or even slightly down. And I knew from personal experience that Alan wasn't an easy person to work with; what he was like to live with, God alone knew. Alan was a natural born worrier, a fact which amused me when I thought of how important it must have been for him to be positive when representing his clients.

"Alexander, I'm done – come through." The door to his office was ajar and he'd called out as soon as his phone call was finished. Alan was sitting behind his desk and got up as soon as I walked into the room.

"Oh God it's good to see you. But how are you, how are you? You're still feeling okay - still on the mend? Things working out better, yeah?" He didn't leave much space to breathe. I tried to pay attention to how my newly acquired listening skills could help me with the ball of nervous energy that was Alan.

"I'm feeling very well Alan. Thank you for asking. And you? How's life treating you?"

"Well, that's why I needed to see you Alexander." He poked his head out of the door. "Darling – can you come in?"

Julie-Anne came in and sat in the chair beside me.

"We, er, need your advice Alexander. Urgently. You're aware of my political leanings, and you'll remember that about nine months ago we were approached by representatives of the government with a view to helping them improve their profile with the teenage market. They wanted to start reaching more pre-eighteen year olds by working with an agency who had their finger on the pulse of what's going on in teen world. We're the obvious fit."

"Yes, Alan, I remember it well. I assumed nothing had come of it since I never heard anything more. What's the problem?"

Julie-Anne replied,

"It took us ages, but we put together a proposal for them which they seemed to like. It involved some suggestions as to the types of teenage-targeted events that high-level party figures could attend, getting some fluffy media profiles going on some of the cabinet's more interesting teenage children, staging music events and all that sort of thing."

Alan stood up. I was impressed with the way they moved seamlessly from one to the other as they delivered the story. Here was a team working and living together. How I yearned for that type of connection.

"We've invested a lot in this pitch Alexander. A hell of a lot. We got film shorts done, staged a demo event at a club near Whitehall, laid out and printed up God knows how many different flyers and promo packs. Contracts had been drawn up and we've just been waiting for the phone call to say the deal is officially done. Instead, at nine o'clock this morning, we got an email telling us the deal was off. As soon as we got the email - a bloody *email* for Christ's sake - Julie-Anne thought we should contact you. So here we are."

Julie-Anne had thought of me, and I immediately thought of Helen. Whether that was because of seeing the two of them working so closely together and my harbouring some romantic and wildly absurd notion that I could one day be in a similar working relationship with Helen, I don't know. Or maybe it was because I knew I still had more to learn from Helen, and the part of the technique she hadn't yet taught me was what I needed to help these two. I started to lean upon the simple step I had already learnt and been practising.

"Okay, so you've spent loads of money and time pitching for this job and now you feel really hacked off because they've pulled the plug. Have I heard you right?"

"Spot on, Alexander, spot on. We really need this gig. And the profile it will give us – can you imagine?"

"Yes, yes I certainly hear that Alan." Questions. Questions. What bloody questions could I use to draw some more information out? What would Helen say now? Damn it, Claude, where are you when I need you?

"Julie-Anne – why do you think they've pulled the plug?" I was fishing. I didn't know what else to say, so I thought I'd keep the conversation going and hope that I received some Divine inspiration along the way.

"It's a good question Alexander" she replied. "One we've been tossing back and forward ever since the email. We have absolutely not got a clue. I just had a really strong feeling that you might be able to help us – though I've no idea how or why."

"That's why I called you." Alan put in, looking fondly at his wife. "A woman's intuition. Tell you what, she hasn't let me down yet."

I felt strangely reassured by their confidence in me, even though they had far more faith in me than I had in myself.

"Okay – so what have you responded with so far?"

Alan looked at Julie-Anne. She shook her head,

"Nothing yet, Alexander. We didn't want to panic. Alan wanted to ring up our lawyer straight away and see if we couldn't do them for something."

"Well bloody hell, they've got us spending so much time and money and then suddenly they don't want to know? I mean there's got to be something in there. At the very least I'm going to give the bloody government office a piece of my mind."

"Alan, I understand that you're really angry about this. You've done loads of work on it and – why wouldn't you be mad? I do think though that you've got to try to find out some more information. There's got to be a reason for all this and maybe the right type of questions will give you a bit more of a clue as to what, if anything, can be done."

"I agree with you Alexander. We mustn't panic. Alan, you know that – when has panicking ever got us anywhere?"

Alan stood up and went over to the window. He looked down on the street below. Julie-Anne looked at me and put one of her thumbs up. I didn't really feel like I'd done anything.

"What do you suggest Alexander?"

Now I had to give him something. I took a deep breath and, to my surprise, shut my eyes briefly. The room remained silent. About thirty seconds later I opened my eyes again.

"Are you okay?" Alan looked genuinely concerned.

"I'm fine. I'd like to suggest that you use email first, the tool that they have chosen to use. Just to get heard initially. Who sent the email?'

Julie-Anne had been the one to open the email earlier that morning.

"It was Trevor. Trevor Larken. He's been Alan's champion throughout this. He's worked really hard with us to help get as far as we have got. That's why it's so odd."

"Alan, what do you make of Trevor?"

"He's a nice enough bloke. Quite straight I thought for a civil servant. Not a great sense of humour, but nice enough. Show's how wrong I can be."

"Not necessarily Alan. Let's just assume he's the messenger; let's not shoot him. Chances are that if he's got to like you both throughout this, and let's face it who wouldn't, he's probably feeling crap right now about what he's had to do. That's probably why he used email as opposed to a phone call. Couldn't stand to disappoint you personally."

"Yes, well that's possible I suppose." Alan looked at Julie-Anne who nodded as well.

"Okay, well let's say he's gutted right now too. The last thing he needs, or wants, is to have you come back in a right old two-and-eight telling him he's wasted your time for the last several months. Truth is, he's probably feeling his time has been wasted for the last few months too if it hasn't been his decision. So here's what I suggest. Email him and start off just repeating back to him what you've understood from his communication. Something like – *Dear Trevor, thank you for the email. From what you have written, am I right in understanding that the whole deal is definitely off?'*

Alan was looking a little perplexed. "Is that it, Alexander? Is that the best you can come up with? Just repeat his words back to him?"

"Alan hold off for a minute. Give Alexander a chance to finish." Julie-Anne asserted her authority with such calmness that she was impossible to oppose.

"If you start off by showing him that you've heard him Alan, he'll be more open to talking with you. He'll feel listened to. Anyway, you haven't got enough information yet to know what to do next - so you've got to find out more somehow. And most importantly, Trevor won't be bloody terrified that you're about to send the boys round. People just want to be liked you know."

People just want to be liked. If only it was as easy to do as it was to say. It struck me that, in spite of chasing stuff and results most of my life, all I had really wanted was to be liked. To be the kid that everyone wanted to play with; the bloke who everyone knew they could rely upon; the man who everyone wanted to become.

As I spoke, I knew the words had merit. Inside Trevor, was living little Trevor, and little Trevor ultimately wanted to know that he was still loved. It wasn't that I knew this intellectually, I was beginning to feel it. I *knew* it. I had no idea where this certainty was coming from, but it started to flow as easily as the champagne at a Knightsbridge ball.

"Once you've got his ear, that's the time to ask your question or questions. Nothing confrontational mind you, just something polite, calm, non-judgemental that goes to the heart of it. Can you think of an appropriate question Alan?"

"Yes. Why the fuck have you pulled out of the deal?"

"Alan, will you be serious." Julie-Anne was more ruffled than I had ever seen her. "Please Alexander, go on."

"Actually, if that's the question that goes to the heart of the matter, then that's the essence of what you need to say. Maybe we could just take the rough edges off it. How about something like '*If the deal is indeed off, could you let me know what has changed and if there is anything that we have done that has caused this rapid change in circumstances?*'"

"You don't need the word rapid in there Alexander. It's superfluous." Julie-Anne was not only listening to me, but she was even writing down my suggestion. I felt good.

"And then what?" Alan looked right at me expecting another piece of wisdom to spring from my lips. I paused again and waited for some flash to come. It didn't.

"Then you wait." Yet again, I couldn't think of anything else to say. Alan sighed. Julie-Anne stood up.

"Alan we have no choice. Alexander is absolutely right. Before we find out some more information there is nothing we can do. And if you go shouting at them you'll lose them forever. You know that. Thanks Alexander – probably what I knew anyway, but it helps having another perspective."

Alan was noticeably less thrilled.

"I hope you're right. I still think they need a good sharp shock – let them know they can't treat small companies like this. Go on then Jay – send the email before I change my mind. Alexander, are you around today if we need to talk to you again?"

"I'll be available most of the afternoon. You've got my mobile." I shook hands with Alan and left the office. As I got out into the street I breathed deeply and went away from the noisy street to a small public garden nearby, where I sat on a bench. I reflected on what I had just advised one of my top clients to do. Where had those words come from? Was I right to suggest such a softly-softly approach? After all, we were dealing with big business and politicians. And what would I advise them to do next? I needed to talk to Helen, and quickly. I urgently needed to know what the next step was in her model before Alan called me again.

I no longer had to worry about waking Helen from her sleep during the day. Long gone was the stop-start regime of night duty, the pattern that ended up being one of the reasons why our relationship had become untenable. I remembered how I used to ache sometimes to see her upon my return from foreign trips, only to be disappointed by a note announcing an earlier start than expected. Now, with her own counselling business and the boys to look after, she worked a fairly regimented day, finishing around three to give her time for school pick ups and shopping.

I called her practice number but got the answer phone. She must have been with a client. Bollocks. The meeting could have just started, or could have been near the end, I had no idea. I left a message asking her to call me. I sat on the bench for another few minutes and closed my eyes. I did a simple exercise that Helen had taught me, but that I had failed to do regularly; counting my in-breath and my out-breath. As I did so I could feel myself becoming more attuned to the sounds around me. I wanted to open my eyes to check out the source of each new crackle or beep, or voice. But I managed to resist. While London went on around me, I sat on my bench, in my own silence, counting my breaths in and out, and in and out.

Before long, all the sounds seemed unimportant. I no longer desired to investigate them nor was I even wanting to separate them. They were merging into a background, low-level hum, while I was being overtaken by an evolving sense of peace. It was like a series of gentle waves washing over the chaos of my mind, and as the waves lapped onto the beach, so the receding waters were taking with them the rubbish that was my anxiety.

'There's nothing wrong. There never has been and there never will be. There are only our judgements of what we perceive to be wrong. Every problem is an opportunity waiting to reveal itself.'

Some people talk about hearing voices. I didn't hear a voice saying these words; I felt them. And, while I didn't fully understand their meaning or know how much even to value them, they increased my sense of calm. I stayed there on that bench, with my eyes shut, for what turned out to be another twenty-five minutes. I couldn't see Dada nor hear him speaking, and yet I felt his presence. I received no phone call from Helen and, amazingly, had no fear of receiving a phone call from Alan.

Just as I was coming out of my altered state, lo and behold my blackberry announced another call from Alan. Perfect timing. I was feeling calm and centred.

"Well Alexander. Interesting. Very interesting. We've heard back from Trevor already. How soon could you get back here?"

Not long ago, I would have made all sorts of mumblings about how difficult it would be, the effort involved, how I was already half way across London. Why? Why did I always feel I had to prove how much bloody effort I would have to put in to meet someone's needs? Why did I always feel prone to exaggerating so much? Just to make out what a good person I was?

"I can be back in a few minutes, Alan. Is that okay?"

The voice down the end of the phone was nothing if not grateful.

"That would be great. Thank you so much."

This new honesty felt good. No more show. No more pretending how important I was and how many other people needed me. Ironic, considering I was going to a meeting with a PR agency whose daily job was to show the world how important their clients were.

When I got back into the office I was still feeling energised from my quiet time in the garden. I was sensitive enough to be able to tell that the atmosphere in the office had already changed slightly from how it was during my earlier appointment. Julie-Anne greeted me and we went straight into Alan's office.

"Hi Alexander. Coffee?"

I didn't want a coffee. My God, I didn't even want a coffee. I used to live on the stuff.

"Any chance of some water?"

Water? This was turning into a strange morning. Julie-Anne returned with a glass of water and Alan leaned over his desk passing me a piece of paper.

"Here's Trevor's reply Alexander. Interesting what he has to say."

Hi Alan, thanks for the email. Thanks in particular for not throwing all the toys out of the pram – I was dreading your response after all the work you've put into this. I was informed last night by a senior colleague that the reason they were pulling out was because their budget has changed dramatically due to the increasing economic downturn, and so they're looking for an agency who can provide more outreach than one just into the teen market. We've always seen you as a specialist teen agency, so the plug got pulled.

I'm really, really sorry and will do my best to get some of your exes covered if you want to get me over some details of what you've incurred to date.'

"So, as you can see, the goalposts have moved. The bastards. And they never even told us." Alan's face reddened again as he spoke. Julie-Anne tried to be the voice of reason.

"Still, one step forwards since earlier this morning – at least they're offering to pay some of our costs."

"I don't want the bloody costs darling, I want the gig." Alan remembered he was talking to his wife. "Sorry. You know what I mean though."

I sat there and listened while the two of them exchanged views on the merit of getting some expenses back against the disappointment of missing a great opportunity.

Opportunity? *Problems are opportunities waiting to surface.* The words flashed across my mind with such clarity that I ended up saying them out loud.

"Problems are opportunities waiting to surface."

The two of them ceased their dialogue mid-sentence.

"You what?"

"There's an opportunity here Alan. I know there is. We're just not seeing it yet. It's just down to how you're perceiving this." I found my mind now beginning to race again in search of the next step. Oh God, if only Helen would call me back.

"Alan what are you thinking of doing next?"

"Well Julie-Anne thinks we should bung in an inflated invoice for expenses and I was thinking about going over Trevor's head to his boss. Trevor's clearly just a puppet. They've got to know they can't treat people like this."

I didn't like either of their options. One involved lying to the government, which could never be a good thing; the other would involve alienating his only good contact, and one who had already started to demonstrate that he was willing to communicate.

"Alan, you need more information. I think you should call Trevor this time – make personal contact. Let him know that you've heard what he has to say, what a difficult position it must have put him in etcetera etcetera. Tell him how much you appreciate the fact that he let you know why they pulled out. And then ask him for a bit more about what they're really looking for. You've put together a package for them tailored around young people. That's all they know AS PR for – they've probably only ever looked as far as your association with Rocco Records. But I know from our work together, that you can handle a much broader scope. I think you should question him a bit more to find out exactly what they're looking for. Just use questions to start with. No promises of what you can or can't deliver. No blame. And no shouting."

Alan shuffled in his chair. I felt strength coursing through me; I felt amazing. I didn't know what the hell I was doing, and yet I felt amazing.

"Call him huh? Are you sure about this, Alexander?"

"I've never been more sure. Do it. I'll go for another walk outside. I'll come back in ten minutes."

I ended up giving them about twenty minutes. When I returned, Alan met me in reception.

"Well, I did it. And I just about managed to stay calm."

"I was very proud of him Alexander. I listened to the whole call." Julie-Anne was smiling.

"You stayed calm – that's great. And how did you feel and how do you think it went?" I was fascinated to find out what my unexpected approach had brought about.

"Well, funnily enough, I felt okay. It felt good being nice to him, which is weird considering what's happened. He sounded pretty relieved and was really apologetic – quite something for a civil servant. Anyway, the long and the short of it is that they didn't know much about what else we did, and he's going to have a chat with his bosses with a view to sending over more details of what they're now looking for. He's hoping to get something over tomorrow morning."

"Do you think that's a good result Alan?"

Julie-Anne interjected. "Well, it's a better result than the one we would have achieved earlier if Alan had rung them up and given them what for, as he wanted to."

"Yes, well thanks for reminding me darling. Just got to wait and see now. You don't recommend anything else right now?"

I wished I had some gem up my sleeve, but I didn't. I still hadn't heard from Helen and so had winged my way through this so far. I noticed with some surprise that at no point did I feel like using my old tools for dealing with the situation. That would have involved getting heavy and getting heavy quick, just as Alan wanted. This was entirely new. And it was interesting. We hadn't got any concrete result yet, but it was definitely a step forward.

"No, nothing else right now Alan. Sleep on it. Wait and see what you hear from them. Let's take it from there."

"Okay Alexander. My wife seems to trust you even if I have my doubts." I shook Alan's hand and he disappeared back into his office.

"Thank you so much. He listens to you. What you advised, I feel it's right too. But he needs to hear that from a man sometimes, and, quite honestly, I was worrying too much to have put it as clearly as you did. We'll speak soon I've no doubt." Julie-Anne gave me a hug and a kiss on the cheek. Somehow that gratitude meant as much to me as anything else. She'd never done that before. Or at least if she had, I had never experienced it like that. I virtually skipped out of the office even though I was still completely uncertain about how it would all end up. Little did I know.

30

Once I'd told Yao that I had lost my job at FiveStar, I was immediately offered a full-time job with Tang, to be based in Hong Kong. Helen and I had long talks about this; she loved her job at Guys, although she had been finding the nights increasingly difficult to cope with. I was also a little concerned about leaving my father, although he seemed so unbothered himself about receiving help from me that the decision became easy. Helen seemed more upset about leaving my mother behind than I was, such was the connection they had formed in their occasional meetings and phone-calls.

And so it was that we found ourselves upping sticks and moving to the other side of the world. There was no fanfare farewell waiting for us at Heathrow, nor was there any to greet us at the other end. Unless you call a waiting taxi driver a fanfare.

I was given the post of Junior Executive of Overseas Development, together with a substantial salary and a basic apartment a couple of miles from the business centre of the city. Helen had decided to apply to all of the city's hospitals and soon found herself being offered three different posts, each with an increased salary to the one she had in the UK.

One of the projects I co-managed was Jaksic's Croatian business; the cause of Steve's sacking at FiveStar. I still found it hard to hear mention of Jaksic's name without some minor tremor spreading its way down through my body. Still, the deal with Tang had gone through, I'd received my bung from Jaksic who had been as good as his word, and I also had my bonus from Tang which helped us to get off to a pretty luxurious start in Hong Kong. Helen naturally wondered how I'd got all the extra cash, and I was able to explain simply that I'd received a bonus, which of course I had.

Indiscretions behind me, but not forgotten by me, Helen and I settled into whatever sort of rhythm it is that you settle into when you are working and living in a culture that is totally alien to you. I found the travelling surprisingly hard to start with; I hated leaving Helen in this foreign city, cooped up either in her immaculate, sanitised, working environment, or in our immaculate, sanitised, little apartment. My heart would ache when I was away and I could only find respite in the occasional fix or by getting drunk, or by keeping myself exceptionally busy. The good thing was I could follow any of my vices while I was away, and have plenty of time to get rid of the evidence before returning home. *Home?* No, before returning to Hong Kong. The downside was that I then had to be able to cope without them once back with Helen.

One thing I didn't do was get involved with any more women. It was easier than I had expected; my foreign trips kept me very busy and I was still reeling from the guilt of that night-time visit back in Chelsea from Melissa, or Melanie or whatever she was called. It was Melanie wasn't it? Of course, the same name as my first ever girlfriend.

But as the trips went on, and our working lives seemed to conspire to keep us apart at the appropriate times, I found the desire to scratch my itch growing. By now of course, in my mid twenties, I had learnt volumes from my education and those around me as to how to scratch itches efficiently. I was very good at it. But what I had been given almost no guidance on at all, was how to develop and increase my levels of self-discipline, the one skill I clearly needed in order to resist scratching. And so I just learnt to satisfy myself, and my bed-partners once again became the cold and distant celluloid images of magazines and films. At least I wasn't being unfaithful again, and somehow that made it seem okay.

The Croatian project was developing at a pace. One day I was called into Yao's office. Zhu, his ever faithful assistant, was present too, but no Ma which was unsurprising considering his importance in the company. He was always off meeting with foreign dignitaries and international business leaders. Zhu started the conversation.

"Alexander, how are you thinking the Sunsure organisation is doing?"

Autopilot time. I had found my Hong Kong colleagues initially gentle in the way they got to the point of something, just as they had when we first met with them in New York prior to the alliance with FiveStar. However as I became more a part of their culture, I had noticed how they were coming to the point much more quickly.

"Yes, fine. All seems to be going okay. Why do you ask?"

Yao stood up from his chair and walked around behind me, which I found mildly unsettling.

"Over the last few months the numbers of hotel guests appears to be up by twenty percent on the previous year."

I knew this from the latest figures I'd seen from Jaksic's accounts department.

"I know, it's good isn't it?"

"The strange thing is, the turnover figures we received last week, which show staff costs are rocketing, don't appear to be matching the footfall increase. Can you imagine why not Alexander?" Yao moved back into his seat, crossed his arms and looked straight at me. "And there is something else odd. Jaksic has told us that big cracks have suddenly appeared in their biggest hotel – as part owners now we're liable for some of the building costs which could be big. Insurance for subsidence in Croatia may not be that effective."

Declared income not matching footfall and cracks in the structure. What had my feelings told me ages ago? What had I sensed about the workers and the vibe at Sunsure? What had I felt about Jaksic? But no-one had ever told me to listen to an intuition, to a mere *feeling*. Shit. I couldn't help feeling something was coming home to roost.

"Alexander, we first employed you because the three of us felt you had an awareness of hotels and people that was unique and fresh. You work for Tang in order to provide not only your business judgement, but also your personal judgement. You know Jaksic and Sunsure as well as any of us; what is your sense of their organisation? Because here in Hong Kong, when we hear a building has cracks developing, we tend to look at the structure of the building first. We don't go reaching for the cement to fill the cracks."

I found myself caught between a rock and a hard place. Not dissimilar to the one I found myself in with Steve back at FiveStar about the whole Tang and Sunsure involvement. What was it with this bloody Croatian deal? I was beginning to wish I'd never heard of Croatia. Should I tell Yao about my concerns and then leave myself open to criticism for not telling them earlier? And then of course there was the payment I'd had from Jaksic for giving Sunsure the thumbs up. My survival instinct kicked in.

"I'll deal with it, Yao. I'll have a word with Jaksic, and maybe a couple of his managers that I know, see if I can find out anything. They're sound – probably just experiencing teething problems."

Yao sat back in his chair and made the shape of a triangle again with his hands, reminding me of the crystal pyramid he'd brought to our first meeting in New York. Zhu remained quiet. The silence was deafening. Yao stood up and walked over to the window which overlooked the streets of Hong Kong.

"But you see, Alexander, that wasn't my question. I appreciate your kind offer, but that definitely doesn't answer my question. My question was what do *you* sense about their organisation? I can speak to Jaksic. I can speak to managers. I don't want to hear their reasons or thoughts at this moment. I want to know yours. They want us to put in more money, but I'd like to hear your views on them before we get in any deeper."

I suddenly felt nauseous. Yao wasn't going to let me escape from his office without telling him what I felt about Sunsure. But, business wasn't about feelings, it was about facts. It was about numbers. It was about profit and loss accounts. Jaksic had me over a barrel because I'd received that payment. If I fouled things up for him here, he could so easily screw things up for me by letting it be known that I had taken a bribe. Although would he really risk his own name by doing that? My brain was doing overtime. I had to act.

"My sense is that they have probably had problems adjusting to the expansion. I think they may need more help in managing their expansion. There is also a question as to whether the current management approach is too rigid and maybe needs to become a little more flexible. Jaksic is pretty strict with his staff, maybe they've been kicking back a bit and demanding better pay."

"So you think we can invest further?" Again Yao looked directly at me.

"Yes. But maybe we should look at more hands-on involvement." I lied. If I had the choice the whole deal would be shelved. But I was in too deep and I couldn't stop it now.

Zhu and Yao stood up. Zhu had not said a word throughout the meeting since her opening question, and yet her presence had added something to the weightiness of what we were discussing. I could lie to one person, but could I lie to two?

"Thank you, Alexander. Tell me, how is Helen doing?"

"She's well thank you, Yao. She's adjusting fine to Hong Kong." Another lie. Helen was struggling with the loneliness of her existence in the City but was, for the sake of us, putting on a brave face. She hated our separations as much as I did. It was all very well having money, but there were only so many things either of us wanted to spend it on in Hong Kong. Our goal was to earn enough to be able to return to the UK in a few years and buy a decent house without the need for a mortgage.

I left the office and returned to my desk. It seemed that almost everywhere I turned I was having to deceive someone, somehow. Was I born a liar? Or had it just been passed down through family genes? I thought of my mother and her lesbian secret, and of my father with his hookers. I thought of gristly meat again and exams. God, I had even lied my way through exams. I hadn't known, as in really *known*, any of that stuff, I had just learnt it. And as quickly as I had learnt it and got my exam results, so I forgot most of it. It didn't live in me.

One Thursday about seven months later the Croatian deal imploded. Literally. It started with the cracked wall hotel partly collapsing following a minor tremor in the region. We were told it wasn't a tremor that should have caused any structural damage, as virtually no other buildings in the vicinity were affected. As a result of the collapse, which fortunately happened out of season, three members of the hotel staff were trapped and one of them died later that day in hospital.

For Tang, this collapse was a very bad omen. As a consequence they were seeking to sell on their share of the chain with immediate effect to another hotel group, or back to Jaksic.

Things got worse however when word reached Yao that seventeen members of staff were already in the process of suing Sunsure, and therefore Tang, for various breaches of health and safety. Ironically, this only became common knowledge on the day after the collapse. As if that wasn't enough, it then turned out that the member of staff who lost his life was an illegal immigrant who had been rooming with three other immigrants in a basement. That was where he died. The press had a field day and made sure that news of Sunsure's poor staff practices were broadcast throughout their client markets both at home and throughout Europe. Almost overnight, Sunsure lost their reputation for providing the best that Croatia could offer in accommodation. Tang's stake suddenly became a lot less valuable.

I watched this all unfold with a sense of dread and helplessness. I couldn't count myself responsible for the earthquake, or even for Jaksic's failings. I couldn't even count myself responsible entirely for Tang's decision to invest, I had after all been one young voice in a long chain of more experienced consultants and advisors who had contributed to the decision. But what I couldn't escape for all that, was that I had gone against my better judgement. And that the one thing that Yao had asked of me, my sense of what was right, I had failed to share. I had acted out of self-protection and, ironically, probably made myself even more open to attack.

It took a while for the axe to fall but, inevitably, some months later it did. Tang gradually extracted itself from Croatia, and a little while after, gradually extracted itself from me too. I managed to escape with no major recriminations from either Jaksic or Yao; just a future of having to live daily with the knowledge that I had lied to protect myself. The simple little lie that had been sown over two years ago and that had been regularly fertilised by a series of equally minor untruths had cost me my friendship with Steve, my job at FiveStar, my job at Tang and an ever-present sense of both emotional and physical discomfort. I would like to say that I learnt from it and immediately changed my ways. But it wasn't that simple, because while I can see it all more clearly now, to me then it just seemed unfortunate that things had worked out as they had. I was acting no differently from anyone else in business.

And so, some two years after first arriving in Hong Kong, Helen and I found ourselves with no pressing reason to be there. I had lost my job, she had hers still but wasn't that enamoured with the ex-pat lifestyle, and to cap it all we found out something else that would change our lives forever. Helen was pregnant. It was time to return home.

Our homecoming to England was difficult. Helen's early pregnancy was burdened with morning sickness, and for the first four weeks after our return, we had to stay at my father's house in Notting Hill. He had been out to see us a couple of times in Hong Kong and had managed to avoid any more collapses. He was also getting very close to retirement, and in seeing him less often, I had begun to notice the inevitable changes that age brings.

I had not forgotten about finding the pornography in his paper that day of his collapse, and I was as much concerned about him embarrassing me in front of Helen as I was anything else. While I had still allowed myself to forage in the glossy world of celluloid escapism, mainly when I was abroad, for some reason the thought of my ageing, single father doing the same thing was still upsetting. Also he and Helen, while getting on okay, seemed to have some sort of blockage between them. I couldn't put my finger on it, but Helen commented to me that she didn't think that he trusted her. Maybe his experience with my mother had made him wholly unable to trust any woman ever again.

After three months looking for work I had still found nothing, which, with Helen not wanting to work either due to her difficult pregnancy, had a disastrous effect on our plans for bigger and better. My Chelsea flat was alright, but I had bought at the height of the market and soon after prices in that area had dropped quite significantly. They were beginning to recover now, but not to the extent that we wanted. I tried not to let on to Helen how worried I was becoming about the financial side of things, seeing it as my role to shoulder the burden of concern. Another useless part of my education. Why hadn't I been taught to share the worries as well as the spoils? We were a partnership after all. Why did I feel the need to project this image the whole time of everything being under control?

After a month of being with my father, and then another couple of being in my place together all day and every day, Helen and I often found ourselves getting in each other's space. The ever expanding internet had become a refuge for me and I started surfing the net for solutions to all my ills. When I tired of that I'd go down to the local pub in search of anything that would help me escape my gathering gloom. She was beginning to reconnect with some of her old London friends, and so if I went out, she'd often spend the evening on the phone chatting.

On one of these occasions I was sitting in the corner of my local boozer, reading a copy of a management journal that I had been getting regularly since my return. In it there was an article about a young whizz kid from the City who had made a fortune out of starting a business on the web that offered students the best deals available on travel, cars, bank accounts, concert tickets and the rest. He'd started off by contacting one or two companies who wanted to reach the student market with their products and managed to get them to advertise on his site. From there the idea had exploded and he had recently sold his company for a seven figure sum.

As I read his story, I could feel myself tingling all the way down my spine. There was something in this. I knew nothing about websites, but I knew plenty about hotels and I suddenly thought about creating an online guide which provided a unique insight into the world's most luxurious hotels. It would cater for the mid to high end of the market and I would secure advertising from companies ranging from the hotels themselves, to cosmetics suppliers and airlines.

I ordered another drink and started to list some of the hotels that we could feature. I ran through a hundred or so different web names and wrote each one down, crossing through any that on second look struck me as unsuitable. By the time I left the pub some two hours later, considerably the worse for wear, my mind was as awash with ideas as my body was awash with beer. I was desperate for a fag and, reasoning to myself that Helen would be fast asleep by now, I walked down to the river to grab a smoke, blow the smell of pub out of my hair, and sober up.

It could only have been about ten o'clock or so, and the Chelsea Embankment was bustling with traffic. I stood beside the river and lit up, my website idea now firmly fixed in my head. A couple of river boats with night-time revellers passed by. I realised I was standing in almost the exact same spot where Helen and I had first met. I looked up the embankment towards Westminster Bridge and there was the coffee hut, all shut up for some reason. I looked back to the river and my heart ached to feel the way I had about the night-nurse all those moons ago. I shut my eyes and tried to see her in her long coat with her nurse's outfit just peeping out underneath. I longed to experience the freshness of her face and her voice and to watch her back as she first disappeared across the road on her way home that first night. To think she had become mine was almost unbelievable. And where was she now, my night-nurse? Tucked up in our bed, in our flat, just waiting for me to go home and curl up alongside her.

I felt something in those moments that I hadn't felt in a long while. A longing for my night-nurse. A longing for the woman that was carrying my baby. A longing for my wife.

I ran nearly all the way back. It was probably about ten-thirty or so when I made it home. The lights were still on which was unusual because, during her pregnancy, Helen was normally in bed by about nine-thirty to ten o'clock. I fumbled a little with the keys but managed to get the door open eventually, making more noise than was necessary.

"Mother? What on earth are you doing here?" If there was one person I wasn't expecting to see as I walked up the stairs into our living room, it was my mother.

"Hello Alexander – lovely to see you too. How are you, my darling?"

Helen looked uncomfortable and I was suddenly very worried that all was not well.

"Helen, are you, are you okay?"

Helen smiled and breathed out.

"Yes Alex, yes I'm fine. Your mother was just up the road for the evening and so she called me to see if we were in and I invited her over. I've offered for her to stay, but Jenny came up to London with her and is visiting someone else, so she's picking her up any minute."

Thank God. I so wanted to tell Helen about my revelation in the pub. I went and gave her a kiss and sat beside her on the couch.

"You've been smoking. Alex you've been bloody smoking. You bastard. You promised me. Oh Christ."

And in a few simple words my hopes, my dreams, my vision of our perfect future were, temporarily at least, snatched away in a moment of complete horror. I was not on my guard, probably because of the combination of the beer and the surprise of finding my mother at home. I'd run home so fast, I'd completely forgotten about the fag I'd had.

"How can you tell?"

"So you have. You admit it. Shit Alex – and I'm bloody pregnant. I thought I could smell something. I'm so sorry you have to witness this Elizabeth."

My mother sighed and gave her a look that contained the solidarity of sisterhood.

"Please don't worry on my account Helen, I've seen far worse. I think I'll wait outside for Jenny, she won't be long. I should leave you two alone."

For once I actually didn't want my mother to go. Not yet anyway. I wanted her protection from my enraged, hormonally-charged, pregnant wife. Bollocks, why was I such a dumb-arse? How many years had I got away with it so far? How many times had I managed to hide the tracks? How often had I gone for days, sometimes weeks without a fag because I knew the danger was too great?

"Stay, please, until Jenny comes. Alex and I will sort this out after you've gone." Helen didn't look at me as she spoke.

I went out to the kitchen in silence and put the kettle on. I felt in my pocket and pulled out the cigarette packet. I really was slacking – I would never normally risk bringing a packet back into the house. I stuffed it under the other rubbish in the kitchen bin and cursed as I did it. I put down the creased magazine on which I had scrawled my vision. At that moment my dream felt as crumpled as the magazine. I could hear them talking quietly next door, but had no desire to hear the content of their conversation.

I made myself a cup of coffee and went back, with trepidation, into the lounge.

"You shouldn't be drinking coffee at this time of night Alexander. It's not good for you." My mother still had a way of making me feel about ten years old when she wanted to. Could I do nothing right at all? Funny thing was, once she'd said those words I wanted Helen to back her up to show that she cared as well whether I was up all night or not. But she didn't. She remained silent.

Just as the quiet was becoming extremely hard to bear, there was a knock at the door downstairs. My mother wished us goodnight and left us, knowing full-well that she was leaving her son to the mercy of a raging bull.

Attempting to seize it by the horns, I launched into a description of my brainwave.

"Helen, I don't expect you to understand but I - I think I've come up with an idea. For our future. One that could make us seriously wealthy. You know, get us our place we've talked about. In Hampstead. It's genius. I just got over-excited, had a couple of beers and then suddenly wanted a cigarette. First one in years. I don't know what got into me."

Here we go again. Is lying an illness? An addiction? Why did I find it so difficult to be honest? To be me?

"You lied Alex. You promised me – twice – that you would never lie and you would give up smoking. You lied and you smoked. I saw my mother die of smoking. Have you ever seen anyone die of emphysema Alex? It's not a pretty sight. I have no intention of going through that again with my own husband. I don't want to nurse you Alex. I don't want our child to grow up with a sick father. And I don't want to bury you young either."

I went over to her to hug her. She pushed me away.

"You stink Alex. When you're pregnant you become more sensitive to everything. I can't be near you. I'm going to bed and if you're thinking about joining me, you better work out a way you can come to bed smelling of roses."

I took her at her word. While she went to the bathroom I whipped out of the flat and, at the risk of getting done for drink-driving, I drove up to the local garage that mercifully had one small bunch of red roses in a bucket on the forecourt. I managed to get out and back within about ten minutes.

I went quietly back into the house, dumped my smoky clothes in the laundry basket, showered quickly and towelled myself dry, brushed my teeth and gargled with mouthwash, and finally walked naked up into the bedroom balancing a couple of roses upon my head and carrying two in my mouth.

The bedside light was still on when I went into the bedroom. She was facing in the opposite direction but I could see in the mirror that her eyes were open. She saw me standing there, totally naked except for the roses. I tried to speak which wasn't easy with prickly flower stems in my mouth.

"Oo wanted me smellin o roses madam?"

She turned over and started laughing. The roses fell off my head and onto the bed. I spat out the others and she reached out her hand to pull me in.

"Ow, bloody hell that hurts." I'd rolled onto one of the fallen stems. Helen laughed even more.

"Karma, if you ask me."

"Kama Sutra, if you ask me."

That night we had the best sex we'd had in two years.

The next day I tried to tell Helen about my internet idea, but she didn't get it, probably because she had never used the internet. But I so wanted her to understand and to be behind me, that her antipathy stabbed like a dagger in my heart. She said she could understand a job that involved people, but one that only involved computers couldn't excite or interest her. And yet I knew this idea was a winner. Maybe I shouldn't have talked to her about it first thing in the morning when she was feeling awful.

Undeterred by her ambivalence, I set off on my journey of research and finance-raising. I became the lonely warrior, equipped with an idea that couldn't fail, but without the real backing of the person I most wanted behind me. It's not that Helen tried to stop me, only that she showed virtually no interest in what I was doing or trying to achieve.

Over the next few months as she became more and more focussed on having the baby, I became more and more focussed on creating the business that would support the baby. She'd lie in bed in the evening looking at catalogues for slings and natural baby products, and I'd lie beside her studying hotel catalogues, web design printouts and cash-flow forecasts. Every now and again she'd thrust a picture under my nose saying we must get one of those, and I'd parry her thrust by shoving a photo of a luxury hotel room in Dubai in her face.

As Helen got bigger and bigger, so my idea got bigger and bigger. I used my contacts to secure me appointments with some of the top chains, and, by a freak of nature, Divine Intervention or something, on the same day that Daniel Baker was born, *www.muststayhere*.com also went live in the world. Helen and I were both in raptures, but I'm not sure it was about the same thing.

I have to confess though, that something happened to me at Daniel's birth. I was present throughout, and Helen gave birth remarkably easily. As I saw that little slimy baby emerge from her, something in my heart was shouting so loudly that its call became deafening. It was so loud that I couldn't decipher the words. Doctors, nurses, a crying baby on my wife's chest, a shattered looking but exuberant Helen, a screaming inner voice. What was it saying? Something about Daniel. Something about his future. Something about us. Melanie. Jaksic. BMP. Jessica Strang. Guilt. The noises all merged into one and I couldn't separate the inner from the outer. I wanted to celebrate and to be present with Helen in her moments of joy, but the shell that had become established to prevent me from experiencing my guilt and 'bad person' stuff, was also stopping me from being able to embrace and celebrate fully what had happened.

We very soon slotted into our roles. Helen became house mother, and I was on my travels again, visiting luxury hotels throughout the world in whistle-stop tours that left no time at all for real pleasure. I started to fall back again on my instant fixes; cigarettes, pornography, the occasional joint, and, if I was feeling very stressed, I'd hunt out a club in whatever city I was in and dance and dance and dance.

Within weeks of going live, the website started getting hundreds of thousands of hits, and I now had to keep it updated every week and add new deals, offers and hotel information and photos. As the workload increased, so did the need for me to remain well. I could feel the pressure of that, and just as Steve had taught me years ago, as soon as the first sign of a cold came along I'd go straight to the doctor, demanding some sort of quick fix. The thing was, I was doing it as much for Helen and Daniel as I was for me.

As our respective 'babies' grew, so did their neediness of each of us. Helen had gone down the natural parenting route; a decision which I tried to respect even if I didn't understand it. Everything she was doing in her parenting, and that she wanted me to be a part of, seemed to involve the long way. Everything I had been trained to do in my life and was now doing in my work involved the short way. She had tried on many occasions to explain why breastfeeding was so important, and why we had to have Daniel sleeping with us in our bed, and why sticking a dummy in his mouth as soon as he started crying wasn't the answer to anything, but I was generally too tired to be able to listen. And each time she went off on one of her parenting lectures, I would try to get even by telling her about the latest website developments. It was earning our keep for Christ's sake. Without my new company and the investment I'd secured, God knows where we might have ended up. But none of that seemed to wash with Helen; she wanted me, not my money. Although I never asked her, I really think she may have settled for being poorer, if it meant having me around more.

It was a good time to have had a sound internet idea. Before long my little baby was *the* site for the wealthy to explore their overseas accommodation options and dreams. I was being bombarded with offers from businesses around the world, wanting their hotel or product to be reviewed on the site. It was a great triple earner; I got paid advertising revenue; a fee for anyone who booked the hotels or bought the products featured by coming through our site; and free, or heavily discounted, accommodation at any number of hotels throughout the world.

The shame was Helen rarely wanted to take Daniel outside of the UK, and, to be fair, I was travelling for my job, so the last thing I wanted to do was travel for my holiday. Also the Hong Kong experience had more than fulfilled our travelling ambitions for the time being, so maybe it wasn't surprising.

And so it was that, by what seemed to be a mutual yet unspoken understanding, we established our parallel lives. She got on with becoming a mother, I got on with my business. She showed no real need of my services, and I couldn't get much help or involvement from her. I guessed this was just how relationships were when children came along.

To my chagrin, my mother featured more and more in Helen's life, and Jenny became Daniel's second grandma. Helen said she needed them to support her, that being alone with a baby-come-toddler all day every day was more than any one person should have to cope with. I often thought about how she should try doing my job for a day to see what real work involved, and occasionally this frustration spilt out into our increasingly infrequent conversations.

It was dawning on me that Helen seemed to have no interest in pursuing her career. She was so adamant that Daniel's needs would be best met by her being around him constantly, that I felt no desire to challenge that. With the company going so well, in fact almost too well, finances were no longer a major issue, so I was happy to let her make sure everything was alright at home and with our son. I got on with the business of making the money to support us. I thought I was doing the real work of course, but enjoyed providing Helen with an allowance to look after the domestic side of things. She met my needs, and Daniel's of course, and I provided the cash to meet hers. I thought I was now beginning to understand what long-term relationships were about.

My father and I were drifting apart again. His health had been declining very gradually and I hadn't wanted to observe the decline at too close quarters. Since spending that month at his house, it had become clear how difficult we both found it to reach out to each other. I remember one shocking moment when I was watching one of the adult channels via satellite in a hotel in Berlin, when my mind suddenly drifted and I found myself imagining my father at that exact same moment, sitting on his bed watching an x-rated video. I was so distressed I had to switch the television off immediately. That night my heart ached more for Helen than ever. I so needed to be next to her, to feel her body tucked up against mine. But it couldn't be. We were miles apart physically, and becoming miles apart emotionally. And yet I was helpless to do anything about it. We were merely dancing to the hypnotic tune of modern life.

And that's how the first two years of Daniel's life passed; as though we were both in some sort of trance state. On his second birthday we had invited the grandparents, although Jenny still couldn't attend anything that my father was coming to. We had all the normal stuff; cakes, balloons, and far too many presents. My father seemed determined to outdo everyone each time. The previous year he had turned up with three huge presents, this year he kept on returning to the boot of the car after each opening, and ended up giving Daniel five gifts, including a train set way too advanced for a two-year old.

I was struck by my father's insensitivity; and by the clear expectation that he projected that a toddler should be able to show gratitude for the gifts he was being given. Daniel was still as interested in the packaging as the contents. But the old man just didn't get it.

"Now then Daniel, this is the best gift of all."

Daniel was playing with some wrapping paper.

"Come over here Daniel, I want to tell you something."

Daniel carried on playing with the wrapping paper. He then moved on to one of the plastic trays that had recently been holding an express train. My father went over to him instead, and spoke so that the whole room was obliged to hear what he was saying.

"This morning I set up a bank account for you. Do you know what a bank account is? Well, it's a thing that you save money in. Every year I'm going to put some money into your account and then, when I feel you're ready, if I'm still alive that is, I'll give you the keys to the account. How about that eh?"

I noticed my mother staying quiet. Helen was also silent. This wasn't a comfortable quiet. I had to say something.

"Thanks Granddad – that's so kind, isn't it Daniel? Darling, isn't that generous?"

And on the face of it, my father's offer was generous. But there was something deeper going on here; a subtle nuance of manipulation of which both Helen and my mother were aware, and to which I was still oblivious. I could feel a slight jarring as my father had made his announcement, but I couldn't understand why, and my uncertainty only highlighted a further separation between Helen and me, and our differing parenting ideas.

We needed something that would pull us back together. The night-nurse and I had grown apart. I hardly knew how or why; she was still the most beautiful woman in the world as far as I was concerned. But it had happened, just like a crack in the ground that one day suddenly becomes big enough to fall into.

That night, after my parents had gone and Daniel had fallen asleep from the effects of over-excitement, Helen uttered the words that should have brought joy back into our lives.

"Alex, I'm pregnant."

My first response was '*oh God, just when we needed to get our lives back on track.*' I didn't say it aloud. My actual response was to hold her close in my arms, her head tucked in by my shoulder. My head went on thinking '*Was this the fix we needed? Was this the solution? Would having another child bring us closer together again?*'

What I said aloud was, "Darling, I'm so happy. That's wonderful."

Another lie had begun to weave its way into my life.

31

A few hours after my last meeting with AS PR, I was back at home and settling down to yet another meal for one, when the phone went.

"Hi Alex, so sorry not to get hold of you earlier – I've had a mad day and I've only just got the boys their food."

Here we were, however many years later since we first met by the river, and her voice still had that effect on me. My dinner was waiting for me, but I didn't want to miss the chance to talk. Just hearing her voice made me feel good.

"Helen – thanks for calling. I wanted to talk to you about a client I met with today. I started using the listening model. It definitely helped and they got a pretty immediate result. I was surprised – amazed actually - at how easy it was." I went on to tell Helen exactly what had happened and how I had played it. I could tell from her frequent questions and sounds of approval that she was not only pleased, but impressed that I had really started to take this seriously and was risking using it with a client.

"The thing is, I had no idea what the next steps were. You've only taught me the first one and I was caught off guard when we applied that, and then the client asked me for the next move. Since they're waiting for their client to come back with a bit more information about their potential requirements from an agency, all I could think of saying was to let it go over night. Reflect on it and see what the client comes back with in the morning. Then they could consider that and discuss it again. So what have I missed?"

"Alex, you haven't missed a thing. You've just done the next step, and you've even advised them as to what to do for step three. That's why this system works so well once you get it going – it's entirely intuitive. You got your client to validate the civil servant by acknowledging how hard it must have been for him to send the initial email of rejection; you got your client to ask the questions that led to the information about the broader scope required in a PR agency; your client has already shown what a great, and fearless, listener he is and he's made the government official feel heard.

"Step two is where you reflect on the information that you have received. Your client has already done a measure of that and will now be reflecting on what has happened today. It might not be comfortable for him overnight because he still doesn't know how it's going to work out, but by the morning he will be feeling quite different about the day's events. And the likelihood is, he'll act from a place of strength and calmness tomorrow, provided he continues to be reminded to demonstrate his listening skills.

"Alex, can you imagine how different our lives may have turned out if either of us had really questioned each other about our grievances and then reflected on that information before jumping off at the deep-end?"

Her words rang true. If we didn't shout each other down in those final months of our marriage then one of us, normally me, would run off with our fingers in our ears. I had always found it particularly hard to hear what Helen had to say about my life, and there were also times when Helen wasn't much better. I don't know what either of us was so scared of finding out. But whatever it was, the fear had taken over from the ability to listen, big time.

"Yes, okay, point taken. So what I said, about doing nothing overnight and just waiting for their response, that ties in?"

"Ties in, Alex? I would have told you to do nothing different at all if you had got hold of me. When someone takes away the information that they've received and considers it, the other party really feels valued. You couldn't get hold of me earlier because you weren't meant to. You've already started living this. And that makes it very real."

Yes, that made sense. And it was what I had observed happen to a certain extent today. I had questioned and validated Alan and Julie-Anne. I had reflected on what to do as well, and that had shown them I wasn't panicking, and that I was valuing their concerns. Alan had already avoided making a complete arse of himself by not blowing up at Trevor and that in itself was a victory. And I had demonstrated my faith in things becoming clearer, by not suggesting any further action until Alan heard back from Trevor. Faith? Well now, there's an alien concept. At least what used to be an alien concept.

"So Alex, the third step? You've already given them a clue. Once they get the next set of information in, they need to take their time and reflect on it again. Repeat step two first - no diving in. Sometimes people find that problems dissolve after these first two steps have been carried out properly. Sometimes people just need to feel heard or to hear the other side of the story. In this particular case I have a feeling that you'll need step three, which involves your client then going back to the civil servant and discussing their response to this new information, asking any further questions they may have. Your client must continue to show his listening skills – questions and validation are two of the best tools for this."

Not so long ago I would have recoiled at the thought of taking advice from Helen. That was partly what had driven us apart. Why I had found it so hard I was only just beginning to understand; the ego is a wily fox. But now I was listening to her in such a way that I was beginning to *hear* her.

"One point to remember Alex. When a person starts to use step three, discussing, it is very important that they come from a place of truth. They mustn't lapse into telling someone what they think they want to hear, and nor must they start getting into blame and guilt trips. Sometimes gathering all the information and being truthful means saying no, and that needs to be okay."

I was writing down notes as she was speaking. I felt like I was back in school, although this time I genuinely wanted to learn my subject, rather than fill in time between rugby matches.

"Can I go over this so I'm clear? Step one – listen, using validation and questions. Step two – reflect, take time out and consider things. Sometimes problems will just dissolve at either of these steps. Step three – discuss, using validation, questions and truth. Have I got that right?"

"Perfect, Alex. Each time you get new information in, go back over the same steps. But don't expect everyone to get this as clearly as you have. That's what I was saying about the problems I have getting people to remember to apply it. We slip into old habits so easily."

"Yes, that's true enough. Helen, how exactly did you learn all this stuff?"

"I've told you many times Alex - reading, seminars, my teacher. Listen, I must go – Joel's calling for me. I just want to say well done – and thanks for listening to me. I feel quite, well, humbled really. Must go – lots of love."

"Yes, of course. And thanks – so much. Say goodnight to the boys for me."

I put the phone down. *'Lots of love.'* I wish.

That night, I sat in the bath pondering the events of the day, and my phone call with Helen. Something she had said towards the end of the conversation was bothering me; the bit about how people have a problem remembering to stick to the model. I shut my eyes and drifted off into that other world with which I was now becoming more familiar, the world of peace and rest and not-doing. As I did so, I found myself walking in an imaginary world, a world of vibrant colours, peace and tranquillity.

I was standing on a gentle, sloping path that wound itself around the side of a mountain. The views across the surrounding landscape were spectacular, taking in other mountains, waterfalls, lakes and, in the far distance, an ocean. Intensely green trees and shrubs decorated my walk, and I was accompanied by a chorus of bird-song. I came to a shelf on the mountainside, in which shimmered a beautiful pool of turquoise water, and into one end of which a small waterfall cascaded. I put my hand down into the water and it was as warm as a bath. I lay down in the water and rested my head back on the bank, reaching my arms out to either side. From where I lay I could see across a large part of the valley.

The sun shone down onto the pool, bringing further warmth, and I shut my eyes. The water felt like it was penetrating every cell of my body, rejuvenating the tired and broken parts that had suffered so much abuse over the years.

"Alexander – what do you think of my little place then?"

I opened my eyes, and there emerging from the waterfall was Dada. He swam over to me and lay beside me, taking in the same view that I had been enjoying.

"Dada?"

"Yes, it's me Alexander. There are some things I need to tell you. I should have told you years ago, when I was still alive, but I just couldn't quite do it."

The striking thing was, even though this was all clearly insane, I felt absolutely cool about it. I just went with it. No fight.

"That night you asked me to come back with you and we found your mother kissing her friend – do you remember it?"

How could I not? That night had haunted me for most of my life. The way I had screwed up my parent's future and my own. From that moment on, I had taken it as read that I was to blame for my parents' divorce. If Dada hadn't seen them together, everything may have been different.

"Yes Dada, yes, I remember. What of it?"

"Ah, Alexander, things are not always as they seem. I don't think you can blame your mother entirely for her infidelity to me with other women."

Now I was confused. What did he mean?

"You see, the thing is Alexander, I can say this now, you're a man and I'm, well, I can see from where I am that I just didn't know any better. But I want to help you now and I can, because you've got important things to do. And you must know this." There was such calmness in his voice. I had no idea what he was talking about yet, but he was completely at ease, his translucent body floating effortlessly in the water beside me.

"So, what do I need to know?"

"Well now. All my life, I always had a - a predilection for ladies, shall we say."

Well, that was perfectly normal. So did I.

"What of it Dada?"

"I liked the ladies to be together Alexander, I liked to see women cuddling each other and kissing and things. And I always had quite an active sex drive, while your mother would be interested occasionally, and then the rest of the time she'd be more interested in reading her books than in me."

This was weird. I knew perfectly well that in reality I was lying in my bath, at home, in Hampstead. But another part of me, a lighter part, was away floating in a warm, mountain lake listening to my dead father talk about his sexual leanings.

"Just before my fortieth birthday she asked me what I'd like as a gift. I must have been a little drunk, because I told her I'd like to get a couple of lady performers around to 'entertain' the two of us. Apart from being a little shocked by my request, I suppose she wasn't that surprised, because she had lived with me for years by then. I didn't really think she would take me seriously, mind you. But she did. Of course, she had no idea where to go looking for such entertainment. I made out that I had no idea either, and pretended to fish a number out of a directory of mine. What she didn't know, was that I had been entertained by these two before, nights when you were at school and she was away."

My mind returned to the evening when I had returned home early to find him with Cleopatra and the schoolgirl.

"Anyway, one night, you must have been back at school, I came home from work to find the house lit with candles, and two women in nurses' outfits in the darkened sitting room. Your mother was sitting on the sofa, holding a birthday cake with forty lighted candles on it. She was shaking and smiling."

This information should have been freaking me out. I'm sure the Alexander in the bath was freaking out. But the me in the pool was listening in respectful silence.

"No-one had ever taught me how to go deeper with love, Alexander. No-one had taught me that the satisfaction we all crave is not to be found in quantity, but in quality. That the perfect partner will provide you with the best and most satisfying experience of love you can ever possibly want to imagine. Way beyond your wildest dreams. Can you believe that, Alexander? I never would have. Not that anyone ever told me. No-one. And so this itch was just something that I had to scratch over and over again. I wanted to satisfy myself by having as much and as often as possible. I thought the answer was lots of girls, lots of the time. I seriously believed that my appetite could only be appeased by large helpings, featuring lots of women."

The water continued to lap around me. My eyes were fixed upon the waterfall. Dada lay there serenely, telling me all the things that he hadn't been able to tell me when he was alive. Somewhere, I could hear a telephone. Peculiar. I couldn't understand where they would have a telephone up a mountain.

"A few months later, I asked the girls again. I didn't mention it to your mother until the night, I so wanted her to be a part of it too, and I didn't want her making other plans to avoid it. I even went to the extent of booking the car in for a service, so she couldn't suddenly drive off.

"I soon became hooked on doing this regularly, but mainly because your mother was involved. It was her I always wanted. It was never the same with just the girls, although, after we split up, I desperately hoped that I'd find the same degree of enjoyment without Elizabeth there. I never did, of course.

"I never knew you could deepen a relationship, Alexander, beyond a certain stage. I thought that once you'd had kids, you just had to learn to maintain what you had as best you could. I got bored easily Alexander, I needed new challenges, new excitement. But I was too lazy and too ignorant to look for those new challenges in my relationship with Elizabeth. Outside stimulation was the only way I could see of getting it. I had no idea there were still layers to peel off in our relationship that could have revealed the mutual pleasure and excitement we were probably both craving."

All the time he was speaking I was thinking about the night-nurse. I was seeing occasion after occasion in my adult life flashing across a screen beside the waterfall, replaying moments when I had failed to engage with Helen, choosing instead to accept as inevitable the decline of our once passionate relationship. I too had sought comfort in the arms of another, and in the cold and ultimately heartless images of magazines and films. I too had totally failed to search beneath the surface of my relationship with Helen.

It had been passionate for a while. It had been loving for a while, undoubtedly. But when it most needed us to hold in the discomfort that major life changes like having children brings, we had failed to remain still and peel away the next layer to see what lay underneath. The pain had been too uncomfortable and all my training had taught me to fix it. So I had fixed it, and predictably, divorce had followed.

My father continued,

"My little treats increased, and your mother was in no doubt that she was always expected to be present. I see now what that must have cost her to give to me. Ironically, I got my way at the ultimate cost to me. The woman with whom we saw her that night was one of the girls that used to come round to us. Thanks to me, Alexander, your mother started to enjoy the company of women more than mine. It's not her fault that she left me for another woman. It's mine. It would never have happened had it not been for her trying to help me meet my perceived, superficial needs."

That wasn't a perspective I was expecting. Oh. Somehow I couldn't swear in this lake. I was too mellow, and this place was too sacred. I glanced at the screen. It was still showing the film of my relationship with Helen. Paris, Chelsea Embankment, Joel's birth, Melanie, smoking, BMP, caring for a dying father, Paris again, Claude.

"Why is this happening Dada?"

"Why do you think, Alexander? How long have you been making your mother wrong? And how much do you love Helen? You don't need to answer those questions to me, but you do need to find the answers in yourself."

I shut my eyes. The water had become cooler and I suddenly felt quite alone. I opened my eyes again and I was back in the bath in Hampstead. Fully back. No mountains, no waterfalls, no birds, no Dada. I got out and dried myself on autopilot, trying to take in the information that this dream had imparted. Had it been real? Did I need to do something with this? Had Dada truly been the cause of my mother's departure? If so, then I had spent much of my lifetime making her wrong, and she had never once tried to defend herself. She had accepted my judgement without trying to prove or disprove anything. If it was true, then was her acceptance the ultimate act of her respect for my father?

I went out of the bathroom and into the living room. The answer phone was flashing. So, I had heard a telephone ringing. I hit play and listened while drying my hair with the towel.

"Hi Alexander, it's me again. Tom. From school, and the funeral, and stuff. Your mother told me you're in Hampstead – well, I'm in London for the night and I got a real nudge to call you. I know you might not want to speak, but I thought I'd try anyway. Can you call me back if you're there?"

I wrote down the numbers and looked warily at them. Having just connected in the strangest way with one ghost, I was now looking at the few random digits that separated me from connecting with another.

This was one ghost that it was time to lay to rest.

32

If anyone ever did state that having a second child is a good way of addressing the problems in a relationship, and a way of bringing people back together, they were lying.

Helen suffered again during this pregnancy, leaning more and more on my mother for support as I continued to do what I was good at; going away and growing my business. It's interesting how easily a relationship that contains two people who once loved each other so passionately, can very gradually unravel, almost unnoticed, over time. You take your eye off the ball, and one day you wake up and find everything has changed.

Joel's arrival did little to improve things between us. Maybe I was wrong to hope that this beautiful baby boy would bring with him a miracle. I don't know whether Helen hoped for the same thing or not. We rarely talked about us any more, and life had become much more about childcare arrangements and coping, than about spontaneity and fun. And as far as sex was concerned; on the rare occasions when she was in the mood I was often too shattered to be able to give her the sort of attention that I knew she wanted. She was talking more and more about wanting to make love, not have sex. I tried to understand, but never really got it. For me, sex was sex. Everything for me had become about *getting it done*, whether it was meals, sex, business or relationship issues. I had become a man whose goal was to survive the journey, rather than to experience it.

My trips abroad now started to offer me respite from the demands of fatherhood and being a husband. I can't believe it now, but I remember actually looking forward to leaving the house even if I knew I had a two-hour airport wait followed by another three-hour flight. It took me away from the consistent message I was getting that I was failing in my domestic life. Hopelessly. And when abroad I was able to fall back again on occasional drink, drugs and porn to bring some sort of respite from such gloomy thoughts. The trouble was, these boosts were always short-lived. And while I knew it was important sometimes to give myself a taste of the pleasure that I was no longer getting anywhere else, all I was really doing was dealing rather pathetically with the symptoms of my own unrest rather than the causes.

The business was growing at an extraordinary rate and this helped me to avoid spending too much time worrying about what was happening to Helen and me. Over the course of only five years, my little business went from nothing to one valued at over four million pounds. The website had become a global phenomenon in the leisure industry and I had received two offers of a buyout, the latest of which sorely tempted me. However I wanted to make sure I sold at the right time, not too early, and so I kept the potential buyer dangling, while I tried to increase the company's value even more.

Having discovered that Joel's arrival had not fixed the problems that existed between us, Helen and I both looked for something else that could be the panacea to our pain. We had talked often of our dream house in Hampstead, and with the boys and my business growing, and house prices on the up and up, we decided it was as good a time as any to move. My flat had recovered its value and shot up over the course of the last few years, and with my thriving web company providing the extra funds, we were able to move into a four-bedroomed house, close to the railway line in Kingsford Street.

The weeks leading up to the move were chaotic. Helen was trying to cope with the boys, I was trying to cope with the business. We met sometimes over a packing box in-between our two worlds, but the meeting would be strained and centred around the job in hand. Joel was a light sleeper and once awake, whatever the time of night, would think it was the start of a new day and would keep Helen up for hours. The wooden floorboards didn't help, everything echoed around so much, and we developed techniques for packing and wrapping in almost total silence. Were we not both so tired, we may have seen the funny side. That rarely happened.

Added to our difficulties at that time was the legal and practical nightmare that is involved in house moving. Although Helen had offered to help out with the business side of moving, I perceived her offer as half-hearted, and, knowing this was my domain, I shouldered the entire responsibility for it. Apart from letting her book the removal company, I didn't request her help on any aspect of the organisation of the move prior to the event. I was the negotiator, I was the one with the business head, I was the one who understood surveys and mortgages and bridging loans. I thought I was doing the brave thing, the chivalrous thing. I thought I was doing what she would have wanted, and allowing her to focus on the boys. I thought I was doing what men are meant to do. The trouble was, in taking everything on myself, I was beginning to resent her. I didn't want her help and yet I wanted her help. I wanted her to share the responsibility for it all, but didn't trust her to do it as well as I would. Moreover, I was in no way aware of these mixed feelings at the time. How fucked up was I?

In hindsight, I can see one incident illustrated my contradictory state of mind. It was the day of the move. It was November, though why we had allowed ourselves to get involved in moving amid the short days and damp of pre-Christmas weather, I do not know. I suspect it was born out of our desperation to make everything okay again.

I had taken three days off work to oversee the move. Helen had driven the boys out to their respective kindergarten and toddler groups and had arranged for them to go back to a friend's house in Chelsea that afternoon. Completion was due to happen at noon, and the removal firm was booked at eight o'clock in the morning.

By eight-thirty, there were still no removal vans and I was beginning to fret. I was deeply tired because of the months of broken nights, but the adrenalin had kicked in for the day, and it swept along with it a sense of excitement, and hope that things were now really going to change for us. If only the removal firm would come.

I picked up my mobile and called Helen who was still trying to deliver children in the rush hour.

"It's eight-thirty and they're still not here. What's their number?"

"Hello Alex."

Bugger. I hadn't even said hello.

"They're probably stuck in traffic. It's terrible along the Fulham Road this morning."

"Hello Helen – hello?" The signal was breaking up.

"Hello Alex, I'm here. I shouldn't worry. If you really want to call them the number is in the…"

The line broke up again.

"Where? Where's the number, Helen? You're breaking up."

"What? I can't hear you, Alex, the phone's breaking up."

The signal went dead. Seemed we were having communication problems on more than one level.

I went inside to look for the removal company card. I couldn't find it anywhere. Shit. They should have been here by now. I tried to remember their name and then recalled that Helen had the quote in the house move file. Now where the hell was that? I was surrounded by boxes and crates and house plants. Where in the name of God could our paperwork be?

What if she'd booked them for the wrong bloody day? Well, that would be typical wouldn't it? The one thing I don't do, the one thing I leave to her and she gets the wrong bloody day. I knew I should have done it all. I started running round and round the house looking frantically for papers. Why did she have to be so inept? Why couldn't she do one simple thing? Why did I marry her at all?

Ten minutes later Helen appeared through the front door. I was already run ragged. In her hand was the file with the paperwork. She saw me looking at it.

"You took the fucking paperwork with you? Well that's a fat lot of bloody help. Christ, couldn't you have just got the boys off for the day without causing chaos? I mean bloody hell Helen, give me a break."

Helen thrust the folder at me and burst into tears, before running up the stairs. She was shouting at me as she disappeared:

"I've called the bloody firm and there's no-one in the office yet. They won't be open until nine, so don't bother calling, you'll be wasting your time. And I'm sorry you think I'm inept. I only did what you asked me to do." And with that, she slammed the door to the loo. It was the only place where she could sit down without being on a box.

269

Needless to say, a few minutes later the removal men turned up. They had been stuck in traffic on the Fulham Road. Helen was right, but the damage had been done and I had no idea what I could do to repair it.

The rest of the move happened without mishap, and before long we re-established the same old routines, but in a new environment. Months went by during which Helen immersed herself in the world of children and I immersed myself in work. We both thought we were doing the right thing. I suppose it shouldn't have surprised either of us that Hampstead wasn't the answer to everything, but there was no doubt we were both clinging to the hope that it might provide some sort of tonic to our ailing relationship. It didn't. Nowhere could have done.

I had become a spectator in the boys' early years, even more so once Joel had arrived. I did what was expected of me and stayed out of areas that Helen seemed to handle better without my input. I can't say it pained me; I was much too numb by this time to feel pain. I couldn't even feel the shell closing around my heart any more; I suppose it had rusted into place and was permanently protecting me from experiencing feeling of any sort. I found myself waking at two, three, four o'clock in the morning and then my mind would be buzzing with business concerns and worries about things I thought I had forgotten to do. Before long a pattern had set in and I would become so agitated that I started sleeping in the spare room so as not to disturb Helen.

One night, about three-thirty in the morning, I was lying awake in the single bed going over and over in my mind whether or not I had finished a Powerpoint presentation I was making to the Forte group the next day. I could remember most of the slides, but there were at least three in the middle that I kept muddling up. I was about to get my laptop out, when I heard Helen come into the room.

"Alex, you can't sleep again, huh?"

I loved it when Helen became the night-nurse again. I wanted her love; I wanted it all for me. I loved my boys but they were taking the attention that I had craved for so long.

"No, not really. I've got this meeting tomorrow, with the Forte group, I just need to make sure everything's ready."

"Alex, this has been going on for quite a while now. You can't function properly without sleep. Don't you think you might need to get some help?"

Oh here we go. It's *my* problem again. *Need to get some help?* How come it was always me who needed to get the help? Didn't she realise this anxiety was because of us? Oh, shit. Because of us? Is that why I was struggling so much?

"I'll be fine. I just need to think that's all." And I turned over, shutting her out as completely as I could, short of physically pushing her back through the bedroom door.

"Alex, look this might not be the best time to tell you this, but I think you should know. I'm seeing someone else. Another man. Nothing's really happened yet. But it might. I like him Alex – he listens to me. I'm sorry."

I heard Helen walk back into her room. I stayed rolled over on my side. I didn't move. I didn't move for three hours. I couldn't even cry. My mind went over and over the words that I had just heard my beloved night-nurse say. She was having an affair. She. Her. Helen. How? When did she find time to meet anyone, she with a now seven and a four year old? If anyone should have been having affairs it was me. But, other than that one indiscretion all those years ago, I had remained faithful. For years now I had battled the desire to rent hookers, or to return the advances of amorous business contacts. Yes I had used porn as a prop to help me deal with my pent-up sexual energy, but I hadn't got involved with another *person*. I wasn't seeing someone. And I certainly wasn't expecting to find out that my night-nurse was. I thought she was safe. I thought I'd done everything, well, almost everything, that she had asked. How the hell could this have happened?

Another eight weeks elapsed before my shell finally cracked. Outwardly, not much had changed in the weeks since the night-nurse had presented her terminal diagnosis of our relationship. But then, one morning, she asked me if I could pick the boys up because she was going away for the night with her friend. For two months, my shell had done everything it could to hold back the tidal wave that had started life all those years ago as a small droplet. *One flicked match to start a fire.* This simple request, an inevitable development of our new situation, was the catalyst in the collapse that followed.

Bravely, or foolishly, I had tried to play it cool about picking up the boys. I'll be fine, no worries. I'll sort it. And I think I genuinely believed I would be fine. All day I had fought back the thoughts of Helen together with this *friend* of hers. And I had partially succeeded so far, even though every few minutes I'd find myself imagining how she was feeling about seeing her new man that evening, and having the whole night with him. And then I'd wonder how I'd be feeling come midnight when I knew they'd be in bed together and I'd be desperately trying to get to sleep, alone, in our bed. In *our* bed. Not mine. Ours. That's how it was meant to be. And then it would strike me how completely I had lost her.

Thus far into the disintegration of my marriage, I had managed to avoid any form of public humiliation; my shell was doing its job. But I hadn't seen the children yet. And that's when it all started to kick off.

That afternoon, having picked up both the boys, I had put them in the back of the car. Joel, as usual, was a nightmare to strap in, his arms flailing as he described his fight with Brad Taylor, the new American kid in town. As ever, they were both over stimulated from the effects of a day of being surrounded by other children, and for the first few minutes of the drive, were both talking simultaneously at me and each other.

But then, when we were roughly ten minutes from home, the question that I had been dreading was asked.

"Why isn't Mumma picking us up?" Daniel was the first to notice that Dada was chauffeur for the afternoon.

"Yeah, where's Mumma – I want Mumma." Joel suddenly realised his main carer was missing.

"I said it first – you always have to copy." Daniel's tone was withering.

I put the radio on to try to divert their attention. It normally worked. Radio Two was doing one of their hits-of-the-nineties playlists, and Celine Dion's 'Think Twice' had just started up. I hated Celine Dion but at that moment, who cared? She was an entertainer for my children.

"Mumma, I want Mumma. Where's Mumma, Dada?"

"Yeah. Where's Mumma? Why are you picking us up? You never pick us up."

I had to stop at some lights. I tried not to but, with the lights red, I loosened my belt and turned round intending to tell them that Helen had gone to see a friend for the night, and that they were going to have me all to themselves. Something about the combination of them using the same names that I used to use for my parents, something about those great big eyes staring so innocently back at me as I turned round, something about their so innocently asking the whereabouts of their mother; what could I say? *'She's off screwing her new lover – the man who's going to become your new Dada. Is that a good enough answer, kids?'*

And then Celine bloody Dion broke into the chorus.

'Don't say what you're about to say,
Look back before you leave my life
Be sure before you close that door
Before you roll those dice
Baby think twice'

And all I could do was think of Helen and the decision she was in the process of making about our own lives. Tonight would be the night she would shut the door on us. And, God, I wanted her to think twice. At that moment, I felt my whole inner self explode. It felt exactly as I imagined that a heart attack would feel, except this was rocking every single part of me, physically, emotionally and, if there was such a place, spiritually. I was still facing my boys, mainly because I didn't feel able to move, but also because I now didn't want to let them out of my sight. I had lost one part of my family; I didn't want to lose another.

Car horns beeped and the children started crying, with Daniel shouting at me to get going. I could barely hear them through the noise that my pain had generated. Thank God, there was still one frail part of me anchored in the real world, and with tears streaming down my face and noises coming out of my throat and mouth which shocked even me, I managed to turn around again and drive on. Neither the boys nor I stopped crying all the way home.

When we finally arrived at the house, I sat there in the driving seat unable to move. Still the tears and the heaving came, but soon I was crying solo. The boys had cried themselves out, and the silence from the back was ominous. But I couldn't think what to do. Every vein, every bone, every cell was in agony. This was pain on an unprecedented scale. Pain that had been locked up for so many years that it had turned into a monster. And that monster was now slaying me.

Daniel was able to tell me later that it was he who unlocked his seat-belt and climbed into the front of the car to get the keys. He apparently then went up to the front-door and unlocked it, returning the keys to the ignition before helping Joel out of his seat and taking him into the house. It is astonishing that children, whom we often don't even trust to know when they want wee-wee, can get it together in moments of crisis as confidently as any adult.

All this time I sat there in the front of the Mercedes, crying and crying and dry heaving. Dusk started to fall and still I was there. I don't know how many people went past me, but I'm not sure we're very good in England at dealing with awkward situations like a grown man crying in a car. Anyway, no-one stopped. And still the damn tears came. And I couldn't do anything other than let them come. I'd got the boys home and that was it. Daniel was having to be the man now.

I don't know what time it was when the door opened. I didn't even turn my head.

"Alex? Alex?"

Somewhere in the distance I could hear Helen's voice. Or maybe I just wanted to hear Helen's voice.

"Alex? It's me. Helen. Alex, speak to me."

But I couldn't. I could hear the words. I could tell she was beside me. But I couldn't speak. I couldn't do anything.

"Alex, I couldn't do it. I couldn't go away with him. I got in the car when I left work and I put the radio on. Celine bloody Dion was singing. It was like she was singing straight at me. Think Twice. Do you remember the song Alex? You hated it. *'Look back before you leave my life, be sure before you close that door.'* I couldn't bloody do it. I was going to be shutting the door tonight, Alex, and I couldn't bloody do it."

But I was too far gone to be able to make any real sense of what she was saying. She thought she was talking to Alex, her businesslike husband who would take this new bit of information, deal with it and get on with life. But she wasn't. She was talking to someone who had little idea of who he was and no idea as to how he was meant to react. I was broken. Completely broken. And it would be some years before I would feel like I was mending again.

33

It was strange that just pressing a few numbers on my phone could so easily connect me to an experience that had long ago started to shape my life. I felt not only scared, but powerful; powerful, because at my fingertips was the equivalent of a time-machine that could take me back into another life with which I had lost touch.

The numbers piled up alongside each other on the little display. All I had to do was press the green button. I stared and stared at it, wondering if I had the courage. Speaking to Tom would bring me face to face with the reality of what I had done. Was I ready for it? Or should I leave this ghost trapped in between two worlds for a while longer?

The numbers disappeared off the display. I had waited too long. I went and made a cup of tea and thought about what I would say. Nothing came. I sat at the kitchen table, the mug of tea standing beside the upright phone.

Suddenly it rang. I nearly had a heart attack.

"Hello?"

"Alexander? Is this Alexander?"

It was Tom.

"Christ, Alexander, this is Tom, Thomas, your old school mate. I wasn't sure I'd left you my number, so I was just ringing again."

"Tom, I was about to call you." I stared at my cup of tea. Was I? Would I have been able to make that call?

"Look Alexander, I'd prefer not to do this over the phone, but I really want to talk to you. How would you feel about getting together? You're in Hampstead I gather – well, so am I tonight. Any chance you can make it this evening?"

"Uh - yeah, sure." And so I gave him directions and he told me he'd be over in about half an hour. Thirty minutes between me and my history. There was only one way I could prepare and that was to sit. In silence. And let the chaos that was my thoughts, and that still wanted to consume me, run its course. No tears, yet. Just breathing. Controlled, deliberate, mind-aware breathing.

I sat there, not moving, for what seemed like at least an hour. Eventually there was a knock at the door and I knew the moment had finally arrived. The moment when my past would become my present.

I opened the door to find my old friend Tom, Tom the now blind man, standing on my front step with a white stick. I had no idea what the protocol was with blind people – did you have to take their hands and guide them past all the obstacles in a house, for instance?

"Tom, well, we've finally done it. Come in – would you, would you like a hand?"

Tom smiled and shook his head.

"Alexander, thank you for letting me come round. I'll be fine with my stick, I'm used to it. A house in Hampstead eh? Well, you've certainly done alright for yourself."

What was I thinking of, offering him a hand? A man who had just completed a year-long walk, half way across the world. Like he'd need a hand to get into my house. How insulting could I have been? I might as well have said *'Hi Tom, you're disabled. I'd better help you find the chair.'* Another example of the inadequacy of my education.

Tom followed me in, even shutting the door behind him. It was remarkable what struck me in that brief time he was with me. The things that I so regularly took for granted, things that I could do easily, and yet for a blind person must have posed continually new challenges; shutting the door, walking in between the grandfather clock and the hall table, taking off a coat and putting it on the side of the couch. Simple things. I suddenly valued my sight more than I ever had.

"Can I get you a drink, Tom – a beer, whisky, tea?" It was the least I owed him. After all, I had made him blind.

"A beer would be fantastic. Thanks Alexander. Can I call you Alex, or do you prefer Alexander?" At that moment Tom became the first person I could ever remember to ask me what I preferred being called. It demonstrated a sensitivity and freedom from embarrassment that I admired. Helen had never asked if she could call me Alex, but from her I had always liked it. And she was the only one that I allowed to call me by that term of endearment, for that's what it was between us. Alex was still Helen's word.

"Well, I prefer Alexander if that's okay with you. Are you okay with Tom or do you prefer Thomas?"

"Tom is fine. I've been just about everything in my life."

I went out to the kitchen and came back with a couple of beers. "Bottle or glass?"

"Bottle sounds good to me. What's the beer?"

"Czech Bud – hope that's okay." I handed Tom his beer and we chinked bottles.

"It's one of my favourites. Cheers."

I sat down again and looked more closely at Tom. His face didn't look right even now. Plastic surgery had probably done wonders, but you could tell that his features were a little distorted. The black shades didn't help; they lent an air of mystery to his appearance.

"I was sorry about your father, Alexander. Although, I have to say, in some way his death was rather fortuitous as far as I was concerned."

"What do you mean, Tom?"

"Well, that's how we were able to get back in touch with you. I had an experience on my trip that was very powerful, and it involved you in some way. I knew upon my return that I had to contact you. I had only been back a few hours when my parents mentioned the death of your father to me; they'd remembered him from his current affairs programme days. We managed to contact your mother via the television station, one of the benefits of being in the news too, and that's why we went to the church."

"Why didn't you speak to me then? Why the wait?"

Tom shuffled on his seat.

"I wanted to, Alexander, but I couldn't quite do it. For years after the accident the whole thing was never discussed in my family. My life was one of operations, waiting, operations, more waiting, more operations. As my early years drifted away, so did my memory of what had happened. But one day, when I was eighteen, I had to know the full story. I had to know, because of a note that your father sent me. I made my mother tell me every detail that she could remember and, although she said you were absolutely not to be blamed for what had happened, I did blame you, Alexander. I don't know what I would have done to you if I'd met you again back then. I was furious with you, for I believed that you had truly ruined my life."

I sat and listened and felt unable to comment. Worst case scenario. Tom did know it was my fault he was blind, and he hated me for it. And why not? Reverse the roles; how would I be feeling?

"Alexander, you're now having to come to terms with facts with which I dealt years ago. I learned that our parents were in regular contact over the course of my treatment. Such was your parents' guilt about what had happened that I only found out when I was eighteen that they had paid enormous sums to make sure I got the best treatment possible. My father tried to resist accepting the money, but I gather that Peter was insistent. They said that he was almost as desperate as they were for me to regain my sight via the various operations. Your father took each failure personally."

The things I didn't know. What our parents never tell us. I had had no idea that they had been trying to make up for my childhood moment of madness by sacrificing their own savings. Was that why we had taken that small house when we moved so quickly after the accident?

"Yes, I can imagine Dada struggling with that. I had no idea they had been contributing to your treatment. Well, I wouldn't have done, would I, since I didn't even know I had blinded you."

"Of course not, Alexander. Each year, on my birthday and at Christmas, I would receive a cheque from your father. My parents always told me he was my Godfather. But when I got to eighteen, I received the final cheque from him for five thousand pounds and a note. The note was very brief:

'We can never make up for what happened to you, Tom, but I hope you can make something of the enclosed.'

"That was when I had to ask mum what it was all about. Five thousand pounds, Alexander. People don't just send you five grand without good reason."

Guilt money. The five thousand was clearly my father's way of trying to deal with the guilt that he had carried ever since I had committed my first crime of innocence.

"Well, for what it's worth, Tom, I'm pleased. Although it should have been me sending you the money not him. I set the shed on fire after all."

I'd said it. *'I set the shed on fire.'* And I'd said it to the man whose life it had shattered. I felt strangely relieved.

"Yes, you did set the shed on fire, Alexander. And it could just as easily have been me setting it on fire, and you on the roof. But it wasn't, and it wasn't meant to be. For years, I thought that I was the unlucky victim of a terrible accident. I now know that I was meant to be on that roof, at that precise time. I was meant to be injured. I was meant to go blind."

I took a large swig of my beer and nearly choked. I didn't understand what Tom was saying. *'He was meant to go blind?'*

"Tom, I admire anyone who has a positive attitude in life. But how on earth can you say that you were *meant* to go blind?"

"I've learnt a lot in the last twenty years, Alexander, and I can thank your father for much of that. When he sent me that money, I was just finishing school and wondering what to do next. Having the five thousand set me free to dream. I knew I wanted to go travelling without my parents. I had no idea how I could travel abroad, alone, as a blind person, but I knew I wanted to do it. My parents helped me to research the idea and we figured out that I could travel abroad as long as I had guides."

I was silent. He had awoken me to another painful truth about his blindness. Tom could never have seen mountains, oceans, rivers – no matter what beautiful spots he had visited.

"So I booked my first trip to India and the Himalayas. I had guides every step of the way. I quickly learnt to understand their broken English; I started to grasp bits of their language too, and on that first visit, I began to acquire the ability of seeing the world through another's eyes. They told me everything about the environment I was in. The feel of the water, the freshness of the air, the thinning of the oxygen as we climbed higher, all their descriptions matched my own senses perfectly. These people became not just my eyes, they were my angels. Sure, they were receiving a good wage for doing it, but for me it was peanuts, and it was worth its weight in gold, because I wasn't just having a holiday, I was learning a whole new language. I was developing a sensitivity that I would never have acquired with sight. And I'm not trying to make you feel better."

I could tell he wasn't. A softness had come over his face as he had started talking about India. He sounded authentic.

"This is both difficult and wonderful for me to hear, Tom. Just bear with me huh?"

Tom took a drink from his bottle and smiled straight at me.

"Of course, Alexander. Let me carry on though, okay?"

I nodded my head without thinking. But he even seemed to know that.

"There's something about the Himalayas, Alexander. Something magical. Something ancient. I found myself in a place of what I know is unmatched beauty, and yet in a place where being blind just didn't matter. I should have been screaming inside that I couldn't see this breathtaking landscape, and yet all I could sense was a fast-developing intuitive understanding of nature and a growing gratitude for the beautiful people in this world. I had intended to go out there for six weeks initially. But it turned into six months. Soon, word got round about the crazy, blind Englishman who was climbing the mountains, and each time I arrived at a new village or base camp, there would be a new welcome awaiting me, and someone else wanting to be my guide.

"This warmth and respect energised me so much that I wanted to do more. I had never climbed anything in my life until the Himalayan trip, but after three months I was already getting quite accomplished, finding myself under the tutelage of a wonderful man called Sherpa Sangmu. Sangmu means the kind-hearted one, and in this man was embodied the very essence of giving and patience. Day after day, he taught me how to master my environment; I soon learnt how to recognise dangerous terrain by the movement of the stones under my feet; I learnt how to anticipate a change in the weather by the feel of the air upon my face; I learnt how to tell safe water from polluted water just by smell. I never knew water had a smell, Alexander, until I went there."

The more he talked, the more animated he was becoming. He reached up and took off his black glasses, revealing two deep set, bright blue eyes. I finished my beer, but Tom was barely half way down his, he was talking so much.

"Don't forget your beer, Tom."

He reached out and expertly took it from the table in front of him. What I assumed would have been a relatively complicated task for a blind person in a strange place, was executed with ease.

"So, I started writing about my travels and experiences, Alexander. Sherpa Sangmu had a nineteen-year old daughter called Pema, which means lotus tree. Pema was studying English out of books that she had got from travelling friends of her father's, and both she and her parents were delighted for her to get this opportunity to practise her writing.

"I began writing a series of articles which I called *The Blind Leading The Blind,*' and she transcribed every word for me."

The Blind Leading The Blind.' It was a vaguely familiar title. But I couldn't put my finger on it. Books hadn't exactly been my thing since leaving school.

"So, for two or three days at a time I would go out with her father, and then for the next couple of days after I returned, Pema and I would sit together and I would recall my journey, and what I had learnt about how a blind person can experience this most beautiful of all the world's environments. I only sent them back to my parents, who, much to my delight, seemed to think they were something special. What I didn't know at the time was that they then sent them off to your father, as he was the one person they knew who had contacts in the travel journalism world. And of course, he had always shown so much desire to help me."

All this new information I was finding out about my father. One minute he comes to me in a vision, confessing that his failure to get a grip on his voracious sexual appetite was the cause of my mother running off with another woman, the next I'm told that he, clearly with my mother's support, had been a wonderfully generous, silent benefactor to the boy I had maimed when aged nearly six. Nearly six. Not five. Nearly six. It still lived in me.

"He knew of an American publisher who he thought would like my material, and got directly in touch with one of his contacts there. They asked for the manuscripts to be sent over immediately, and the next time I spoke to my parents by long distance, it was to be told that I had been offered a worldwide publishing deal. At first

I couldn't believe it. They were offering me one-hundred and twenty-five thousand dollars as an advance, and talking about film rights as well."

Oh, crap. *'The Blind Leading the Blind.'* There had been a film. I'd never seen it, but I remembered Helen mentioning it at some point during our marriage. A Hollywood film about the boy I maimed. It was the story of a blind man finding his way across the world, helped by complete strangers acting as his eyes. It was a story of the essential, innate goodness of mankind; a theory to which I'd never given serious thought. My little mate Tom's story had been made into a film.

"Who was in that, Tom? I never saw it, I'm afraid."

"Another Tom. Cruise. I still can't quite believe it. You'd think they could have got someone better looking, but I suppose he was the only bloke available at the time." Smiling, he took another glug of beer, and I went and got two new bottles from the kitchen. As I was in there, I looked back into the lounge at him. He had a peace about him, an ease and confidence that somehow I didn't expect to see in a blind person. I don't know why I didn't. He was, without doubt, one of the calmest people I had ever met. I opened the beers and took them back into the lounge. I didn't need to say anything, he just reached out as soon as I was within touching distance of him and took the bottle from my hand.

"I've never looked back, Alexander. This last charity walk I was on, the one that brought me back to London and enabled me to come to your father's funeral - this was just the latest in a series of walks I have done over the years. All raising money for the blind. But also raising consciousness about blind people. We're capable of experiencing so much more than people realise. And now, by my side, walks my wife, Pema. I returned to the Himalayas only two months after I had come back after that first trip, and she was there, waiting to take more notes. The family welcomed me back into their house with open arms and I stayed for another six months, during which time Pema and I fell in love. She wanted to go to University, so I bought her back to England, and, with my parents help, we got her into Reading University where she studied English. She stayed with us and took the bus every day to the campus. As soon as she had finished her course we married and we now have two beautiful children, a boy and a girl. We called them Peter and

Tashi. We named Peter after your father, Alexander, because it was thanks to him that I was able to make that first trip. And ultimately, of course, it was thanks to you."

This was shocking, heart-warming, confusing stuff. I could see how Tom had grabbed life by the scruff of the neck and made it into something, even with his disability. And I could tell by his voice and his body language that here was a man at ease in his world. A blind man who had seen as much of the world, in fact far more, than I had. And he had really seen it. Using these friendly strangers, Tom had connected with the world. He hadn't just seen it on the surface like the rest of us, hurrying from one 'must-see' to another in order to tick them all off the list. Tom had seen the world through the eyes of those who know it and love it. He'd seen it in tune with their rhythm, at their pace and with their knowledge.

"How come Pema wasn't with you when you came back for the funeral?"

Tom put his bottle down and sat back in the chair.

"She had to return home. She had accompanied me with the children on some of the trek, but then news reached us that Sangmu had been taken seriously ill. She returned with the children immediately and she is there now with them. We've been living over there for years, Alexander. We decided that it is a much friendlier place to raise children. Our children have grown up with a very natural sense of what is right in this world, and with a veneration for their fellow humans. I wanted them to have that quality living in them, the same quality that I had perceived in the people on my first trip to the Himalayas. I don't think you can find that easily in the West."

I wondered about the truth of Tom's statement. And as I thought about my own life, I saw how that very quality, the one of deep reverence for the very presence of another human being, had been missing from my life. I had dismissed people from my life because I was angry with them; I had used people to suit my needs, irrespective of the impact of my actions or words upon their own lives; and I had shut people out from my world for fear that they would find out what I was really like, rather than letting them into it and allowing them to see me, warts and all. I was in awe at how my kindergarten friend had turned from victim into victor.

"Tom, you seem - well, really, really at peace. How did that happen?" I was agitating to know if there had been some magic formula that had helped him to move out of the anger of which he had spoken, and into the place where had become accepting of what had happened, and of me.

"I can tell you that easily. Of course, the people and the landscape were weaving their magic on me every day while I was out there so that I started to feel less hatred for you. But when I met Sherpa Sangmu and his family, I found a whole new level of peace. I was sitting in their hut early one evening when their youngest child came running in having hurt himself badly on a rock. He was screaming loudly. I could tell that he had run straight into the arms of his mother, Karma, Sangmu's wife. All the time he lay in her arms, Sangmu just repeated over and over an expression that I later had him translate for me: *'Pain is the breaking of the shell that encloses your understanding.'*

At that point I stood up. Tom heard me and stopped talking immediately. I knew those words. Those exact words. I had heard them recently, someone had said them to me.

"Tom, where do those words come from? I've heard them before."

"It is just as he said it would be. Now this is exciting." Tom was smiling.

"Just like who said what would be? What are you talking about, Tom?"

"The Swami. Soon after the beginning of my walk, I stopped with Pema and Sherpa Sangmu for the night. We were burning a fire, when I heard the sound of someone or something approaching. I knew there could be dangerous animals prowling at night and so I alerted Pema and her father. I have developed even better hearing than either of them after all these years of training. But it wasn't an animal. I heard them welcome someone to our camp and whoever it was sat down beside me. He spoke in Hindi, which Pema translated. I later found out that he was a Swami – and that neither Sherpa Sangmu nor Pema had ever met this Swami before, although they had both heard of him.

"The Swami had barely sat down when he started telling Pema that I needed to do this journey to walk off the remaining anger that still lurked in my soul. Soon, the anger would be all gone and would leave only love. And he said that the old friend who was the reason for my anger would be waiting for me at the other end. I was to give him a message. He said the message was known best by Sherpa Sangmu, for it was his favourite saying, the saying that had got him through crisis after crisis in the mountains. Words penned, ironically, not by some ancient Swami but by a Twentieth Century Lebanese American called Kahlil Gibran. Alexander, Sherpa Sangmu's favourite saying is *Pain is the breaking of the shell that encloses our understanding.*'

Now I remembered my dream about the plane and the elephant. That was where I had heard that quote before. And then my mind was jumping back to Dada's speech, and what he had said about the blind man. I'd heard that speech so often now, I had memorised almost every word: *Look out also for the blind man for he holds the first key, and, without that key, the way will soon become obscured by the gathering dusts of inertia.*'

"Yes, I know that phrase, I was told it in a dream – by an elephant, as it happens. Tom, from the experiences that you've described, I don't think what I'm about to say will freak you out. I think this message is somehow linked to something that my father said just before he died. A clue about something I'm meant to do."

Tom picked up his beer again and sat back in the seat.

"Go ahead, Alexander, I'm all ears."

34

It's a deeply strange feeling in life when you suddenly realise you haven't got a grasp on anything at all. And that was precisely how I felt following my journey back from school that day with the kids. The information from Helen that she couldn't do it, she couldn't go and spend the night with her new friend; it didn't seem to slot into any particular compartment in my brain. I couldn't process the very fact that should have been making me feel better.

I went to my local GP and got prescribed six months off work and some anti-depressants. Rather than take the first piece of advice, I decided to put in place the sale of *muststayhere.com,* handing the whole thing over to my lawyer to deal with. It cost me a lot in fees, but then the price they ended up getting was substantial, so maybe that was the best way of doing it all along. I was to remain in a consultancy role and even maintained a share holding with options. I tried to keep my hands dirty a little during the months leading up to and following the sale, though it didn't really matter. Nothing really mattered. All I cared about was getting rid of things; starting again. I was realising that the person I had been all my life was not the person I wanted to keep being. Everything I had previously valued was no longer important to me, whereas the things that I had not valued enough suddenly meant everything. And I was close to losing the lot. I'd already lost my wife. I didn't want to lose my boys too.

The hardest decision was the divorce, but I knew I had to do it. Helen and I were already in separate bedrooms, and all the time she was under the same roof, I knew I couldn't become this new person, for in her reflection I would still see the old Alex. Blind Alex.

Much to my relief and amazement, Helen agreed that I should stay in the house. She and the boys moved out into a small three-bedroomed, rented house near to where my mother had relocated, in Crouch End. Again, I wanted nothing to do with the legal proceedings and so handed it over to my solicitors. We were no longer Alex and Helen, but the petitioner and the respondent. We went into it with the intention of not being drawn into a legal wrangle, but my solicitor in particular, acting out of desire to secure the best result for her wounded client, created only animosity and ill-will between us. And I was in no state to cope. I just let her get on with it and advise me as to how much I could hang on to, how much I deserved, how much was rightfully mine. Basically, she was advising me on how much I could screw out of this sorry mess.

Each time we went back to Helen's solicitors with further demands or rebuttals, my solicitor would come back to me and tell me we'd won again. Helen put up no fight. She'd ask for stuff, we'd generally refuse, and she'd accept it and shut up. It was easy money for my brief, which was probably annoying as it meant her fees weren't as high as they might have been had we been in lengthy, disputed negotiations.

Having sold the company, we both ended up with plenty of cash out of the arrangement, but my solicitor told me that I could have ended up a lot worse off than I did. I even managed to keep the Merc. She wanted me to be pleased, but I couldn't have given a damn at that point.

At no point during the divorce, once I'd kicked it into action, did we discuss whether we were doing the right thing. I was as certain about it as I could be about anything at that point in time. I knew I had to burn my bridges, do something radical that would set me free of my history, set me free of my lies and guilt. The company, conceived and birthed alongside my first child, had become my first child. Thanks to my conditioning, I knew how to value it much more than I knew how to value Daniel, or for that matter Helen and Joel. And then there was my marriage. A relationship built originally on simple principles. *'Don't smoke; don't do drugs; and never lie or cheat'*. And I had ignored them all. That's why both the marriage and the business had to go, for they represented so much of what was fucked up in me. They were symbols of transactions done by an ignorant and confused man. And, as the law says, ignorance is no defence.

And so there I was, a man stripped bare of his identity. I had children but no wife; I had a house but no real experiences to fill it with; I had money but no real need or desire to spend it; I had occasional work if I wanted it, but no real desire to do it.

About nine months after Helen and the boys moved out, we each received a notice stating that we had a decree nisi. That was it. My relationship with Helen had been consigned to a few lines of Times New Roman on a form letter. The divorce was made absolute six weeks later and we were free agents.

Contact with Helen, immediately following the formalisation of the divorce, was restricted to the interaction we had regarding child arrangements. To start with, I couldn't deal with the boys at all, so for about eight weeks I barely saw them. I underwent counselling, but got fed up with being taken back into my painful past and being asked questions all the time. I didn't want to answer any more bloody questions. I couldn't answer questions. I wanted tools that would help me deal with how I felt *now*, and the counselling approach I was receiving didn't do it for me. I tried the anti-depressants for three months, but felt like they only increased the fog, or more appropriately smog, in which I was living my life. Without this support the pain was excruciating, and yet somehow I felt that I had to, and almost wanted to, experience it. At some level I knew that it was by understanding the shit I had got myself into, that I would be able to find the ladder to climb out of it, and I could only do that by becoming more aware of where I was. I sometimes wished I could have someone guiding me through this, but without such help, I forced myself to learn the way of most suffering that, I hoped and prayed, would result in most reward.

Very gradually, I started to wake up from my nightmare, and as I did I became more able to be with the boys, and soon became almost dependent upon my weekend fix of youthful engagement. I also got my father in to help me out from time to time, and found that he and the boys had a rapport of which I soon became quite jealous.

Helen would sometimes come to the door with the boys when I went to pick them up. She had been looking a pale shadow of the night-nurse that I had met on the bridge all those years ago. Not that I could talk. I felt like all the life had been sucked out of me, and that I was, very, very, slowly being resuscitated.

One Saturday morning when I went to pick them up, I was met at the door by my mother. She seemed to be helping Helen out even more often than my father was helping me out. It was like a boy versus girl thing. Peter and Alexander clubbed together, Elizabeth and Helen clubbed together. That particular morning, it struck me how vibrant my mother was looking. Maybe it was the contrast with our own weakened and shattered states. Or maybe she always looked that good and I was only just beginning to be able to notice.

"Hello, Alexander. The boys are just getting ready."

"Hi, how are you?" I didn't give her time to answer. I wasn't interested in the answer. In my mind she still represented so much of what had gone wrong in my life. "So where's Helen this morning?"

My mother didn't so much as blink as she answered. She looked directly at me and spoke clearly.

"She's away for the weekend Alexander. I stayed last night so that she could leave during the evening and avoid the Saturday morning traffic."

I took a deep breath. And so, this was the confirmation I had been waiting for. I knew it would happen sooner or later, just as I expected it to happen for me again, one day. And now that it had, I felt a sadness that was no longer destructive in its nature, but that was somehow empowering. Part of me felt pleased for Helen that she had found someone, and while I didn't want to dwell on who, or how long, or where, I found I could allow myself to be happy for her. A tear rolled down my face as Joel appeared at the door. I quickly wiped it away, not wanting him to think that Dada was about to lose it again.

"Dada's here, Dada's here!" Joel's joy was palpable. Daniel came down the stairs a little more slowly, but before long we were off in the car and heading for another testosterone-filled weekend of play-wrestling, mini-rugby, take-out pizzas and Match of the Day.

The same routine went on for several more months. Helen never said anything about a partner, and I never saw her with one. The boys never mentioned one either; under scrutiny from me they said that sometimes Mumma went out with her friends. That reminded me how my Mumma had said the same thing to me many years ago, and it had turned out that her friends were more than just casual acquaintances.

I had absolutely no interest in other women; it was as if my libido had run dry from years of over-exertion and abuse. Occasionally, and much to my embarrassment, my father would ask if I was getting any, and when I replied in the negative, a look of great concern would come over his face and he'd utter some moronic, hide-myself-under-the-nearest-stone comment like *'well, you know, you mustn't let yourself get too much out of practice Alexander. Keep your hand in so to speak.'*

I'd like to say that the pain eased throughout this period, and I suppose at certain points it did. There was a very gentle increase in moments of peace. But when I felt the pain, when I allowed myself to feel it, it was there as big and as wide and as tall and as black as ever. I *had* to feel it. I had to learn that the Alexander who had been shaped by a sequence of seemingly random life events, was a man who could gain something significant from these experiences.

In the first two years following the divorce, I felt like a snake very slowly sloughing its skin. However in my case, what lay underneath was not another protective layer of skin, but raw, agonising, profound uncertainty. I started to become much more interested in the people in my life. I started reading about coaching, and the way that coaches trained people to make the most out of difficult situations. I started adopting one or two techniques that I found on the internet, and soon found myself using strategies to get me through this emotional breakdown that had at one stage seemed as though it would rip me apart. I cut down on my drinking, I ceased drugs of all sorts, even prescribed ones, and one night, in a moment of steely resolve, I piled my collection of porn magazines in a heap in the back garden and set it alight. It was a small fire, but it was enough to help me realise the significance of what I had done.

Once I was feeling better in myself, I even joined the local running club which met early on a Sunday morning and took in the paths around the Heath. *'Joined the club'* sounds too formal. I had simply gone out jogging one morning when I'd woken up early, and found a group of other runners at the entrance to the park. They said I could tag along and I've been tagging along, on a very occasional basis, ever since.

On one summer Sunday morning, I had met up with my other runners as usual. It was a good turn out that morning. We were a motley bunch, ranging from a nineteen year old male nurse called Tony to a seventy-three year old former Olympian known only as Speedy. It was a pleasant enough morning, although there was good cloud cover. We had run around the paths as usual, all going at our various different speeds, some with headphones on, others just enjoying the freshness of the morning air and the sounds of the Heath.

As I closed in on the gate which marked the end of our run, I could see a group of people gathered together, including Tony, Speedy and two of the other runners who had already completed their morning exercise. I came to a halt by the crowd and saw a young man with a video camera on a tripod. Once I'd regained my breath, I asked Tony what was going on.

"This bloke says he's making a short film to inspire prison inmates about what they're really capable of. He's asking anyone to write down something good about themselves on his board, then he's going to stitch all the different shots together and set it to music."

I managed to stand up straight enough to be able to see over the crowd and into the middle where Speedy was holding the whiteboard up just below his face. He had a broad grin on his face. On the board were written the words 'I am alive.' And he was. If there was one thing Speedy very much was, it was alive. He was remarkable for any age, let alone a septuagenarian. The film-maker then got Speedy to run towards the camera and lift the board up as he came to a halt, smiling yet again.

Some of the people were less willing to engage. It was interesting to observe how difficult it was for them to write something good about themselves, or anything positive at all, on the board. But then two young, pretty girls who were out walking tiny, designer dogs, picked up the board and, scrubbing out Speedy's writing, wrote their own words. 'We are fun.'

The other runners were drifting back and soon we had all eighteen back at the gate; the late arrivals wondering what the commotion was about. We had a running strip which made it easy for us to identify each other amongst the walkers, other runners and cyclists, and this didn't escape the attention of the film-maker. For some reason he came over to me first.

"Look, could you get your team together? It would be fantastic to have you all run in, and then a couple of you pick up the board and have everyone else gathering around pointing at it. We'd need something suitable on the board of course – can you think of something that you think would inspire prisoners to think more positively about their abilities to co-operate and get along with others?"

"We make a great team." I don't know where from, but the words popped into my head. And suddenly I entered a world of co-operation and mutual respect for my fellow human beings. Here was a man trying to lift people's spirits. Trying to bring that simple thing, a smile, to people's faces. Speedy had sussed it straight away. I had no idea what this little film would be like, but I felt I understood what he was trying to achieve.

We got the runners together and ran back about a hundred yards. The film-maker got his camera ready and held his hand up asking us to wait until everything was perfect. In that moment I suddenly had the idea that we should all run in a line, with our hands on the shoulders of the two people on either side. By now a large crowd had gathered around the cameraman.

His hand went down and we jogged in beautiful, bumbling synchronicity towards the camera, each person smiling for all they were worth. Some were laughing, some were singing. We ran closer and closer to the camera and when we arrived there, Tony and I picked up the board while everyone else closed in around us and pointed to the words *We make a great team.'*

"It's a wrap. At least, I think that's what I'm supposed to say. Thanks so much, everyone."

There was a moment's silence, followed by a single person clapping. Suddenly the whole crowd was clapping. The atmosphere was like nothing I had ever experienced on a Hampstead Heath Sunday morning, or for that matter, anytime, anywhere else. Now everyone wanted a go, and within a few minutes, a crowd of about seventy-five people had linked hands and were huddled around a board that pronounced in great big letters, *We are loved'.* The director then got us all to hold our linked hands together above our heads while a young, black cyclist held the board aloft with the help of a white-haired gentleman in a suit and tie.

Something about this 'director' intrigued me. Who was he? What had happened to him to make him risk ridiculing himself by coming out on a Sunday morning in Hampstead with a whiteboard, some pens and a lot of front? How had he managed to unite a group of disparate strangers in such a short space of time? What did he do when he wasn't making wacky shorts? I decided to ask him.

"Me? Well, at the risk of sounding very transatlantic, people normally call me the Coach. I quite like my anonymity. Makes me remember it's not about me. I'm a life and business coach – I help people to achieve their highest potential. I've got some good contacts about the place these days, and I thought it would be fun to put together an inspirational film for inmates. I'm pretty sure I can get it distributed throughout the UK's prisons once it's done. Remind them of who they really are, rather than letting them invest any longer in the fucked-up personalities that they've become through a series of probably random incidents and unfortunate events."

He could have been talking about me rather than prison inmates. And he had reminded me of who I might one day still be able to be, just as he was also holding out a message of hope for those prisoners. All the time I was running towards '*We make a great team*', I had been thinking of the teams of which I'd been a part over the years; the teams that I had either let slip into nothingness, or that had been ripped from me. In that brief one-hundred yards, I connected once more with my teams and I saw them as that; me with my mother, me with my father, me with Golly, me with Steve, me with Daniel, me with Joel. And as I grabbed for that board and held it beneath my chin I thought of the greatest team I had ever been a part of. Me with Helen. And I felt proud that I had been a part of her team for even one day.

"That's a great idea. Where did you get it from?"

He smiled at me. "These things, they just come. Sit still and learn to listen to yourself for long enough, everything comes. You can go out chasing after it, but ultimately I reckon it will probably find you, if it's meant to. Take the sequence just now. I couldn't have planned that. It just happened. It came to me. All I had to have was the intention of making an inspiring film for prison inmates – the rest is already beginning to take care of itself."

"How did you get into coaching?"

"Easy. I had to go through my own shit. Once I'd experienced what it was to suffer, I found I had a talent for helping people get through their own crisis. People think when they're going through hell that once it's over they can just go back to how life was. Well, I don't think you can. You change – for the better. I just chose to ride with it. And now I spend my life helping people and making them smile. By the way, there's talk that one day you'll be able to distribute films via the internet, so you never know, this little film you've been in, maybe people will be seeing this as far away as Australia in years to come. I've got to go – good luck finding you."

And with that intriguing comment he was gone. *'Good luck finding you?'* Did he mean it was good luck for him finding me or was he wishing me good luck in finding out who I really was? And if he was, how the hell did he know I was even looking?

35

Whether it was anything to do with being blind I don't know, but Tom demonstrated in the next few minutes what an excellent listener he was. He kept silent as I told him all about Dada's illness, his strange and yet enlightened speech, my reunion with Claude, and my trip to Paris with Helen and the boys. I told him about the first three steps of Helen's communication system, and of how I was already beginning to use it with impressive results, and how Helen and Claude both felt there was still something missing.

As I told the story, I found myself believing in the mystical elements of it all more and more. And in telling it, I could also see on what a bizarre and intriguing journey I had embarked. And maybe, just maybe, in the same way that Tom felt he was the one who had to be blinded, I was the one who had needed to experience loss and despair. Recounting the events of the last few weeks made me feel alive, light, full of energy; and that was in spite of the fact that I was still confused as to whether or not I was meant to be doing anything with this. I wondered whether I should be taking it seriously, or had my mind just got carried away on some flight of fancy, born out of a need to have something different happen in my life?

Tom stood up and went to the loo, which he found with consummate ease. He left me in silence, contemplating the story I had just told. I didn't feel anxious. But I did feel curious. And I wanted him back in that room to complete the jigsaw.

"And so Alexander. I'm the blind man in your father's speech. That much is clear. Haven't you got a question for me then?"

"Yes Tom, I have." I felt a mixture of confidence and concern surging through me. What if he didn't know the answer? What if he wasn't the right blind man? What if all this was claptrap; my father's feeble attempt at having the last laugh? I put my anxieties into a bottle and then imagined smashing the bottle to pieces with a sledgehammer. "What's the key, Tom? What's the first step?"

Tom looked at me and then picked up his bottle and took another final drink.

"I have already given it to you Alexander. The Swami. What the Swami said. What the elephant said in the dream. You have to make that work for your model. That is the key. That is what I was told to come to give you."

My heart sank. My brain started doing somersaults trying to work out what the hell it really meant and how on earth I could apply that to Helen's model to transform it into a tool that could help achieve global change. *Pain is the breaking of the shell that encloses your understanding.'* I could grow to hate that sentence.

"I can tell you're disappointed, but it's in there somewhere. None of this is coincidence, Alexander, you've got to trust it. Listen to those words, make them real for you. The answer will be there if you can just ask the right question. What do those words mean for you?"

'What do those words mean for you?' That was the question. That was what I needed to sit with.

"One word of advice. Relax. The answer will come if you can allow yourself to be patient. Stop reacting so impatiently to everything." Tom then stood up as if to leave.

"That will be my lift. Alexander, it's been a real pleasure. We must stay in touch now. I'd love you to come and visit us one day."

I had heard nothing, but then sure enough I heard the sound of a car pull up outside. I went over to Tom and hugged him. In that hug I could feel years of guilt and shame evaporate, and I hoped that, for his part, he would no longer be damaged by the anger that he had carried about me for so long.

That night, I lay in my bed reflecting on our conversation. I didn't watch television or put on music. I lay there in silence. For the first time since my mother had told me what I had done to Tom, I felt able to breathe deeply. He had been honest with me, and demonstrated such a sense of contentedness in himself. His life had turned out well as far as he was concerned, remarkably well in fact. To think, I was once best mates with someone whose life story had been made into a film starring Tom Cruise. Tom had truly excelled at living; his determination to engage with people, to forge relationships where many would have given up, leading him to a place of personal satisfaction and happiness. Material success had followed, and when it did, he'd had a secure enough hold on what was important not to let the trappings of fame or wealth tempt him off the path of being true to himself.

He had said so many important things that I wanted to recall the whole conversation, to replay it word by word and look for any clues that might help me to decipher the key. But the words that seemed to stick most were some he uttered towards the end of the evening; the bit about being patient and letting the answer come. He had told me to stop reacting to everything and I could feel the value in that. It was in essence, precisely what I had been advising Alan to do; by getting him to listen more closely to his client he was no longer reacting to what his client was saying, he was purely gathering information. I was helping him to arrive at a point where he would *know* what to do, rather than reacting instantly to the first bit of bad news and *thinking* he knew what he was doing.

The dream I'd had about Dada flicked back through my mind. Did he really come to me and tell me that he had been partly, if not mainly, responsible for my mother's infidelity? Had he had groups of women back to his house just to satisfy his needs of the moment? If he had, it was outrageous. But I could also see now that this information could be healing for me. Had he appeared in order to help me achieve some form of forgiveness, of peace?

I dropped the idea of looking for any of the answers, as Tom had advised, and fell asleep thinking about mountains, lakes, a smiling Sherpa, and Tom Cruise.

The next morning I went for my run on the Heath. It was beautiful, and I had awoken feeling full of hope and energy. The events of last night were ruminating somewhere in my mind, but I was trying to engage with the moment more and more. I tried to imagine what it must have been like for Tom, blind and in a strange country, having to make new relationships with people whose language he didn't speak and whom he couldn't even see. And yet he had turned it into a positive and had even ended up finding his wife by surrendering to his vulnerability and trusting in the essential goodness of people.

As I jogged up Parliament Hill towards my favourite resting place and view-point, I purposefully made eye contact with people that I passed and smiled at them. I wanted to see if it worked for me, in stiff-upper-lip England.

When I got to the top of the hill, I was almost disappointed to find sitting on my favourite bench, a mother with two young boys who were probably of a similar age to Daniel and Joel. At first I was going to keep running and pretend I had no interest in the view. That's certainly what I would have done in the past. But I didn't this time. I stopped and smiled at the three of them.

"Good morning. No school today?"

The mother smiled back, and so did the boys. I'm not sure my two would have done the same if a strange man had started talking to them.

"They don't go to school. They're home educated."

"Mum, we're radically unschooled. We don't home educate." The older boy looked bothered that his mother had used the term 'home educated'.

"Can you do that? I mean, is it legal to have your children learn at home?" I had vaguely heard about home education but had never taken it seriously.

"Yes. If you really want to know, it's a parent's right in the UK to educate their children as they see fit. As long as you equip them with an education that will help them take their place in society, you can pretty well do as you please. And that means, on mornings like this, we can decide to do geography and history and exercise all in one go, by coming up to a place like this and studying London for real."

I wasn't intending to get drawn into a conversation on education, but this mother had an interesting point. I had all but wiped out my lessons from my memory, they had been so unforgivably dull. Dry facts, learnt from text books; an education cold in its delivery and ineffectual over the long-term.

"So do you two enjoy it then?" Both boys looked at me. I was struck by how alert they seemed, how together. There was no indecipherable grunting here. These boys could speak.

"It's good."

"Yeah. It's cool." Short, sharp, to the point. They obviously had confidence, and felt under no pressure to explain themselves.

"So what made you take this option? I mean, it must be pretty hard work isn't it, teaching two boys twenty-four seven? Do you get a chance for a life?"

"Well, to be fair I don't really teach them. They're discovering their own appetite for learning, so when they're ready to learn something they come to me or their father…"

"More often the internet." The older broke in, smiling as he spoke.

"Yes, and we provide them with what they need to explore the subject. You see, my husband works in the city. He was getting more and more graduates coming to him who could work to a set task provided it was all laid out for them. But as soon as they had to think for themselves, they would flounder. The school system is producing robots who are very capable of solving linear equations but who don't have the capacity for lateral thinking. We want our boys to grow up knowing themselves, knowing that you don't only need to check your answer, you need to check whether you really want to answer the question you've been set in the first place."

The boys got up and started playing football.

"That's their way of saying '*oh God, mum's off on one of her lectures again*'."

We both laughed. I started playing football with the boys.

"So, about three years ago we decided to take them out of school. At first it was really hard because we thought we had to do school at home. We thought we needed a curriculum to get them to learn, and set lessons at set times. But we soon discovered that everything provides an opportunity for learning – even a trip to the supermarket. Maths, communication skills, orienteering, nutrition – all wrapped up in an hour's visit to a shop. And when the two of us talked about our different experiences during the day, Jack in the world of reaction, us three in the world of discovery, we started to understand the massive difference between their education and our own."

I was engrossed in her words. London lay stretched out before me, her two boys chasing the ball as it rolled down the hill. I had reached out like Tom had all those years ago, and I felt like a man in a new world learning a new language.

"What do you mean by the world of reaction?"

"I mean that we have been educated from year dot to react to problems. That's what's wrong with the world. Think about it – from kindergarten onwards we're asking children to answer questions. What happens when the teacher asks a question in class?"

I jumped back to my earliest days in education. Even in Miss Baines's class I could remember the feeling of joy if I knew the answer and my hand would shoot up, or the feeling of terror if I didn't know the answer and I would try to shrink lower than my little table.

"Kids stick their hands up."

"And if they don't know the answer?"

"They, er, well, I used to try to hide. I don't know if other kids would do the same."

"Of course they do. That's precisely the point. We've taught children that they're only good if they know the answer; if they don't they try to run away from the situation. We didn't want our children feeling superior for knowing things, nor did we want them hiding from life just because they haven't learnt something yet. We wanted them to feel that it's okay not to have all the answers. We couldn't change the system, so we decided to take them out of it."

This woman, whom only a few minutes ago I didn't know at all, was becoming more animated by the minute. She stood up as if she was addressing the whole of London; in fact she was keeping a subtle eye out for her boys.

"We've never looked back. My boys aren't spending their childhood cramming useless information any more in order that they can answer some arbitrary tests that prove nothing about who they really are. They're looking for the questions that live in them. Who am I? Who am I here to be? How can I help contribute to this world? Oh, looks like we're off."

And with that she said a hurried goodbye as she followed the two boys who were now dictating their own new course down the hill.

"Goodbye – thanks for the education. I think."

I sat and looked out over London. And that's when it all suddenly made sense. The first step. The reason people struggled to sustain the model was because the first step wasn't about becoming a better listener. The first step was about understanding why we're such crap listeners in the first place. You can't go where you want to go if you don't know where you're starting from. That's what Helen's model was missing.

I understood now that the quote that the Swami had wanted me to know, the Gibran quote, was all about staying in your place of discomfort, and allowing wisdom, knowledge, to come naturally. That's precisely what this mother was describing about her boys' education. As a mother and a businessman, she and her husband had recognised that the years and years of conditioning that we receive in our education equip us to become two things – brilliant at fixing when we think we know the answer, and brilliant at developing withdrawal techniques when we meet something for which we don't have an answer. But in developing our reactive qualities, we've lost something far more important. The ability to analyse the information to find out whether we need to do anything at all.

I looked back over my life as I had developed into an adolescent and young man, and how I had taken that conditioning into every area of my life. Why wouldn't I have done? Having no other model to fall back on,   as I started to grow into relationships I had reacted to problems in the same way as I would have approached a classroom test. I either sought to fix them immediately, seldom with long-lasting results, or they became situations from which I ran a mile. And as I went into business, I blindly applied the same linear methodology. In fact, the learned habit of reacting to problems had undoubtedly been one of the greatest causes of unhappiness in my life.

I had only recently developed the courage to rest in my uneasiness and it was already providing dividends. Dada's peaceful death at home was a classic example of this change. Years ago, when I was in fix or withdraw mode, I would have had him carted off to hospital where he would probably have died an anxious old man in the company of strangers. But, by choosing to disengage from the need for a solution, and by choosing to engage instead with my own discomfort, my own uncertainty, I had him stay at home and in doing so I had discovered a whole new world of understanding and magic. I had received many benefits throughout that dying time. Dada's speech was one thing in a sequence of minor miracles with which anyone who has cared for the dying will be familiar. How different might I be feeling now, had he never made that recording?

I now knew that it was this new understanding that was the missing link in Helen's model. For people to grasp the tool, they had to know that the first step was in the identification of why we react like we do. The first step was to identify our conditioned reflex, the knee-jerk response we all have when something challenging happens in our lives. We have to stop trying to fix, and stop running away from things which scare the living hell out of us. It sounded simple, and yet I already knew from my own limited experience, that it takes a lot more courage to remain calm and engage in a challenging situation than it does to get in there and fix it, or run a mile.

My mind jumped back a few years. The life-coach. The bloke with the film. I'd met him here too. Funny, the people I had come across on the Heath. He had struck me at the time as an interesting man. Hadn't he said something about sitting and waiting until things became clearer, until the answers came to him?

I got back to my house as the phone was ringing.

"Hello?"

"Alex, it's me. I had to call you and I don't even know why. Has something happened?"

There hadn't been time to tell Helen that Tom was coming round; there was no way she could have known.

"Bloody hell, Helen, how do you do that? It's freaky. Mind you, what isn't in my life right now?"

"All part of my training, Alex. I'll teach you how one day. So come on, what's happened?"

How could I tell her about my meeting with Tom over the phone?

"I met with Tom last night, Helen. The blind man in Dada's speech. And something else just happened today too. It's all a bit weird, but I think I've found the missing link."

There was a silence at the end of the phone. After a few seconds I could just make out what sounded like a few tears and Helen blowing her nose.

"Alex, that's - that's wonderful. It must have taken a lot of courage to meet with Tom. Are you okay?" Her voice sounded soft and caring. For a few brief seconds she was my night-nurse again. I wanted to dive into those moments and swim in them for eternity.

"Yes Helen, I'm fine. Listen, can we meet? I can't do this over the phone."

"Come round tonight – I'll do dinner. The boys have got something to show you anyway."

"It's a date. I mean, not a date, but, well,…"

"Yes, Alex, it's a date. Come at seven."

36

By the time my father became ill, I had been working as a self-employed business coach-come-consultant for about three years, having managed to extricate myself entirely from consulting for my old business. I had attended a couple of workshops, read some motivational American books on the subject, and other than that, had put the rest together with my years of business experience. I didn't feel entirely in control of what I was now doing, but I knew that I had to work with people and this seemed to be the best way of utilising whatever skills I did have.

At first, clients came through my previous business contacts, and later through word-of-mouth. Stress levels mounted again for me. I put off dealing with my issues again as I found distraction in my new work. My diary was filled very quickly, and, once again, I was trying to juggle the requirements of being a father with the requirements of my fledgling business. I don't think I did particularly well at it, and the old man's illness was all I needed.

The first I knew of his health problems was one Saturday when I had taken Joel over to his house to watch a rugby international. Daniel remained at home with his mother doing an art project, something he chose to do in preference to watching a live game, which was anathema to my father and me, and Joel for that matter. It never ceased to amaze me how different from each other Daniel and Joel were turning out.

England versus France games seemed to have featured a lot in my life. This one was no exception. At half time, Granddad asked Joel if he'd like another drink and stood up to get us all refreshers. As he rose, he let out the most piercing yelp I had ever heard. His face turned white and he fell straight back in the chair. Rightly or wrongly, my first thought was not about him but about Joel.

"Joel, you might want to leave the room."

Joel didn't move. "I'm staying right here, Dada. Should you call an ambulance?"

"Yes."

"No. I'll be alright. It happens sometimes. It's not the first time. Just - just give me a couple of minutes. Get me some water, Alexander, will you?"

I rushed out to the kitchen and returned with a glass of water. When I came back into the room I saw my father differently. He was Dada again. He was vulnerable, he was suffering, he was approachable, he was weak. And he needed me. He really needed me.

He was right. It only took him a few minutes and the worst of the problem seemed to pass. But I had seen enough to know that, for all the things I couldn't give him, the one thing I could give was my love, and I determined there and then to do that. I took him out of his house that night, with Joel carrying his overnight bag. Dada thought he was coming to stay the night. But he never went back to that house, the house in which he had established his own mysterious, lonely life. He came back with us that night, and he stayed for the rest of his life.

37

I could hear the boys shouting at each other from inside the house as I rang on the door-bell. They arrived at the door simultaneously, fighting each other to drag me in by the hand.

"Dada, Dada, we've got a surprise. You have to see this."

"I'm showing him, You said I could." Joel was pushing for my attention, using his body to get in between me and Daniel.

"Boys, I know you are both excited. Just let your father come in first and take his coat off." Helen came up to me and gave me a kiss on the cheek. She spoke softly this time. "Hi."

"Hi Helen, thanks for the invite. What's all the excitement about?"

She smiled at me and followed the boys into the living room, where one table was given over to the computer. I marvelled at how she managed to keep everything running smoothly in this small space with two boys and their growing needs, while I struggled to keep a much larger house in order.

"Dada, you're famous. Look what one of mummy's friends found on the internet."

I looked at the screen. Daniel hit the play button. Over the course of the next four minutes, I watched as a series of random individuals and groups of people, from an undertaker to a milkman, from a group of nurses to a cluster of policemen, held up signs in front of them on which were handwritten positive statements. And then, as the music built and the film neared its end, there I was with a bunch of runners, standing in the middle of the shot holding up my words, the words that I always wanted to say to Helen but somehow had never been able to.

'We make a great team.'

At that moment Helen took my right hand and squeezed it tightly. The boys were watching the screen intently and I kept my eyes fixed firmly forwards.

"And here you are again Dada, here you are again."

And there I was, in the middle of my family, and there I was, in the middle of the crowd. Surrounded by smiling faces and waving arms, a hand squeezing a hand in the secrecy of celebration.

'You are loved.'

The film ended with our crowd walking away in slow motion. Helen removed her hand quickly from mine. I looked at her. Tears were in her eyes. It might have been wishful thinking, but I couldn't help sensing they were tears of hope.

"I want to see it again, I want to see it again."

"We make a great team Dada don't we?" Joel came and flung his arms around my waist, followed quickly by Daniel.

"Yes, boys we do. That is, I think we could make an even better team, because I'm just beginning to realise the part I'm meant to play." I couldn't help but cry a little too, but these were tears of joy more than anything else.

And then the magic happened. Helen came over to her boys, all three of us, and wrapped her arms around us all.

"You can't be a team without me, you lot."

And, as the video started playing again, we held our own space, three men and a woman united by a common force. Love. I felt like a dying man who had found an oasis in the desert.

Later that evening after the boys had gone up to bed, I told Helen all about the meeting with Tom, the message from the Swami, my meeting with the home-educating family and my subsequent conclusions about the first step.

"Alex, this is brilliant. You've caught on so quick. This is what's been missing."

"Are you sure? I mean how can you be so certain I've figured it out correctly?"

Helen leaned back on the couch and took a sip of her red wine.

"Because of how you've arrived at the answer. Because of the sequence of events and the lateral thinking that followed. You didn't go looking for this answer, it found you. It was always going to. You just had to be ready to receive it, and intelligent enough to know that you had. You've changed, Alex. The man I used to know would never have allowed any of this to happen."

She was right. I had changed. And I was changing.

"Helen, how have you become so certain, so clear about everything and so giving? I mean I've put you through crap and you're still talking to me. You're a nurse and yet you never once tried to get me to take Dada to hospital, nor did you tell me how to treat him or what to do. You've never complained that I'm living in a bigger house or drive a better car. You didn't become confrontational on anything in the divorce. How do you do it?"

"Alex, when we were married I went through hell. From Hong Kong to Notting Hill, I did everything I could to support you, and to help us be a great team. But I couldn't reach you, Alex. My heart broke every time you went away and left me with the boys. But after a while, it stopped breaking. There was nothing left. I stopped feeling anything. And then I decided I had to do something for me because that was all I really had. I knew I was no good to the boys if I was broken, and so I started looking for help. That's when I started reading what you'd have called weird books and that's when I found my spiritual teacher. From that moment on, I started to see a bigger picture, and I was able to detach from needing you to be anyone different from who you are."

I'd never thought of the struggle she was going through all that time. I was so caught up in my own story, I had assumed Helen was coping. This was a perfect reflection of the same realisations I had come to myself in more recent times. They say women mature more quickly. Helen had certainly got there first.

"As my heart started to open again to this bigger picture, I started feeling more love in my life again. At first I didn't know quite how to handle it and that's when I nearly left you for Phil. Remember the Celine Dion moment?"

How could I ever forget it? *Look back before you leave my life.* I only ever listened to that song anymore if I knew I badly needed to cry.

"But now I've got a better handle on it. It will sound corny Alex, but I feel much more love for people now. I've realised that relationships are where it's at, which I think I've always known - it's just that my experience with you nearly put me off them for life. In truth, relationships are all we have. And I want to get the most out of all mine while I can."

I guess, even if it takes you half a lifetime to realise something so significant, that you can call your life a success. *'Relationships are where it's at.'* I loved the way she talked. I always had.

"Alex, I think you should meet her."

"Who?"

"My teacher. She can probably explain things better than I can."

"Oh Helen. You know, I'm not sure I'm really into all that sort of stuff."

"What sort of stuff? What do you think might happen? She's not going to turn you into a frog you know."

I suddenly felt uncomfortable. It was a shame, the evening had been going so well.

"You know, spiritual stuff. Like you said, weird things."

Helen raised her eyebrows. "So going away to Paris with your ex-wife to meet a French Priest in order to discuss a bizarre speech containing references to him and me, and recorded secretly by your dying father; that's not weird? Finding out that a boy you blinded at age five, was instructed by an Indian Swami over thirty years later, half way up a mountain, to give you a message; that's not weird? Being filmed four years ago on the Heath holding up a message that is meant to speak to you and me now, today; that's not weird? Just what is your interpretation of weird, Alex?"

I was silent. Helen had named only a few of the many things that I had recently come to accept as normal.

"Checkmate."

I shut my eyes and was silent for a while. I thought about the first step again and realised that my brain was desperate in that moment to say goodnight and leave the house. So this was what it was like not to react immediately. I could see how tempting it was to get this sorted now, and how I was conditioned to do precisely that. Helen remained silent too. And in that peace, I felt like our silences reached across the room and joined. If this was what she had been learning from her teacher, then maybe I needn't be so scared.

"You would really like me to meet her, Helen?"

Helen opened her eyes slowly and nodded her head. "I think the time is perfect, Alex, yes."

"Okay, I'll do it. But could I ask you to be there too? I don't want to be left alone with any crazy weirdo."

Helen took another drink from her wine and laughed.

"Of course I'll be there. And she's not some crazy weirdo."

I finished my wine and wished Helen goodnight.

"Alex, that message, on the film, the one you held up about making a great team. Who wrote that?"

"I did. He asked us to come up with our own statements, something that meant something to us."

"I liked it." She kissed me on the cheek and showed me to the door. As I left, I couldn't help feeling that, had I been even half-awake, we truly could have made a great team.

One of the first things I did the next day was to ring Claude in Paris to let him know about the first step of the system. He talked about reacting in terms of the Church's response to anything that didn't fit its model and how that knee-jerk action had evolved over hundreds of years of dogmatic and fear-led instruction. He said he didn't know what he would do with this new information, so I suggested he follow the structure we had developed so far.

"Claude, I understand that you want to start creating change straightaway. It's hard, isn't it, when you can see so much that could be improved and how things could be brought up to date?"

"Yes Alexander, it is very hard. Sometimes I just feel like giving it all up you know, it is such a daunting task. Other times I want to get to work immediately and start tumbling down the walls." Claude's English still occasionally made me laugh.

"Claude, do you feel confident enough in the system to know exactly what to do?"

"No Alexander, I do not."

"Then, maybe this is a time for waiting for the answer, or the right action, to become clear. Someone once said to me, *we spend too much time looking for the answer, and not enough time asking the right question.*' Are you clear what your question is, Claude?"

There was a silence at the end of the phone. I could almost hear Claude thinking from over a thousand miles away.

"Thank you Alexander. That was what I needed reminding of. I haven't found the right question yet."

We said goodbye and I managed to leave a discussion with the outcome unsolved again. For the second or third time in just a few days. This was against everything that I had grown up doing, and it felt surprisingly good. I was no longer providing answers everywhere I went. And now that I knew *why* I had developed the instant-response-or-run-away reaction, I found it much easier to start validating, and asking the questions that helped lead Claude to a place where he knew he had to focus.

The next few days with clients was subtly transformational. Remembering why I reacted, I found myself listening more closely to their stories, and as a result, was able to ask them questions that helped them, not me, to come to what I can only call a greater state of consciousness about their situations. What was particularly interesting to observe, was that clients started opening up more about themselves and their bigger pictures, rather than talking only about numbers and contract issues.

I hadn't heard anything from Alan or Julie-Anne for a few days, and a voice inside me was niggling away, wanting to know what had happened with the government pitch. Many times I picked up the phone to call, and each time I managed to resist. No news was no news after all. If he needed me he'd call.

And, eventually, he did.

"Alexander, we finally got the government's spec. They're looking for an agency that will raise the party's profile in a completely new way across the board. They want to give politics a makeover, basically. It's a terrifying and wonderful opportunity and one that I feel I was born to do, if that makes any sense. This feels right Alexander, both Julie-Anne and I agree. We want this. And we think you could help us to make sure that we're not missing anything. Could we get together and talk?"

Alan and I arranged to meet the next day. When I arrived, Julie-Anne gave me a pile of papers to look through while I was waiting, papers that the whole team had already been studying for two days. A few minutes later I was called into his office. I put the papers on his table.

"What did you make of them Alexander?"

"There's a lot of material there Alan. Probably based on years of an old way of doing things. You're the PR expert – what did you make of them?"

Alan promptly launched into a tirade about wasted taxpayers' money, useless marketing schemes and failed spin stories. His eyes shone as he spoke about the territory he knew so well. I didn't need to know the technical aspects of PR to know that here was a man talking with integrity and passion. He cared about the subject, he cared about the client, and he cared about the end result as much as he did about the financial size of the contract.

"Alan, I don't think I'll need to study these papers. You're the experts on the material; listen to yourself, you already know it inside out."

Alan smiled. "So that's why I pay you; to make me feel good about myself. Fair enough."

"Alan, sum up in one sentence what you think the government wants from their PR agency."

Alan went quiet for a minute. "To encourage more people to vote for it at the next election. To win voter confidence."

"And they think that throwing a shed load of money at a sexy makeover is going to do that, yes?"

"Well, surveys have shown that voters can be affected by how politicians look, speak, dress, whether they have high-profile entertainment connections and the like, yes."

"And would you say Alan, in your view, that this is precisely where the government should be spending its money to win voters?"

"God no. I mean yes, sure, spend some money continuing to make sure that present voters have reason to feel confident in continuing to vote for the party. But no, I'd be looking at how you get more people to vote in the first place. The year Two Thousand and One saw only fifty-nine percent of possible voters turning up at the polls, while four years later the figure had slightly increased to sixty-one percent. Did you know, in Belgium, the election turnout since the war averages over *ninety-two percent*? Imagine how different our political landscape might look if we were getting those sorts of figures."

"And, presumably, how much more engaged with our government the nation would feel if, in the first place, most of us had voted it in."

Alan rubbed his hands together. "Exactly, Alexander, exactly."

"So Alan, your intention is to follow the government brief, and tender on the basis of what they're asking for, even though you say it has failed to serve them for years. Are you sure you want to do that? Are you sure they're seeking to answer the right question with this brief?"

Julie-Anne had joined us and was listening closely. "Well, we can hardly tell the government they've got the brief wrong."

Alan leant forward. "Can't we? Or can we? Go on, Alexander."

"From what you've answered so far, you're putting together a tender to provide a service to the government that will basically be answering the question 'how do we raise the public profile of the government?' Have I got that right?"

Julie-Anne and Alan both nodded their heads.

"But your personal view is that the government should be spending a decent whack of its PR budget on reaching out to the mass of people who don't bother to vote, right?"

"Yes, but that's my personal view."

"A personal view, *as an expert* Alan. That's why they might employ you, because you're the expert. Your job is not just to match the client's brief, it is to make sure the client is asking the right question in the first place. Help the client to be a more effective client. Maybe the question the government needs to ask is 'how do we encourage more people to become interested enough in politics to want to vote?' It's subtly different from their brief, but could have a massive effect on turn-out. Of course, it could work against them if it succeeded – greater turn-out might mean greater loss."

Alan and Julie-Anne were quiet as they thought about what I had been saying. After a couple of minutes Alan stood up and looked out of his window at the people below him.

"We could help them to care more. To feel they have a role in shaping what sort of country gets handed down to their children. And bollocks, what have we really got to lose anyway? I'm a risk-taker Jay, and so are you. That's why we married each other. Let's do it. Let's tell them we think they've got the brief wrong. It's radical. Alexander, I think we should try to arrange a face-to-face with whoever we can get in cabinet. I'll talk to Trevor Larken and explain why. All or nothing. If we get something, will you join us? As our communications advisor?"

I felt a rush of adrenalin sweep through my body. The thought of even sitting in on a high-profile meeting, possibly with government members, was exciting.

"Count me in." I stood up and we shook hands. I gave Julie-Anne a hug and left the office, feeling on top of my game.

Over the next few days I got heavily drawn into emails, conference calls and meetings with Alan, Julie-Anne and Trevor. I asked if Helen could sit in on some of the meetings to be my co-consultant on communications, explaining that even the process of formulation of the tender needed to demonstrate a new willingness to listen and not react. Although I was feeling more confident all the time about the listening model, I was still quite new to this methodology, and I knew that Helen could help us to identify if any of us were being drawn into fix-it mode in particular.

Civil servants are not known for their risk-taking, but Trevor seemed very excited about the thought of refocusing their strategy towards capturing the interest of the non-voters. The more we talked about it, the more it became clear that this could be a legacy for future generations of which any government could be proud.

Trevor gradually brought in higher powers into the game and throughout this period, Helen and I insured that the process was not only transparent, but also that every contribution was heard and noted. Alan started to notice how he was much less inclined to hurry into decisions when faced with situations that would previously have freaked him out, and out of all the information and exchanges emerged not just a tender for work, but a vision for increased future public engagement in the election process.

If the government bought it, we knew it would demonstrate incredible self-belief on their behalf. This was an altruistic model, a model with the sole focus on educating, informing and inspiring the general public to engage with the excitement of choosing the very people who run the country. Alan and Julie-Anne had come up with various ideas, ranging from a TV reality show, to poster campaigns and school and university tours featuring celebrities and leading thinkers. All with the view of encouraging a vote; not a vote for their party, just a vote. It had risk written all over it.

After a concentrated fourteen day period, the tender was formally submitted. With Trevor's boss's input and guidance, it was a tender which knowingly broke the rules of the accepted tender process and guidelines. But such had been the excitement stirred up by the simple identification of one key question, that the proposal was allowed to stand, and went in alongside the other bids. Now all we had to do was wait.

I had so enjoyed working with Helen on the government project. I had always been so threatened by the thought of her ever being on a level business footing with me, as if that had to be my domain. But the reality of it was that it felt good, not at all how I had been programmed to think it would feel. I liked learning from her, and I liked having her support; and I think she enjoyed the new level of importance that this pitch had given her. I needed her in a way not related to looking after children, I needed her skills and her aptitude. I had never allowed myself to need her like this during our marriage.

About four days after we had helped Alan to complete the bid, Helen called.

"What are you doing tonight?"

I no longer felt my heart race at the thought that she was asking me out on a date. I knew we were in a different place now, and it was a relief that not every conversation needed to contain some sort of relationship innuendo.

"Well, apart from saving the planet between six and seven, I think I'm free for the rest of the evening. Why?"

"I've got my teacher coming round tonight and the boys are at sleepovers. I thought you might like to join us. I'll do dinner. Can you bring some wine?"

This time my heart did race a little. Nerves. Did I want to meet this self-styled guru of hers? I had started to feel comfortable in my life again, did I really need to shake it up? Helen could sense my uncertainty down the phone.

"Alex, you owe me. Come on – there's a free meal in it anyway."

"Okay, I'll be there. Seven-thirty?"

"Seven-thirty it is. See you then."

The rest of the day passed, but not without the spectre of Helen's spiritual teacher hanging over me and entering my thoughts every now and again. I decided to follow my own advice and accept the uncomfortable feeling. I didn't try to change things. I didn't run away by cancelling. I allowed myself to feel nervous. After all, how bad could it be?

As I walked up the path to Helen's front door, I experienced a feeling that Dada was close to me. It was so strong I had to stop and check behind me to make sure there wasn't anyone there. My heart was thumping, a feeling I had experienced only recently when waiting for Tom to arrive.

I'd picked up some white lilies on the way to Helen's which I held upright in my left hand as I approached the door. I grasped the bottle of Rioja firmly in the other and bent over to press the bell with my nose. It didn't work, all I succeeded in doing was to squash my nose. Why did I feel so nervous? Why did the thought of meeting a spiritual teacher scare me so much? Was it purely because I had no point of reference for what such a person might be like? I remembered a quote from Lord of The Flies that I had used often over the years whenever I felt fear taking hold in business; *'Fear can't hurt you any more than a dream.'*

I put the wine down on the step, and rang the bell.

Helen came to the door. Inside the house I could hear soft, relaxing music playing, and the sweet smell of lavender wafted through the hall.

"You came. I knew you would. What beautiful flowers. Come in, come in." Helen took the flowers and the wine and disappeared into the kitchen with them. I took off my coat as slowly as I could and stood still, waiting for her to return. The house felt like an oasis of calm. The music wasn't too sappy, it was the sort of chill music I played occasionally at home, and the smell of lavender was not overpowering.

"Well, come in Alex. Don't be scared now – like I said, she won't bite." Helen had put the white lilies in a vase which for some reason she then gave to me again.

"I think you should present them to her."

I took the flowers without thinking and walked towards the living room, Dada walking, it seemed, right behind me.

"Alexander, welcome. Ah - white lilies, my favourite."

I nearly dropped the flowers. Standing opposite me was my mother, my Mumma, her vibrant appearance and purple and pink splashed shawl belying her seventy odd years. That's why I had chosen white lilies. That's why I had brought Rioja. That's why I felt Dada at my shoulder.

"Mother, Mumma. But what are you…" I looked at Helen, then back at Mumma. "You mean, all this time, you've been Helen's teacher?"

Mumma nodded her head. I put the flowers on the table and sat down on the couch opposite her, without waiting to be asked.

"Did you never notice how much time Elizabeth and I started spending with each other once things started to turn bad Alex? I was desperate and I reached out for help. Elizabeth was able to provide that help. I was furious with you Alex and I wanted revenge, but your mother showed me another way, a way where I would not end up losing my respect for myself by getting even with you. It was Elizabeth who was my guide throughout the whole divorce procedure; she guided me to come from my truth, to ask you for what I deemed to be fair and then she helped me to let go of my demands as soon as it looked like we were descending into war."

I looked at Mumma in shock. She sat there serenely, listening to Helen's eulogy, and sipping on a glass of wine that Helen must have given her before I arrived. When she spoke, her words were measured and calm.

"You see, Alexander, when there are children involved, they are the ones who are hurt when divorce turns into war. I should know, I've been there. And so have you. I simply asked Helen to be brave by asking for what she wanted and to allow you the opportunity to give. That's why you ended up with the house; that's why you've ended up with more money; that's why you have been able to spend more money on the boys. Helen has had to learn not to resent or hate you for that."

Helen sat down on the couch next to me. "And I've also had to learn that, just because I couldn't buy the boys the same size presents, or take them on such expensive holidays as you do, they wouldn't love me any less. Elizabeth told me how it had been with your father in their divorce and how nasty it had become, and what damage that had probably done you, Alex. I had an opportunity to break the pattern, so I learnt how to state my truth and then surrender to what would be. Ultimately, I suppose, Elizabeth taught me to trust in the essential goodness of life. As you know, I could have pressed for much more in our divorce but, for the sake of the boys and the wellbeing of our family, your mother helped me to wage peace."

"Alexander, it takes two people to have a fight. I taught Helen how not to be one of those two people."

I thought back to the divorce. All that time I was thinking I'd been clever; that I had out-manoeuvred her. The congratulatory letters and phone calls from my solicitor to tell me that Helen had conceded on yet another point. And now I knew why. She hadn't been giving in because she was trying it on; she'd been giving in for the sake of the family. She'd trusted me to be fair, and I had failed. I'd taken advantage. And she didn't seem to hate me for that. Could I have behaved the same way if the roles had been reversed?

"Mumma, I don't understand. How on earth did you get into all this stuff? How did you become a teacher in the first place?" I liked hearing myself calling her Mumma again. I had started to let her back in to my life at the funeral, but time and distance had let her slip away again since then into being 'mother'. But now she was Mumma, and I was glad.

She looked at me and leant forward in her chair.

"Alexander, how long have you got?"

I took a deep breath and stood up.

"Am I going to need a drink for this?"

Helen and Mumma both answered simultaneously.

"Definitely."

I went to the kitchen and opened one of the beers that Helen had started keeping again in the fridge in case of my visiting. I liked that. She still thought of me, still anticipated my arrival. I walked back into the lounge, beer in hand.

"Okay, I'm all ears."

For the next two hours, Mumma gave me the most powerful history lesson I had ever had in my life. She told me how she had felt about the shed incident with Tom. How Dada had reacted badly and decided to withdraw us immediately from the area, because he was so embarrassed and upset by what I had done. He was deeply concerned that if I ever saw Tom again, blind and disfigured, that I would never be able to cope with life. For her, leaving that community was deeply painful; it was about all she had at the time.

"It was alright for your father to leave, he was always travelling anyway. His life was essentially based in London. But for me, a virtual single mother with a young boy, leaving the only people I knew as friends was hard. And yet Alexander, I'll never forget that summer we had together either. You could only have been five or six. And the house was tiny. But it was magic. We had a wonderful time."

I remembered that summer. Somewhere a warm, cosy feeling stirred in me. And as I glanced at Mumma I saw again that caring, loving soul who surrendered everything else that mattered to her in order to protect me.

But the sacrifices didn't end there. The dream I'd had recently, the one where Dada had come to me and confessed his sins. It was all true. She didn't go into too many of the gory details, but it was clear from what she had said that Dada had all but driven her into the arms of another woman. He had failed to pay attention to her for years, and eventually she looked for love elsewhere. For most of my life I had believed that she had wronged him. Now I knew, beyond doubt, that living with him had become untenable. I told Mumma about the night that Golly got knocked down when I had returned to find Dada in the house with two women. She shook her head and sighed.

"I had to do something for myself Alexander. The pain was crucifying me. You didn't know it but I was drinking more and more, just to escape reality. You won't remember, but I started to find it increasingly hard to get out of bed in the mornings. With what I was faced with for the rest of the day, was it any surprise?"

I did remember. I often wondered why she was still in bed, when the day was already half done.

"I could no longer be a part of this lie and I had no tools to deal with it. Thank God, that before I totally destroyed myself, I saw a local talk advertised called 'Transforming Mediocrity'. The poster spoke to me. I went along and heard about how we can *choose* happiness. I had never heard such outrageous talk. And yet I felt excited by the thought of it. I started reading books and looking into metaphysics. I started meditating. The books I read were a mixture of mysticism and science. Alexander, no-one had ever told me anything like this before. I think the most significant lesson I learnt, was that I was responsible for what was happening in my life, and that I could therefore choose for something different to start happening. So I started to choose happiness.

"I started doing all this, and soon found comfort in a bigger picture of this world. A picture that suggested that your father was acting out of ignorance, not malice. I realised I had to stop blaming him for my depression, because the blame was only destroying me. And I had to start working on forgiving myself for being found by you both that night outside the house. That experience nearly killed me, Alexander, but I don't regret it. I now see that it was meant to be. You were meant to see me that evening and so was your father, so that we could both stop living the charade that our marriage had become. It was time to move on."

Mumma was using words that had a strong resonance with the words Tom had spoken to me. *'It was meant to happen.'* Could I really allow myself to believe that?

"It hurt me Mumma. Badly. I couldn't tell anyone at Freestone that my mother was a lesbian. I was livid with you. You represented everything that I despised."

Oh, the relief of saying these words aloud. They had been dispatched in some bottle years and years ago; but the bottle had survived, and floated the oceans of my inner world before coming back to rest right in front of my eyes. Now I was strong enough, and wise enough, to uncork the container and set them free, without fear of their impact upon either of our lives.

"I know. And I know that you hated me throughout the divorce, and for splitting up the family; and I know that you blamed me for the unhappiness in your father's life. And I have had to learn to accept that I couldn't change your perception, Alexander. Only time and truth could do that."

"But - why didn't you tell me all this years ago? Why allow me to go on living the lie?"

Mumma took another sip of wine and looked at me.

"Would you have listened? Could you have listened? And if I had got through to you at all, which I doubt, what would have then happened between you and your father? I didn't want to hurt him, Alexander, in spite of everything that had happened. I could see that he had already hurt himself quite enough."

She was right. I would have been in no way equipped to hear this story while Dada was alive.

"As soon as I started to focus on my role in what was happening, instead of seeing myself as the victim of your father's behaviour, I dropped my fight against who Peter was. I knew I had to focus on me, not on trying to get him to be someone different. That's when I got into what you and he used to call my weird stuff. And I was amazed to find that, by allowing myself to acknowledge the terrible pain I was in, hope started to surface in places that I least expected to find it. I learnt to embrace the pain of having a son who despised me, even hated me. As I became more accepting of that, I realised that I had to be kinder to me. That what was done, was done.

"As soon as I learnt to drop the fight against all these painful things, as soon as I was able to stop needing your approval for what I had done, my life started to change. And very soon I found I had something to say about life; I had something to share. I had been in the worst pain imaginable, the pain of losing a child, and I was coming out the other side. I became my own teacher Alexander, and it wasn't long before I started helping others to transform their own, apparently hopeless, lives."

I sat there in silence as Mumma talked. Helen sat beside me, and I realised that her left hand had been on my right hand for some time. She was looking at me, trying, I felt, to sense my reaction to what Mumma was saying.

"It's thanks to Elizabeth, Alex, that I didn't throw the book at you in the courts; it's thanks to Elizabeth that you still see the boys; it's thanks to Elizabeth that I'm still able to be in the same room as you; and it's thanks to Elizabeth that I was able to create the listening system that you have completed. The system that just might make a teeny, tiny difference in this world."

How could I have got it all so wrong? How could I not have allowed myself to investigate all the possibilities, rather than just jumping to the obvious conclusion? I shut my eyes for a minute and took a long, deep breath. I felt Dada right there. He had screwed up, he knew it. But he had also decided to take responsibility for his mistakes. He'd learnt. He might have learnt it when it was too late to do anything about it physically, but he had learnt. And I was pleased about that. And I was pleased that I'd been aware enough to listen to what he had to say in those final moments of wisdom, rather than dismissing his words as meaningless.

"Helen has told me all about Peter's speech, and the journey you've been on recently. I even understand that your old friend Claude has become involved to help you unravel the mystery. Peter would have liked that. He would have enjoyed watching you solve the clues. Ultimately, it's only a game, Alexander. We can either choose to play or choose to watch. You've chosen to play. So have we. After all, it's more fun playing."

Playing. Games. It was disconcerting to look at all the serious things that had happened in my life that had helped to shape me, and think that they were all part of some game; a game of which I had only now become aware. As soon as I had lost sight of the game itself and thought it to be real, I had started forming the shell that I hoped would protect me from feeling any pain. The shell that would conceal behind its solid exterior, the guilty secrets and bottled up emotions of a lifetime of denial and ignorance.

Of course, one day the shell would shatter. And then all that would be left would be the choice between oblivion and self-knowledge. I knew even then, that, ironically, the easier choice was oblivion. It was the choice my father had made. The choice of most effort, and ultimately most reward, was self-knowledge

My parents had, in some miraculous way, done their job. This wasn't a choice I had to make, it was a choice I had already made. A choice I started to make when I shared my truth with Yao all those years ago, when I had told him from my heart why I liked FiveStar hotels so much. A choice I nearly reneged on when I tried to bluff my way through cheating on Helen, and when I lied about the Croatian deal; a choice that nearly disappeared off the screen during the divorce, but that hung around just long enough to enable me to engage with one of the most powerful educations of all; the dying process. I made the choice to be with Dada, to be present for him, and that choice was now changing the future direction of my life. Everything had happened recently because of that choice. Helen had known what it meant. That's why she had supported me, but not taken over. She knew I had to experience it to get the rewards. And the rewards were coming. I had been courageous, and I could, for the first time in years, feel good about who I was.

With a head full of information, and a heart full of life, I sat for the rest of the evening enjoying the close attention and positive energy of the two women in my life whom I had most loved and hated.

When the news came through that Alan's pitch had been successful, nothing could have surprised me. Here was a government saying that it was prepared to spend a considerable sum of its outreach budget just on making the public more aware of the need to engage with politics. The idea had grown to such an extent that word had filtered out through the House and all the major parties had decided to throw their hats into the ring and offered their own contributions towards the marketing campaign. All of a sudden, Alan's PR budget had tripled, and, amongst the people that knew, our team was being talked about as a groundbreaker in a new world of transparent communication.

The celebratory meal had been wonderful. Helen and I were lavishly entertained and very nearly ended up in her bed at the end of the evening. But this time it was I who called a halt to the proceedings. Things were going well with her, but I knew I had to continue to allow my own new knowledge to grow before I could be certain that I wouldn't fail her again. I was growing, I was learning, and I realised now that time wasn't an issue. It would be clear when, and if, we should take things further, and we both needed to be certain about that. I didn't feel I could have that certainty until I had acquired more self-knowledge. But I was happy to know she was there. The night-nurse was back. I had won her respect again.

The next morning Alan had called, sounding slightly the worse for wear, saying that some ministers and a couple of MPs wanted to meet with the team who had put the communication system in place. They wanted to meet Helen and me. They wanted to know about the tool that had enabled them all to unite behind a common cause. And they wanted to see whether it was something they could start rolling out in their own departments. I was both delighted and terrified. I called Helen, whose only response was *'Holy shit.'* The meeting was arranged for the following week in Alan's boardroom. Two ministers were due to attend, with two MPs from each of the other leading parties, and Trevor with his boss.

The following Monday afternoon, the night-nurse and I arrived at Alan's offices in Knightsbridge. She brushed a speck of fluff off my collar as we stood in the lift, and gave me a brief kiss on the lips just before the doors opened. We walked into reception to find Julie-Anne standing in front of the desk.

"Are the ministers here yet?"

"Yes. Yes, they're all here."

"Will we all fit in alright? It's going to be a bit of a squeeze."

"We'll all fit in fine."

I turned to Helen who looked younger and more beautiful than ever.

"Right, well, this it. Are you ready?"

"Ready as I'll ever be."

"Let's do it then."

"Yep, let's do it."

"I love you."

"I love you too."

9 780953 006359